Here's what readers and reviewers are saying about
The Legend of the Firefish, book one in the Trophy Chase Trilogy...

"Swashbuckling is the best way to describe Book One of the Trophy Chase Trilogy. Without wasting time, Polivka's first novel drops readers into a fantasy world filled with action, where chivalry is alive and well, and sword fights are frequent...With the nonstop action that cuts between multiple story lines, readers will be flipping pages eagerly."

—**PUBLISHERS WEEKLY**

"A ripping yarn with the feel of the open sea and glimmers of eternal wisdom."

—**KATHY TYERS,** AUTHOR OF *SHIVERING WORLD* AND THE FIREBIRD TRILOGY

"*The Legend of the Firefish,* first in the Trophy Chase Trilogy by George Bryan Polivka, is a winner... This is a story filled with action, adventure, danger, intrigue, surprise, suspense. It will keep readers turning pages to find out what will happen next...The characters Polivka created are fresh and interesting...A must-read for fantasy lovers and a highly recommended rating for others who want a good story."

—**REBECCA LUELLA MILLER,**
A CHRISTIAN WORLDVIEW OF FICTION WEBSITE

"This was one of the most amazing reads!...I have to put this up there as one of my favorites!...It's been a very long while since I've picked up a book that I literally could NOT put down. My family was clamoring around me for milk, cookies, dinner, but no, all things had to wait because I could NOT put the book down."

—**BETH GODDARD,** AUTHOR OF *SEASONS OF LOVE*

"I cannot say enough how much I enjoyed this read...I would rank Polivka's novel with the elite in Christian fantasy and sci-fi. His is unique, but I enjoyed it just as much as C.S. Lewis's *Narnia,* and just as much as Walter M. Miller's *A Canticle for Leibowitz.*"

—**BRANDON BARR,** COAUTHOR OF *WHEN THE SKY FELL*

"George Bryan Polivka has effectively created a lush and rich world of life on the high seas...filled with vivid descriptions and engaging dialogue. Polivka masterfully weaves a story that draws the reader into this mythical setting from page one."

—**MIKE LYNCH,** COAUTHOR OF *WHEN THE SKY FELL*

"The plot...moves quickly, full of imaginative twists. The protagonists struggle with real-life issues dealing with guilt in the struggle to obey God but sometimes failing. Although the antagonist seems to embody evil, Polivka successfully brings a sympathetic element to her character as her story unfolds."

—**CHRISTIAN LIBRARY JOURNAL**

"This book will be a surprise hit for many readers...Highly recommended. Read it or be prepared to walk the plank!"

—**BOOKS-MOVIES-CHINESEFOOD.**BLOGSPOT.COM

"George Bryan Polivka has crafted an extraordinary tale of high sea adventure and peril that grabs on tightly and never lets go. Packer Throme's breathtaking journey is full of action, suspense, and inspiration, and his character is engaging and captivating. Polivka effortlessly transports readers into a new world of pirates and swordsmen, where evil is frighteningly real, and faith, honor, and love are worth fighting for. Fabulous heroes, creepy villains, scary sea monsters, epic sea battles... this one has it all."

—BookShelfReview.blogspot.com

And praise for book two in the Trophy Chase Trilogy,
The Hand That Bears the Sword...

"Polivka's characters are real. He makes these people come alive; gives them adequate motivation; shows their struggles, failures, successes, fears, hopes...The plot is full of action and suspense, twists and surprises...There is an unending list of what to like in this story."

—Rebecca LuElla Miller, A Christian Worldview of Fiction website

"*The Hand That Bears the Sword* moves beyond adventure...It capably takes its place beside those ageless, classic Christian novels which look profoundly into the deeper ideas of Christian philosophy. Even if you have not read the first story in the Trophy Chase Trilogy, *The Hand That Bears the Sword* will hold your interest, sending you back to the first one, *The Legend of the Firefish*."

—ChristianBookPreviews.com

"Filled from the first page to the last with action, adventure, and a beautiful portrait of God's perfect love. I would highly recommend this book to all fantasy lovers."

—FlamingNet.com

"This book can be enjoyed by any adventure-seeker or those who enjoy reading about life on the high seas. It is wonderful to see that, through a very entertaining story, real truths about God's existence and faith through trials can be presented."

—ReaderViews.com

Wonderful words for the conclusion of the Trophy Chase Trilogy,
The Battle for Vast Dominion...

"Polivka weaves piracy, adventure, fantasy, and faith together in such a compelling manner that readers may not immediately recognize they're simultaneously being taught biblical theology."

—*CBA Retailers & Resources* Magazine

"This story is fun, unexpected, powerful, satisfying. Of the three books in the trilogy, this one had the most tension, kept me engaged and eager to come back to it quickly, curious to see how it could all be resolved. And it was, in believable fashion."

—SpecFaith.ritersbloc.com

BLAGGARD'S MOON

GEORGE BRYAN POLIVKA

HARVEST HOUSE PUBLISHERS

EUGENE, OREGON

Cover by Left Coast Design, Portland, Oregon

BLAGGARD'S MOON
Copyright © 2009 by George Bryan Polivka
Published by Harvest House Publishers
Eugene, Oregon 97402
www.harvesthousepublishers.com

Library of Congress Cataloging-in-Publication Data
Polivka, Bryan.
Blaggard's moon / George Bryan Polivka.
     p. cm.
ISBN 978-0-7369-2537-2 (pbk.)
1. Pirates—Fiction. I. Title.
PS3616.O5677B55 2009
813'.6—dc22

2008045617

Printed in the United States of America

09 10 11 12 13 14 15 16 17 / LB-SK / 10 9 8 7 6 5 4 3 2 1

For Weeks and Lag, and Eeker, for Rodge,
for Mark and Dan, and Jimmy,
and for all the fellow pirates of my youth.

I'd like to acknowledge all the wonderful folks at Harvest House Publishers for their support.

Specifically, Bob Hawkins, president of Harvest House
LaRae Weikert and her excellent editorial team
Barb Sherrill and her fantastic marketing department
John Constance and his energetic sales department
Gary Lineburg and the creative guys in design and layout
Jenn Butenschoen and the very efficient production staff
And all the behind-the-scenes people at Harvest House who work hard to make a book successful.

A special thanks to Paul Gossard for his invaluable input on copy and story

And to Aime Polivka, for her nautical knowledge and know-how

And to Nick Harrison, whose editing and encouragement are always energizing.

Contents

*The Lord hath made all things for himself: yea,
even the wicked for the day of evil.*

—The Book of Proverbs, 16:4

CHAPTER ONE

ONKA DIN BOTLAY

"ON A POST. In a pond."

Delaney said the words aloud, not because anyone could hear him but because the words needed saying. He wished his small declaration could create a bit of sympathy from a crewmate, or a native, or even one of the cutthroats who had left him here. But he was alone.

It wasn't the post to which he'd been abandoned that troubled him, though it was troubling enough. The post was worn and unsteady, about eight inches across at the top where his behind was perched, and it jutted eight feet or so up from the still water below him. His shins hugged its pocked and ragged sides; his feet were knotted at the ankles behind him for balance. Delaney was a sailor, and this was not much different than dock posts in port where he'd sat many times to take his lunch. He was young enough not to be troubled with a little pain in the backside, old enough to have felt his share of it. No, the post wasn't the problem.

The pond from which the post jutted was not terribly troublesome either. It was a lagoon, really, less than a hundred yards across, no more than fifty yards to shore in any direction. He could swim that distance easily. He peered down through the water, past its smooth, still surface, and eyed the silver-green flash of scales, lit bright by the noonday sun.

The piranha, now, they were somewhat vexing.

"Nasty little fishies," he said aloud. They were a particularly grumpy strain of the meat-eating little monsters. They were so grumpy that he

9

wasn't even sure they were piranha. Each one was about the size of a blue-gill, not much bigger than Delaney's hand, and each boasted an impressive set of teeth. But where piranha were flat side to side, these were flat top to bottom. And while piranha had small mouths and a few sharp teeth, these had wide mouths, all the way around their heads, and their teeth were triangular and interlocked, like little bear traps. They could use them, too, as he'd just witnessed. That had been a gruesome show, put on by the pirate captain just moments ago. Now the irritable little critters were swimming around his post like angry bees. Wanting more.

But even the piranha were not the worst of his troubles.

Belisar the Whale.

Delaney did not say those words aloud. Belisar Whatney was the rotund pirate captain, soft of jowl and hard of heart, wide of girth and narrow of purpose, who had left his sailor here.

"Big in his britches, maybe," Delaney told the fish, "but small in…" he groped for the words, "…other ways." He thought a while longer, then said, "Low enough to raise a man to the top of such a pole." He nodded once, content. And it was a low thing, he felt, low and wrong to sentence a man like Delaney to such a mean and calumnious end. No, he would not say that man's name aloud.

So instead he said, "Monkeys."

He said it with a release of breath that seemed to let steam out of his soul. His narrow shoulders sagged. And then he rested his chin on his calloused palm, and he pondered the word, and the world that could harbor such beasts. Here was what troubled him most. Not the post nor the pond nor the piranha nor even the pirates, but the monkeys. And not the furry little creatures that clambered around humorously and screamed maniacally in the jungle canopy in the woods. No, he was not speaking of them.

Looking down past the fish, he saw under the green water piles of broken white bones lying on the bottom. The biggest pile was heaped up around his post, just where it met the floor. Piranha couldn't do that. No sir. No little fishies, not even ones with big teeth, could break bones into splinters and chips, shards of skull and scraps of jaw, slivers of hips and shoulder blades and ribs. Here were arm and leg bones split lengthwise, the marrow eaten out. The bones of men. Something far more powerful than a fish's jaws had done this. Something had come here to feed, fearing no fish. Something strong enough to crack and split human bone. Something with arms and hands like steel. Something with claws.

Blaggard's Moon

Sea monkeys.

Delaney had never seen one. And he wasn't the sort of man who could imagine such things on his own. But the pictures had been carefully, even ruthlessly planted in his head, just last night. The local natives, the Hants, had spoken of all this in solemn voices as they sat around their cooking fire sharing their strong drink, their *andowinnie* in the little wooden cups, and passing around their big *hoobatoon* pipes. They had conjured sea monkeys with their words in such a way that no man who heard could unconjure them again. Now he saw them in horrific detail, and he couldn't stop seeing them. His mind had an eye that he couldn't shut.

Oh, he saw them.

The mermonkeys swam toward him underwater from their submerged caves, with their skinny but powerful arms held back at their sides, squinty white faces puckered like skin too long in a bath. Near the post, they reached out with wrinkled hands and he saw the steel sinews of their forearms, the fanning rods of bone that were their hands, their fingers long and crooked, curving claws where fingernails ought to be as they grasped the wooden pole in slow, deliberate movements. One, two, three mermonkeys—six hands sinking pointy hooks into the hard flesh of the wood.

And then they climbed. Those claws bit deep, and tore out little chunks of post that swirled away under the water. And then the wrinkled flesh of their scrawny hands broke the surface, gleaming white and dripping, and then pale arms with muscle writhing under the skin, and then pasty, doughy faces, white and hairless monkey faces. And then he saw the dark intentions behind those blind, slit eyes, which were white like an overheated poker, and he felt the ravenous hunger of the screeching maws behind those wicked, pointed teeth.

Delaney shuddered.

Mermonkeys. That's what the crewmen called them. But in their own tongue, the Hants called them *Onka Din Botlay.*

Rippers of the Bone.

"Stories to scare the kiddies," Delaney said aloud with a sniff. He was hoping that these words, spoken by his own mouth here in the warmth of a fetid forest where lazy dragonflies buzzed the surface of a serene green pond, would sound believable. But they did not. They did not reach from his head to his heart; they caught in his throat, barely squeaking past. And then those words just made him seem smaller, more alone, on his post in his pond.

He looked down at the marks, the chunks ripped from the aged, gray wood, some fresh, some faded, above and below the waterline. Triangular punctures not much bigger than what an iron nail might leave, leading up, up, up to where he sat, to the crimson-black stains that colored the open grain of the wood…

Yes, this was what worried Smith Delaney. This was what he found most troubling. *Onka Din Botlay.* They attacked only in the blackest darkness. Nightfall was hours away, but it was coming. And tonight, there would be no moon.

After a while the images faded and Delaney's heartbeats slowed. A man can think on his own gruesome death for only so long, he concluded. He rubbed his nose, then shifted from one buttock to the other and back.

He wished he had his knife. Belisar the Whale had wanted to leave Delaney with a knife. Not that it would save him. Pirates should die fighting, is all—so Belisar believed. But that lamebrain Lemmer Harps had botched the throw, careening it off the post, where he'd meant to stick it within Delaney's reach. Lemmer had thrown it from the shallop, the small ship's boat that had brought him here. He'd thrown it from only a short distance, close enough to be sure not to miss, but just far enough away that Delaney couldn't try anything other than maybe to throw it back again from his awkward perch.

But Lemmer had missed. Now it was useless, a good knife gone, *kerplunk*. A true shame, too. He'd bought it in the Salmund Islands, the ones that ring the Sandavale nation. They could make a knife, the Sandavallians. That blade would hold an edge. It was balanced and hard as diamonds, sleek to look at and sharp as a razor to cut with. Delaney ran a hand over his stubbly chin, and felt a pang of sorrow that he'd never feel its cool steel on his whiskers again.

Lemmer had paid dearly for that poor throw.

Delaney didn't want to think on it, but as the events were fresh they came into his head anyway. He didn't mean to remember, but when he started thinking about his knife, and then about Lemmer, well, what Belisar had done just came next like a wagon follows a team of mules. Hungry piranha feeding on a live man's hand was not a good thing to think on. He closed his eyes against it, but his mind rolled on anyway, and now he saw Captain Belisar Whatney's bulk in the back of that little boat, making the prow point upward like a scolding finger, and he heard the pirate captain's words.

"There's the knife right there, Mr. Harps." Belisar's was a high-pitched voice, with just a touch of a whine.

"I don't see it, Cap'n," Lemmer answered, peering down into the dark waters. His chin shook a bit as though he already guessed what was coming, and it made his jutting beard quiver. His eyes were small and sharp, and they were placed close in, right next to the thin bridge of his long, crooked nose, so close in fact that Delaney often wondered if Lemmer saw everything like he was looking from two sides of a wall at once.

"Just reach in the water there," Belisar said, almost gently, the fat flesh under his eyes rising up with dark pleasure. "I'm sure you'll find it if you just reach your hand in."

Then Lemmer's head jerked upward as his pinpoint eyes searched his captain's, recognizing only too well the dancing gleam he saw there. "But Cap'n…"

"You lost it, Mr. Harps. You left our dear Mr. Delaney to die without a fighting chance. So just reach in the water, and fish it out for him."

"But…there's them *Chompers* in there…" Lemmer said pitifully. The Hants had called these fish the *Jom Perhoo,* but never explained what that meant. Lemmer had translated it directly into a word he recognized. It certainly fit.

Belisar leaned back against the small boat's high stern planking, quite at ease. "Blue, you may need to help our reluctant Mr. Harps."

Blue Garvey had the oars in his calloused hands. He was a big man, master at arms aboard Belisar's ship, and just the sort of man a pirate captain would trust with all his ship's weapons. He was loyal as a collared bulldog, though it was rumored aboard ship he had no heart at all. Word was he'd lost it in a poker game with the devil. Delaney didn't believe that sort of talk. Still, if ever there was a man who would hand his heart over on a bet, Delaney figured it would be Blue Garvey. He was merciless as sunrise on execution day.

Blue took Lemmer's arm above the wrist in an iron grip.

"No!" Lemmer squawked.

"You'd rather your hand, or all the rest of you?" Belisar asked with a satisfied sort of smirk. "Mr. Garvey won't be letting go his grip till one side or the other of you goes in the drink."

Lemmer couldn't parse the meaning of that, so Belisar explained it patiently, like a schoolmaster. "Do you see where Mr. Garvey has his grip on your wrist, Mr. Harps? Well, he can put the short side in, which would be from your wrist to your fingertips…Or, he can put the long side in, which would be from your wrist to your heels. It's your choice, but I suggest the former. I'd hate for you to lose that nice pair of boots."

Blue emitted a guttural hiss, sounding like a snake with poor sinuses, that Delaney knew from experience to be a laugh. "I'll take 'is boots, Cap'n, then chunk all the rest of him in for ye!"

"I'm sure you would, Mr. Garvey, and I thank you for the offer. But Mr. Harps will make the right choice. Won't you, Mr. Harps?"

And he did. The *Chompers* were in fact exceedingly vicious, or exceedingly hungry, or both. Inside of sixty seconds of blood frenzy, Lemmer's hand was nothing but white bone and gristle, still attached at the wrist.

Delaney shuddered. It was Lemmer's face, for some reason, and not his hand, that stuck in Delaney's mind. It wasn't pain there, not really. It was more like…amazement. And at the same time…sadness. It was odd. It was as though Lemmer was amazed to be losing his hand, and grieving for the loss of it at the same time.

Delaney shook his head to clear the image, which didn't work very well, because after the shaking he wondered if that's what his own face would look like when the end came, when the mermonkeys took out his bones. He looked at his knobbled knees, his scarred knuckles, and he flexed his fingers. He'd broken several of them, plus an arm and a leg and a toe over the years, but they'd all healed fine. Gnarled and rough as his bones might be from the hard labor of hauling sheets and tying off lanyards and climbing ratlines in the rain, fighting and falling and rising up again bruised and bleeding and battered, they were still good bones, with a lot of years left in them. He'd be sorry to see them go. Sorrier even than he was about his knife.

Then he looked up through the hole in the cloud canopy to the sky above. He needed to find a better place to put his mind. His whole life had come down to a post, a pond, and a few hours of daylight, and all he could do was think on the worst possible things, both what had already happened and what was yet to happen. He squinted against the sun that flamed down into this dank hole. It looked like a torch against a blue background.

Yellow light in a blue sky.

A blue-eyed little girl in a yellow dress. Eyes shining.

Now there was something to think on! Delaney brightened and inhaled the dank air as if it were suddenly fresh and pleasant. Her face came back to him now, and it was a mercy. Her eyes were sad, but not like Lemmer's had been sad. Hers were blue and sweet and made you want to pick her up, protect her, take her back to her mama. How could anyone see such a sad, sweet face as that little girl's and remember his orders? It's no wonder he didn't obey. Those eyes had little white specks in the blue parts, like she had inside her a whole world of sky and clouds, all shining out.

She'd be dead now if he hadn't done what he'd done. He knew that. She'd be dead if Delaney had followed Belisar's orders the way Belisar had meant them. But now she was alive. He grinned, showing the piranha the gum line above his teeth. She was alive, and he was the reason. That was a good thing.

But now Delaney was dead, or nearly so. And that was a bad thing.

His grin faded. His face bunched up, and he scratched behind a ragged ear. There was something all akilter in the world when obeying orders would have got her killed and disobeying would get him killed instead. And it was doubly akilter when neither he nor the girl deserved such a fate. He hadn't been given his orders aright. *Go take care of the girl,* was what Belisar had said. If he had wanted her dead, he should have said so plainly.

Delaney hoped she was running far away now, far away and safe aboard the *Flying Ringby,* running from the pirates, far north out of the Warm Climes, north toward the Havens Tortugal where the Kingdom of Nearing Vast held sway, and at least some sort of law could be counted upon. She'd be safe there. She'd be out of the Warm Climes, where nothing was as it seemed.

How she got mixed in with pirates, and how Delaney got mixed in with her, and how she got away, and how he got here on a post in a pond way upriver among the Hants, so far away from his home in the Kingdom of Nearing Vast…that was a story. That was the kind of story Ham Drumbone would be telling for years to come, speaking soft and low to silent sailors deep in the forecastle, as they swung in their hammocks at the end of a long day's watch.

"Good old Ham," Delaney announced, happy again for another pleasant turn of mind. Hammond Drumbone. Oh, Ham would tell this tale. He'd already told much of it, up to the point where the little girl came in. These last parts now, he'd have no way of knowing. That wouldn't keep him from making something up, of course. But the rest of it, what had led up, that was a bigger story. That went back years. It was a big tale, too, with pirates and pirate-hunters, and fights at sea and on the land, and then of course that whole tale of love and woe. Some was a famous story, known by all, but some wasn't. Some Ham picked up from bits and snippets that Delaney and others told him. Ham filled in a lot of it himself, no doubt. But no one ever minded. No one ever asked which parts were true and which parts weren't. Didn't matter. It was all true, the way Ham told it.

Delaney could almost hear Ham talking now, a shade of melancholy in his deep voice, calling up both lonesome longing and high hopes at the same time, painting those word pictures like only he could paint them. He was as good as the Hants were at conjuring images. He'd wait until there was quiet, there under the decks, quiet but for the creaking of the ship's timbers. And then he'd begin.

Where did it all start? he'd ask. *Where do such tales ever start?* It was what he'd always ask at the outset of a story. Then Ham would answer himself. *Deep in the darkest part of the heart, where men don't know what goes on even inside their own selves. That's where every story starts.*

That Ham. He could tell a tale.

"Dark and clouded it was," Ham began one evening below decks, "with the sky iron gray and restless, the misty sea churning beneath it, throwing off white foam as far as the eye could see." Smoke rose from his pipe as the men lay silent, hammocks in tight rows swaying together with the movement of the ship. "A storm was brewing, aye, and a big one, too. And then a thundering came, and it echoed, and then a voice came, carried on the thunder. But the voice was not like the thunder. The voice was high and beautiful. The voice was a girl singing sweet, and lingering on every note, a pure voice from far away, from out of the rain, out of the storm, out of a dream."

"How old was the girl?" a young sailor asked in hoarse whisper.

"Don't matter her age," Ham answered easily.

"What'd she look like?" asked another, bolder.

"It was just a voice, gents. A disembodied voice, as they say."

"Ye mean she ain't got a body?" a third asked, somewhat shocked. "It's a ghost, or what?"

Ham sighed. "It's all happening in a dream. The ship, the singing, the girl…I'm telling you about a dream that Mr. Delaney had. When he wakes up you'll know where he is, for some of you were there. But I'm trying to build some mystery into it, so shush and let me tell it."

The pirates went silent again, and Ham continued. "And then the lightning flashed, and there was a ship. An enormous, sleek thing, sailing toward our Delaney at uncanny speed, sails full and billowing white in the sudden gale. And the voice sang words, radiant words that almost seemed to make sense, if only one could listen aright. But they didn't make sense, not to Delaney, and he was listening close. 'A true lang time,' she sang in the dream, as sad and distant as lost love." And now Ham's big bass voice sang out a melody, and Delaney imagined it many octaves higher, the way he'd heard it in his dream:

> *A true lang time,*
> *A lang true la,*
> *And down the silver path into a rushing sea,*
> *Where moons hang golden under boughs of green,*
> *And the true heart weeps*
> *As she sings her song…*

Ham's voice echoed into silence.

"What does it mean?" the young sailor asked. He was a boy of "almost thirteen," the youngest of these cutthroats, and with his older brother, the newest.

"Mystery, Mr. Trum. Let there be mystery."

"He means shut yer yap," an elder added helpfully.

"Thank you, Mr. Sleeve. Though you do take a good bit of the poetry out of the language." The others laughed. "But the song is done, for you see, just then a gruff voice broke that dream all to bits, like a gunshot shatters the silence of a night watch. 'Time to pay for your sins!'"

Delaney closed his eyes, and he remembered being there, then. He remembered how those words had pierced through hazy, cluttered layers of deep sleep, and how he had jolted awake that day, up to the harsh and grating recognition that this voice had an owner, and the owner was a jailor, and the jailor was glaring down at him from the other side of grimy black bars.

The jailor clanked a tin cup along those bars, an angry clatter penetrating Delaney's pounding skull. The jailor was dark-skinned, bald, with arms like a bull's forequarters, a round brass cuff tight above his bicep. "What, you think you kill a man then sleep 'til noon?" he asked. "Not in this town! Judgment in Mumtown comes at dawn!" And the dark man's skin glistened and his eyes were afire. Then he laughed, all echoing and hollow.

"Who's kilt?" Delaney asked him, sitting up painfully, his own voice screeching in his head.

"You don't remember? Why, the *Stellat* man, what you would call mayor! And so it is death to the lot of you." His sweeping gesture went beyond Delaney.

"Hang on, now," another sailor piped up. Delaney turned his head, wincing with the accompanying pain. There were half a dozen shipmates here with him. His heart sank when he saw the two boys, the young Trum brothers, here among the newly condemned. The sailor who spoke was in his twenties, not quite as big as the jailor but probably as strong. Nil Corver, trembling amid his complaint, continued. "We din't kill no 'stellar man.' We din't kill no one, not till we was fired upon!"

"Aye!" his fellows added. "Defendin' our own selves!"

"The mayor? The mayor fired first?" the big jailor asked, teeth blazing at the absurdity of such a suggestion. "The mayor of Mumtown pulled out a gun, and fired on you?" The nods were universal, if not terribly confident. "Through the floor of his room above your heads?"

Now there was silence. Then all eyes swung to the gaunt man leaning back against the corner of the cell. Spinner Sleeve met their accusing gaze with disregard. "Didn't know about no mayor up there," he said coldly. "How could I?"

"We're real sorry about what Mr. Sleeve did, then," offered another, a kind-faced man of middling age, hoping to win some pity.

"You shut it, Avery!" Then to the jailor, Sleeve said, "We ain't admittin' to nothin'! None of us!"

"Fine. Tell it all to the *Horkan* man. What you call the judge. Oh wait, that's me!" He showed them his teeth again, and several sailors groaned audibly. "Clean yourselves up as best you can. You'll want to impress me. Trial right after breakfast!"

"Yer givin' us a trial?" Sleeve asked suspiciously.

"Yer givin' us breakfast?" Nil asked hopefully.

Their jailor and judge, the *Horkan* man, just raised an eyebrow.

"*His* breakfast, ye ninny," Sleeve grunted from his corner.

"Oh." Nil grew glum again.

"Delaney, do somethin'!" Nil pled, as soon as the jailor had left them alone again.

"Are we really going to die for our sins?" a Trum boy asked.

Delaney blanched. The men looked to him because he could fight. But he was weaponless. "I don't even recollect rightly what happened." His

Blaggard's Moon

head pounded some more and he closed his eyes. But as soon as he did he saw that ship again, heard that sweet song. *A true lang time…*

"Well, it was like this," a somber voice interrupted. Delaney kept his eyes closed, but recognized the gentleness that was Avery Wittle. He was a deliberate and thoughtful man who always worked within his abilities, large or small though they may be. Mostly, they were small. "We anchored *Tomorrow* in the bay for a little shore leave. Found a nice little tavern. Remember? We were singin' to King Reynard. There were a few foreigners around, I grant that."

Delaney opened one eye. Avery had his cap in his hand. His expression was more earnest than any man over ten has a right to wear, as though Delaney could absolve them all if only the events were recalled in sincere enough fashion. "We sang songs. You remember that?"

"Them foreigners didn't take to it," Nil suggested. "Not our fault!"

"They ain't the foreigners," Delaney countered crustily. "We are."

There was a pause as the men considered that possibility.

Delaney remembered the songs. He recalled the bitter faces at the other tables as a dozen careless men from a far northern port stood up, puffed out their chests and raised their mugs, singing out their own superiority. A proud moment for Nearing Vast. But this was Mumtown, in the island nation of Cabeeb—a dangerous port if a man had any money, and more dangerous if he didn't.

"They fired first!" Nil insisted.

"Sleeve fired first," Delaney said. He remembered that part clearly. "Didn't ye, Spinner?" It all came back now, in a rush. His heart sank like a lost anchor. The mayor left, headed upstairs with a wink. Then the shouting commenced. Accusations. Threats. A fistfight. Shots fired. Then more gunfire. The haze drifting over the silent room. A man's leg propped up on an overturned table. Another man facedown, draped over a chair.

More than one man had died last night.

"There's a trial!" Nil offered. "Cap'n Stube will come. Cap'n, he's a good man. He'll vouch fer us all!" His eyes brimmed with sudden hope.

"The *Tomorrow* has sailed. Stube's gone and left us." A bald man spoke, not much above a whisper. His deeply tanned skin was lined with hard years, his head was wrinkled and dry. Silence fell as they all looked to Mutter Cabe.

"Is it true?" Dallis Trum asked Delaney. "Did the Captain leave us?"

"Naw!" his older brother told him, punctuating the statement with an elbow to the ribs. "Cap'ns don't do such as that!"

Sleeve harrumphed.

Delaney's heart sank further. "Ye don't know he left us, Mutter."

Mutter's dark eyes were blank with certainty. "He came. Stube came in the night. He spoke to the warder. Paid gold. Took Blith. Took Peckney."

The men in the cramped cell looked around them. Blith and Peckney were the first mate and the navigator. They had been here last night, had been a part of it all. Now they were gone.

"May their souls writhe in red blazes," Sleeve hissed.

"Don't say that!" Avery blurted.

Sleeve looked Avery up and down. "May they all writhe in the red blazes a' hell, until the end a' time. And you right with 'em."

"Look," Avery offered, "I don't want to die any more'n you do. But if it's dyin' we got to do, then we got to be of a forgivin' sort of mind. I don't want to go to my Maker otherwise. Do you?"

"I ain't goin' to no Maker!" Sleeve stood. "I'm gettin' out of here if I have to kill every last Cabeeb on this rat-infested pile a' sand." He scratched at a bug bite for emphasis.

The other men looked back and forth between the two voices, hovering in their opinion.

Time to pay for your sins!

"Not the startin' place," Delaney explained to the fish. He felt a crick in his back, and straightened up a bit. The sun was hot, the post was hard, and he'd been slouching over as the story ran through his mind. But it had suddenly occurred to him, as he got to the hard part, to that point in time when a life of crime had seemed the only honest way out, that Ham had not started the story there. He hadn't begun it with the dream and the jail. That was just the place where Delaney had gotten caught up in it. Those were things Delaney himself remembered. But there was a whole lot that had gone on before. It had wound its way around for many years, having nothing to do with him until it met up with him there in Castle Mum. Those earliest things, the ones Delaney had had no way to know, those he'd learned from Ham Drumbone and his stories.

Delaney stretched again, then looked down into the water. The fish were hungry. "Starve, ye little wretches."

He might have died there, that day in Mumtown. It would have been a better death than this, better than what awaited him now, after nightfall, in the dark of the new moon. He rubbed his nose with vigor and sniffed. He wasn't a man to feel sorry for himself. But it did seem odd. Back then, his sins didn't deserve the fate that the *Horkan* man had pronounced upon him. But now they did. They deserved it precisely. A clean hanging or a simple firing squad was more than a pirate could ask for, all he deserved. But now such an honorable end was no longer an option, and now, Delaney didn't deserve *this* fate. He didn't deserve to be left to the *Onka Din Botlay*, the Rippers of the Bone. Who did? Not even Belisar the Whale, if what the Hants said was true...if the mermonkeys really did strip away a man's meat to get at his bones, without bothering to kill him first.

The Hants knew how bad this place was. They knew how horrible it was to die here. These were their *Jom Perhoo*. This was their post. This was their pond, a place of dark legend that scared even them. It was what they called *Kwy Dendaroos*. Doorway for the Doomed.

Belisar, plenty articulate but less poetic, dubbed it Blaggard's Hole.

Delaney closed his eyes, trying to go back to the beginning, trying to remember where Ham had started the tale. But he couldn't. It didn't seem to be anywhere in his head. He sighed and cursed softly. He was never much for getting his mind to do what he wanted it to do. He knew other men, captains and officers mostly, who could direct their minds wherever they wanted, and then direct yours there, too. But Delaney wasn't like that. His mind needed a captain to tell it where to go, and he was but a common sailor.

Telling stories, though, that took directing your mind, and your words. Not like a captain directs things, but more like a mother instructing a youngster. Not that he knew much about mothering. He recalled little of his own ma. She had a warm way with him. And a kind smile, sort of peaceful and easy, whenever she wasn't whupping him.

He didn't even know her name. *Ma*, that's all he ever called her. *Yer Poor Ma*, is how his Pappy called her. Delaney had been taken away from her when he was only, what, five or six? Not old. Just old enough to pinch liquor and vittles for his Pap, but not old enough to get jailed or beaten for it. At least, not bad beatings. Not usually.

Pap had taken full advantage of his skills for a few years, then left Delaney alone in the City of Mann when he was ten or twelve, when he got old enough to get into real trouble. Then his Pap didn't need a kid who couldn't carry his end of the log. That's what Pap said the last time Delaney saw him. So off Delaney went to learn how to carry a log like a man. He lived on the streets for a while, happy for handouts when someone was generous, just as happy to steal when someone wasn't.

That was when the priests came after him. Lawmen he could avoid, but the priests were tricky. Wearing those gray robes with their somber faces, they'd lurk around corners, then pop out smiling, speaking real nice like they were just coming around to help, reaching out with open hands, trying to grab you. He knew what they wanted. They wanted to scare him. They talked about hell. They said bad things about his Pap, said God was watching, and disapproved. One time a big priest caught him by the scruff of the neck and hauled him off to church. Afterward, he scared Delaney for hours on end. Talking about demons and torment and damnation, and how he was sure to drop straight to hell just any moment, unless he repented.

Delaney determined then to get as far away from priests as possible. When he heard that priests didn't sail much in ships, he signed on to the next one floating out of the Bay of Mann.

Odd. When he'd started sailing, he would have been about the same age as Dallis Trum was now. Funny that had never occurred to him. Dallis seemed like such a green young dolt.

But that was not the beginning of the story, either. That was too far back. Any man hanging in a hammock in the forecastle deck of a pirate ship would be fast asleep in no time, listening to a story like that, about some chucklebrained youngster learning how to grow up. Ham would never tell a story like that. Ham's tales were about battles and ships and lovers and losers, gambling and fighting and winning and getting killed trying. *Good* stories.

It was an odd thing, Delaney thought, how a deckhand like Ham with no particular skills otherwise, who could hardly keep up with his own pistol and powder, could somehow keep track of a thing as slippery as a told tale. But he could do it. Night after night. When he started speaking, all went quiet. He'd lie face up in his hammock, legs crossed at the ankles, one hand across his big chest, or under his head for a pillow, pipe in his other hand, smoke rising up from his mouth as the words intermingled with the gray swirls. His broad nose, broken at least twice, twitched now and then, and his beard bounced a bit, but other than that he'd just lie there and talk to the ceiling. Like he was reading a story written on the beams overhead. He never seemed to doubt where to start, or how much to say about what, or which pieces could be left out and what had to be hurried through and which parts he could meander around in slowly, just savoring it like a fresh meat stew.

That was one thing Delaney remembered about Yer Poor Ma. She sure could cook. And so could Maybelle Cuddy. Seemed like all the women he ever knew at all could cook.

The girl!

Delaney remembered now, and it felt good remembering, that Ham had started his story with the girl. The crew always liked a story with a girl in it. Didn't matter what kind, whether mother, daughter, sister, wife, widow, lover, or tramp. Though most men favored one kind over the others. Ham would always put a girl right in the big middle, if ever he could. And there was a girl in this story. And not just a girl, but a woman. That was how he got it all going, the port at which Ham had set sail.

And it had all started just where Ham always said it did. *Deep in the darkest part of the heart.*

Chapter Two

THE DEFENDER

"Our story begins on the day that a mysterious young woman met the eyes of a bold and battle-tested young sailor." Ham puffed his pipe. "It was a sunny midday in June, in the fair City of Mann back in Nearing Vast. The docks were bustling, seagulls were careening and cawing, flies were buzzing around fresh stocks of fish that were being unloaded and gutted. Altogether a glorious day. This fine young lady was boarding a ship, and at that same moment a fierce young warrior wearing the blue naval uniform of a Vast marine was disembarking from another. She glided up the gangway to the main deck of a heavy-laden merchant vessel, which was bound for the southern seaports of the Warm Climes."

"What's her name?" one of the men asked.

"Tell us what she looked like!" begged another.

"Aye, and don't tell us there's mystery to it!" another called out. Laughter rose. Ham was always shrouding some fact he easily could have explained, just so he could produce it later with a flourish, making his listeners feel satisfied after a long hunger.

"Oh, she was a mystery," he said. "She was indeed. The sort of mystery that a man could look on and talk about and study over, and know every detail about, and still not fathom. Aye, our young lady was a mystery with a fine feminine cut. She was dressed in velvet and silk, bodice and gown. Her waist when it was all trussed tight was no bigger around than...well, than a soup bowl is around its outer edge. But she was not a skinny lass

24

otherwise, no sir, but of good proportion. Her face was kind and serene and wise. And she had long, wavy blonde hair, not light nor yellow, but golden, like fine sherry."

"What's a fined cherry?" a sailor asked his neighbor.

"It's a fancy drink, ye lowlife," the neighbor answered. The others laughed.

"Aye," Ham continued, unthwarted. "She was a fine and fancy drink. But for you lads, let's just say her hair was the color of an excellent malt amber beer."

"Ooh, that's nice."

"And as she ascended, our man descended the gangway of a thirty-gun frigate, just in from those same southern shores. They turned and saw one another in an instant, who knows why? Maybe it was a songbird behind the one, a bosun's cry behind the other. Or perhaps, perhaps it was the call of something deeper. Perhaps it was a destiny neither could avoid. But if so, it was a hard destiny, a fate that would lead them both through unimagined battles and hardships and vicissitudes."

"What's the sissitudes?" young Dallis Trum asked.

"Means hardships," Sleeve answered.

"He already said 'hardships.'"

"So I did. Now shush. Whatever the reason, they turned in that moment toward one another, and their eyes met. And they recognized one another, for they were not strangers, but had a strange past together. And this is what he saw in her, in just that moment of sunlight. He saw beauty, fresh and unspoiled, radiant and sharp-eyed, but with sorrow somehow bound up deep within. And what she saw was a dark-haired, scruffy warrior just in from the wildness of the seas, fresh from the fight, but with some unquenchable thirst, a drive she couldn't name."

"Wait, wait, did you say a fight?" one of the men asked. "What fight?"

"You are a hard bunch to tell a story to, and that's a fact. If you must know, that very morning Damrick Fellows had had his first battle against a pirate. It wasn't much, really, just a—"

Now the cramped room exploded.

"*Who did you say?*"

"Hang on now!"

"You sayin' it's *Damrick Fellows*?"

"This story is about Hell's Gatemen?"

When the room calmed, Ham puffed his pipe for a moment. Then into the tense calm, he spoke the single word, "Aye."

The room erupted once again, this time in glee. "Tell us the *fight!*"

Ham savored the moment. "But gents, we were about to learn of fair Jenta Stillmithers, and her travels, and how she was first introduced to the world of pirates and scalawags."

"*Jenta?*" and "Wait, ye mean the pirate's woman?" and "We want to hear Jenta!"

"No!" and "Hang on, tell the fight!" others countered.

And then the forecastle was in an uproar, men shouting at one another from their hammocks, until a few rolled out and stood, the better to argue their points, particularly should their own position on the matter require proofs of a somewhat more forceful nature.

"All right, shush now! Shush or you'll hear neither!" Ham bellowed. The room quieted some. "You'll get the Whale down here thinking there's fisticuffs broke out amongst us, and we'll all be feeling Mr. Garvey's lash. Just furl some sail, boys, and ease up a bit."

The men grumbled but settled quickly, then waited impatiently.

Ham cleared his throat. "Aye, the tale is of Damrick Fellows, and Jenta Stillmithers, and Conch Imbry and his gold. And you shall hear it all."

Grunts and mutterings of approval now lapped over and filled the gaps between opinions.

"As for Jenta, many say she was the pirate's woman true and sure, and many say she never was. But none can argue that she was drawn deep into the darkest lair of the greatest pirate of the age, and from within that lair drew to herself the heart of the greatest of pirate killers. Her tale begins earlier that day, in the hours before her eyes met Damrick's on that gangway, with words spoken in urgency by her dear mother. Those words were these: 'Girl, our ship awaits! Pack your things, we're headed south!'

"As for Damrick, it could be truthfully said that his calling, which as all pirates know by now was to draw hard lines and sharp swords against the likes of us, began within sight of land earlier on that very same day, his last as a uniformed member of his majesty's marines. And while it is true that many to this day find reason to doubt the final allegiance of his heart, no one can question his early mercenary zeal. And he knew the first stirrings of that deadly fervor when he heard words shouted out with urgency—perhaps at the very same moment that Jenta heard the particulars of her own fate, though the pair were far from one another across the seas. What he heard were words that have stirred men's spirits for timeless ages. And those words, gents, were '*Battle stations!*'"

A rumble of anticipation went through the forecastle. "Now we'll hear it!"

But Ham did not quench their thirst just yet. "And thus on one day began the true story of Jenta, and of Damrick, and of Conch Imbry...a tale of love and destruction, of deception and betrayal and the death of dreams. For this is the story of the great battle between the pirates of the world and the band of merciless men who would purge us from the seas, and make the name 'Hell's Gatemen' a source of terror to us all."

A great colored bird flapped and cawed up to the canopy above. Delaney watched it wing through the air until it disappeared into the blue beyond. Below him, the fish still looked hungry. He absently checked his pockets for a morsel of food.

It was a funny thing, how pirates loved to hear stories of their great enemies. He supposed it wasn't much different than how good men and women, upright folks with children in tow, would sit around listening to tales of cutthroats and buccaneers, men who in actual life would flay them and quarter them and feed them to sharks, given half an excuse. Maybe it was the thrill of fear, he didn't know. But there it was, and it worked the same way with pirates.

"Bah," he said to the *Chompers*, realizing suddenly what he was doing—looking for food to feed that which mostly wanted to feed on him. He held up an empty hand. "I'm hungry, too. Don't mean I'm eatin' nothin'."

Delaney was in fact hungry, but not as hungry as he was thirsty. He knew that the more he thought about it, the thirstier he'd get. That was the way these things worked. He'd told younger sailors plenty of times just to focus on the work and quit bellyaching about being tired or hungry or thirsty, and sooner or later it would all come. But now he had no work to do. He had nothing but his own thoughts, and they went where they wanted. Right now, they wanted a drink. He worked a little moisture up and swallowed it down in a sharp lump, trying to think of something, anything, else.

Jenta Stillmithers came right to mind. Now there was a distraction. Women like her seemed all delicate, especially when they were frilled up and fancy as she was, walking up that gangway, looking like they were woven together with some fine thread. Somehow, those delicate, fragile things turned the strongest men weak as babes. Men who couldn't be beaten with a sword or a club or a fist could be taken down with an eyelash, and a certain sparkle in the eye behind it. Even men like Damrick

Fellows. And women like Jenta Stillmithers, they could be shattered with a silent turn of the heel.

It was a mercy, Delaney thought, that he himself didn't have the swash and the swagger to draw such a woman's fancy. Smith Delaney wasn't such a man as Damrick, and Maybelle Cuddy wasn't such a woman as Jenta. But even so she had managed to stick a pike deep into his heart that was somehow still there, even after all these years.

And then, as Delaney relaxed into it, Ham's story began to flow again.

"Battle stations!"

Damrick, the young marine, heard the cry from the bosun, collected his long rifle and ammunition from the armory, and climbed to the fighting top halfway up the foremast. The seabreeze blew back his hair, and his heart was pumping even faster than his feet. Arriving ahead of his squad, he attached his safety line to the mast with a large brass toggle. It couldn't protect him from flying musket shot, cannonballs, and shrapnel, to which he would be completely exposed. But it could keep him, or what was left of him, from falling to the deck or into the sea.

Damrick did not know this from experience. The thousands of drills and maneuvers in his three years at sea had gone like clockwork. The Kingdom of Nearing Vast had not been at war for decades, and while the Kingdom of Drammun postured and threatened and encroached and spied as always, the only actual bloodletting enemies of the Vast people were pirates. And in Damrick's experience, pirates flew like rousted pheasants when a royal navy frigate like the *Defender* topped the horizon.

Today, though, on the final leg of his last voyage, a sleek little brigantine flaunting the skull-and-bones was revealed suddenly when the *Defender* rounded the western tip of Fire Island, on a northwesterly heading. In full view of the Vast man-o'-war, the pirates unloaded a salvo into the belly of a fat, slow merchant vessel. These pirates, intent on their prize, were caught sails struck, stern to their new foe. The brigantine began a turn to windward, hard to port, abandoning her would-be prize in an effort to avoid being run upon from starboard astern, hopeful to get her prow around far enough to manage a broadside engagement, port side to port side.

She moved quickly, but in error. The *Defender*'s captain immediately ordered his helmsman to steer the ship between the pirates and their prey.

Blaggard's Moon

The brigantine's port turn and the man-o'-war's forward momentum would conspire together to keep the outlaws' stern exposed for the entire pass. With only one aft cannon facing a broadside of fifteen guns, the conclusion was foregone.

The *Defender* was at two hundred yards and closing, all her guns primed and loaded, when fire belched from the brigantine's stern cannon. An orange blur whirred over Damrick's head, passing through the heavy sailcloth as though it were frayed gossamer. The echoing boom trailed behind like a lazy watchdog finally aroused. Damrick felt heat in the wake of the shot, as though the midsummer sun had suddenly crossed the sky in a flash.

"They aim to burn us down," muttered the compact, red-faced Lye Mogene, kneeling to Damrick's right. This young marine wore a thick, ragged brown beard under round, ruddy cheeks that pushed up against deeply creased, sunken eyes. The combination made him look healthy but always tired. Now he swore at pirates in general and nestled one cheek firmly into his rifle stock.

Damrick looked at the round hole in the canvas above him, saw it was blackened around the edges. A few red embers still struggled to catch the canvas. He had heard stories about red-hot cannonballs, how they'd pass through a man and leave him dead with a clean hole and no blood. He raised his own long rifle, sighted down the barrel at the approaching ship. He saw a thin plume of smoke rising from her afterdeck. That would be the furnace in which her crew heated the shot.

"*Savage Grace*," Damrick read aloud the words painted in faded, flaking gold leaf across the stern of the pirate vessel. Damrick's dark eyes scanned his adversary as his mind turned.

"Pipe down," his lieutenant ordered. This was Hale Starpus, a broad man with a big brow, a strong belly that rode high on his torso, thick arms and legs, and a wild tangle of sideburns that looked as though they had never been trimmed. "Ready your muskets and fire on my signal." Then after a pause he said, "That's Sharkbit Sutter's ship, lads."

"Sharkbit!" The pirates listening to Ham's tale in the forecastle shouted out their delight. "Sharkbit Sutter, the madman!"

"Aye, the very one," Ham confirmed. "He was new to the world's oceans, and his reputation was just beginning. But that name already struck fear into simple hearts whenever it was uttered."

"Is it true he used to be a priest?" one of the sailors asked Ham.

"Nah," Sleeve groused. "He was a pirate from birth. That was just a lie."

"Oh, but it wasn't, Mr. Sleeve," Ham countered. "I know men who know, men who knew men who knew our Sharkbit well, so rest assured it's true. A priest he was, until one night he was praying at a ship's rail in a storm during a missionary voyage, and was washed overboard. Left behind, he survived…but only to be attacked by sharks and swallowed whole by one of them, a huge and ancient beast. So he found himself alive in its belly. But unlike the repentant Jonah, this priest went mad and fought against his fate, ripping in a blind fury through the thing's flesh. He killed it from within, and surfaced without a scratch. Still punching and flailing, he raged at the other sharks until they abandoned him as just too much trouble. When his shipmates hauled him from the water, there was a dark wildness to him, a danger that ran deep into his soul. He stripped off his robes and never prayed another prayer."

The forecastle deck was silent, pondering. "But let's continue our tale," Ham finally suggested.

The pirates grunted their agreement.

The hammers of eight long-range muskets cocked back, and all bores aimed down line from high on the foremast fighting top.

"Ye know why they call 'im Sharkbit, don't ye, when not one shark ever bit 'im?" Lye asked. Damrick had heard, but said nothing. "It's 'cause he cut his way out of that shark's belly usin' naught but his own teeth."

Damrick was no coward, but he felt sweat on his gunstock. He noticed that his own knuckles, where he gripped his rifle, were bloodless. *White knuckles.* In the back of his mind he acknowledged that this meant fear. He'd never before considered that the phrase might be literal.

Another flash and a hot orange blur flew from the *Grace*, this one below Damrick and the fighting top, this one on target. It crashed through the hull at the bulkhead, just below the quarterdeck, amidships. Sailors on deck streamed down through doorways, headed to the ship's belly with buckets. They were followed quickly by the ship's carpenter, looking like an iron-monger in his heavy gloves, carrying huge tongs, the surgeon sent to remove a deadly foreign object from deep within his patient's wooden flesh.

Suddenly, scores of lead balls whistled through the air or smacked into nearby masts and spars. Puffs of smoke and hard cracks, pistol fire mostly, erupted from the *Grace*'s stern. The men instinctively lowered their heads and pulled in their shoulders to avoid the barrage.

Lye Mogene cursed, then shook his right hand as though he'd been stung.

"You hit, sailor?" their lieutenant asked.

"Nah." He settled his cheek back into his gun stock. But Damrick saw blood seeping through Lye's sleeve, just above the wrist.

"Ready and steady," came the order. Intermittent pistol and musket fire whistled and pattered, pinging all around them.

Damrick found and sighted on a ragged-haired pirate who stood on the weather deck of the *Grace*. He waited for the rifle to steady itself. Accounting for the rhythm of his own ship's rise and fall on these small waves was easy enough; he could feel it all, through his right knee, his left foot, his whole body. But taking the measure of the opposing ship's movement, that was the art. That was the skill at which Damrick had labored, through three years of practice in drills and maneuvers. He knew the moment would come, if he would wait, and watch, and relax, and let his eyes lock on the target while his mind and body made their own peace with the seas.

And then it came. Suddenly he no longer sensed the movement of the *Grace;* he saw his sights lock down, stopping dead on target, as though his rifle knew its business and needed him not at all. All else in the world moved, everything but his rifle sight and one ragged villain.

"Fire at will!" came the cry from below.

"Fire when ready," grumbled Lieutenant Starpus. He knelt to Damrick's left, Hilly Manders between them.

Damrick eased the trigger back. When the hammer hit the flint, the powder breathed out a menacing hiss. And then it exploded in anger, propelling its missile in a roar of fire and smoke.

The ragged pirate's head jerked backward, his long hair flipping up. And he was gone.

There could have been no other outcome, and Damrick nodded at the simplicity of that fact. He had a new powder charge in his hands and down the smoking gun barrel without thinking, without willing it, and then he had the shot packet, wad and patch and ball, rammed home and ready. Cannon thundered below him.

Damrick found his second target quickly, and his rifle sight settled almost instantly. Another squeeze of the trigger, another pirate down. *Pirates,* he thought dismissively. *This is why they run.*

Then the marine to Damrick's left jerked suddenly and dropped his rifle. His hands quivered before him as he reached out, fingers clawing the air as though searching for a wall in the darkness. He moaned once in dismay, hardly more than a whimper, and then tumbled forward off the fighting top. His safety line jerked taut with a sound like the plucked string of a bass fiddle.

"Fire on, sailor," the lieutenant ordered.

Eyes wide, Damrick nodded, reloaded. *Hilly Manders,* was all he could think. *That's Hilly Manders, shot dead.* And then that thought turned to hot anger. *A good man shot dead by worthless cutthroats.* Damrick took aim at the first thing moving and fired, but missed. He took a deep breath and choked on black powder smoke. Now amid the crack of pistols, the roar of muskets, and the boom of cannon he heard for the first time cries of men in pain, the death throes of comrades below him. Had this madness just now descended, or had he somehow, until now, ignored it? He calmed himself and reloaded. His hands shook as he replaced the ramrod.

Scanning for a target, he saw one of the *Grace*'s stern windows drift open, gently, as though blown in the wind. He rammed the packet home, raised his rifle, searching inside the darkness behind that open frame. He saw a shape, perhaps a face, hardly visible, rimmed in darkness. As he aimed, the face moved suddenly into the light. And then it looked at him. Damrick froze. He saw wild eyes. Not wild in the way of the lunatics who lurk on street corners in Mann, reciting incoherent complaints against the world, but wild like the feral dog he'd shot once in the woods as a boy. Wild like a growling wolf. And he saw the man's teeth in the growl.

Damrick's finger squeezed the trigger, and the musket exploded.

A hunk of wood blasted away beside the iron frame, and glass flew. But the face was still there, teeth still visible. Damrick wasn't sure if the look had changed or if he had imagined it, but he was quite sure now that this was no growl. Damrick was being mocked.

Moving quickly, wanting this prize, he rammed another packet home and raised his musket.

But the face was gone.

He moved his sights around the stern of the ship, the rails, every window. Nothing. And then he settled in on another target. But before he could fire, a dark figure in a hooded cloak appeared on the weather deck, the highest point astern. Damrick aimed, and waited. His sight drifted down from the man's bleeding face and stopped dead, covering his heart. A shark's tooth hung there, just where a priest would wear a cross. As Damrick's finger squeezed down on the trigger, the man raised an arm, and in his hand was a white bit of cloth. No more than a handkerchief. But it was white, and he waved it.

Damrick froze, uncertain.

"Cease fire! Cease fire!" came the call from below.

"Hold your fire, men," Lieutenant Starpus repeated, closer by.

Damrick did hold his fire, but he also held his aim. He could see now that the man did not wear a cloak, but rather a long black riding coat, the kind cut in the back all the way up to the belt so that both a man's legs could be covered while astride a horse. It boasted a hood that its owner wore up, loose around his face, keeping him in shadow.

"Do you surrender?" the bosun called, following the captain's orders.

"Aye, on condition!" shouted the man in the hood. His voice was hoarse, and ragged.

"Identify yourself!" the bosun shouted back.

"Why, I thought you knew!" came the gravel-throated answer. "I'm the worst seafaring captain of the sorriest ship ever to sail these dismal seas! And I have under me the least disciplined lot of savages ever called a crew!" His pirates grunted out in unison, a sound of agreement and dark joy, in a cadence that would have seemed rehearsed had it been at all less brutal. As it was, it sounded like a single snort of derisive laughter.

Lye couldn't contain himself. "And they're all plenty proud of it, seems like," he muttered. Then he spat on the floorboards at his feet.

"Quiet!" the lieutenant ordered him. "Ready and steady."

"Are you the one they call Sharkbit?" the bosun called.

"Aye, ever since that brute ate me and I gave it reason to repent!" His men now laughed.

"What are your conditions?"

"Parley! A simple parley with your captain."

"And then surrender?"

The grin again, and a right hand raised in a gesture that looked to Damrick like the mockery of a solemn vow, "As God is my judge!"

Rumbles and mutterings could be heard from below, on the *Defender*'s deck.

Now it was the lieutenant who couldn't contain himself. "God'll be his judge, soon enough."

"Not soon enough for me," Lye answered.

"Terms accepted!" shouted the bosun. "Prepare to be boarded!"

The man in the hood bowed, then made a sweeping gesture. "Welcome, honored guests!" And he disappeared from the deck.

Damrick shifted his position, trying to look over the lip of the fighting top to see what had become of his companion.

"Steady, now," the lieutenant reminded.

"Permission to…" Damrick started. He glanced at the taut line beside him. "Corporal Manders, sir." His words did not form a question, but his tone did.

"You and Ensign Mogene, then," the lieutenant granted with a nod. Damrick quickly laid down his rifle, and he and Lye hauled Hilly Manders' lifeless body back up onto the fighting top.

"It wasn't two hours later that the *Defender* sailed away," Ham offered next, in the tone of a conclusion. "She left the *Savage Grace* behind to repair her broken rudder and refit elseways as best as she could. Her rear was shot all to pieces, but only one or two holes needed to be patched at the waterline. So Damrick Fellows, Lye Mogene, and that entire crew of fine, fighting marines watched the ragged pirate's ship shrink away behind. They were mortified, gents. They were aghast. For Sharkbit had been let go."

"Pirate's parley!" shouted one of the sailors who had been listening in rapt attention to Ham's account. The other men laughed aloud and hooted. The men had wanted to hear a fight, and they had heard one. While it was good as far as it went, it was lopsided, and it did not lop in their preferred direction. The sudden escape of Sharkbit Sutter was therefore a particularly agreeable turn.

"Aye, it was a pirate's parley," Ham affirmed. "But not like you boys may be thinking."

"What's a pirate's parley?" asked Dallis Trum.

"You tell him," Ham suggested to the old sailor who had first called out the words.

"Not me. I ain't good for no stories." The sailor's neck turned as red as the bandana tied around it.

"I'll tell 'im," Spinner Sleeve said in a voice cold enough to douse a cookstove.

After a pause, Ham said, "Well, have at it, Mr. Sleeve."

The gaunt man spoke to the darkness above him as he lay still in his hammock. "Pirate captains ain't like regular folks, boy. They have different rules. You parley with a pirate, you parley with death."

There was a somber silence.

"Well, that's a fine bit a' storytelling, Mr. Sleeve, and I thank ye." Ham's voice was full of mirth, and the men laughed, both in relief and approval.

"But our Captain Sharkbit Sutter did not kill, nor did he even threaten the brave naval captain. Rather, he used a bit a' guffin', which had been worked up a while earlier to prepare for just such a strait. It was no more than a rolled piece of parchment that did the trick."

"A letter from the king?" asked a sailor.

"That's been heard about before," another suggested.

"Aye it has," Ham acceded, "for the king has had some dealings in the past with those of the pirate persuasion. So it is said. But nay…it were no letter from the crown, though it was sealed by the governor to prove the truth of its verity. This seal was broken before the eyes of both captains, right there on Sharkbit's main deck, and there both saw together that the parchment within had been signed and pressed with yet another seal—the seal of a man all of you shall hear much more about soon enough. A man with dealings far and wide, and no lack of plans and schemes by which to line his own pockets. A man who would happily invite a fine-looking young woman and her mother into the very lair of the devil, and them wishing only to better themselves and their lot." Ham paused, waiting. Not a soul had a guess. "The sort of man who would invite a lady far south to the Warm Climes, while she supposed him a gentleman of noble character."

"The one that took Jenta on board that ship headed south?"

"Excellent! Mr. Roe, our fine helmsman, has not been asleep at the tiller. Aye, the document was signed by one Runsford Ryland, of Ryland Shipping and Freight. For you see, Sharkbit carried with him a signed affidavit. That's a legal document, in case you were about to ask, a bit like a contract except it just writes down a man's words so no one can question that a man said them. And the words written down were these…" Ham cleared his throat and stroked his beard, closing his eyes as though recalling it all precisely.

> For all men hereby, who may come to these portents and in due course meet with Captain Stansfield Sutter, better known as Sharkbit, I heretofore and with all due legal conformity herewith state for all men present that this same Captain Sharkbit Sutter be now in my employ, to ensure the performance of duty by my own ships and captains thereto, of any vessel sailing under the banner and in the register of the Ryland Shipping and Freight Company. Furthermore, I wherefore acquiesce that empowerment hereunto has been given, which allows said Sharkbit to halt

and board for commercial purposes said ships of the Ryland line,
using force as necessary to inspect and to confiscate such goods
and materials as deemed by him necessary for the enactment of
his said duties, heretoforeupon.

"What's all that mean?" Trum whispered in the dumbfounded silence.

"It means, young pup," Ham quickly answered, "that Sharkbit can do as he blame well pleases with a Ryland ship, and Mr. Ryland himself gave the orders. And being as how the fat merchant vessel that was being attacked by Sharkbit was flagged and chartered by Ryland, it means what Sharkbit did was all good and legal, and so our courageous men o' war could do nothing but let him go."

"How'd Sharkbit ever get such a paper?" a sailor asked.

"Why, in a pirate's parley, of course."

Much laughter, much whooping. A fine fight well told, they all agreed.

Chapter Three

A WOMAN OF SECRETS

"AND NOW TO JENTA'S VOYAGE south to the Warm Climes," Ham began the next night in the forecastle.

"I'm sleepin'," one said. "Wake me up when there's another fight."

"All right, if you don't want to hear about her wedding."

It had been a long shift in the sun, and a blustery wind had kept them busy furling and unfurling canvas, hauling and tying sheetlines. They had done no business today, no pirate's business, but were on their way to the Stella John Shoals off the Bandamin coast, where business was always brisk. Muscles ached and eyelids drooped. They all needed rest.

"She marries Damrick," a tired sailor said. "Who couldn't guess that. Tell us a fight, or let us sleep."

"Nah, ye dolt, she marries Conch Imbry. It's Jenta, the pirate's wench." This was Spinner Sleeve. But even in argument he sounded weary tonight.

"So she's been called," Ham answered. "But sometimes the truth is not what it seems."

"No mysteries tonight," another weary voice implored. "Just tell us who she married, and we can sleep."

"Hmm." He thought a moment. "No, that would be tapping the keg too early, and spoiling the ale. But I'll say this, and then let you rest: The next man to fall in love with Jenta was tall and skinny. The son of a rich man, raised to run a rich man's business. Heir to the Ryland Shipping and Freight Company. And Jenta, well, many thought Jenta lucky to have found favor in the eyes of such a man as Wentworth Ryland."

Snorts and epithets rose. "Lucky?" and "*Wentworth?*" and then "Are you kiddin'?" and finally "He ain't man enough!"

Ham just tugged on his crooked pipe, let the smoke rise and the ire settle. "See, boys, that's just it. That's just the kind of woman she was. Men took to her, took to defending her, just as you're doing now. Many wanted her for themselves. Many others just didn't want the under-deserving to have her. She carried herself with an air of easy nobility, and when she looked at you, you felt the light of it in those blue eyes. Like not only was she noble, you could be noble too, just by standing close enough. But I'll tell you, Jenta Flug was not born noble. No, that rumor was false. She was in truth born poor, raised poor, and by a mother who dreamed she'd become more."

"Wait, who's Flug? I thought you said her name was Stillmithers. If she married this Ryland, wouldn't her name be Ryland?"

"Aye, yer messin' it up. How many names she got?"

"Ah, it's a wee bit hard to answer all these questions at once, and still let you nod off after only a few minutes time." He sighed and stroked his beard. "But I'll try. See, Jenta's mother, name of Shayla Flug, had made what fine people in up-and-up society call a bad, bad mistake. She wasn't more than sixteen when she'd latched on to a man above her station, a gentleman who was...kind to her. But he turned against her and turned her out, soon as he learned she was with child."

Whistles and low whoops stole through the forecastle.

"He swore the baby wasn't his, and all believed him. The young man's family promised to pay handsomely for her to keep it all quiet and secret and send the baby off to an orphanage, but she refused. And then her own family gave her the boot. And so that left Shayla Flug to fend for herself, a scarlet woman now, and a baby on the way."

"What'd she look like, Ham? The scarlet mother?"

"Well, she had raven-dark hair and clear green eyes. Her skin was like the finest white porcelain, and her heart, they said, was the same. But who could blame her for turning cold, making her own way like she did in a world where she was scorned? She took the only honest job she could find, with a wealthy man who let her have one small room in his basement for raising her child. She became the lowest of household servants, no more than a washerwoman, her delicate fingers ever raw and callused from scrubbing the master's silk stockings and the mistress's dainty underthings."

"Dainty underthings," one listener repeated. Men chuckled and glanced sideways at one another.

"It was a hard life for Shayla Flug. But she loved her little girl, and gave her the name of Jenta in the hope that one day, some way, she'd become a gentlewoman herself. And Jenta grew to be a beauty. Tall and comely, with blue eyes that pierced."

"And hair like a mug a' beer!" a young voice noted.

Ham winced. "Ah, the analogy is apt, even if the words fall somewhat short of perfection, Mr. Trum. But let's rather again say that her hair was the color of a fine sherry, and leave it there."

"Okay."

"Jenta, now, she was softhearted. And she learned something her mother had lost somewhere along the way. Jenta knew how to laugh. She would seem quiet and serene, politely listening, and then something would strike her, and her blue eyes would spark like a flint on powder, and she'd laugh, and her laugh would light the darkness. And the world would be drawn to her. And by the world, I mean the world of men.

"But Shayla protected her daughter ferociously. This one, *this one*, would grow up a lady. And so while Shayla cleared the teacups and crumbs of crumpet cakes, she watched the wealthy women carefully, and she listened close and studied how they worked their polite magic. And when she wasn't washing the linens or polishing silver or scrubbing fine marble tiles, she was schooling her daughter in the ways of gentility, teaching her how to sip from a porcelain cup with her pinky finger raised."

A few of the men, lost now in the tale, raised invisible cups to their lips and dutifully protruded their little fingers.

"And Jenta learned how to proffer a limp hand for a gentleman to kiss at a garden party." Several men kissed invisible hands. One or two absently held up limp hands toward the dark timbers above their hammocks.

"Eventually, she taught Jenta all the manners and mannerisms, and Jenta learned to be a perfect lady. But as Jenta came of age, neither her lessons nor her skills brought her a single invitation to any of the fine events in town. For in Nearing Vast, in the City of Mann at least, the doors to such society are shut upon those not born to rank and privilege."

There were grumblings about the unfairness of society's doors.

"There was one dance, though, just one, a cotillion held for new recruits into His Majesty's Navy. It was local girls saying their goodbyes to local boys, mostly, but it had an air of respectability to it. Jenta was sixteen, versed in all the ins and all the outs of polite banter, knowing the fine dance steps of ladies and gentlemen, and ready to put such skills to use. So Shayla said yes, and Jenta went. And there she danced with many a young sailor. Several caught her eye, but only one caught her fancy."

"You're a quiet one."

Jenta said it to the dark-haired boy who leaned against the wall near the bowl of sugar punch. He wore the same blue uniform as the others, but standing there by the drapes where the wall angled in, he fairly melted into the shadows. She had noticed him some time back, tall and aloof, calm eyes that spoke of some larger purpose, something deeper. He seemed more aware, somehow, than the others. He had held her gaze when she glanced at him during a dance, not in a challenging way, nor in a hopeful way as most of the boys did, nor in that hungry way a few of them did, but just in a questioning way. As though he felt she was different, too. He hadn't seemed the least interested in dancing; she even saw him shake his head when chatting with several girls who came by and then left him alone again.

Jenta spoke the words after she had finished perhaps her fifth dance, a slow and melancholy thing, throughout which she had needed to assure her partner that no, he hadn't hurt her toes and yes, he was doing just fine, both of which he seemed quite willing to believe. She had graciously declined the young man's offer to continue their partnership into the next tune, citing a sudden thirst, and when he asked if he could accompany her to the punch bowl she had quickly agreed. But on the way she introduced him to a young lady with whom she had spoken earlier in the evening, and who afterward seemed to watch with something that looked a bit like envy. So after a brief conversation, during which it was discovered that the young lady very much enjoyed dancing and the young man very much wanted to learn to dance better, she was able to complete her quest for punch unaccompanied.

She did not pick up one of the empty cups beside the bowl, however, but instead stood nearby watching the dancers, close enough to the quiet young man that he must be quite aware of her presence, but not so close as to be considered forward. He made no move to introduce himself. She sighed, fanned herself, and even caught his eye with hers once. But he said nothing. So she was the first to speak, a simple observation, not an accusation, regarding the apparent disparity between his level of interest in the affairs of the evening and his actual participation in them.

"I'm sorry," he said in answer. "I'm afraid I'm not very good at this sort of thing."

"You don't dance, then?"

"No." He was not apologetic about it.

"But you don't mind watching others."

The fiddler hit three sour notes by way of tuning, then started in, joined by a bass fiddle in a much more spirited tune.

"I don't step on toes when I watch others." His raised eyebrow spoke of experience.

She laughed. "Not a risk taker, then?"

He did not answer. Instead he studied her.

She turned her attention back to the dance, letting him make his assessments, hoping she had not offended him. But she thought not. She waved at the couple she had recently put together. The young man smiled as he danced by. The young lady winced.

"What are you doing here?" Not curt or cold, but curious.

She turned her head toward him, looked away again. "Certainly you know. You've been watching me all night."

"Well, there's only one way you could know that." His tone was not defensive.

She laughed again. "I did wonder why you're standing here alone. I thought perhaps you were assigned to guard the punch bowl."

He shook his head. He was not smiling, but he was not angry, either. He picked up a cup, scooped it almost full, then held it out to her.

She put her hand on it. He held it just a moment longer than he needed to. "You didn't come over here for the punch. Did you?" he asked.

His directness took her off guard. She heard no accusation and no pretense. She glanced around to see if any of the others had overheard him. It was rude behavior, she knew, but no one was paying attention, and she found herself unable to react negatively. In fact, it had the opposite effect. "Well, my mother tells me I have a bad habit of picking up strays."

"Is that what I am?"

She looked into the cup, studying the deep red liquid. She smelled strawberries. But she did not drink. "I don't know what you are."

He looked into her, studying her bright blue eyes. He smelled the honeysuckle of her perfume. "But these others belong here. You don't."

"Do you know me?"

"No. But I don't belong here, either."

She felt suddenly his sense of purpose, and it surprised her. It was startling. It was not unattractive.

A talkative crowd now gathered around the punch bowl, surrounding them, ignoring them. He made a quick gesture with his head, hardly a formal invitation, but when he walked away she walked with him.

They stood on the back porch of the inn, looking out over the street. It was quiet here, a perfect summer's evening. The music sounded farther away than it was, and more melodious, more wistful somehow, from this distance. A watchman in a soiled frock coat walked to a lamppost, set down his stepstool, climbed up, and began trimming the wick, brightening the street by a shade or two. Now from behind them, a matronly woman creaked heavily onto the porch and crossed her arms.

"There's your guard of the punch bowl," Damrick whispered, cutting his eyes to the chaperone.

She smiled, but did not laugh.

"What's your name?" he asked. He seemed much more at ease out here.

She wanted to tell him. But for some reason, she didn't. "Do you ship out in the morning?"

He nodded. He looked out over the street again. "Three years of service, starting at dawn."

She wished she hadn't brought it up. That was his focus. That was his sense of purpose. Of course. "Will you look for me when you return?" She asked it impulsively, but she held his gaze when he turned to question her. She felt a sting as he searched for an answer. His eyes grew distant again, though he looked at her still.

Finally, he looked back down the street. "It's hard to know what three years will bring." Then they spoke about the Navy, about pirates, then back to cotillions. But they never got back around to her question.

"That was a conversation Jenta never did forget," Ham informed his audience. "She talked to her mama about it, and when she spoke about the dark young man, her pulse quickened. Shayla saw it, and warned her about the risks, the attraction that a woman could feel for a dark, mysterious fellow with a trace of danger about him."

"That's us!" someone called. The others sang out in hopeful agreement.

"She told her mother he'd behaved as a gentleman, but Shayla was quick to point out that in fact he was not one. Jenta countered that neither was she a lady, and what ensued was…a serious clash of conflicting convictions."

"A serious *what?*"

"An *argument.* The upshot was that there would be no more cotillions for Jenta unless they were truly of the higher social order. And so, there would be no more cotillions. Three years later, the most beautiful young woman in the city, nearly twenty years old and refined of heart and mind, lived with her mother and two cats in a cramped, dank cellar below a rich man's house, smelling of lye and linens, not even allowed the light of day of the servant's quarters."

Many of the men growled and groused on her behalf.

Delaney was one of them. He had seen a fair number of those born to rank and privilege up close, after he'd turned pirate. He had brought the favored, the slammers of social doors, to unfavorable ends. He had done his part to blast those doors down, using cannon fire and gunpowder. He had watched as gentlemen, and even a few ladies, trembled with fear when set upon at sea.

Fear and terror, that was something Delaney expected. But disgust, that he did not expect, and it had chafed him raw inside. More often than not he saw disdain in the haughty faces of the rich, heard scorn from lace-trimmed throats, felt contempt in their defiant refusals or grudging compliance. It made Delaney feel bitter and small and exposed somehow, even though it was he who held the pistol.

The truth was, the haughtiness of the high and mighty could make pirating a satisfying line of work.

"Damrick, on the gangway that day," Ham continued, "looking into her eyes as he'd done years earlier, felt the fanned ember of that single evening years before. And just as the slightest spark falling from a flint can smolder on a forest floor among the dry leaves and pine duff, almost invisible, in the same way, that evening spent in conversation on a porch burned within each of them. Now the winds of fate that drew them close once more also blew that ember to flare up suddenly, a flame that could not be denied by either, drawing them silently but surely back toward one another.

"But let's not jump ahead of ourselves. For Jenta's voyage south began not on that gangway, nor with that rekindling moment. No, it began just a bit earlier that same day, when Shayla rushed down to the cellar and announced to her daughter that all must be left behind. She hurried them both through the packing of clothes into laundry sacks, and they rushed out and up toward a waiting carriage, fleeing at last the servant's life in Nearing Vast."

"Mama, is that carriage for us?"

"Try to act as though you've seen one before. And I'm your mother, not your mama. We are in public."

Jenta stiffened, looked at the driver, a man quite a bit older than Shayla but plenty spry. He hadn't overheard; Shayla had been discreet, as always. A striped tabby cat wandered up, eyes questioning. Her long tail flicked back and forth at the tip. "Poor Moggie," she said, picking her up. "Who will feed you table scraps?" The cat let herself be held tight.

The driver stepped down and looked at the two sorry sacks, stained and ragged. "Are these your traveling bags, madam?" Shayla said nothing in response to his bewilderment, but instead waited silently at the carriage door. He shrugged, put out a hand, and helped Shayla in.

"Come, girl," her mother said from within. "And no, we cannot take that with us."

"She wouldn't be any trouble. Would you, Mogs?" She scratched the cat behind the ears.

Shayla gave her just a moment, then said, "There are strays everywhere. Pick one up on the way."

Jenta whispered softly to the cat. When she set it on the ground, it promptly ran toward the house. "Won't even miss me, will you?" she said after it. But Moggie turned and sat, and watched.

Jenta admired the carriage even more on the inside, though she kept that to herself. It was polished mahogany and walnut wood, smelling of lemon oil and leather. The upholstery was blue velvet. She heard the thuds of the duffels hitting the roof, the creak of leather straps as the driver buckled them down tight, and then the cluck of a tongue, the slap of reins, and finally the plod of hooves on the dirt street. The carriage lurched and creaked.

"Wait!" The voice came from the lawn behind them.

"Don't stop, driver!" Shayla called out.

But the carriage ground to a halt.

Jenta, facing backward, watched the approach of a familiar white-haired man, slightly bent, whipping his cane ahead of him and planting it with conviction at each step. He popped his head into the window. Thin white hair flowed back from a lively face punctuated with bright, kind eyes. Shayla looked calmly at her employer.

"Ma'am," he said by way of hello. Then to Jenta, "Miss."

"Good morning, Mr. Frost," Jenta answered as brightly as she dared. She had always liked him.

"You seem to be leaving in quite a hurry. Is everything all right?"

Shayla blinked once. "Yes, thank you. I apologize for our haste, but we must not miss our ship."

"Your ship? I see. So it's Runsford Ryland taking you...where? South?"

"We are his invited guests. And yes."

He nodded. "I don't suppose I could talk you out of it?"

"I don't suppose you could."

"You don't know him well." Now the old gentleman looked concerned.

"I suppose not. But he has promised us...introductions. And a place to live above ground."

"Yes, I understand. A step up." He fumbled in his pocket. "I don't blame you for that. Here, take this." He held out two gold coins.

"For what possible purpose?" Shayla asked, as Jenta watched in silence.

"You may find you need independent means."

Shayla looked at him carefully. "For nineteen years I have washed your socks and changed your bed linens and served your tea. You and Mrs. Frost have kept me in a cellar. I care not about myself, but I would have liked some small foothold for my daughter, so that she would not be condemned to the same life. And yet you could not, or would not, provide it."

"We have tried."

"Have you?"

"*Mother!*" Jenta whispered. She had felt the sting of Shayla's displeasure often, but had never known her to aim it toward Mr. Frost.

Shayla didn't pause. "You lent us money to buy the clothes we wear, which I repaid in extra hours and extra duties. And you introduced me to Runsford Ryland. For those two things I thank you, but you will excuse me if I find your parting gift rather dubious. Now that your scrubwoman is already gone, you offer her independent means?"

Jenta's jaw dropped.

Mr. Frost closed his hand around the coin, but did not retract it. "Dear

Shayla. I have given you a place of refuge in which to raise your daughter, protected from the scorn of society. You need not know the scorn I myself have received for my troubles, but I can tell you it does not reflect well on the society you are so eager to join. And I apologize if I have been unable to alter centuries of social stigma. But you must be aware that you are leaving troubles you know for troubles you do not. I am not stopping you; I am simply offering you a hedge against those troubles, whatever they may be." He opened his hand again. "Take it. Please."

"I will not." Her face showed no emotion, not even determination. "Driver?" she called.

"Mother, take it!" Jenta intervened.

"Accepting a gift binds you to the giver, girl. The greater the gift, the greater the bond."

Windall Frost closed his hand around the coin again. "And yet you accept the gift of an entire new life from a man you barely know."

Shayla's right eyebrow twitched. Jenta could see anger in her mother when others could not. It ran dangerously deep at the moment. "Runsford Ryland is a gentleman with a reputation to uphold," she said, perfectly controlled. "And *he* did not offer me *money.*"

"I see." Windall Frost withdrew his hand and his offer. "Then I wish you the best, both of you."

"Thank you," Shayla said. She knocked on the hardwood above her head. Still the driver didn't move.

"Thank you for everything you've done for us." Jenta had never said a word that she meant more.

"You are welcome, dear girl," he answered. "And don't worry about your cats; we'll take good care of them." His eyes danced.

"That would be so kind."

"Please instruct the driver," Shayla said coldly. "He apparently cannot hear a woman of few means when a man of many stands nearby."

"Write to me, Shayla. Should you need anything."

"Do not wait at the post office."

Mr. Frost stepped back. He tapped the wooden door frame with his cane. The carriage creaked and lurched forward.

"Who is the gentleman?" Jenta asked after a respectful pause.

"What gentleman?" her mother asked calmly.

"Mr. Ryland."

"Runsford Ryland is a man of good family and better connections."

"You must have impressed him greatly."

Shayla heard the shade of accusation. "It's not like that. He's married. His motives are selfless. He is a centerpiece of society on the island of Tortugal. He has a home in Mann, but he lives most of the year in the south, where he conducts his shipping business."

"The Warm Climes." It was so far away. "Is there a city?"

"Yes, of course there is a city. We are not farmers or fisherwomen."

Now Jenta was silent, brooding. The horses' hooves clattered against stones as the carriage moved from the dirt road onto the paved streets that would take them through town to the docks. "And what are we, mother, exactly?"

Shayla watched her daughter. "It's not what we are, it's what we can become. Not so many questions will be asked down there, about family trees and histories. It is possible to start over."

None of this impressed Jenta. "And what is the name of this great city of hope?"

Shayla could find no way to couch the news. "We're going to Skaelington," she said at last. "Skaelington City."

"Skaelington!" Jenta exclaimed. "But mother, Skaelington is—"

"Yes, yes, I know, it does have…a bit of a reputation."

"A bit? There's not a savagery known to man that doesn't happen in Skaelington!"

The pirates crowed their agreement.

Delaney took a deep breath, remembering the moment. A pair of dragonflies buzzed the surface of the pond, zigzagging in and around one another, like an angry dance. It was a funny thing, how Ham Drumbone could keep a shipload of pirates in a silent trance with a tale of two ladies in a fancy carriage. But he could do it. One reason was that pirates weren't that different than merchant sailors, at bottom, most of them having been exactly that at some point in the past. A fish jumped at the pair of bugs, huge teeth snapping, clicking loudly. It missed its snack by a hairsbreadth and plopped quietly back into the water.

Another reason, Delaney figured, was that everyone knew Ham would be getting to a fight sooner or later. Most often sooner.

"And how will Skaelington be better than Mann?" Jenta asked, incredulous.

"The city has much to its shame, of course. But there is a cornerstone of Vast society there as well. We will be able to start anew, as Shayla and Jenta Stillmithers, from a good family in Nearing Vast."

"Stillmithers?" She was shocked. "You've changed our name?"

"'Flug' is not exactly poetry."

"But *Stillmithers*? Did you make it up?" She felt something escaping her, something she wanted at all costs to hold onto.

"It's a gentleman's name." Shayla went quiet. Then she said softly, "Now it's your name. It's our name. I will hear no more about it."

Jenta understood her mother, and knew there would be no changing her mind. This was the life for which she had been groomed. But to leave everything, every familiar thing, even her name, invited by a stranger into a wild world far away, all in the hopes of some great and permanent improvement in their station? It seemed beyond absurd.

She watched the city streets roll by, wondering if this was the last time she'd see them. Citizens were buying and selling and chatting in the warmth of an early summer day. All of them doing what they knew, being precisely who they were, pretending nothing. It was gentle; it was easy; it was what she wanted. She couldn't imagine desiring anything more.

The docks rolled into view soon enough, and the increased bustle of the shipping trade only deepened her melancholy. The carriage rolled to a stop. "I don't want to leave," she said.

"Of course not. You can't see how it will benefit you. But you will see, in time."

A coachman opened the door; not the driver, but another servant sent to greet them. The carriage had been driven directly onto the pier, and had stopped at the foot of the gangway. Neither woman moved.

Jenta wiped at an eye. "Mama," she said in barely a whisper, "maybe I don't belong at fancy balls." There, she'd finally said the words.

"I thought you adored that cotillion you attended."

Jenta blanched. Her mother had not mentioned it in years, ever since forbidding Jenta to mention it again. "I did." And now it came back, as though summoned…the young man with the dark eyes watching, the cup of punch cold in her hand, the sense of serenity and possibility as she spoke to him on the porch. "But Mother, why isn't such society enough? I don't ask for more. I can serve. I can work. You do it, and you're the best woman I know. If I can do that and stay here…who cares what people think?"

Shayla stared hard at her daughter, trying to will some sense in her. For just a moment, she sincerely wished she had been one of those brutal mothers who convinced their children at all costs to flee from their parent's example. Almost anything seemed better than having Jenta aspire to be like her. Then Shayla sighed. She moved across the carriage to sit next to her daughter, moved a wisp of hair off the girl's forehead, then put an arm around her, pulled Jenta's head softly to her own shoulder. "Don't fear this. If life in Skaelington isn't all it should be, if within a year there is no promise of a future even there, then perhaps we shall return."

Jenta raised a sad face toward her mother. "But you didn't take Mr. Frost's money, did you?"

"Ladies?" the coachman asked. He put his hand into the carriage.

Jenta descended with easy grace. One servant walked alongside her up the gangway, while another took her mother's arm. Halfway up, the heartbreak within her became unbearable and she turned to take in one last view of the city she was leaving behind, perhaps forever. But she didn't see the city. For just across the dock, not thirty yards away, was another ship, a naval vessel.

She saw Damrick Fellows.

She had just seen him again, so clearly in her mind, as she had spoken of the cotillion. Now suddenly he was here, returned, arriving as she departed, descending his gangway as she ascended hers. And he saw her. His eyes were penetrating, severe, focused. He was little more than a stranger, and yet he did not seem to be. He seemed like someone she knew well. And he seemed to see through her, to the heart of her pain. He offered her something with that look. A different way out, perhaps. A society in which she'd be welcomed without seeking anyone's permission.

After a moment in which time seemed suspended, her face flushed, and Shayla was at her elbow, pulling her away. Jenta turned and ascended to the deck.

And from across the dock at that moment, Damrick watched that beautiful, forlorn young woman as she walked up the gangway. She had turned to look at him, but then she looked farther, he felt, searching through him for something else, something that he wasn't. And then she turned away.

But everything came back. Her dress had been gray satin with little white beads, gray ribbons. She smelled of honeysuckle. She was present, poised. *Poised*, that was the word, as though she stood at the edge of a precipice in perfect balance. Her laugh, her voice, her eyes as she glanced at him sideways, accusing him of watching her. He remembered everything about her; everything but the sadness. That was new. He wanted to go to her. He wanted to protect her from whatever had hurt her, whatever threatened her.

But she had remembered herself, had lowered her eyes and turned away from him.

And why wouldn't she? A fine lady like that, facing a bold look from a scruffy marine across a dock. It took her a moment to assess, to gain her bearings, is all. She probably didn't even recognize him. Worse, perhaps she did. The woman with her, her mother, was there to remind her of her station, should she forget it for an instant.

"Pretty girl," Lye Mogene said.

Damrick's anger flared, but he saw nothing more than a man making an idle comment to pass the time.

"What? You know her?" Lye's round face was serene and without concern—an unusual condition for him. But they had just been mustered out of the Navy, and were in no particular hurry to do anything at all.

"I met her once." Something went hollow within him as he realized the folly of his hope.

"Rich man's daughter. Don't be messin' there 'less ye want to get throwed in jail, or dead."

"Hmm." It was a grunt of agreement. But it didn't remove the hollowness.

The pair walked down to the dock and sat on their duffels. Damrick rolled up his trouser leg to look at the wound in his left calf muscle from that morning's battle. He hadn't even known he'd taken it until Lye noted the blood. The surgeon had removed the shrapnel; what was there now was hardly a scratch. Wouldn't leave much of a scar, if any. He rolled the pant leg back down.

"Mine's better," Lye said, showing Damrick the stitched gash in his forearm. "Least I'll have somethin' to remember the Navy by."

Damrick's eyes wandered from his friend's wound to the ship's deck across the way, but the young woman was long gone. She'd be in some fine cabin by now, served by six or eight waiters or stewards or whatever they may be called. He ran a hand through his hair. What he felt now was more like anger.

It wasn't just the girl, either. The fight had worked on him, like shrapnel still lodged in a muscle. He'd lost more than one friend in the skirmish; and even though he'd made others pay the debt, the idea of letting those pirates go...he had no knife that could cut that event out from under his skin.

The captain had explained it, of course. And Damrick understood. They couldn't overpower a peaceful vessel, couldn't stop a captain doing what he was licensed to do, even if that captain went by the name of Sharkbit Sutter. So the *Defender* had turned and headed for port. Voyage over. And now Damrick's tour of duty was done.

"We goin' to see your papa?" Lye asked.

Damrick grunted. His father's dry-goods business beckoned. The store was a thirty-minute walk from here. He'd promised Lye there'd be work there for him, at least for a while, until his friend could find more permanent employment. But Damrick couldn't bring himself to set out on that short journey. Not just yet. "Let's eat," he suggested instead.

With Lye Mogene at his elbow and dark thoughts on his mind, he took his dinner at a small table in one of the quieter pubs near the docks of the City of Mann. As they ate in silence, they overheard two sailors standing at a long, smoke- and ale-stained bar.

"Sharkbit, ye see, he's luckier than the rest of 'em," one of them was saying. "Give me luck over brains. Luck over pluck. He'll live longer than Skeel Barris, or Dancer Clang, or Conch Imbry, or any of 'em. You can write these words down."

"Luck, pluck, brains," said his partner dismissively. "Give me fight any day. Give me Scatter Wilkins. There's no man alive who fights, or gets his men to fight, like Scatter. I'll take Scat Wilkins on any sunny day, and twice on a stormy night."

"Nah. What would Scat a' done today against the *Defender*? Fought 'til he was bloody, and got most all his men kilt."

"And then gone and got some more and gone back 'til he won the day. He wouldn't never give up. He'd a' never parleyed, neither. And he's got some Drammune sailing with him now, what I hear, makes him even dangerouser. Them Drammune…they fight like a cannon full a' grape-shot fired down a hallway."

"They do, I'll grant it. But it don't matter. Scat can bring the whole Drammune Glorified Army, or whatever they call it. But it takes luck to do what Sharkbit did. Taken prize by a Vast man-o'-war, outnumbered, outgunned, and still he sails off with a whole crew alive, and tip o' the hat and how-do-ye-do to the king and his whole flag-wavin' Navy! Scat couldn't a' done it."

"His whole crew wasn't left alive," Lye seethed. "We killed a third of 'em anyway, or he'd never parleyed."

"Shh," Damrick answered, listening close.

"See, the Navy thought they had 'im," the first man continued, "but no. It was Sharkbit had *them*. He's wanted for piracy, don't ye know? Got at least four warrants and a price the size of the king's palace on his head. But somehow, he convinces a full naval captain that a piece a' paper signed by some shipping boss means he should go free. He's got a spell on 'im, I'm tellin' ye. Or a curse. Call it luck. Call it being looked out for from above. Or from down below."

"Ah, you're dreamin'. It wasn't God or the devil, but somethin' a little more down to earth…" he rattled some coins in his pocket, "…somethin' with a little glint to it."

The first man laughed. He raised his mug, "Enough gold, and you can buy a chest a' luck!"

"Here's to that kinda luck…and may our pockets ever be full of it!" And they drank.

Lye Mogene watched the change come over Damrick. His whole body tensed. His dark eyes grew black as he stared off into nothing, as though seeing a world he had never seen before.

"What? What are you thinkin'?"

But Damrick Fellows could not speak. He had just assumed that there were no warrants. Sharkbit was new to piracy; it was easy enough to believe. But if there were warrants, their captain would have known about them. Damrick stood and walked to the bar, his hand on his sword hilt.

Lye swore under his breath, rose, and followed.

"What do you know about those warrants?" Damrick demanded of the first man.

Both sailors stood tall and raised their chins to what felt like a direct challenge. "What warrants?" one asked.

"For Sharkbit Sutter."

"Who wants to know?"

"We're marines from the *Defender*," Damrick said with a seething ease, "and we killed a couple score of pirates today, and should have killed them all. And if you know all about it, and you weren't one of us, I'm thinking you were one of them."

The man swallowed hard, emptied suddenly of bluster. "No, we just heard tell. Heard people talkin'. Didn't mean nothin' by nothin'. If we insulted your ship or your captain, then we're right sorry, and we take it back. Don't we, Shoe?"

His partner nodded. "We take it all the way back, to where it ain't no more. Won't you boys have a mug with us?"

"I'm not looking for a drink or an apology. I want to know about the warrants. How long have they been sworn out?"

"How would we know that?" He looked at his partner.

"Days? Weeks? Months? Years?" Damrick demanded.

"Months, anyway," Shoe offered. "I guess. The sheriff's office is up in town. He'll know, if you need it for certain."

"And there's an office here at the docks," the other said. "You could check there. If it ain't closed down on account of the riffraff floatin' in."

"Why would it be closed on account of riffraff?"

The man shrugged. "Gets a little wild when certain ships pull in. Then the deputies take their prisoners up to Mann. They come back when it settles."

Damrick's jaw tightened. He turned and walked away without another word. He stopped at his table, tossed a small coin next to his mug of ale and his bowl of half-eaten stew. "We're going to see a deputy," he told Lye.

Lye looked down at the table. "But why not finish the stew first…?"

"I don't have the appetite. Do you?"

Lye blinked at his own steaming bowl and swallowed. "I guess not."

Damrick's look suddenly turned darker. Then he walked back over to the bar. As he did, Lye levered a large spoonful of stew into his mouth. And then another.

"What ships have pulled in recently?" Damrick asked the barkeep. "What ships would cause the deputy to take his prisoners to the city?"

"Well, the *Savage Grace,* for one."

Damrick studied the man. "You're saying that ship is here?"

"Not in port, no. Anchored near the marshes south, they say. Out by the Dark Inn over that way."

Damrick scowled and left them again. On his way past the table, he looked at Lye, who was barely visible under the large cloth napkin he was using to wipe his mouth. "Finished?" he asked.

Lye nodded, wiping his mouth furiously, unable to speak for the quantity of stew within it. He followed Damrick.

"Mr. Ryland, this is my daughter, Jenta Stillmithers. And Jenta," Shayla said, turning a warm look in his direction, "this is our benefactor, Mr. Runsford Ryland, of Ryland Shipping & Freight."

Jenta bowed her head as the elder of the two men in the plush stateroom took her hand, and kissed it. She was sure that Mr. Ryland must be a very powerful businessman; she could feel it in his presence. He struck her as truly sophisticated, more so than the sunny, playful Mr. Frost had been. He was not at all unattractive, even though rather plump around the belly. His clean-shaven face was ruddy and healthy. His hairline receded, but went gray only at the temples. His features were long and narrow, holding spectacles that seemed mostly ornamental. She curtsied.

"Charming," Runsford said, looking carefully at Jenta. "Truly. Miss Stillmithers, allow me to introduce you to my son, Wentworth Ryland."

The elder passed Jenta's hand to the younger, who kissed it with evident pleasure.

A shipful of pirates booed.

"I'm very glad to meet you both," Jenta answered, withdrawing her hand as quickly as she dared. "And I thank you for your generosity."

"Infinitely charmed," Wentworth said. He was lean like his father, leaner and paler and taller, but with slightly stooped shoulders. His manner was aloof and refined, but he smiled just a bit too broadly. His teeth were imperfect, and this, together with his grin, gave him just a bit of a wild, hungry look.

"And where is Mrs. Ryland?" Jenta asked, looking around the stateroom.

"She's ill…and so I'm afraid she's stayed back in Mann," Runsford offered quickly. He shot a glance toward his son, a look that seemed to Jenta like a warning. Jenta then glanced at Shayla, who displayed no surprise, not the merest trace.

"And do you find your quarters comfortable?" the elder Ryland asked.

"Quite agreeable," Shayla answered quickly, and now she cut her eyes toward her daughter—definitely a warning. In fact, the cabin they shared aboard ship was far below decks, dark and cramped, hardly big enough for one. And though it seemed generally clean, they had found a dead rat in the bottom of their one small cabinet, and being ladies they had required the services of a cabin boy to remove it—an earthy young man who had found the situation highly amusing.

"I'm so glad," Runsford said easily. "Thank you for dining with us. Come have a seat, won't you?"

Jenta looked around her, finally feeling that it was appropriate to do so. If Runsford's intent was to quarter his two guests in a cabin that encouraged them to linger here instead, it was working. This stateroom was more elegant than any room in any house that Jenta had ever seen. One deck below the captain's quarters, and running the width of the ship across the stern, it had all the comforts of a luxurious apartment. Walls were draped in tapestries; thick woven rugs covered polished wooden floors. A small dining table stood in the center, covered with white linens. A bar with four stools stood to Jenta's right. To her left and back, up against the stern windows and behind a modest silk screen, was a large double bed complete with decorative headboard, a tall post at each corner.

"My, what wonderful accommodations," Shayla offered. "Quite comfortable for the two of you."

"Yes, though it's just me at the moment. My son has his own stateroom. Would you like something before dinner? I have a fine sherry…"

Pirates winked and nodded at one another.

"I'd love some," Shayla answered.

"How about you, Miss Stillmithers?"

"No, thank you. My stomach is a bit unsettled as yet." This was only partly true. The other part was that Jenta simply did not have any desire to imbibe here, now, with the younger Ryland still ogling her. He made her very uneasy. Her mind drifted to the young sailor she had seen descending the gangway. She still had no idea of his name, or he hers, but nothing about Wentworth survived the comparison.

"I will pass as well," the young man said quickly. Not only had he yet to take his eyes off the girl, he still held his hand aloft, half open, where she had pulled hers away. As he spoke he closed his fist delicately.

"Come, sit," Runsford repeated, holding out an arm toward the table.

Wentworth rushed ahead to pull out a chair. "Miss Jenta, please." His intense eyes urged her toward him. As Jenta sat, he took the napkin from the china plate, shook it open, and laid it in her lap.

"He ought not to be doing that!" one of the pirates shouted.

"The blaggard!" answered another.

"But you see, he didn't touch her or nothing of that sort," Ham said easily. "It's a polite thing, that about laying out the napkin, but usually done by a steward or a servant."

"He ain't no stewart! Who's he think he's foolin'!"

The others murmured agreement.

"Ah, and unfortunately, the lot of you are all quite correct," Ham confirmed, "though how you figured it out I wouldn't know, utterly unfit for making judgments about staterooms and napkins and sherry as the sorry likes of you are."

Self-congratulations could be heard amid confirming laughter.

"Aye," Ham sighed, "Wentworth Ryland was smitten, from his first look at Jenta."

Delaney felt a twinge in his thigh, the left one, and he unlocked his ankles to stretch the offending leg out before him, wiggling his toes to keep the blood flowing. He didn't need to be getting a cramp. He moved back and forth on the post from one buttock to the other.

"Smitten," he said aloud, letting the word linger as he watched his toes curl. That's what Wentworth was. Jenta too, but not with Wentworth. Delaney knew what that was all about. He'd been smitten with his girl, Maybelle—"Smited," he concluded after a moment's ponder. He remembered when the priests had used such a term to threaten him, telling him that God would smite him if he kept stealing for his Pap.

Delaney now looked down at the swimming fish. They had risen to the surface, and were watching him. "Ignorant bunch you are. Ye don't know nothin' about nothin'. See, if a man don't do right, then he gets smited. Sounds bad. But it turns out that being smited feels all warm and tingly at first. But then, it goes on to make a man start to thinking and doing things he never thought he'd think or do, and all for a lady's attention. After a few years he realizes just how bad he's been smote. And by then it's too late."

As he watched the fish he realized that it was his wiggling toes that they were eyeing so hungrily. "Ye like these little critters?" He wagged his whole foot now, and the *Jom Perhoo* began buzzing around at the surface of the water, agitated. "Ha! Yer smitten! Fall in love with my toes, go ahead! See what it gets ye! Whole lot a' heartache is all." He thought for a moment, then drew his foot back to its place on the post. "Leastways, I hope that's all it gets ye."

Gloom settled back down on him. Maybelle Cuddy. He had been smitten, and so had she been, but he had let her go. They had ended for no reason. At least, no reason that seemed like reason enough.

Maybelle was a barmaid. Just a simple barmaid in a simple pub near the docks of Split Rock. Maybelle was plump, and Delaney was skinny. She was young and full of laughter, and he was older and more serious.

She had family, and he had none. She'd been schooled and he had not. But he had loved her, and she had loved him. Just for a while. A few short weeks in port, while his ship was refitting and repairing. Their hearts had melted together, somehow. That was how it felt.

Her daddy had put an end to it when he found out. And respecting him, and knowing himself, he had kissed Maybelle on the cheek and held her soft warm hand in his and looked into her eye, and then he'd sailed away. He'd turned his heel.

It was years later, next time he came to Split Rock, that he found her married and nursing a tiny baby boy. She was sad to see him, though there was still a trace of that same light in her eyes. They had nothing much to say as she dandled the baby, showing him off. Delaney grinned and clucked and made faces until the baby laughed. He didn't touch the child, though. He reached out once, thinking he'd pat its head or something, but then he remembered himself. This was another man's son.

He didn't touch her either, though they did speak to one another in sweet tones after that. And he remembered fingering his cap as he talked to her, and it felt like silk in his hands. And he saw, or thought he saw, that same longing in her eyes, that same spark that once was.

That was something.

But then he said goodbye again. He'd kissed her the first time he left, but this time he just kind of wagged his fingers toward her. He turned back to see her one last time, when he'd reached the door, but she wasn't looking at him anymore. She was cooing at her little child.

And he knew he'd never, ever kiss her again.

Why hadn't he stayed, that first time? Why hadn't he decided to make himself into a good man, to prove to her daddy he'd make an honest, true husband? He could have, back then. He was still a true hand, then, like Avery Wittle. He could have made a stand. But he had sailed away, and he'd broke her heart. And his own. She'd married another. And he'd gone from bad to worse and then to piracy, and now would die a bitter death.

Something in the undergrowth moved. He watched for a moment, his heart heavy. But nothing more happened. Just a critter. Darkness was coming, and it would swallow him up. It would rip him apart.

It would eat him alive.

He wished all of a sudden he'd fought harder when he'd fought. He wished he'd taken crazy chances like Damrick Fellows did. Then maybe he wouldn't be here, waiting to get killed. He didn't have the skills of a Damrick, so he'd have gotten himself dead a lot earlier, and a lot better, surrounded with sweat and blood and men, his lungs sucking in gun-powder smoke and blowing out steam, his hand flashing and jabbing and slicing, doing something he was good at doing. Then maybe he'd have been worth at least a story or two, if not a song.

After the jail, Damrick's next stop was a general store, where he had the clerk lay out on the counter every weapon he had for sale—an arsenal of swords, pistols, knives, axes, adzes, and muskets.

"Who you so mad at?" Lye asked him.

Damrick didn't answer. He chose two small pistols and two large ones, a skinner's knife with a sawtooth back ridge, a short blunderbuss, and a three-inch boot dagger.

"You ain't thinkin' about turnin' against the Navy, are ye?"

Damrick stopped. "No. I'm going to do what the Navy didn't. You better stock up, too, if you're coming with me."

Lye blanched. "Those are just for you?"

"The Navy left me with a sword. Not near enough for this work."

"But how is this work your work? Let it be, Damrick. I thought we were done with all that."

"I *was* done with it. Now I'm not." He started stuffing a burlap bag full of ammunition, sacks of musket balls and scattershot, tins of powder plugs and wads and patches, just as fast as the storekeeper could get them onto the counter.

"You expect to kill the whole lot of 'em?" Lye asked. "A whole ship a' pirates?"

"I expect to bring Sharkbit Sutter to justice."

"So you're a deputy now, or what?"

"Bounty hunting is legal in this kingdom, unless they outlawed it while we were away."

Lye hesitated. "We could get killed," he pointed out.

Damrick checked his sack, making mental notes. "So could he."

Lye Mogene's eyes searched the weapons, the ammunition, his partner and friend. "How are you payin' for all that?"

The proprietor showed a sudden interest in their conversation.

Damrick turned his attention across the counter. "Put it on account. My father's store, Fellows Dry Goods. Lye, pick out a few."

The clerk crossed his arms.

"On Halver Lane," Damrick told him. "You know it, don't you?"

"I know it. You're Didrick's son."

"I am."

"Does he know what you're up to?"

"He doesn't even know I'm in port. And he won't know, until I'm dead or Sharkbit's gone." There was a shade of warning in his voice.

The merchant sighed. "I'll have to charge you for the weapons. But take the ammo for free."

"I can't do that."

"Yes, you can," the merchant insisted through tired eyes. "You get yourself killed from my goods while I bank the profits? No sir, your old man will never speak to me again and I won't blame him. Take the ammunition, no charge. That pretty much wipes out my profit."

"I'll do it your way, if you'll let me pay when I return."

The merchant nodded. "Deal."

CHAPTER FOUR

SAVAGE GRACE

"WE CAN'T SWIM IT," Lye whispered in the darkness.

Damrick and Lye stood in the marshes, up to their knees in cold, muddy water that had overflowed their boot tops. Peering through a curtain of reeds that towered over their heads, they saw the darkened outline of the *Savage Grace*. Her sails had been struck and her anchor dropped, and now she floated alone in a backwater lagoon two hundred yards from shore.

"We need a boat," Damrick agreed.

"We ain't got a boat," Lye pointed out, hoping this might end their journey. He was tired from the long walk from Mann on rutted, darkened roads while carrying heavy, awkward duffels. But his partner was, if anything, more eager than he had been all night.

"There's a watchman," Lye told him. "Crow's nest."

"He's asleep."

"How can you tell?"

"It's the people on deck we need to worry about."

Lye squinted, but could see nothing. After a moment, he said, "Well, we can't swim it."

Damrick turned toward him, eyes flashing. "We need a boat. As I said." And he waded quietly back through the tall marsh reeds to firmer ground. After emptying their boots of water, they started hiking again, not back the way they'd come, but further down the road toward the notorious inn that was the only reason for any man to wander through this wilderness, the only destination in this direction other than the wide ocean beyond the bay.

Suddenly Damrick stopped, put a hand up, halting his partner.

"What—"

"Listen!"

Lye heard the buzz of insects, crickets mostly, and the bleat of a bull-frog. He said as much.

"That's not a bullfrog." Damrick pulled a small pistol from his belt.

"Then what…?" but Lye knew. It was a snore.

Damrick moved slowly through the dank water toward the sound. Parting the tall grasses with his pistol barrel, he waded out only five or ten yards before he found the rowboat. Two pirates slept off the effects of what smelled like great quantities of rum. Damrick cocked his pistol and pushed the barrel into the temple of the closest one, a haggard-looking scarecrow of a man, with more scars than whiskers. For a moment, Lye feared his partner's recent foul mood would drive him simply to pull the trigger. But the pirate was out cold, lying in three inches of murky water, his head propped against the stern planking. Damrick shook the boot of the other man, the one whose snores they had heard. He snorted once, then snored on.

Damrick pulled the boat toward shore.

"What'll you do with 'em?" Lye asked.

"Nothing."

"Nothing?"

And sure enough, Damrick climbed into the boat, found two small paddles, and when Lye had stepped uneasily over the gunwale as well, they headed out toward the dark ship, two dead-drunk pirates with them.

"Sharkbit's not likely to be on board," Lye pointed out. "Just a skeleton crew. It's shore leave. Don't you reckon?"

"We'll find out where he is."

"He's at the inn, Damrick." After a pause, "This is crazy, you know." Then after another pause, "We gonna kill all these pirates, or what?"

"You think we shouldn't?"

It sounded like a question, but Lye got the impression it wasn't. "I'm just sayin', Damrick. We should have a plan. They're like to shoot us without askin' a load a' questions."

"They might."

Lye sighed, and pulled on the paddle with little enthusiasm. The *Savage Grace* had seemed small and inconsequential when they'd run up on it out at sea in the man-o'-war, *Defender*. She hadn't looked much bigger from the reeds. But now as they approached in the pale moonlight she seemed enormous, towering, forbidding. An evil king's castle, surrounded by a wide moat and protected by those who knew all about dark magic.

As they approached, a hoarse voice suddenly pierced the darkness. "Welcome, honored guests!"

It was the dark king himself.

Ham Drumbone sighed. "Well, I'm sleepy. I'm afraid that's all for tonight, lads. More tomorrow if I've a mind and you've—"

"No!" The voices pounced on Ham almost in unison. "The fight! We wanna hear the *fight*!"

"The fight, eh? It'll be just as good tomorrow." Ham tapped red embers into his hard palm.

"Relight that thing, ye big oaf, and on with the story!" a sailor insisted.

"You have a rather ungainly method of persuasion, Mr. Garvey," Ham said as he crushed out the embers with a calloused thumb. "Generally, a man with a request refrains from insulting the one of whom he's requesting."

"Aye, well, sorry." Then a burst of irritation, "But blame it all, ye do it to us ever' time! How'm I gettin' to sleep with that hangin' over me?"

"A true point," Ham admitted. "But if I go on with the tale, how are you getting any sleep then?"

Blue pondered. "Well, I guess I won't," he admitted. "But at least I'll hear the tale!"

"Hmm. Very true. All right, then," Ham acquiesced. "If the other boys agree."

They did.

"What business do you have here, two wayfaring strangers?" Sharkbit asked, leaning over the rail. "Or is it four?" His harsh voice was cold and casual.

"Just two, and we come to join up!" Lye blurted.

Damrick turned to look at him. Lye ignored his friend, fearing that anything but a highly believable lie would get them killed instantly. He

Blaggard's Moon

kept his neck cricked and his eyes upward, watching the hooded figure who hovered above them, dark as death.

"You have in the boat there the evidence of where such a life will lead. Why would two such robust young men in the prime of their lives desire the spiritual poverty of piracy?"

"Um. The money?" Lye managed.

"Temporal riches, then. You'll trade your mortal souls for filthy mammon?"

Lye was silent, sensing some trick behind the question. He shrugged, finding none. "Sure."

"Is that a trade you demand of all your sailors?" Damrick asked. "That they sacrifice their souls to you?"

"Your tone is a bit harsh for one who seeks but to serve," Sharkbit replied.

"I'm a bit harsh," Damrick told him through clenched teeth.

"Then you'll do. Come aboard."

Suddenly two sailors appeared, one on either side of Sharkbit, and a knotted rope was thrown down. In what seemed to Lye like an unnatural hurry, Damrick put an arm through the loop of his duffel, threw it over his shoulder, and climbed. The weapons within clinked and rattled. Lye watched the pirates above as Damrick used a hole left by the *Defender*'s cannon for footing. Then Lye took a deep breath and followed, grunting aloud and swearing silently.

As soon as his two feet were firmly aboard, before his partner had even cleared the rail, Damrick had a large pistol in each hand, the muzzle of the left one hovering three inches from Sharkbit's forehead. The other was aimed at the nearest pirate, to his right. "You're under arrest, Sharkbit. Please, resist."

Sharkbit showed his teeth. "I recognize you. Your aim was not so good this morning."

"It'll be plenty good now."

Lye fairly fell over the rail, trying to get his pistol from his belt as he scrambled aboard, his heavy pack falling on top of him. He came up with the weapon in his hand, aimed it at the other sailor, the one to Damrick's left. To his dismay, however, he realized that both the pirates had pistols in their hands as well. It was a standoff.

Then shadows started drifting up from below decks. As the bounty hunters stood, ready to take their prisoner, they were gradually being surrounded.

"Lord, why aren't all your men at the inn having some fun?" Lye muttered irritably.

"Lord, indeed," Sharkbit answered. "They serve me and do as they're told. Despite my statements at our earlier meeting today, which were made to maintain my reputation as a madman, my standards are actually quite high."

"Yeah? Then who are those drunks in the boat?" Lye asked.

"Applicants. Supplicants. Rejects. Drinking off their disappointment, I presume."

"Get in the boat, Sharkbit," Damrick ordered without emotion.

The captain of the *Savage Grace* shook his head. "Dear man. You have misjudged much. Do you believe yourself so superior that you could climb aboard an enemy ship and take its captain ashore with a pistol and…a poor opinion?"

"You about through talking?" Damrick asked.

"You do have some courage," Sharkbit acknowledged. "No. No, I don't think I am through talking. Why don't you come to my parlor, little fly, where we can talk further. I begin to think you might make a very good spider yourself."

"You want me to join up with you?"

"It does occur to me. You have the cold heart and the steady hands required. You could become great. You could become very rich."

"I'd never follow you."

"Because you're a leader. That's what I like about you."

"I'd take everything you have."

"You can have all I own."

For the first time, Damrick paused. "Why?"

"Because I want a lot more than I currently own, and I have the means to get it. I'll have greater means yet, with you captaining a ship for me."

"You sail under Conch Imbry, is what I hear."

"You hear right."

"Why?"

"Power. Wealth. Protection."

A trace of a glint from Damrick's eye caught Sharkbit's eye. Sharkbit grinned. "It's a powerful temptation for any man. But you, you carry the fire of destiny within you."

Damrick lowered his pistol.

Lye Mogene gripped his more tightly, swung the barrel around to aim it at Sharkbit. Then he stared holes into Damrick. "You're not seriously…" He trailed off. Damrick ignored him.

"Come," Sharkbit said. "Let's have ourselves a drink."

"Lead on."

Sharkbit nodded, then glanced at his men, who lowered their weapons as well.

"I'll be tarred and feathered," Lye said aloud, but mostly to himself. He was the only one now with pistol raised.

But as soon as the dark captain turned his back, Damrick swung his pistol butt, a straight right that caught Sharkbit at the base of the skull and crumpled him to the ground. A fraction of a second later, two blinding cracks of fire dropped the two pirates closest to Damrick. Their heads snapped backward and their bodies thudded to the deck. Lye, recovering himself, took one step backward as he aimed and fired. He killed a third pirate before the rail caught the back of his thigh and he tumbled over it, somersaulting backward into the lagoon with a thudding splash.

Damrick, alone now with his enemies, dropped his two empty pistols and dove for the unconscious body of the pirate captain. He heard hammers click back, saw two flashes from pirate pistols, heard two shots and the ring of a ricochet. He landed on Sharkbit's back, blasting air from the man's lungs as he did, and then he rolled him over so that the hooded pirate was on top of him, his closed eyes and blank face aimed upward at the moon. From that position, under the captain, Damrick reached down to his own belt and found a third pistol, pulled it, and aimed at the nearest pirate. As he did, Sharkbit's limp arm jumped into the air, his palm open. It appeared to be a gesture of command, a signal to halt. It worked as precisely that, freezing the pirates where they stood.

Wrapping an arm around Sharkbit's chest, Damrick pinwheeled himself around, clicked the pistol hammer back, aimed the pistol at pirate after pirate, each of the half dozen who now had him surrounded. Seeing that they were for the moment unwilling to fire for fear of hitting their leader, Damrick pushed the pistol's cold muzzle to the temple of their captain.

"Lower your weapons, boys, or I'll empty his skull of all but lead."

"You do that, yer dead right after," one pointed out.

"Then I'll die happy."

They pondered this, glancing at one another.

"You don't think I'd have come aboard like this if I cared one whit whether I lived or died, do you?"

They pondered some more. It seemed a reasonable line of argument.

"You want your captain dead, you just keep standing there with your mouths agape and your pistols pointed."

One of them lowered his weapon. Then another. Then all of them did.

"I want those pistols on the decks."

They dropped them to the floorboards.

A dripping Lye Mogene grunted up over the rail again, pistol still in hand. "Good," he said, panting. "You got 'em."

"Pick up their pistols," Damrick ordered.

Now with both feet on the deck, Lye waved his gun menacingly. "Don't try anything!" After he had collected nine pistols from the deck and stuffed them into Damrick's duffel, Damrick rolled Sharkbit off of him. Lying face down on the deck, the dark captain took a hard breath, writhed a bit, then winced.

"Check him for weapons," Damrick ordered, now standing, still pointing his own pistol at Sharkbit. When Lye had checked the captain and had come up empty, Damrick gestured toward the sailors. "Check them, too."

"All right, lads, off with yer boots," Lye ordered them, still waving his own pistol at them.

The men sat, and those who were wearing shoes or boots removed them. A couple of derringers and three or four knives hit the planking.

"Now your belts," Damrick commanded, as Lye collected the weapons.

As the men untied or unbuckled belts, several more pistols and knives fell to the flooring. Lye collected these as well. "Got 'em all," he reported, holding up the bulging, heavy duffel.

Now Damrick pulled the last pistol from his belt, his fourth. "Here, take this," he said, holding it out for Lye.

Lye took it. "Why?"

"Give me yours."

Lye handed it over. Damrick looked at the wet weapon, then tipped the barrel down. After a moment, a dark gray goo, wet gunpowder, dripped from the barrel. A second or two later, the ball dropped to the floorboards.

"You might have traded with me a tad earlier," Lye seethed, turning red.

Damrick's eyes shone in the moonlight.

Sharkbit sat up, held the back of his head, and looked around through slitted eyes. "What happened?"

"I declined your offer," Damrick told him. "Now, get in the boat."

"Wait, I always heard Sharkbit was shot in the back!"

"Aye, from a coward's pistol! Everybody knows that story."

"You're gettin' it wrong again. Tell it how it really happened!"

The men were restless, unhappy. "You boys need some sleep, is the problem here," Ham informed them with infinite patience. "I should have quit the story when I said."

"But ye got it wrong!" another complained.

"Did I now?" Ham asked.

They all answered him in the affirmative, adding a wide variety of colorful intensifiers.

"Well, let's just put the story away and lock it up for the evening. Before I do, though, I'll say this: Sharkbit was not one to go quietly."

"Aye!" and "Now yer sayin' right!"

"He carried on him a weapon that Lye Mogene had not found. A dirk, tucked down the back of his hood. So as he walked to the rail, he reached up as though to scratch his skull, and he pulled the blade. He wheeled around, meaning to kill Damrick Fellows. But he failed, lads. For ye see," Ham continued in the brooding silence, "our Captain Sharkbit believed he could not be killed. And a man who believes he cannot be killed has no reason to believe he can be taken alive. Sharkbit's long knife came around in a flash of silver, but Mr. Fellows was ready. He had the pistol. He had the will. He fired. And you already know what a crack shot he was. Could be but one result. Sharkbit tumbled over the rail, landing smack on top of our two drunken would-be pirates, a pistol ball clean through his head, entering at the left eye.

"'Go home,' Damrick then says to all the other pirates gathered there, as they stared in stunned silence at their fallen leader. For they too had believed that Sharkbit Sutter could not be killed. 'Go home,' he says, 'or die likewise.' Then he and Lye threw all their boots into the drink, so as not to be followed, and climbed down the side of the ship, rowed to shore, and carried Sharkbit's body all the way back to Mann for the reward. And from then on, Damrick Fellows never thought about any line of work other than ridding the seas of the likes of us."

"I don't like 'im," Sleeve said aloud. "All righteous-like. He's a killer, and likes to kill, I say, as much as any pirate ever did. Don't he?"

"Maybe so," Ham said. "Certainly, he killed more men than all but a very few of the most legendary cutthroats. But I tell you this story so you'll know who he is. So you'll know what we're up against, when he comes to fight a man like Conch Imbry."

"The Conch!"

"Aye, the Conch!" others echoed. "He'll take 'im down!"

"Aye, the Conch," Ham confirmed. "So what we have now, gents, is what's called a bit of drama. It means that when we do get a fight between the chief of the pirates and the chief of the pirate hunters, it's likely to be a good one."

Delaney sighed. His anger had dissipated. Fighting like a madman would get a man killed off right enough, but it wouldn't get him out of a jam. Foolhardy as it may have been to climb aboard a pirate's ship, once he had gotten himself on deck Damrick hadn't just started shooting. He hadn't just gone wild with blood frenzy. He'd used more than his weapons; he'd used his wiles. Guns and guile together. Delaney didn't know much about how to do that, but he thought it was a good combination, one that might work for him yet if he could figure it out.

So Ham's story wasn't about remembering, all of a sudden. It wasn't about keeping his mind occupied, either. Delaney didn't need drama. He needed ideas. Not to kill off pirates, but to beat the Hants and the *Chompers* and the *Onka Din Botlay*. And maybe, just maybe, Ham's story could help him do it. Damrick had had a whole string of ideas right in a row, hadn't he? First, he'd pretended to go along with Sharkbit's bid to turn him. Then, he'd pistol-whipped the pirate from behind. Then, he'd dove onto him and used the pirate's body like a shield. Then, he'd put the pistol to Sharkbit's head, rather than aiming it around at his enemies when he was outnumbered. Those were all ideas, one right after another, and together they'd saved him.

But unhappily, the more Delaney thought, the more he knew he could not have done what Damrick had. Had it been him, he might not have pitched over the rail like Lye Mogene, but he sure wouldn't have pulled off all of Damrick's deeds, either. And not for lack of physical skills, but for lack of mental ones. None of those ideas would have come to him, he knew, not if he'd had a year to sit and scratch and ponder. And worse, not one of those ideas was the least bit useful secondhand, though he tried every one of them like stray keys into a stubborn padlock. But mermonkeys weren't likely to ask him to join up. Nor would they care if he

Blaggard's Moon

pretended to join them. And they weren't likely to hand over their teeth and claws just because he held a gun on them. A gun he didn't have anyway. So after further contemplation, he came to the conclusion that he needed a set of new ideas.

And he had no idea where to get them. How did people ever imagine something that wasn't, and then bring it to pass? No answer came to mind. None ever did. He couldn't imagine, because he had no imagination. He couldn't even pretend, hadn't been able to even when he was a boy.

Except once.

He remembered that time vividly. It was before his Pap took him away. He remembered the little house where he'd lived, and he was lying on his belly on the one rug, which covered a small part of the dirt floor, right at the center of their one room. Yer Poor Ma was sitting beside him, smiling down on him. Her face was warm like the sun.

"It's a soldier, don't you see?" she said to him. And he looked at the big wooden spoon in her hand with the napkin tied around it, and the small table knife tied to the napkin. She had used some charcoal to draw a face on the big scoop of the spoon. "He's standing tall, and that's his rifle right there," she explained, pointing at the knife. Her voice was smooth and full of light, carrying him with it. "And he's holding it against his shoulder. For marching." And as she moved it across the floor, just for a moment Delaney could see it. For just a moment the spoon was a soldier at attention, and his charcoal eyes were alive, and he was proud, and Delaney saw it! He took the soldier from his mother's hand and marched him clumsily across the rug. And as long as he marched that spoon, it was no spoon at all, but a soldier.

Then his Pap came home and picked up the spoon and whacked him with it. He just snatched it right away, untied the spoon from the fork, cussed Yer Poor Ma for marking up a good ladle and for filling a boy's head with nonsense. Then he thumped Delaney's skull for an idiot, raising a bump. It hurt and he cried, and for crying he got a true beating.

And that was the end of play-pretend. It was the last time he ever did such a fool thing. But Delaney remembered it, so clearly after all these years, how that wooden spoon came almost to life. He knew what it meant to imagine, he sure did. For he'd done it once.

But a smiling spoon wouldn't help him now, either. He had to have not just an imagination, but a true idea. For some people, it seemed like ideas popped up in their heads like their minds were gardens, somehow, where ideas grew like tomatoes, and there was always a ripe one to pluck off the vine whenever it was needed.

Delaney's head wasn't full of tomatoes like that. He'd *never* grown a tomato in there, as far as he knew. Instead, his garden grew whatever it wanted, and that was weeds, mostly. Even now, now that he'd thought about tomatoes, the more he tried to think of ideas, the more he ended up thinking about tomatoes.

He'd had a crewmate once who told of growing tomato plants in his backyard at home. When you poured water into the dirt, he said, it didn't all just disappear into the ground—no, a lot of it went into the plant through the roots, and then it went up the stem and into the vines. Sucked up like little kids with cut straws suck up lemonade and ginger beer. And then the water collected up into the tomato as though that tomato was a wine bladder, and that's what pooched it out so much, so it got big and fat and red. When that sailor described his tomatoes, you just wanted to bite into one and let the juice drip down your chin.

Delaney decided at that moment that he would climb down and get some water. No sense trying to have ideas when all a man can think about is tomatoes, and especially when those tomatoes needed water to grow. If tomatoes were like ideas, then ideas needed water, too. So maybe that's why he couldn't have ideas. Maybe he was too thirsty to think up ideas.

He would shinny down the pole. He didn't need much of a drink, he figured, because the tomatoes he wanted to grow weren't real tomatoes, just idea tomatoes, and they likely wouldn't take nearly so much watering. Once he had a little water down his throat, then he could shinny back up and sit for a while, let that water get sucked up into his brain, and he could grow some ideas. He wasn't sure it worked that way, but since he didn't really know how it worked, it sure made sense it might work like that. And besides, he was thirsty.

"I don't want no trouble," he told the piranha in a tone meant to calm them. "I'm comin' fer a drink, nothin' more." He untied the blue bandana from around his neck as he spoke and opened it up. "I'm parched, ye see?" It occurred to him that fish probably knew very little about being thirsty, but he could think of no way to address the issue with them, so he remained quiet about it.

He gave the cloth a little shake, and then immediately wished he hadn't. The fish grew agitated at the motion and gathered closer to the post to investigate. Several even surfaced. "I ain't food, I tell ye," Delaney said, irritated with them. "Dumb little *Chompers.*" He shook his head at their ignorance as he tucked the bandana into the rope that served as his belt.

Once the fish seemed to have settled again, he slowly unknotted his ankles from behind the post. Surprised and a little worried by how stiff his legs had become, he stretched his bare feet out in front of him and wiggled his toes, keeping his balance by holding the post under his buttocks in both hands. Feeling a little more confident, he put the soles of his bare feet against the wooden sides of the post, then lifted up his right buttock and slid his right hand, palm down, onto the cross-cut surface under him. He shifted over so that he sat with his right buttock on just the edge of the post. Pushing up with his feet and legs as well as his hand, he raised himself enough to reach his left hand over in front of him and place it palm down beside his right hand.

"Here's the tricky part," he said aloud, less to the fish than to himself. The pole shook and trembled, but with agility gained in flinging himself around the rigging of tall ships, he loosed his feet and turned himself around to face the post, his feet quickly but carefully finding the post again, inside arches pressing tightly to the rounded sides. He lowered himself until he was hugging the post in a shinny. There he waited once again for the hungry fish to calm themselves.

"I'm tellin' you boys, leave it be."

Slowly, inch by gradual inch, he shinnied down until his toes were about two feet from the surface of the water. The *Chompers* seemed highly interested, but not highly agitated. He paused again to remove the bandana from his belt, which he did quite slowly. By now, his mouth felt dry as dirt, his throat hurt him just to think of swallowing. The worst part, though, was that he could smell the water now; he could feel its coolness rising upward. The thought came to his mind that he could just let go and plunge in, drinking in all the cool water in the world before the inevitable, before it was all just over and done, but he shook that thought away with a start. It was the sort of strange imagining that dying men did.

He looked down again, saw the silvery blue fish moving from sunlight to shadow, shadow to sunlight, circling, bobbing up to the surface for a better view, waiting. Taking the bandana in his right hand, hooking the post in the crook of his left arm, he squatted down on his haunches so he was sitting on his own heels. Then he began, ever so carefully, to lean down, down toward the water, his left arm unwrapping itself until he clung with his two feet and his left hand, reaching out to dip the bandana in with his right. All he needed was to get it wet, and then he could suck its moisture into his mouth. It was a plan that couldn't fail, he thought. He had seen how high the *Chompers* could jump when they took Lemmer's hand. His bandana was a good twelve inches long, and none of those fish ever got more than six or eight inches from the surface unless they were pulled up out of the water, with jaws clamped on—

"Don't think on that," Delaney whispered to himself.

As he lowered the bandana, the fish grew agitated again, sure now that here at last was a morsel on which they could feed. They swarmed so thick under the cloth that Delaney suddenly wondered if there was any water between them at all. Then he worried that so many of them would try to take the bandana, it would be shredded before they could determine it was naught but cotton.

But as he held the bandana poised above their heads, a strange thing happened.

The piranha disappeared. They turned in an instant and were gone, fleeing in all directions. Delaney looked at the bandana for a moment, wondering how it might have scared them. Then he realized this was his chance, whatever the cause, and he plopped the cloth into the water. It was a bit of a greasy thing, and floated on the surface at first. So he waved it a few times through the water to be sure it had soaked up some moisture. Then he pulled it up and put it in his mouth. He closed his eyes and felt the cool liquid pour down his throat. No ale ever tasted better.

Suddenly the post lurched, as though something had slammed into it hard under the surface. Delaney lost his grip and fell sideways with an awkward splash, into the lagoon.

Panicked and under the surface, he turned back toward the post and kicked hard with his feet, pulled with his hands, coughing out a great bubble, willing himself back to the post the way a man in different straits would have shot upward for air. His head still underwater, he felt the post with his hands, pulled it toward him...

And then he saw it.

It was right below him. The face, doughy and puckered, blind white eyes, bared teeth, hugging tight to the post not eight feet under him.

Scrambling upward with strength and speed born of terror, Delaney shot out of the water up the post, slipping as he went, sliding back down the wet surface, twice as far as he climbed it seemed. But he reached the top alive, and was instantly seated again on its upmost end. He peered down into the darkened water, dripping wet, heart battering his ribs like a flurry of cannonballs hitting a hull broadside. He pulled his feet up under him as far from the surface, as far from that thing, as he could possibly get them.

The dark water was silent. And then the *Jom Perhoo* came back, arriving lazily, unconcerned. As though nothing had happened.

But nothing had *not* happened. It was not *nothing* that had happened. It was *something*. He had seen that something, and that something was the *Onka Din Botlay*, Ripper of the Bone. Sure he had—he hadn't imagined it. He was no good at imagining. Besides, he was wet; his clothing was soaked. He had fallen in and he hadn't been eaten by *Chompers*. So it had happened.

He had seen its face.

That was going to stay with him a very long time, he knew. That is, if he in fact had a very long time, which now that he'd seen the face, he realized he undoubtedly didn't. That face had howled at him, Delaney was sure. But he was also sure it had made no noise. It was shrieking like the monkeys of the forest, with mouth wide, eyes blind in anger, a vicious cry. But it was silent. Its claws were dug into the post. Long fingers, just as the Hants had said, that came to points like carpenter's nails. It was whiter, pastier, older, uglier than he had known how to envision. Hollow cheeks, sunken like it was starved. Eyes deep and piercing. Like there was hatred in them.

Delaney's breaths came a little easier now, now that it seemed the thing wouldn't follow him up the post. And the *Chompers* were back, which he was very glad to see. They suddenly seemed like old friends. "Good little fishies," he told them, hoping they'd stay around. So long as the piranha surrounded him, he was safe.

The lagoon had grown placid again. The mermonkey was gone.

Onka Din Botlay. Why hadn't it ripped out his bones? Why had it showed up at all? They come out only at night, is what the Hants said, under blackest moon. But it was day. And the thing was definitely out.

No, that's not what the Hants had said. He remembered it now. The fire was burning, casting its flickering light on the faces of those seated around it.

"*Onka Din Botlay* attack only under the black moon," the leader had said, the one with his face tattooed black-and-white in the shape and figure of a skull. He was their chieftain, or their priest, it was hard to know which. He said it, then he let the sickly old man translate, then he took a great tug on the long *hoobatoon* pipe. He blew the swath around him in an odd, ceremonial fashion and handed the pipe to Belisar the Whale. The pirate took it, nodded, and did the same.

They *attack* only under the black moon. That's what the man had said.

Delaney took a deep breath now and exhaled. He had gotten his water, but so far it had grown no idea tomatoes in his head. In fact, it had pretty much run everything out of his head but mermonkeys. Mermonkeys that would come in the dark, and climb the post, and eat his bones.

It would have been better to die that day in Mumtown, like Avery Wittle did. That would have saved him this horrible end. And saved the world a load of piracy. Avery hadn't turned. Avery had made his stand there, in Castle Mum. And though Delaney didn't want it to come back, didn't like to think on it, there it came, a memory from four years back that seemed so lifelike, it seemed it was happening all over again.

"I need your hands," the *Horkan* man said, picking bits of beef breakfast from his teeth with a twisted splinter of wood. "You first."

The *Horkan* man wanted to bind them all, and he wanted to bind Delaney first. His head still pounding, Delaney stood to face the challenge, then glanced over his shoulder at his fellow captives. They were all watching to see what he'd do. He swallowed once, filled his lungs, then did the only thing he could think to do. He extended grim fists between the bars, just as the jailor demanded. He had no other ideas.

The big man tied Delaney's protruding hands at the wrist with a thin leather thong. The sailor admired the handiwork in spite of himself, the firmness of the wrap, the quick, careful frap that drew it tight, the easy, firm double half-hitch over his right fist to secure the end. Here was a man who knew his business.

"You next," the *Horkan* man said, attempting to pull Sleeve from the corner with a bent finger. Sleeve swore at him, but didn't budge.

"No trial for you, then." He pulled a pistol from where he kept it in his belt at his back and aimed it between the bars. "And I'll kill two others here, just for spite." He pointed it at the Trum boys.

"Whoa now!" Delaney offered. "Let's not be hasty. Sleeve moves slow, is all. But he's movin'. Ain't ye, Sleeve?"

Sleeve snarled his displeasure, but the encouragement of cellmates convinced him to follow Delaney's example. After Sleeve, the jailor bound Mutter Cabe, and then big Nil Corver. Delaney furrowed his brow. Something about the order in which his fellow captives were summoned struck him as odd. Then he knew what it was. The Cabeeb jailor had somehow assessed the danger his captives posed and was securing them in order, from best fighter to worst. Information bought with Captain Stube's gold, no doubt.

Least and therefore last was young Dallis Trum, eyes wide and unseeing, lower lip trembling as though saying as many prayers as he knew, as fast as possible.

"It's all right, young pup," Delaney tried to assure him. "It's just a bit of a pinch, that's all. Pinches come and go." He winked in what he hoped was a knowing sort of way, but there was a sting like a particle of dust in his eye, and all he could think was that he wished he hadn't taken the two boys under his wing quite so thoroughly.

Dallis put his pudgy hands through the bars next to his brother without being requested, having seen all the others do the same.

"Oh, not you," the jailor told him. "You will be the first to die."

"Whoa, wait!" Nil trembled. "What about the trial?" The corners of his mouth drew downward, pulling his eyes into a blank stare. "You *said.*"

Sleeve harrumphed. "Ain't gonna be no trial, ye blame fools." He rattled the bars vigorously and vainly, using all of his strength and most of his vocabulary. The others just watched.

"Trial, yes," the jailor told them once Sleeve's bile was spent. He stared deep into Sleeve's eyes from the free side of the bars. "Yes, we must do things in the proper order. My mistake. First, the trial. *Then,* you die. Sometimes I forget and do it backward." But the humor was now gone from the *Horkan* man, replaced by flat, dry death.

Sleeve reached out to grab the jailor by the throat, but the big man stepped back easily, out of reach.

Now the jailor turned to the wall behind him, which was fashioned from rough boards tied together with lengths of hemp, and to the surprise of his prisoners he slid it aside as though he were opening a curtain at some theatrical show. When their eyes adjusted to the sudden stream of blinding sunlight, the doomed men saw an empty dirt courtyard fenced around by stone walls, darkened from decades, maybe centuries, of dirt and smoke. The sunlight that fell here seemed only to make the grime more dismal.

In the center of the little space was a platform, the broad remains of a huge cedar or some other gnarled tree, its long-dead roots twisting up here and there from the sandy earth like gray snakes that had died sunning their bellies. The platform this trunk created was six feet across and a foot or two high.

The jailor unlocked the iron padlock with a rusted key and went into the cell, binding Dallis Trum's hands behind him. Then he walked the boy out and stood him in the center of the stump, turned him to face the crewmen.

"Witnesses," the jailor said. Delaney thought he was addressing the sailors until two men stepped toward the stump into view. One was of no particular distinction, average in height and weight, middle-aged, no beard, dressed like any merchant of Nearing Vast.

The other man, however, was a sight to behold. He overshadowed his partner in every way. This one was tall and broad-shouldered and was dressed in a cream-colored silk shirt, silvery satin breeches, and white silk stockings to his knees. His calves bulged; his knotted muscles almost made the jailor's proportions seem small. He wore no hat, and his light brown and sun-streaked hair fell in glorious curls to his shoulders.

His face was leathered and tanned by the elements, and it was broader from ear to ear than it was from hairline to smooth chin. It was not a handsome face. His mouth was wide and his eyes were narrow. His moustache was long and waxed, points stretching outward. None of his facial features were attractive, but somehow they combined to make him striking, even arresting. Maybe it was his demeanor more than his look; he was a powerful presence. He was self-consciously sure of himself, even vain in that assurance.

Then Delaney heard the words that escaped Sleeve's lips, whispered with equal parts certainty and dread:

"Conch Imbry."

The pirate captain heard and turned toward Sleeve, touching what would have been his hat, had he been wearing one. Delaney's mouth went dry as dust, and his knees trembled.

CHAPTER FIVE

AVERY'S END

"CONCH IMBRY AND his pirates," Delaney said to the fish. "Now there's piranha for ye. Put you little boys all to shame."

The fish reacted to this news with dull stares and lazily flapping fins.

Delaney tried to think about something else. He did not want his mind to go back there, did not want to think about what had happened next. So he thought of a big glass of ale, and when that got him remembering the Cabeeb pub where the shooting had happened, he switched to thinking about a jug of cool water. That made him think about the water in the lagoon, which he'd just tasted, so he looked at the fish and tried to think about fish that weren't piranha but were regular fish that men killed and ate, instead of the other way around. Grouper and tuna and blackfish.

For a while he succeeded, remembering his favorite dinner. A great steaming plate of grilled seafood. But then he thought of a big hunk of boiled shark meat, which he'd eaten once and was strong and tasty. Then when he'd thought about shark meat, the old legends about Firefish rose in his head, those sea monsters that could eat a whole ship but whose meat could double a man's strength, if only one could be caught and killed. But they couldn't be caught or killed, because only if a man could eat Firefish meat, they said, could he become strong enough to kill a Firefish. But he wasn't strong enough otherwise, so until he did it, he could never do it. And that was a puzzle Delaney couldn't piece together.

But after he'd thought about Firefish eating sailors for a while, wondering what that might look like, whether those sailors would die like fighting men aboard ship, which he'd seen a lot of, or like Lemmer Harps getting his hand eaten, which he'd seen only once, he ended up thinking about piranha again. They weren't as dangerous as bigger predators, because they were just little fish, really, and hungry. Not greedy to kill men, like Firefish. Or sharks. Or bears, or lions. And once he got to thinking about the worst kind of predators, he thought again about pirates. And then he thought about the worst pirate he'd ever met so far, which was Conch Imbry.

And so after only a few moments his mind flowed back to Conch and the Cabeebs. And there he was, watching the poor Trum boy once again.

Dallis was on his knees now on the stump facing the jail, his hands bound behind him. The jailor stood over the boy, to his left. Conch Imbry stood to the boy's right. Standing beside Conch was the unimpressive man, who now pulled a pistol from his waistband, checked its load, then held it down at his side. Delaney felt a sudden awe. This unimposing man was the executioner, then. Would he take the life of so young a boy, just like that, right before their eyes? Delaney couldn't imagine he would, but then he could see no reason why he wouldn't, him being a pirate.

"What's yer name and what's yer rank, sailor?" Imbry asked. His voice was a croak on top of a rumble, nothing at all like the pure baritone note of the seashell trumpet for which he was nicknamed.

The wide-eyed youngster looked up from between the twin mountains, the pirate and the jailor. His eyes were round in fear. He was younger than almost thirteen. He was barely twelve.

"Ye have a name, do ye?" Conch asked again.

"Yes, sir. I mean, *aye,* sir," he offered in a squeak.

Conch waited. The Cabeeb jailor kicked Dallis in the thigh, and the boy yelped.

"Just say your name, son," Delaney suggested firmly, to push Dallis into obedience, but gently, so as not to rile the pirates further.

"Dallis Trum, sir," came the boy's thin reply. Then, taking strength from Delaney's intervention, he straightened himself up, put his chin in the air and announced, "I'm a tried hand, sir, and a seasoned sailor." He made a very brief effort to salute before the cords that bound his wrists stopped him.

Delaney grinned in spite of himself. The boy had grit.

Conch seemed thoroughly unimpressed. "Yer accused a' murder," he offered, as though that fact might be unknown. "What's the penalty, *Horkan* Meeb, for murder in Mumtown?"

"Death, Captain," Meeb replied. "Death to the lot of 'em."

At this cue the unimpressive man stepped forward and put the pistol barrel to the back of Dallis's head. He had to lean over to do it, and when he did, Delaney saw that the back of the man's shirt had blood seeping through it in long stripes, as though he was wounded. As though he'd been whipped. But he didn't act wounded or whipped. He acted as though he was just fine. Which was not at all unimpressive. "Now, sir?" he asked evenly.

Conch did not reply but watched the young sailor carefully. Dallis's eyes wandered from the executioner to Conch to Meeb to the executioner again, then to the crewmen, and finally found Delaney.

It was a look Delaney could not forget, a worse one, even, than that which was far more recently branded into his brain when Lemmer's hand was eaten. This boy's momentary surge of pride was gone. He was not a bright lad, not by any means, and Delaney could see he had not quite grasped the finality of these proceedings until the cold steel of the pistol was pressed to the back of his skull. His look was pleading. It was anxious. It was confused. But worst of all, it was *trusting*. He expected his protector to protect him.

At that moment Delaney wished for all he was worth that he'd never laid an eye on the boy.

"Jes' kids," Delaney said aloud to the fish. Then he clucked and shook his head. "Never should a' come aboard." It was his downfall, he realized gloomily, to pay so much mind to the young ones. Growing up in the rough and tumble of his father's drunken poverty had hardened him to many things, but not to the plight of youngsters. Especially when they seemed lost and afraid and out of their element. He heaved a great sigh. "Should never a' been aboard."

Dallis and Kreg Trum had been taken aboard by accident. As the lines were being cast off, one of Captain June Stube's longtime hands had inexplicably fallen from atop the mainsail yard to the deck, and had to be left ashore in a rather grotesque display of broken bones. The boys had simply appeared at that moment, Delaney recalled, as though delivered from on high, with their bedrolls at their feet. Their faces were grubby and their clothes were filthy, but they swore they were sailors, experienced hands despite their age. Stube doubted, and asked a few pointed questions. To everyone's surprise, Kreg answered them all quite satisfactorily. The captain studied their palms, approved of the thick calluses. He hesitated yet, but then the boys offered to split a share—two crewmen for the price of one. Stube took them aboard and hastily cast off.

They were anything but seasoned hands.

Turned out they were chandlers, the sons of a candle-maker and merchant in some remote village on the Nearing Plains. Their hands were accustomed to hard work and hot wax, but their hearts had led their feet to run from both. They had listened too long and too carefully to an uncle's rum-soaked tales of life at sea, and they had determined to join the Vast Navy. Without papers or commendations, too young and too green, their quest had ended under the wharves at the docks of Mann, where they fought seagulls for scraps, begging every sailor who would listen to help them get on crew.

No one would have them, and now Captain Stube understood why. The boys were aggressively ignorant, showing confidence at all the wrong moments, their judgment in error almost unerringly. Which one of them was worse depended on which one was nearer. They were continually tying off what they should be loosing, coiling what they should be uncoiling, carrying what they should be throwing and throwing what they should be holding onto for dear life. After a cargo pulley missed a crewman's head by inches and crashed through a rum barrel, splaying out its staves like a crunched spider, Stube threw them both into the brig. Bad enough that they had lied, worse that they had bungled, but unforgiveable that they had lowered every man's share of rum.

Delaney had vouched for them, though. Couldn't stand to think of them behind bars. But they'd have been safe there, and if he'd let them be they wouldn't be ashore now. They wouldn't be facing prison, or pirates, or pirate's pistols.

"A seasoned sailor, is it?" Conch Imbry growled. "Now why do that seem so unlikely to me?" He glanced over at the rest of the condemned lot, and Delaney thought he saw a wink. His spirits crept upward.

Conch turned back to speak to the boy, leaning in. His raspy voice softened. "But tell ye what, I'll believe ye, at least till ye prove me otherwise."

Now hope flashed through Delaney.

"And to give ye a fightin' chance to prove yer mettle, I'll ransom yer worthless soul. And here's how. In exchange fer stayin' alive, fair is fair, ye'll have a duty to do me. And it's this. Ye'll swear allegiance to me. Ye'll swear ye'll follow me, like I was yer daddy and mama both. Like yer god in a'mighty heaven. Then, 'stead a' bein' dead, ye'll be alive. And ye'll have all the money ye can spend. Ye'll have trinkets and muskets and women, when ye grow up enough fer 'em, and ye'll have all ye can eat and all ye can drink fer as long as ye live. Ye'll even have fame, fer ye'll be sailin' wif the Conch. But hear me now. Ye'll kill who I say kill. And ye'll die when I say die. So. What say ye, son? Is it a bargain?"

Delaney could see a problem here. Not with the bargain itself, which would save a young man's life and so seemed a fresh wind of mercy. Rather, it was the way Conch had framed it. Captain Imbry had used too many words. He had made a simple choice too complex for the brain of this young runaway. So as the brutal and dashing pirate stood still, waiting for his words to play deep into the mind and heart of the least of these crewmen, it became gradually more obvious to all that the boy was not about to speak.

The executioner clicked back the hammer of his pistol. Conch Imbry's jaw tightened.

"'Scuse me, sir," Delaney heard himself say.

Now all eyes swung to him.

Delaney spoke as though in a fog, his mouth moving around words that seemed to form themselves and escape before his mind had a chance to rein them back. "That is to say, beggin' yer humble pardon, I do believe the boy don't understand the offer."

Conch looked dumbfounded. He looked at the boy. He looked back at Delaney. He narrowed his already narrow eyes. "He's what, a idiot?"

"Oh no. Well, at least not so much that he can't work out the meaning. But if ye don't mind, begging yer pardon again, I'll help explain it."

Imbry waved a big hand. "Help away."

Delaney spoke directly to the boy. "Dallis, son, this here's Conch Imbry, and he's a great pirate captain. Says he'll save ye from the Cabeebs if ye'll turn pirate right now. Otherwise—see that man with the gun there? Well, he's gonna shoot ye dead. So now, son, ye got to decide whether to live a pirate or die right now, being a..." the right word did not come to him, "...whatever you now are," he concluded.

The boy's mouth dropped open as his eyes drifted on their own accord to Conch Imbry.

"I believe he's got it now, Cap'n," Delaney said with a confident nod.

Then the boy did something that surprised them all. He leaped to his feet and ran to his brother.

"Hey!" the Cabeeb jailor shouted, reaching for his own pistol.

"Let 'im," Conch said.

Dallis stopped, his hands still tied behind him, looking directly into his older brother's grim eyes. "What should I do, Kreg?"

"I don't know," Kreg answered earnestly, the predicament too big for him as well. "We din't run off to become no pirates."

"What if Ma finds out?"

Kreg nodded once in earnest. "She'd be real sore if we came home pirates."

After a thoughtful pause, Delaney ventured to speak again. "On the opposite hand, I reckon she might also be a tad put out if you was to come home dead."

The boys looked at him, then looked at one another as they thought that through, their puzzlement complete. "Real put out," Kreg confirmed.

It seemed an impossible knot to untie.

Delaney spoke to the pirate captain, his mouth again running ahead of his brain. "Why start with the boys? Let the men decide, and leave the boys to follow after."

Conch Imbry walked with surprising grace of movement toward Delaney. It reminded him of a cat moving in on a mouse. Conch Imbry's every step seemed to speak aloud, and the words they seemed to speak were, "I'm tired of you, sir, and so now you'll die." And as if to emphasize this silent point, the pirate pulled his pistol and patiently, almost passively pressed its cold, round muzzle into Delaney's forehead. "Yer a talkative one," he croaked. He pulled the hammer back until it clicked. "Talkin' leads to trouble."

Delaney's heart seized up. He thought at that moment that those cold, slitted eyes would be the last things he would ever see.

"Don't shoot him, please!" Dallis yelped, and for the first time in all this, tears appeared in his eyes.

Conch looked over at him, a sudden spark in his own eyes. "I *will* kill 'im, though, ye little bawler. I'll kill 'em all dead unless ye turn pirate and sail with me for all yer days." He did not move the pistol, held in his left hand, from Delaney's forehead.

Dallis's round head bobbed like a cork on the sea. "All right, then. I will. Aye, sir." He looked at his brother Kreg. "For Mr. Delaney."

Kreg nodded. "We're pirates now," he confirmed. "Jus' don't shoot Mr. Delaney. He's a good man."

"A good man, is he?" The right side of Conch's long mouth rose up into something between a smile and a sneer. He reached out his free hand in a flash, and grabbed Dallis Trum by the back of the neck. Then he swung the pistol around and pressed it to Dallis's temple. His grip was firm, too firm to be anything but painful. The boy closed his eyes and grimaced, but said nothing. He'd sworn to die whenever Conch said so. He seemed bound to keep his word.

"And how about you, Mr. Delaney?" Conch asked. "Yer a too-much talker. Will ye save this lad?"

"If I can," Delaney answered firmly.

"Swear it, then. Swear ye'll kill who I say kill, die when I say die, and follow me all yer days."

Delaney had no worries about what his parents might think. Yer Poor Ma was dead and Pap, if not dead by now, was surely dead drunk. "Times bein' what they are, sir," he answered, "it seems a fair bargain."

"Swear it."

A lump rose in his throat. He knew there was no turning back, not from an oath to a pirate. "I swear to follow you sir, live or die, all my days."

Conch nodded. He lowered the pistol. He turned back to the boys. "What's yer name, son?" he asked the older boy.

"Kreg Trum. Dallis here's my kid brother."

"Kreg and Dallis."

The unimpressive man spoke. "More like dregs and ballast, if you ask me."

Conch laughed, which sounded a bit like a bullfrog with the croup. "Aye. That's what they are, no doubt. Dregs and Ballast." And no one called them anything else from that moment on, for as long as they sailed with Conch Imbry.

"How about the rest of you men?" Conch then asked around. "What say ye? Death, or piracy?" He said it with a surge of energy, as though offering a wondrous choice, perhaps selling some healing potion or leading a prayer meeting.

The men spoke all at once, racing one another for the privilege of being first. "Aye, we'll be pirates!" and "Yes, sir!" and "Yers to the bitter end, Cap'n!" and "I'm in, ye can count on me!"

"Swear it!" Conch ordered.

"I swear it!" his new crewmen answered in healthy unison.

All but one.

The good cheer receded as Conch walked calmly over to Avery Wittle. "I din't hear ye swear, sailor."

Avery was short and soft and round and unassuming. If it was possible for a man to have an opposite, Avery was the Conch's. He lowered his eyes. Conch looked down at the pistol in his own left hand. He gripped an iron bar with his right hand, then pointed the barrel at the ground.

"What about it, now?" he said in a low rumble. "Speak up, sailor. No sense dyin' like a hog trussed fer slaughter."

Avery Wittle shook like the last leaf on a bare branch in winter's first storm. But he remained silent.

On his post, Delaney squirmed. Usually he didn't remember all this, this far into the story. He'd kept it far away since the days right after it had happened. Whenever that memory came around, his mind always went off somewhere else, often following his legs to a pint of ale or a card table, or even a deck that needed a swabbing. Anything to avoid what had happened next.

But there was nowhere for his legs to take him now. Squirm or stretch, it didn't matter. The scene went right on.

Avery just looked up at the pirate captain with that same childishly sincere look he'd given Delaney, just hours before when, hat in hand, he'd helped Delaney remember the events of the previous night.

Conch sighed. "What's yer name, sailor?"

"Avery Wittle, sir. Able-bodied seaman, and a true hand."

"A true hand, is it? Well, true as yer hand may be, ye know what I got to do, don't ye, Mr. Wittle? What would it look like to these men here if, after all my talk, I let ye loose alive and no pirate?"

Avery's breaths came in sharp, quick bursts.

Conch watched him a moment, then asked quietly, almost gently, "Not got the stuffin's for a little buccaneerin,' is that all it is?"

He shook his head. "I'm sorry," he said, struggling to look the Conch in the eye.

"It ain't that hard," Conch assured him. "We're just takin' gold from the very men who've taken it from us, and kept it fer themselves. See, these merchants and shipmen, they make the rules, and they make 'em so's men like you and me cain't ever win. But me...I just make diff'rent rules. Ye play by my rules, Mr. Wittle, ye win. You and yer mates. Then we're the ones end up with the gold. That's all it is."

Avery's voice quavered and his chin trembled, but he spoke plainly enough. "I can't tell you how truly sorry I am for this. But I...I can't rightly serve a pirate in this world and be prepared to meet my Maker in the next. And I say that meanin' no offense."

Now Conch's gentleness faded away. His voice was cold and distant. "Ah, a man wif a principle. Well, no offense taken, Mr. Wittle. We all makes our choices. And when a man makes up his mind to die, well, likely he's goin' to die."

And with a single gunshot, that's what Avery Wittle did.

Monkeys screeched and birds flapped upward, and Delaney shivered. Everything had changed. The pond was darker; he was colder. He looked up and found that the sun had now moved in its arc past the opening in the canopy above, and he was in shadow.

Why would Avery do such a thing? Why not pretend to turn, then run the next chance he got? At least that way he'd have lived a while longer. No sense having a principle and then being dead and unable to use it. Who knew, maybe he'd have gotten lucky and made a clean break, disappearing from sea life, and gone on to plow corn the rest of his days far from the reach of pirates.

Fear is all it was, Delaney thought. *Avery was just a coward, through and through.*

Or at least, that's what Delaney had told himself ever since it happened. But now he was remembering it, it didn't seem that way. It seemed...it almost seemed that something else was happening. Avery was fearful; he was trembling. True enough. But something about what he'd done was haunting. Kind of like that little girl's strange and beautiful song was haunting. It was almost like—in some way that Delaney couldn't get his mind around—rather than being pure afraid, Avery was only afraid just on the surface. Like his fear was just the ripple on top of a deep pond. Underneath, it was like Avery was doing something he knew he must do, even though he didn't want to do it. It almost seemed, somehow, when you looked at it that way, *brave.*

And then the song came back to Delaney's mind, and the young girl's pure voice singing it. And though it still made no sense, it seemed now to be a song about Avery, or if not about him, about the sort of man he was. Or maybe, about the sort of thing he did.

A true lang time and we shall meet
On the silver path to the rushing sea
Where moons hang golden under boughs of green,
A lang true la 'tis true...

That little girl had something of the next world in her, Delaney concluded. And it made sense, her being the daughter of Jenta Stillmithers. There was so much of this world's strife bound up in the union that created her, so much of longing for something better and running up against the harsh brambles, so much of the dark in pursuit of the light, that it was only natural the result would be a child connected to this world by a thread.

In her first two weeks in Skaelington, Jenta Flug, now Jenta Stillmithers, was invited to two fine events. The first was a small, private party for a few of Runsford's many business associates, but the second was the city's most splendid dance of the year, the annual Summer's Eve Ball, celebrating the summer solstice. It was the climactic end of the social calendar. Everyone who mattered was there, along with a great many who wished to matter more than they did.

Jenta immediately attracted a flock of admiring young men—and some not so young—all of whom were astounded that such beauty could have been among them and remained hidden. Whispered conversations filled the splendidly decorated room, which she made drab by comparison. She wore a brocaded gown tailored for the occasion, cream with scarlet trim, cut tastefully and elegantly. Her hair was done up and wrapped, leaving one curl of tresses to fall to a bare shoulder. Eyes drifted toward her, then drifted away, or else drifted and stayed.

Her laughter, sweet and ringing, rose above the music. She danced with perhaps twenty different gentlemen and made each one feel he had a direct route to her heart, if only he chose to pursue it.

Jenta was spectacular.

Shayla was in bliss.

Wentworth was in agony. He stood by the wine bar, drinking too much and becoming too jealous. Then when a dashing, muscular man with a wide face, pointed moustache, curling locks, and silk-covered calves took his turn with her, Wentworth could see his prize slipping away.

He marched to where his father chatted with a banker, took him by the sleeve, and pulled him clumsily aside. "She dances with Carnsford Imbry!" he seethed. "The pirate!"

Runsford, having had a few glasses of wine himself, was not prone to let such a fact break his good mood. "Captain Imbry is a businessman, too, remember. Let's not be hasty in our judgments."

"The Conch takes what he wants. Everyone knows that. You brought Jenta here for me!"

Runsford sighed. His mood was broken. "I would remind you that it is your own long train of indiscretions that has made it so difficult for you to win and keep the hand of a lady. Conch has had little to do with that."

At this Wentworth's face turned red. "*My* indiscretions? She's dancing with a pirate! What does that say of her own discretion?"

Runsford eyed his son. "Are you angry with him because he wants to take Jenta for himself, or angry with her for wanting to be taken?"

"Who says she wants him? Where did you hear that?"

Runsford pried the wine glass from his son's hand. "This pique is unbecoming. Stop drinking, and calm yourself. She's a young woman at her first ball. Let her dance. All will look far less sinister in the morning. Captain Imbry will be off to sea again, and Jenta will be living in a cottage outside your bedroom window." He winked.

This calmed Wentworth some, but not much. He watched the remainder of their dance with suspicion, each curtsy, each smile, each touch a knife's blade between his ribs.

"Are you in love?" the whispered words echoed in Wentworth's ear. He didn't know if they were his own thoughts or someone else's, for the answer was obvious, and unavoidable, and a revelation to him. He could not take his eyes off Jenta long enough to turn and find the source of the question. When he finally did, his father was there, but several feet away and chatting with another businessman, paying Wentworth no mind.

In the morning, things did look brighter. Conch's ship, the *Shalamon*, had sailed. Jenta was at breakfast, looking far less formal but no less radiant, her attention focused more or less on him. Wentworth had no stomach for the eggs and bacon set before him, but the girl's laugh, her bright eyes as she recounted her evening, were a healing balm.

"Conch Imbry is a pirate," he told her when she paused in her stories.

"Who?" she asked.

"Captain Carnsford Imbry. Goes by Conch…like the shell. He's the pirate with whom you danced." She still looked confused. "Yellow vest."

She shook her head in disbelief. "The man with the…?" She grasped an imaginary flow of hair above her shoulder.

"*Quite* the pirate, I hear," Shayla said with a tone of warning for her daughter.

False rebuke, jesting, was the way Wentworth heard it. "A dance is fine," Wentworth instructed, "in polite company. But stay away from that one."

Jenta marveled, putting fingers to her lips. "He didn't seem like a pirate at all."

"And yet, he is, and among the bloodiest on the seas," Wentworth scolded. "A pirate king, some call him, with great pirate captains at his beck and call."

Jenta saw the depth of his emotion. "I'm so very much in need of your guidance. How will I know these things unless a gentleman tells me?"

"I shall tell you," he vowed. "I shall tell you all about these things, and much more."

The more Wentworth thought about it, the more he knew he must tell her everything. And not just tell, but vow everything as well, if he were to keep her.

Shayla watched the young man, wondering why she felt a dull dread.

"It's not possible." Shayla said it dismissively, serenely. "It's far too early. I will not hear of it."

"Well, I see we're no longer laughing," Runsford replied, just as placid, from behind his enormous desk. "That's progress."

"Please forgive me. I only laughed because I felt sure it was an attempt at humor. Mr. Ryland, it's a simple matter. He proposed to her and she declined. It's not over between them. She's not uninterested. It's just… well, there has been no courtship." She couldn't believe she needed to explain these facts. "She has only just arrived."

"And with all the eligible men of society throwing themselves at her feet, why, she might not even choose Wentworth."

"She is charmed by him. But it takes time to win a girl's heart. These things must run their course."

"Must they?"

"Mr. Ryland, what would people think, to see such a mad rush to marriage?"

He nodded. "You make a good point there. If the pair were to suddenly become man and wife, it might seem…almost desperate." Ryland placed the fingertips of his hands together before him. "You should know that my son has been at the center of many rumors. I want this to be the end of them, not the beginning of a new round. Perhaps a year of court-ship is the thing to do it."

"Thank you." She smiled, relieved.

A clerk entered with a document.

"Not now!" Ryland barked at him.

"But sir, you asked for—"

The boss snapped his fingers. "Yes, yes, bring it here. You should have stated your business when you entered." The clerk put the folded parchment in Runsford's hand and quickly retreated. If he was dismayed by his employer's behavior, he didn't show it.

Now Runsford Ryland, proprietor of the world's premier shipping line, stood up from behind his desk and walked over to close the door. Outside, clearly visible through the large panes of glass on all four sides of his office, clerks busied themselves along enormous bookshelves, moving ladders to and fro, extracting huge leather-bound volumes, opening them up on gloss-finished tables, inserting new sheaves of parchment here, taking old sheaves out for examination there, making notations and entering figures, reinserting the sheaves, then returning the volumes back to their places.

"Every transaction has a contract," Runsford explained. "Every ship-ment has a bill of lading. Here we account for every barrel of whale oil, every cask of rum, every nail in every crate that passes through Skae-lington or any other port in a Ryland ship. All transactions, all movements are documented here in neat rows of numbers by men whose minds run day and night with sums. They dream of ledgers, I'm told."

"Truly extraordinary," she said drily. But it struck her as an intricate dance, with columns of numbers moving the men's minds and hands and feet, rather than bars of musical notes.

"I do nothing without a reason, Mrs. Stillmithers. I do not spend money foolishly. Nor do I simply invest it and hope for the best. I manage my investments. I expect them to profit me." He returned to his desk, set the folded document at one corner just so, its outer edges aligning with the corner of the desk. "Courtships are delicate things. They break, and they break off, for many reasons. Too fragile. Not a good investment. But courtship it must be. So I ask myself, how might Wentworth court Jenta, and yet there be no chance that she would decide to look elsewhere?"

Shayla's alarm returned. "I shall instruct her according to your wishes, of course."

"Ah, but that would be your bargain, not hers. Young women are willful things."

Shayla waited, ready for almost any piercing suggestion.

"It was Wentworth himself who came up with the solution. Bright lad. Great future. But in truth it was there all along. And it is this…They shall wed immediately, as he proposed. But…they shall do so in secret."

She felt she had been struck. "In *secret?* To what end?"

"You don't see it? Why, they shall appear to be courting for an entire year, when all the while they are married. She will be unable to look elsewhere. She will learn how to behave like a lady. He will learn how to behave as a gentleman. You will help me manage my investment. And then a year from now, perhaps two, we shall have a great, formal, public wedding. And I shall have my return." He folded his hands before him.

Shayla did see it. She saw it too clearly. "Mr. Runsford, I cannot submit to such a scheme. Jenta is a lady whose heart must be won, not jailed—"

"Come now, Mrs. Stillmithers." He walked toward her now, put his hand on the desk near her, and leaned in. He spoke softly. "Or should I say, Miss Flug. I know your history. I did my due diligence. You had your fling with a gentleman nineteen years ago, but there is reason to question whether your daughter is actually his."

"That was settled long ago," Shayla said coldly. "I have made no claims."

"I'm sure of it. For there was another man, wasn't there? Something of a pirate, I believe. And wasn't his name Stillmithers?"

She sat stonily, her eyes focused elsewhere. Then she looked at her hands, folded in her lap. "No. It was Mithers. And nothing happened between us."

"But you still carry a flame for Mithers. It's still Mithers, in your heart, isn't it? Quite clever. And yet, all those years ago you tried to convince your well-heeled gentleman that the child belonged to him."

Her eyes flashed. "It did belong to him! Jenta was…is…not the daughter of Ander Mithers. There were wild rumors, all speculation. Was I attracted? Yes. He was…but I was…"

Ryland straightened up. "He was what? Dashing? Exotic? Dangerous? And you were what? A good girl?"

Her silence was hard, and dark.

"You wanted to move up in society, didn't you? But you failed. You still might have succeeded, until you were tempted by a rogue. Your fiancé found out, and suddenly he couldn't trust that the child was his. But I'll wager he was in love with you, wasn't he?" She said nothing, and he continued. "Of course he was. Just as Wentworth is in love with Jenta. And Jenta's been a good girl, too, hasn't she? But there are many more temptations in Skaelington than in Mann. You of all people cannot afford to see who or what wins her heart. It must be captured and pinned down now, so that she will submit to what's good for her. You must see the wisdom of this."

Shayla's eyes went distant. "She does not love him."

"Yet! She does not love him *yet.* Come, Mrs. Stillmithers. Let's look at it. She is the daughter of a washerwoman, born out of wedlock. And she refuses an offer of marriage from the heir of Ryland Shipping and Freight? Listen to me. *Now* is the time to assure that she does not follow your path. This is the moment when her future can be secured. And your past can be erased."

Shayla felt all her efforts being crushed under the dual weight of his logic and her own failures. This was, after all, what Shayla had wanted; it was precisely what she'd hoped for. But to ask Jenta to marry Wentworth Ryland? She simply could not do it. She could not look her daughter in the eye and ask her to marry a man she could never, would never, love.

So Shayla shifted the argument. "How is it a good plan, though? Such could not be kept secret. The two are both young. An indiscreet comment is all it would take…And there must be a priest at the ceremony, and witnesses. Someone will talk. It will be known."

"No priests. And you and I shall be the only witnesses."

"If not a priest, then who?"

"A ship's captain." And now Runsford beamed. He was proud of his plan. "I know a man who knows how to keep a secret. I know one who, even if he doesn't keep it secret, will never be believed by polite company."

She shook her head, trying to ward off an image that would not go away. "This cannot have been Wentworth's idea."

"No. The secret wedding was his. But the ship and the captain, that was my own."

"Mr. Ryland, I must speak my mind."

"Speak away." He walked back to his chair and stood beside it.

"I came here at the invitation of a gentleman. I brought my daughter here under that same gentleman's protection, trusting to his good faith and kindness, and his promise that he would provide an introduction to society here. But now it seems he has done no more than arrange a marriage for his son, a young man who seems to have a great deal of trouble living up to the title of gentleman."

Runsford's look went cold.

"I'm sorry, but it's true. Jenta is a lady, and both she and her mother have a right to choose whom she marries."

Runsford's eyebrows went up.

"If you insist on this path, sir, I shall be forced to pursue every means at my disposal, including the law if necessary, to alter this outcome."

He waited. "Is that all?"

"Yes."

"You do put on a good show of gentility, I'll grant you that. I'm sure I would believe you actually were a gentlewoman if I didn't know better. But let us not waste any more time. If you wanted to make amends for your past, the church has homes for women like you. But it's not your way to run to priests looking for pardon, is it? No. You run to businessmen, looking for a bargain. Well, here is the bargain you have struck. You will live to see all your dreams come true. All that is required is that your daughter marry far above her station. How is this possible to refuse?"

Shayla was silent.

"You are a foolish, ungrateful woman. You kick and struggle against the inevitable, when you should be thanking me for the sacrifice I am making."

"Sacrifice? What sacrifice?"

"Why, the potential for your past to be known. Stillmithers? Really? This is not just your sham anymore—I share in it now. And I don't think I even need mention what this does to the Ryland bloodlines."

The crushing weight descended within her. "You are not a good man," she whispered. "I will never allow it."

"But of course you will allow it." He picked up the folded parchment from the corner of his desk, and fingered it gently in his hands. "I care not whether you are conversant with the moral principle of chastity, dear woman; that is your concern. But I very much care that you understand the business principle of investment. It is this: One invests so that one might profit. Not so that another might profit. Your daughter will marry Wentworth. You shall be faithful in this, at least."

She stared at him coldly for a moment, then said, "If that is a contract, I will not sign it."

He looked at the parchment in his hands. "A contract? No. Well, I suppose in a manner of speaking. It is a letter from the Sheriff of Mann."

He opened it, turned it so she could see the seal, pressed into the bottom of the page. Then he pulled it back and read over it silently. "It seems you are wanted for some rather heinous criminal activities, both you and your daughter."

Her mouth dropped open. "What crimes?"

"Does it really matter?" he asked sweetly. "But since you ask: extortion, theft, various confidence schemes that entrap gentlemen like myself and my son, using your womanly wiles. Seems you have even lied about your name."

She sat rigid, her eyes wide, the mask cracking.

"Run to the sheriff, Shayla. Go anywhere you like, tell any story you please. All roads will lead back to me, and this bit of parchment. 'She spins a good yarn,' they will say. 'My, she had me fooled.' No, Shayla, you don't want that. You want to see your daughter marry Wentworth. And she will, or you shall find yourselves on the next Ryland ship bound for Mann. And you will not be leaving in finery and accolades, but in chains and humiliation." He set the paper down again, just so. "Is any of this unclear to you?"

Her look hardened again, the mask returned, colder than before. "No."

"Good. I hope that in time you will come to see this as simply a necessary bit of leverage to help you and Jenta leave the past behind, and ease into the privileges of your new, elite positions in Skaelington's refined society."

"I'd like to refine his elite position, that no-good—" The remainder of the exclamations from Ham's audience was drowned in grumbles and oaths, all aimed at the falseness of society, and of rich men with power.

It was odd, Delaney thought, coming back to himself. Ham never seemed to feel the emotions he created. The men could be hollering and swearing, and he was calm as sunset on a summer's eve. Like he could direct their anger anywhere he wanted, flame it up, douse it down. One thing was sure, though. Ham always made the men feel better about pirating.

But that was Ham's job, wasn't it? It was Mutter Cabe who revealed that to Delaney one time, when some part of the story, maybe this very part, made him mad as a hornet and ready to attack the next ship with a Ryland flag and tear it to pieces.

"Ever wonder, Delaney, why a first-rate cutthroat like Belisar keeps a middling deckhand and a worthless swordsman like Ham aboard?"

"Oh, I wouldn't say worthless—" Delaney began to argue.

"Stories lead places," Mutter continued, ignoring the halfhearted objection. "Ham says it himself, all the time. Our job is to cut the hearts out of honest citizens and take their gold. Wouldn't do for us to get thinkin' on that too much, would it? Better if we get all riled up about the likes of Runsford Ryland, who we never even met. Kind of justifies all the men we killed. Not to mention women and children."

Delaney felt a heave in his chest, and knew he was about to feel a great remorse. He'd never killed a child. That he would never do. But he'd helped to put a few on boats, to send them out to sea with their mamas and their papas, without food nor water enough to survive.

It was always the little ones who least understood what was happening, who asked the hardest questions.

"Mama, why are you crying?"

"Why are we getting off the ship?"

"Where are we going now, Papa?"

If they lived, Delaney knew, they'd just grow up to turn pirate one day anyway, in the sway of either the Rylands or the Conchs of the world. For some, like Delaney and the Trum boys, it would come early, and no bones about it. For others it would come later, like it did to Jenta Flug, who lasted more than nineteen years a true young lady, against all odds.

"Innocence," he said aloud. "It's hard to see it, and harder to see it go, in such a sorry world as this."

That's what the song was! Delaney understood it now, all of a sudden.

> *A true lang time,*
> *A lang true la…*

That's why it was haunting. It was the innocence of it. Sung by a young girl, a sweet thing who loved her mama and didn't understand about the wild, cold places of the world, and how they crushed and trampled sweet things, lovely things.

> *…And down the silver path into a rushing sea,*
> *Where moons hang golden under boughs of green…*

That voice didn't know about such darkness, and yet it felt the shadow

Blaggard's Moon

of it. Sure, that was it. A lullaby. A lullaby did that same thing, sweeping your heart away from the hurtful parts of the world, even though it's sung in the very shadow of the rising wave, the crushing that is to come, that always comes. A lullaby like that finds a place where, for just one moment, no bad thing will happen. Just for a moment. *Where moons hang golden under boughs of green, A lang true la 'tis true...*

And then Delaney remembered his own mother. He remembered her lullabies. Not the words, not even the melody so much, but the sound. The feel. The safe place. He remembered. She would hold him. A long time ago, she would hold him tight and sing to him, sweet and lovely and deep and pure, and light was everywhere, and nothing bad could happen.

And suddenly he missed her, oh so much.

He put his face in his hands, and his shoulders shook.

Chapter Six

ACES OVER QUEENS

Captain Carnsford Bloodstone Imbry was known to play cards. He often dropped in on the guests in the private area of the famous Skaelington pub he owned, the Cleaver and Fork. There he would swoop in, make small talk, and encourage both the winners and the losers to continue to gamble, offering a free round of drinks, cigars, and plenty of good food. But he rarely played himself, except in even more advantageous surroundings. Whenever he was in the port of Skaelington, a night was chosen, invitations were sent, gamblers were ushered aboard the *Shalamon*, and poker was played until the early morning hours. When a man received an invitation to the Conch's table, it meant three things. First, he was wealthy. Second, he would pay his debts. And third, he would lose. No one refused the honor of such an invitation, and no one managed to leave the ship with any of Conch's gold. Or much of his own, either.

"But Father," Wentworth protested, looking up from the luminous script of the invitation in his hand, "I understand it's an honor to be invited. But why me? I have no money of my own. Everyone knows that."

"True enough." Runsford paused and swallowed, patting traces of egg from his mouth. "And you will have none of your own until you earn it, and none of mine until you prove you can manage it. And yourself." He drank from a large juice glass.

Wentworth rolled his eyes. The Lecture.

"But you have been invited," Runsford continued, "because I have had a chat with Captain Imbry. I have asked that he invite you. And not just you, but also Jenta. And her mother."

Wentworth paused, his slice of toast hanging in the air. "They're to play cards with the pirate?"

His father just laughed. "No, my dear boy. They will not play." He slathered butter onto bread. "They are invited because you will set foot aboard the *Shalamon* a bachelor, and return to shore a married man."

Wentworth lowered his toast. "I'm to be married at a poker game?"

"Imbry is a ship's captain, registered as such in the Skaelington books. He has the legal authority to join you to your bride. A pause at the gaming table is all it will take. Quiet, discreet, done in minutes."

"But he's a pirate! That's not a wedding."

Runsford grew irritable, swiping his knife briskly across the bread, now leaving jam behind in swaths. "No, it's not. It's a *marriage*. You asked to marry her, if I recall. Did you not? Demanded it. Even the secrecy was your idea."

"Yes, but—"

"Then marry her in secret you shall. You can court her in public, and… here is the important point, son…she will have little choice but to remain interested in you, regardless of your indiscretions. We wouldn't need such conniving if you hadn't sent so many fine young ladies packing with your drinking and gambling and all your indecent—"

"Yes, yes!" He leaned into the argument. "And when those young women found out I had no inheritance, that you will give me none, that's when they lost patience!"

"You have no inheritance because you have yet to earn it! You behave like a drunken rogue!"

"And you treat me like a child!"

"Nonetheless!" Runsford held his forefinger in the air, and took a deep breath. He was not going to argue the entirety of it again. He lowered his hand. "You've got your bride now. She's the girl of your dreams. You begged me to let you marry her. So perhaps she's not the girl I would have chosen. Perhaps it's not the wedding you desire. That wedding, the glorious affair that I'm sure is her entire life's goal, will happen in due time."

Wentworth shook his head, defeated. "To be married by a pirate, though. It seems…like madness."

"Yes, and that is why no one will believe it, even if word leaks."

"Word *will* leak. He'll talk."

"I'm not worried about Conch Imbry. I plan to lose quite a bit of money tonight to ensure that he doesn't talk. Your public wedding could hardly cost more. Captain Imbry is a lot of things, Wentworth, but he is a man who understands that a bargain is a bargain."

Wentworth's look was full of venom, but he aimed it across the screened porch, out onto the yard, at the cottage where Jenta and Shayla lived.

"What is it, son? Say it."

"I don't trust his intentions with Jenta."

"Quite. But you see, that's why I've chosen him, of all captains. He and I have struck a bargain." He put a hand on the table, patted it as though it were Wentworth's shoulder. "She is off limits to him."

Wentworth came back to the moment, and looked hopefully at his father.

"You call it madness. But Wentworth, no policy is madness unless it fails. And this one will not fail. You'll see."

"Gentleman's ante!" Conch announced, tossing five gold coins onto the red felt of the table. The pirate was in fine form, wearing his bright yellow vest over his silk shirt, his wavy hair cascading down to his shoulders, his moustache waxed and drawn out, two perfect tips pointing left and right. His mood was light.

Wentworth gasped. Five in gold? The amount was incredible; it would take him months to spend so much, even in the most expensive alehouses. It was a life savings for many hard-working families. Worse, Wentworth had already bought his chips, a huge investment in neatly stacked slices of colored, polished marble, and this "gentleman's ante" was almost double his chip count. But no one else around the table, all proven and capable businessmen, even blinked. His own father tossed his five coins onto the red cloth serenely, as though buying penny candies.

When it came Wentworth's turn, he reached into his pouch, pulled out five coins, and left two. Feigning nonchalance, he tossed them onto the table. One caught an edge and rolled directly toward Conch, circled twice, then settled in front of him.

The pirate swept the coin away, clinking it into its fellows at the center of the table. "Pot's right," he declared. "Seven-card stud is the game. House rules. Three down, three up, one down. Three bets to a hand: one after the hole cards, one after the up cards, one at the end." Conch turned to his right-hand man, who happened to be sitting on his left, the unimpressive fellow who followed him everywhere. Conch slapped a paw on his shoulder. "This here's Mr. Mart Mazeley, who ye've already met by way of buyin' yer chits. He'll be doin' all the dealin' tonight. Not that I don't trust each of ye with my own life, I do. It's just that I trust Mazeley more. Any questions?"

"Ah…just one," a heavy-set man with long, gray whiskers offered. This was Glemm Gorsus, banker, in his first visit to the pirate's game. "In a friendly card game the deal is generally passed. Is your Mr. Mazeley professionally licensed, perhaps?"

Conch's eyes went cold as stone, making Glemm Gorsus quite uncomfortable. "He's dealin' because I trust 'im. I thought I said that."

"You did, so you did!" Glemm exclaimed happily. He dug into his ear with a finger. "Hearing is the problem. Old age, you know!"

"Age, eh? Well, let's see how old we can make ye feel before the evenin' is out. And so a toast to begin!" Conch announced, his good mood returned. "Where's the rum?" A barmaid stepped forward with a platter of crystal tumblers and put one in each man's hand.

Conch Imbry stood. "To the gentlemen of means who grace this table. May ye leave here with even more grace…and a good deal less means!" He held the crystal high as his targets laughed at their own impending doom, then he swallowed his rum in a single slug. The others followed suit.

"Well I'll be," Imbry exclaimed at the end of the first hand. "An ace on the final card. Ain't that somethin'!" And he raked in the pot.

"He's cheatin'!" the young Trum boy shouted, alarmed. No one answered him. "Ain't he?" he asked into the silence, suddenly less sure of himself.

"Button yer flap," Sleeve told him. "It ain't cheatin' if yer name's Conch Imbry."

The others heartily agreed. "It's just regular ol' piracy," one explained.

"Let us just say," Ham Drumbone suggested, "that the rules of Conch's game were somewhat skewed from what you might consider the usual."

"Aye, Conch skewed 'em. He skewed 'em real good!"

Laughter.

"That is to say," Ham's bass voice rolled out, gently lapping over the others, "in the usual poker contest, the game is to match wits with opponents, all the while testing the fickleness of fate herself, as together you ride the unknown ebbs and flows of blessings and curses known to men as *luck*. Whereas, in Conch's little den of thievery, the game was simpler. More like a child's game, really. For at Conch's table, it wasn't poker at all, but more a game where gentlemen *pretended* to play poker."

Agreement all around.

Dallis Trum nodded. "Play-pretend," he said. Now he understood.

So did Delaney. He'd done that.

"That's it for me," Runsford Ryland said, well after midnight. "I'm cleaned out." Mart Mazeley scooped up one more pile of chips and stacked them before the Conch. Runsford stood, swayed for a moment, then pulled the insides of his pockets out. "Empty," he said to laughter all around. The men were in good spirits. Conch's minions had kept drink glasses full and cigars lit, and Conch himself had kept the stories coming, tales of dark nights and fearsome attacks, hidden gold, close escapes from the clutches of the Royal Navy, and from the jealous husbands of beautiful women. The gentlemen soaked it all in, even as they kept up their extraordinary run of bad luck. As the hours wore on, the inevitable was fully embraced and the mood grew lighter and lighter.

They all watched the amazingly dexterous hands of their dealer as he cut and shuffled, cut and shuffled, then flipped the cards around the table with swift, unerring precision. Unimpressive in most venues, Mart Mazeley was a master here. They never saw a fault. Not that they would have mentioned it if they had, for they all knew what they bought with their time and their money, and it was more than drinks and company. Conch would remember them. His raids on their ships would be few, perfunctory, and generally bloodless. Skaelington's carefully crafted balance between altruism and treachery, liberty and lechery, fairness and foul play, would hold for another few months. A few gold coins at a poker game was a small price to pay for the continuation of a highly profitable way of life for all.

"Perhaps a walk on deck would clear my head," Runsford said, to no one in particular.

The others paid him no mind, and Mazeley kept dealing. But Ryland did not leave, and finally Conch looked up at him.

"All right, I'll join ye, then," Conch said gruffly, tossing his cards onto the tabletop. "I'm foldin' this one in. The rest of ye play on."

"If you're sure" and "Well, why not?" were the responses, as it dawned on the gathered sheep that if Conch wasn't in the game, he could hardly fleece them further. There was a buzz of excitement as they realized that in his absence one of them might actually win something.

Runsford cleared his throat loudly, and finally Wentworth joined his mind to the moment. "I'll walk with you, Father," he offered. He stood unsteadily, wondering vaguely if he had drunk too much, and then followed his elders out of the room.

The pirate led the way to the captain's quarters, but the short walk up from the Poker Deck, as Conch called his richly refitted aftmost cargo hold, had substantially worsened the pirate's disposition. "Where's the wenches?" he growled once they were inside his saloon.

Wentworth stared a moment, not understanding to whom Conch referred, then said, "Oh, right. In their quarters, I'm guessing." He looked from Conch to Runsford. "I'll get them," he offered at last, and went to collect his bride, and the mother of his bride.

Jenta could not remember the last time she saw such sorrow in her mother's eyes.

"Perhaps you'll grow to love him," Shayla told her daughter. She looked at, and then past, Jenta.

"Perhaps," Jenta answered, hoping to ease Shayla's pain. They were seated in the two chairs of a close but comfortable cabin just below the captain's quarters. Jenta had a prayer book in her hand.

"But I hope for your sake that you never do," Shayla continued, from that same place of darkness. Jenta searched her mother's eyes. Something lived there in that distance, something she had never let her daughter see. As Jenta watched, the years were turning back, and an old, deeply wrought memory came to the fore. "When you give your heart away," she told her daughter, "you can no longer protect it." And now, for a moment, Jenta saw the young girl that Shayla once had been. "When you love, dear girl, you give another the power to hurt you." Shayla lived within her memory for a while longer, and then said, "If you love deeply enough, you give another the power to destroy you."

The words were spoken gently, but the force of them was harsh. Jenta shook her head. "Wentworth will not destroy me."

A rap on the door. "Ready, my sweet? My Jenta?" The words were slow and slurred.

Shayla closed her eyes. When she opened them again, the mask of protection she always wore was fully in place.

Jenta stood, handed the prayer book to her mother. She straightened her dress, a gray evening gown with white lace trim. "We shall make the best of it," she said to her mother with, if not great hope, at least a full measure of confidence. Then she opened the door.

Already dark, Conch's mood now seemed threatening. "I don't like doin' yer dirty work."

Runsford blanched. "My dirty...? Dear Captain, marrying a man and a woman is hardly that. It's an honorable duty."

"So is buryin' 'em. I'll want payment for this," he then added in a low murmur.

Runsford's mouth formed unspoken words. Then he managed, "But we've agreed to the payment."

The pirate only harrumphed. He had more to say, but Jenta stepped through the open door, followed by Shayla and then Wentworth.

"Are we ready, then?" Runsford asked, one eye on the Conch.

Conch grunted, barely glancing at the women.

Shayla produced the prayer book, and from it took a folded parchment with the words of the ceremony all written out in careful script. She held out the sheaf. Only Jenta noticed the tremble in her hand.

Conch took the page roughly, frowned at it. "Here gathered," he began, then trailed off, his lips moving. Then he said, "Let's see. This and that, this and that, to be wed in holy mat...matrim...Wait, here we go. Do you Jenta Flug..." he paused, looked at the girl. "Flug?"

Her eyes dropped to the polished planking at her feet. With a look and a word, Conch had knocked all the wind from her sails. The question was ungentlemanly. Even brutal.

She had tried to catch his eye as she walked into his quarters, expecting to see the dashing, powerful man with whom she had so recently danced, expecting to nod and curtsey in pleasant recognition while he formed some appropriate words of greeting. She had prepared for this exchange— how could she not? He was the captain of the ship, the pirate legend of Skaelington, the man who would marry her to her husband. She was a lady. She wanted this moment to be memorable, and everything about it to be as gracious as possible under the circumstances.

She had no reason to believe it would be otherwise. After all, it was less than a month ago at the dance that he had been a perfect gentleman. His grammar might have been poor, but his manners were not. He had bowed to her as he let her go, and said, "Thank ye, miss. We'll meet again,

I hope," and she had responded, "I do hope so, and I hope it's soon." So she had readied her greeting for this evening, hoping to pick up just where they left off, to let him know that she remembered it all precisely.

And so we do meet again, Captain Imbry, she would say, *just as you had hoped. But not, I think, quite as you expected!* She would speak the line cheerfully, a small, shared secret, but perfectly open for all who cared to enter in. This was what she loved about polite society—there was always the dance, always the secret, and then always the opening of the secret.

But the instant she entered the room she knew there would be no small secrets tonight. She saw the dark fire in Conch's eyes. When he spoke, she heard the wolf's growl. And now his first and only word to her, his first acknowledgment of her actual presence in the room, as he raced and fumbled through what was clearly an unpleasant duty for him, was a question—and not any question, but the question of her name, her identity. And it was delivered to her on a hard spike of alcohol and tobacco and annoyance. Here was the pirate revealed after all.

"She goes by Stillmithers," Ryland said at last.

"Well, she can go by Sam Hill if she wants. But if Flug's her name then Flug's her name."

Jenta knew she should meet his eye, but she could not. She looked at her shoes, gray silk like the gray of her dress. Not wedding garments at all. She felt her face flush. She wanted to run from the room.

Conch cleared his throat. "Will you Jenta take this man Wentworth to be yer laughable wedded husband?"

There was an awkward silence.

"Wait. Excuse me?" Wentworth protested groggily. "What did you say?" His eyes were wide, his voice slurred, his stance unsteady. Jenta looked at her mother, but Shayla was far away. The porcelain mask. Jenta closed her eyes and bowed her head again. She prayed it would be over soon.

"Oh, fine. Lawful, then," Conch corrected himself.

There was another long, uncomfortable pause. Then Jenta raised her head, looked straight into the eyes of the pirate. "I will."

Conch Imbry looked back at her a moment too long, Wentworth thought, and at the end of the look he was sure one of Conch's eyes narrowed. Not a wink, precisely, but some shared exchange nonetheless. He searched his bride's face. Her look was intense and riveted, and locked on the pirate. There was fire in her.

"And do you Wentworth Ryland take this here Jenta, whatever her last name may be, to be yer laudable wedded wife?"

Wentworth stared hard at the pirate, weighing the words. But they did not seem to be insulting. "Yes, I most certainly will," he answered, as firmly as he could.

Imbry suppressed a laugh at the drunken twit. "Then I pronounce ye married. Good luck to ye—ye'll need it." He slapped the prayer book shut, crunching the parchment between the pages. "That it?"

Wentworth's head was swimming. This was too soon over. The rum had clouded everything, but surely there was more. "I believe," he offered, finally remembering something, "that it is customary for the broom the kiss the guide."

The others looked at him oddly.

"The groom...I mean, for the groom to kris the bide." He corrected. A pause, then, very carefully, "The groom to kiss the bride."

One corner of Conch's mouth rose, but his eyes were cold. "Why by all means let's do what's customary," he said.

All eyes watched Wentworth, and none were sympathetic. He looked around, surprised. All he'd wanted was to kiss his wife. What was wrong with that? Now completely self-conscious, he could only manage a small, misplaced peck that Jenta returned too late, kissing air.

Now Conch turned to Ryland. "I'll be wantin' my payment. Now."

"But sir..." Ryland trailed off. He had several minutes ago regretted that he had insisted on this particular officiate, and now he repented of the choice entirely. "I...have paid you all that I promised. At the card table, sir."

"*That?* That's not payment. That's money lost gamblin'. I want my ten in gold."

Jenta and Shayla exchanged shocked looks. It was a ridiculous sum, more than enough to buy the entire ship inside of which they all stood.

Ryland was aghast. "Perhaps we should excuse the young couple while we discuss this." He nodded at Wentworth, who took Jenta by the arm, though awkwardly.

But suddenly Conch had a pistol in his hand. He aimed it at the floorboards, but he cocked back the hammer for emphasis, freezing everyone where they stood. "I want my money."

Pulses rose. Chills ran up spines. Runsford spoke. "My dear sir, I'm terribly sorry for the misunderstanding. I don't know how it could have happened. My fault entirely, I'm quite sure. I can pay you as soon as the bank opens in the morning. Mr. Gorsus can vouch for me. He's a banker."

"I know what he is." Conch studied the set of the room. Shayla

Stillmithers stood stonily, eyes piercing him. Beside her stood the girl, looking somehow offended. Beside her, the boy, chin up, trying to look brave. Trembling? Probably. And then beside him, the father, shaking his head, pleading for calm while offering money. Conch sighed. The angry mother, the haughty daughter, the cowering son, the bargaining father. And Conch threatening them and taking their gold. "Ah, the lot of ye make me feel like I'm workin'." Then to Wentworth, "How much do you have left, boy? Down at the table."

"A small stack of chips and two gold coins to spare, I believe." The click of the pistol's hammer had cleared his head with amazing effectiveness. "Not enough."

"Well, you done better than yer old man. Once ye've lost all that, then we'll see what I'm still owed."

"But…" Wentworth looked to Jenta, who stared hard into the pirate's eyes.

She would never hang her head before this brute again.

Conch looked back at her with sudden admiration, as if he had finally found in her the fire he knew was there, waiting to be drawn out. "Back to the game," he said, uncocking the pistol and replacing it in his belt at the small of his back. He slapped Wentworth on the shoulder, then pushed him toward the door. "All else can wait."

"I'll join you," Runsford suggested.

But the Conch turned and put the forefinger of his left hand into Runsford's chest. "Ye got no money. I'll have no spectators. House rules." And he and Wentworth left the room.

Jenta watched them go, then exchanged looks with her mother. Shayla's eyes betrayed a warning. "What, Mother? Say it."

A sailor suddenly appeared, armed, at the doorway, to escort them out.

Jenta did not move. "Tell me what is happening, Mother. What is Captain Imbry going to do?"

"How would I know, child? He's a pirate." She looked at Ryland with a withering scorn, and walked away, ahead of him, out the door.

"It'll be fine," Ryland said after her, sounding none too confident. "He's a businessman at bottom. It'll all be fine in the morning. You'll see."

But the bride slept in a stateroom with her mother, while her new husband went back to the darkened bowels of the pirate's hold, to gamble.

Wentworth tried mightily to lose. Somehow, though, he managed to win against the longest odds. Within an hour, he had amassed more than half the chips on the table. Conch's stack had dwindled while his irritation grew. The other players became visibly nervous for the young man, even edging their chairs away from his. None of this was lost on Wentworth, who appeared more terrified with every hand. It occurred to him, as it did to all the others, that he was being set up. A charge of cheating from Conch, and there would be a duel. Which would thinly disguise a murder.

Conch wants Jenta, Wentworth concluded. *That's what all this is about.* His hands began to tremble uncontrollably. The pirate had made a deal with his father, but that deal wouldn't matter much if Wentworth was caught cheating—and killed for it.

And then, suddenly, Conch went all in. He bet the last of his chips on a hand with nothing showing: a deuce, a seven, and an eight. He turned to his dealer, also his banker, and said, "Give me twenty more in gold."

Mart Mazeley opened the drawer at his lap and produced twenty gold coins. Conch tossed them into the pot.

Everyone around the table folded instantly, stepping on one another in their haste to throw in their cards. Then all looked at Wentworth.

The young man glanced again at his hand. Nothing had changed. He had three aces face up. He peeked at the hole cards. Two queens and a five down. A full house. He looked at Conch, saw the man's eyelids droop lazily, as though he were bored. But underneath his eyes were sharp as honed steel.

"That pot," Wentworth tried, "is too rich for me. I don't suppose I could just fold?"

"Wif yer aces bared for all to see? No. No, I don't suppose ye could fold."

"But I can't cover that bet," he pointed out, a fact that precisely no one in the room had missed.

"How much do you have?"

Several moments passed as Wentworth counted his chips. "Fifteen in gold, twenty silver. I could cash out, pay my father's—"

"Ye need four more gold, and eighty. What's in yer pouch?"

Fingers fluttering like squabbling pigeons, Wentworth loosened his purse strings and emptied two gold coins onto the table.

"Still need two and eighty." The pirate stared hard at the young man. Wentworth couldn't shake the sense that Conch had his pistol out again, this time aimed at his heart. But he could see both of Conch's hands. "What's in yer pockets?" the pirate demanded.

"Nothing…" but then Wentworth remembered. He had the rings. Gold wedding bands, one for him, and one for Jenta. He had forgotten all about them in Conch's rush to conclude the ceremony. But Conch hadn't forgotten about them. He'd seen it all written out on the parchment. He'd skipped over a lot, including the part where he was supposed to ask if there were rings.

"What's in yer pockets?" Conch asked again.

"Nothing I'd want to bet," Wentworth answered.

"Let's see."

And Wentworth reached into his vest pocket and pulled out the rings. He held them out on his hand.

"What'd ye pay for 'em?"

"Two in gold. One for each."

"Still short eighty in silver. Put 'em in."

Wentworth closed his hand around them. He held them for a long time, glancing around the room. The others waited, withholding comment, withholding judgment, watching him work through the problem.

"Ye said vows over them pieces a' gold, or what?" Conch asked.

"No," he answered, too quickly. He looked at his cards again. He still had a full house. A good hand. Nobody had had a better one all night. It was a winning hand. He set the rings on the table.

Conch exchanged glances with Mazeley, who reached out, swept them into the pile.

"What else ye got?" Conch asked.

"Just the clothes I'm wearing."

"Are ye a man of yer word?" the pirate asked.

"Of course I am," he answered.

"Then ye got more."

"What do you have in mind?" Wentworth's heart raced.

"I fancy yer girl."

Wentworth stood. The others held their breaths. Whether he meant to run or to fight, they couldn't tell. Either would be disastrous. "I knew it," the young man whispered at last.

Wentworth glanced around the table, saw no help. But their wide eyes finally helped him find a place to dig in his heels. "I will not bet my…my girl at a card game." The protest came out a bit more like a squawk than he would have preferred.

"I ain't askin' ye to lose yer girl at cards."

"Then just what are you asking, sir?"

"The day ye don't want her no more, she's mine."

"What? What are you saying? You agreed..." but he trailed off. He had too many things to hide.

Imbry spoke slowly, not with irritation, but as a man who wanted to be understood in every regard by a man who was slow to understand. "I ain't askin' ye to bet yer girl. I'm sayin' the bet is this: If ye lose this hand, then the day yer done with her, I'll come for her. And ye won't say a word about it. And neither will yer daddy. And neither will her mama. And neither will she."

Wentworth's chin came up. "I'll never be done with her."

"Then ye've got nothin' to lose. Pot's right. Let's play."

Wentworth remained standing. "She's a free woman, and makes her own choices."

Now Conch leaned in. "Is she, now? Well that's interestin'. A woman of fine means and her mother, come here by theirselves, no menfolk wif 'em. Brought here by yer daddy. And the two of you in that big house with no womenfolk around. And then, just when she's startin' to catch the fancy of many fine gentlemen, Jenta's suddenly yer...girl." He lolled the final word out of his mouth like he was dropping a musket ball down a gun barrel. "But yet, ye say she's free to make her own choices. That's interestin'."

"That is my own business, sir, and none of yours."

"Yer business or mine, the point is, it's *business*. This little bet is just another transaction."

"No, it's madness. You're mad."

Conch spread his cards out on the table. He started turning the hole cards over, one by one.

"Wait, I didn't bet!"

"I didn't say ye did. I'm jus' showin' ye all my cards, all but the last one still sittin' there on the deck in Mr. Mazeley's hand. Just so's ye can make the appropriate choice." He kept turning his cards over. In addition to the two, seven, and eight he turned over a four, another deuce, and a third deuce. "There. Yer aces showin' beats my deuces."

For a moment Wentworth thought Conch was admitting defeat. But then the pirate said, "Well? Are ye bettin' or ain't ye?"

Wentworth pondered as the others waited. No one ever beat the Conch, and everyone knew it. And whatever a man bet here, he couldn't unbet.

"Do ye love her?" Conch asked. The question echoed within him, like the whisper he'd heard at the Summer's Eve Ball.

"Yes!" Wentworth answered fiercely.

"Then what are ye worried after? I'm just a pirate." He seemed almost gentle. "I don't understand how a man binds hisself to a woman fer life. If ye'll always want her, she'll always be yers. And if ye find ye don't want her one day, then what's the harm? Ye won't want her no more, anyway."

Maybe it was the rum. Maybe it was the way Conch's argument struck the other men as humorous, relaxing them. Maybe it was the argument itself. Maybe it was that Conch had left him only the one choice. Or maybe it was the full house he had on the table. "I'm all in," he said.

"Ye heard that, didn't ye?" Conch asked the others, who nodded appropriately.

"Deal one more card down, Mr. Mazeley."

Mazeley did. Still standing, Wentworth turned up his card immediately. It was a three. He quickly turned up his queens. "Aces over queens. Full house."

"Aces over queens," Conch repeated, as though lost in thought. "A good hand." Then he reached out slowly, deliberately, and without taking his eyes off Wentworth, he turned up his last card. One more deuce.

He had four of a kind.

Mazeley rose and swept the winnings toward Conch.

The pirate stood. "And that's it, gentlemen. Cash in whatever little ye have left in front of ye, and Godspeed." As Mazeley exchanged the men's chips for coin, Conch shook hands around the table, chatting briefly with each man. The players thanked the pirate warmly for his hospitality and for the highly amusing, highly memorable evening. A few of them patted Wentworth on the shoulder or said words like "Tough luck" or "I've seen worse" as they collected hats and canes and left the room. Soon it was Wentworth and the Conch alone, with Mazeley counting out the winnings behind them.

"Well, ye got somefin' to say?" Conch asked.

"You had a deal with my father, to stay away from her."

"And now I got a deal wif you."

"I will always want her."

"Then what are we talkin' about?"

"She's my bride. You knew that."

"Aye, and so did you." Conch saw the bitterness of youthful rage. He put a hard, heavy hand on Wentworth's shoulder. He squeezed just enough that Wentworth felt the power, and the control of that power. He stared deep into the young man's eyes. "Don't be gettin' all riled with *me*, son. Ye bet yer wife at a poker game."

Wentworth looked at the hand on his shoulder, then looked sullenly back into the pirate's face. "You coerced me."

"Did I? Don't recall. But even were that so, I'm not the one who bet my bride away like she was worth naught but eighty in silver. And her weddin' ring, to boot. Think on that when ye take yer honeymoon strolls down the beach." He leaned in to give Wentworth the full force of his next statement, hard rum and stale tobacco with it. "Ye bet her away, Mr. Ryland. Ye bet yer new bride away on yer wedding night, not two hours after ye married her. That should tell ye all ye need to know about yerself. And it'll tell her all she needs to know about you as well."

Wentworth recoiled. "Why should she ever know?"

"Ye want her comin' to ye one night all misty, askin' about the rumors she heard from some banker's wife, or the latest gossip at the market? Ye wanna lie right into that pretty face while she sees through ye to the truth of what ye are? If that's yer choice, that's yer choice. But ye'll make good on yer debt, son, when the time comes."

"It won't come."

Conch released his grip, stood toe to toe. "Oh, it'll come, lad. A man who'll make that bet, why, he'll throw a woman away when she displeases him. I oughta know." He grinned. "I'm just that sort of man myself."

Wentworth's mouth formed unspoken curses. Then he said, "You're no gentleman." Then he turned and, buzzing with anger and shame, walked away.

Conch laughed and picked up the closest tumbler of rum. "The game's just begun, boy! Welcome to pirate's poker!" And he downed the drink.

Ham paused for effect. His audience was quiet.

Then one of the sailors exclaimed, "Conch'll get her within the month!"

"He's already got her!" another responded. "Did ye see how she looked at him?"

"No way she wants that wet noodle Wentworth now."

"She's doin' jus' like 'er mama done!"

The forecastle buzzed, and Ham Drumbone listened. When the conversation died down, he spoke again.

"You gents got it all figured, do ye?"

"Well, what'd Conch do?" Ballast asked in the eagerness of his youth. "How'd he get her?" And for once, the experience of age did not descend on him like a ten-pound maul.

"Aye, tell us what he done!" and "Keep talkin', Ham!"

Ham nodded thoughtfully, but he tapped his pipe into his callused hand and mashed the embers out with hard fingers. "I will keep talking, for I'll tell you this. There's not a man alive who knows how to shut me up for long. But gents, we got business of our own tomorrow, and the Whale wants us in fine fettle. Any who lives another day gets another story. That's all for tonight—"

"No, don't say it!" several shouted at once, and a clamor arose.

But when it died down, Ham said it anyway. "That's all for tonight, lads. More tomorrow if I've a mind and you've the time." And once he'd said those words, there was no getting him to unsay it. The rest would have to wait.

"All of 'em's wrong," Delaney told his *Chompers*. "I know what sorta stock Jenta come from, I get that. She weren't high and fine born. But still, a person is what a person is. And Jenta, she was fine." He stretched his toes out again, wriggled them, just to watch the fish roil the water in antici-pation. "See, that's just it. Somethin' appeals to ye, and ye think ye gotta swallow it all up whole right now. Ye dumb fish ain't no better'n Went-worth, or Runsford, or the Conch. Women now, real ladies…" he trailed off as he thought of Maybelle, and her sweet brown eyes, how they seemed like liquid things looking up at him, and how she blinked. Just the way she blinked was like a song. Like a lullaby. There were words there, too, in that song in the blink of her eyes. And a melody too, somehow. If one just could hear it. And Delaney could hear it.

Oh, he could hear it.

"I'll be true to you, Delaney, true for a lifetime." She'd said that to him. Just that way.

"That's a long, long time," he had answered, and his answer was a question, Did she really mean it?

"True for a lifetime," she repeated.

A true lang time.

But he had left her anyway. Hadn't dealt her away, as did Wentworth, but left her out cold all the same. Delaney felt a heave start inside him, and shook his head to clear it. But it didn't come from his head. So he

Blaggard's Moon

took a deep, full breath, and then another. What was he doing, getting all weepy? How was that going to save him?

But there was nowhere else for his thoughts to go. Why did it all seem to mean so much, and yet there was so little point at the end?

A rustle in the forest to Delaney's right, to the south of his post, caught his attention. This time something was moving through the tangled underbrush. Or someone. The tops of fronds waved, and he could trace the movement all the way to the ground below them.

"Ahoy there!" Delaney called out, wiping water from the corner of his eyes. "Can ye hear me?"

The tangle went quiet and still.

"Ye there or ain't ye?"

Nothing.

Delaney watched for a while, then gave up and studied the sky through the gap in the foliage above him. It was still bright blue. Dusk was yet hours away. He studied the *Chompers* instead, still easily visible, though most of them were no longer in direct sunlight. He looked down past them and found he could no longer see the bone pile at the bottom of his post. On the surface of the pond, the line of shadow had moved ten feet away, inching steadily toward the eastern lip of the lagoon. Time turned onward. He looked back to the undergrowth, still saw no movement, heard no rustle.

"Fine, lie still then," he said aloud. He knew it was probably just a critter of some sort. And even if it was a person, it was likely a Hant, and Hants knew better than to wrestle food from their *Onka Din Botlay*. If it was a Hant, he'd only come to check on the blaggard, the doomed, and the doorway through which he would soon pass.

Suddenly Delaney realized he hadn't been thinking of ideas. He'd gotten his water, but those idea tomatoes hadn't come. Unless…unless this was the time. Maybe there was something he could do with that rustle in the reeds.

"Tell ye what," he said loudly to the quiet spot on the shore, "get me outta here and I'll get you all the *andowinnie* ye can drink!" He waited.

No response.

He thought some more. "How about I take ye to Nearing Vast with me," he offered. "There ye'll learn a thing or two about living! I mean real living, with beds and baths and…and pubs!" He thought about explaining a pub, but gave up. Too complicated. "Streets and carriages, how's that! And how about a horse? Bet you'd like to see a horse for once in yer life!"

Horses were simpler. He should be able to describe a horse to someone who'd never seen one. "It's a big thing with four hooves ye ride on." He wasn't sure he'd done it justice. But then, he wasn't sure he could get a Hant out of this jungle and onto a ship anyway, much less get him all the way to Nearing Vast. And even if he could get him to the City of Mann, he'd have a hard time paying for things like beds and baths and carriage rides. Delaney was no longer a man with any means.

It was a bad idea, trying to bargain with a Hant who probably wasn't there anyway. It was no idea at all.

"Anyways," he called out, his voice now lacking confidence. "If ye want to save my skin, I'll do somethin' nice for ye."

Gloom settled on Delaney. He looked up through the hole in the canopy. The blue sky seemed alive somehow. There was a light in it, a glow that seemed it could penetrate anything, if it just wanted to. It occurred to him, from out of that blue, that maybe God was looking back down on him as he looked up. Maybe the God that those priests talked about, the Maker that Avery had worried over, maybe He looked down on it all.

It gave Delaney a very bad feeling, to be watched by God.

He lowered his eyes, scanned the water, hoping to find somewhere else he could take his thoughts. It was bad enough to die here; worse to die with God watching, with God knowing all the bad things he'd ever done in his life. God, who would surely send him to hell just like those priests said. If He was up there.

And then the whole of it, the black darkness that underlay the world while the bright sun shone down, all of it together felt like it would crush him. He looked up again, fearful that he'd see God, somehow, yet unable not to look up.

But it was just blue sky.

"I could be a better man again, like I was once," he said to the round patch of blue. And he felt like he meant it. "Tell Ye what," he said, "get me out of this pinch, and I'll go back to an honest sailor." He thought about that a moment. Why wouldn't that work? Sure, that was something God would want of him. If God would rescue him, he could sneak away through the forests back to shore, and hide out somewhere, and then catch a merchant vessel back to Mann. Or Sandavale! He could just disappear, and turn up honest again. He could go to church, and help out folks who needed it. Help little kids with no place to go. And get himself a new knife while he was at it.

He felt a surge of hope. "If Ye jus' get me off this stump and onto my feet over there ashore, I'll be pleased to be a good man."

He waited. A slight breeze blew, but it wasn't near enough to pick him up and take him to shore. The hole above him was silent. The blue sky did not change. No monkeys screeched, no birds sang out.

"Well. Think on it at least, will Ye? I'll be waitin' right here."

And then he thought of Damrick Fellows. There was a man both strong and good. He never waited on anything. He was a man of action, who took the fight to his enemies. Avery Wittle had refused to join up, and had given up his life for refusing. Damrick also refused to join up, but he picked up a musket and a sword and a pistol and went full after them all. Fighting back the darkness like a farmer fighting wolves off a ranch.

Damrick. Ideas or no ideas, there was a man worth pondering.

CHAPTER SEVEN

HELL'S GATEMEN

"WHAT FAME SHARKBIT Sutter had acquired in his brief sojourn in pirate lore was immediately transferred to his executioner," Ham told his listeners as he picked up the story again the next evening. "Or at least it was so within the limits of the City of Mann. Damrick Fellows found himself suddenly central to festivities that seemed to bloom around him everywhere he went. He drew handshakes and pints and congratulations like a magnet draws metal shavings. You might say it was a perpetual party. Such was the circumstance one evening when he and Lye Mogene were taking their dinner in a modest tavern not far from his father's dry-goods store. But that evening it became plain that neither fame nor glory nor robust vittles could satisfy the sort of hunger that drove our ferocious foe. No, not by a long pull."

"Somehow they seem to know you dragged me along against my will," Lye said under his breath after a young woman, another in a seemingly endless line of admirers, waved goodbye and gushed a beaming apology without a trace of remorse, allowing Damrick and Lye to return to their cabbage and pork.

"I've told every one of them that you were there alongside me, pistol blazing, and that I could never have done it without you."

"I know. And not a one of 'em believes ye."

"But none of it matters."

"Maybe not to you."

Damrick's eyes went hard. "None of it matters, Lye. Who is it offering congratulations and giving us thanks?"

"Every man, woman, child, and dog." He took a sullen sip of ale.

"No. You're wrong."

Lye realized that Damrick wanted a serious answer. He thought a moment, then ticked them off on his fingers. "Men. Women. Children. Barmaids. Vendors. Merchants. Doctors. Bakers. Blacksmiths. Stable hands. A juggler. A fiddle player. Two piano players. Not many dogs, but one or two. What's left?"

"Anyone who has anything to do with the sea trade."

"What are ye talkin' about?"

"Two merchant captains over there in the corner," he said, pointing out the gray-whiskered men in their blue caps. "Six sailors at the bar. That old man with his niece, seated by the fireplace."

"His niece? That's generous of ye."

"He owns the East-West Shipping Line."

"I'll be."

"Not a one of them has come by."

"Don't tell me yer gettin' all sensitive now."

"You don't find it odd? Taking Sharkbit off the seas helps them more than anyone else. Yet they're the only ones that ignore us."

Lye shrugged. "They've seen pirates come and go, I reckon."

"Maybe. But I think there's more."

Lye watched his eyes. "What more?"

"I'm thinking of Mr. Runsford Ryland and his paper, the one he gave to Sharkbit to get him out of the jam the *Defender* got him into. Why would a man like Ryland do that?"

Lye blinked a few times. "Because he was forced to. What are you sayin'?"

"I'm saying the reason these men aren't thanking us is obvious. They aren't thankful."

"You mean the shippers *want* pirates? That don't make sense."

A family of five came by, a firm and respectful father wanting his two sons and his daughter to meet Damrick Fellows, and as they did to shake hands firmly, look him in the eye, and stand up straight. A beaming mother wanted to be sure that both her boys' hair was plastered down and the girl's ribbons were straight, and that all three were polite enough to say hello to "the hero's friend, there."

"He was by my side," Damrick assured them, "Pistol blazing. I couldn't have done it without him."

Five faces smiled at Lye for a second or two, during which he fairly writhed in painful embarrassment. His red face turned redder, and then his scowl turned them all back to Damrick.

"Well, thank you for what you done," the father said with finality, "and bein' brave and bold to do it. That's the both of you. You children remember this day, and these men."

The boys poked one another in the ribs. The girl looked at the bottom of her shoe.

"You're all quite welcome," Damrick said easily. Lye grunted.

Once they were gone, Damrick was quiet for a long, brooding moment. Then he said, "Suppose I live in one town, and work in another. Every day I have to travel the same road twice, once going and once coming back. Say there are highwaymen on that road who know I get paid every day. And let's say there's nobody around who can jail the brigands. I still have to get to work and back home with my earnings. What do I do?"

"Go armed."

"And what, shoot them? They'll shoot back, and I'm outnumbered."

"Get an army?"

"I'm a poor man."

"You move, then."

"Say I can't."

"Well, yer makin' it a hard game to win. I guess you give 'em your money."

"Yes. But if I'm smart, I also make a deal. So they don't take all my money. Just some."

"Why would they make that deal?"

"If they took all of it," Damrick explained, "I'd quit that job and work somewhere else."

"You said you couldn't do that. Yer changin' the rules."

"I'm trying to make a point."

"Okay. So they take only some a' yer money."

"We come to an arrangement where I make enough to live on, and they take everything else. They get all they can, but not so much that I move off, go somewhere else."

There was a long pause. "Are ye talkin' about brigands stealin', or the government taxin'?"

Damrick laughed. "I'm talking about pirates."

The light dawned. "Yer sayin' that's what the pirates are—the high-waymen."

"Yes."

"And the workin' men are all the freighters."

"Not *all* the freighters."

The light faded. "Just some of 'em?"

"Let's say there's a rich man who travels the same road as me, every day. He makes a lot more money than I do, but he's got the same problem. So he comes to the same arrangement. Only the highwaymen like him better, because with him they take away a lot more gold every day."

"'Cause he can afford to give more gold, even though he keeps more himself."

"Right. Now let's say the rich man wants me to go to work for him, and I refuse."

"Why would you refuse?"

"Doesn't matter. Whatever the reason, I don't want to work for him."

"Don't he pay enough?"

Damrick took a deep breath. "He's dishonest. He cheats me."

"Rat badger." Lye's face bunched up.

"The highwaymen have been robbing me for a little, but when they find out I won't help the rich man, who they're robbing for a lot, suddenly they don't like me anymore. Because I won't help the rich man get richer."

"Which means you won't help the bandits get richer."

"Exactly. So what do the brigands do with me now?"

"They shoot ye."

Damrick nodded. "Or run me off."

Lye raised the mug to his lips without looking at it. "Well, I don't like any of 'em."

"When my daddy and yours were our age, everyone with a boat could make a coin or two hauling someone's freight from city to city."

"I remember that. There were a lot a' them tramp freighters when I was a kid."

"Tramp freighters. That's right. But they're gone now. Those that weren't bought out got out while they were still alive, set up a shop, or got themselves some farmland. Somewhere safe."

Lye thought for a moment, raised his mug to drink again, then settled it back down unsipped. "Yer sayin' that when we took out Sharkbit, we took on the pirates *and* the big shipping lines."

Blaggard's Moon

"That's why they aren't thankful. My bet is, Mr. Runsford Ryland is no more pleased with us than Captain Conch Imbry is. We're tipping everyone's handcart."

"You think it's *everyone*?"

Damrick shrugged. "Our own captain let Sharkbit go. And he's Royal Navy."

Lye pushed his dinner plate away as though it had betrayed him. "So the Navy's in it."

"You tell me. Three years we chased pirates. Never caught a single ship until our last day."

"They're fast and sneaky."

"Yes. But we ran up on the *Savage Grace* and caught her fair. Look what happened."

"We let 'er go." Lye looked over at the sea captains, and as he watched them, they turned and looked toward Damrick's table. Their eyes seemed hard and hateful. He looked back at his mug, left it on the table. "Boatloads a' rat badgers," he said in dark awe.

"What are we good at, Lye?"

He shrugged. "Not too much, I reckon."

"But what? What have we been training to do, these three years?"

"Fight, is all."

"Sailing on ships and shooting guns. Big guns. Little guns. And now we come to my point. None of these congratulations matter, not one, until a man with a ship stops by looking for help. Then we got ourselves a real job."

"Go into business protecting the small ship owner."

"Protecting the small ship owner," Damrick echoed.

"From pirates."

"From pirates."

"And from shipping companies."

Damrick shrugged. "Them too."

"And from the Navy." Lye had grown glummer with each additional enemy.

Damrick sighed. "Who knows? When push comes to shove, Lye, it's going to be very hard for the king to order his Navy to attack a ship that's taking down pirates. If everyone knows that's what we're doing."

"Not even the king can stop us doin' God's work, eh?" He didn't say it with enthusiasm. "But the Navy don't need to attack us, Damrick. They just need to stand by while we get attacked."

"Ah well." He took a sip. "What else were you planning to do with your life, Lye?"

"No plans," he answered. He had mulled it as far as he was able. "I guess everyone dies somehow. Might as well cash out yer chips doin' the world some good." And now, finally, he drank down his ale.

The next day handbills were posted along the docks, and in various parts of the city where shipmen—and former shipmen now in the dry-goods business—could find them.

HELL'S GATEMEN
We Safeguard the Seas!
Let the Men who Sent
Sharkbit Sutter
Back to the Devil
Protect your Ship
from Pirates

And down in the lower right-hand corner it gave an address where anyone could find, or join up with, a man named Damrick Fellows.

Conch Imbry had a sheet in his hands and a sour look on his face. "'Safeguard the seas.' Who in yellow blazes is Damrick Fellows? '*Safeguard the seas.*'"

The unimpressive Mart Mazeley shook his head. "A marine ensign and a sharpshooter. Or was. He just got the idea in his head, they say, and took out after Sharkbit."

"Ensign, eh? Got lucky then, I say."

"Perhaps. But he killed Sharkbit Sutter."

"Just him by hisself?"

"There were two of them. They shot three or four sailors, plus Sharkbit. Disarmed the rest of a skeleton crew aboard the *Savage Grace*. Daring raid, by all accounts. He and the other man rowed out in the darkness, pretending to sign on."

Conch's eyes scanned the paper one last time, then he handed the page back at Mazeley. "I want him dead. Kill 'im, will ye?"

"Yes, sir."

Conch twirled a moustache around the tip of one finger. Then he pulled on it. "He get any takers on his offer?"

"We don't know. They're singing songs to him in the pubs."

"Songs?" Conch's eyes were slits as he glanced around his stateroom, finding no place they could rest. "He'll be famous all over the city, then. Go tell the men we're shovin' off fer Mann in one hour. Get all hands aboard, and on deck. I'll show 'em who's famous."

"The men are on leave, sir."

"I know where they are! Round 'em up! How many places could they be in this rat hole of a city?"

"Six or eight, at least."

"Go roust 'em. Get Chasm to help. We're fit and loaded. Just get 'em here on board, I don't care what condition."

"Yes, sir. But I don't recommend leaving port shorthanded. These Gatemen—"

"There ain't no *Gatemen!*" His eyes blazed at Mazeley. "You're believin' this tin hero has what, a whole fleet? You think he's got the stuffin's to take on the *Shalamon*? He's puke in a bucket. I'll kill 'im. I'll kill 'im so dead they'll be singin' songs about how dead he is. They'll sing songs about how no one ever got hisself deader faster than Damrick floodin' Fellows."

Any other man would have backed off. When the Conch started talking about men dying, one or more of them usually did. But Mazeley was unmoved. "Whatever Hell's Gatemen are or end up becoming, Captain, we know what they will *not* be. They will not be afraid. This Fellows met Sharkbit face-to-face and took him down. And Sharkbit was a man who could make the devil seize up inside. Now the whole City of Mann is reveling in this act. He can sign up scores of discontents who can shoot and sail. Don't underestimate this, Captain. Crush him, yes. But I recommend a full complement of men to do it. If you'll pardon me."

This just made Conch sour. "Two hours, then. We sail in two hours wif whatever we can scrounge. You watch me, Mr. Mazeley. I'll put six holes through Damrick Fellows and slice 'im gut to chin before he even knows he's in a fight."

Mazeley smiled. "Aye, sir." He pulled a sheaf of parchment from his jacket. "Thought you also might like to send something like this along to the mayor."

Conch read it. He softened. "Ye got a way wif words. I'll sign it."

The mayor, once he read the note, immediately sent official word to all shipping lines with offices in the city, which meant, effectively, all shipping lines that did business up and down the western shores of the Vast Sea, north and south as far as men could sail. The message was this:

Blaggard's Moon

Any merchant doing business with Damrick Fellows or Hell's Gatemen would lose all harbor privileges in Skaelington, and all associated good-will. The proclamation didn't need to elaborate. Everyone who read it knew what loss of safe harbor in Skaelington meant. It meant the loss of Conch Imbry's protection. Without Conch to answer to, every pirate up and down the coast would be free to attack. They would be effectively invited to attack.

Just that quickly, any ship or shipping company aligned with Damrick Fellows was marked. Fair game, open season.

Damrick looked over the merchandise once again. Every knife, musket, sword, pistol, bow, and crossbow for sale in the small shop was pulled out once again, and then some. And then quite a bit more some. All the weaponry that the store's proprietor could scrounge from all his suppliers and every neighboring store was piled high on countertops, on every free inch of floor space, on top of chairs, barrel tops, sacks of flour—everything that wasn't an armament itself became a display for everything that was. Three hundred square feet of space was now two feet deep in weaponry.

"This all you could find?" Damrick asked, disappointed.

The merchant blanched. "I rounded up all I could, like you asked."

"Can you get more?" He picked up an ancient blunderbuss. "Just new weaponry, though. I don't need to wonder what will work."

"I can try."

"Then try. This won't be near enough. Did you get my cannon?"

The owner crossed his arms. "You paid your bill on the last one, Damrick, but this…"

"I have Sharkbit's reward money. I'm prepared to turn it over to you."

The merchant did the calculations in his head. "All right. I'll see what I can find."

"What are these?" Damrick looked at strips of braided leather, each about two feet long, that hung on a peg by the counter. He took one down, examined it.

"Tie-downs. Lashes. My mother used to make them, and we always found them handy for something."

"I'll take forty. Can you get me forty of them?"

"Sure." Then after a pause, "Damrick, does your daddy know you're doing this?"

"Yes."

"Then why isn't he stocking you?"

Damrick stared at him. "Do you want the business?"

"Sure I want it. It just seems rightly to be Didrick's business, unless there's something I'm missing."

Damrick aimed a long rifle out a window, admired its weight and balance. "Fellows Dry Goods has closed its doors."

"What? Why?"

"Because its proprietor has gone back to his first love."

"Who's that?"

Damrick looked at him evenly. "Not who. What."

"What then?"

"Shipping."

Calliope was not a noble ship. She was not fast, nor sleek, nor maneuverable. She could not hold more than a hundred cubic yards of cargo, and even that had to be weighed carefully or she'd sit too low to be seaworthy. Her hull was heavy, and her beam was wide. She had long been at harbor, tended at no small cost by a dry-goods merchant who sailed her almost never, but couldn't bear to let her go. She was the prize possession of Captain Didrick Fellows.

His son, Damrick, was proud to serve aboard.

"That thing won't hold off a determined shark, much less a pirate, son." The elder stood on the dock, watching as the iron swivel gun was lowered by a boom onto the deck.

"This little cannon will surprise you. It's a long-range gun."

"I thought that barrel was unusual."

Damrick patted the breech. "Tempered steel right there. She can handle twice the powder of a standard swivel cannon of the same size. Twice the power, twice the range."

"What's that, a four-inch bore?"

"Three-and-a-quarter."

Didrick shook his head. "And you've only got two of them. Any pirate ship will have four times that number at least, and all of them twice the size of that popper."

"I know what I've got, Captain," Damrick replied, guiding the dangling weapon to its appointed spot on the deck. "Sharkbit paid well, but not so well as to turn a freighter into a frigate." He and two of his new Gatemen easily maneuvered the small cannon onto its plate and began turning bolts to secure it to the deck at the port rail. The second gun, for the starboard rail, lay in an open box on the dock.

"You think a couple of cannons and a little courage will get you past the likes of Skewer Uttley or Scatter Wilkins?"

"I think I've got an idea what it'll take." Damrick, wiping sweat from his forehead, tucked a wet strand of hair behind an ear. He looked up at his father. "Uttley's retired, anyway."

"They say." The sea captain turned merchant turned sea captain again crossed his arms. He was not as tall as Damrick, but he was broader in the shoulders. With a full head of hair he would have looked very similar. He had the same sharp eyes, which bored into his son now from above. "You've got an idea, do you?"

Damrick nodded. "I do."

"You going to tell me this idea?"

"It's still got a few tangles, Pa. But we'll get it sorted out before we leave."

"You're a stubborn cuss."

"Came by it honest. Don't worry."

"I'm not worried. But your mother is. I'd like to give her some reason we'll come back alive."

"Do you know anything in heaven or on earth can stop her worrying?"

"Nothing I'd ever wish on her. Besides, she prays when she worries, and that's something we'll need."

Damrick looked at his father, then at the small cross he always wore around his neck—given by his wife on their wedding day. "Then let's let her worry."

Once the deck guns were mounted, Damrick hiked back into town, straight to Muzzleman's Shot Tower, where he had left Lye Mogene.

"Any progress?" he asked.

Lye stood at a table in the yard behind the tower, which loomed behind him, casting a shadow across the yard. He poked through a box full of musket balls of various sizes. A brick oven blazed in the afternoon heat behind him, near the wall of the tower. What looked like four iron pokers jutted from the flames. He wore a leather apron and a heavy blacksmith's mitten on his left hand. A dozen muskets leaned against the table, and a half-a-dozen pistols lay in a line across the top of it. To his right, the grass was strewn with twice again that many weapons, as though he had test-fired them and thrown them away in disgust. A hundred feet away an archer's target leaned against a pocked stone wall. It boasted three small holes, none near the bull's-eye.

Lye looked up at Damrick in overheated frustration. "Blew up a good musket." He kicked it with his boot toe. "Breech just shredded." The steel bent outward in fingers at the stock end. "Lucky not to have lost an eye."

Damrick pondered. "You tried double wadding?"

Lye put his gloved hand into a box of cotton wads, the kind used to prepare musket-ball packets. He pulled out a handful. "Double. Triple. Ever' blasted waddin' and ball and patch and barrel..." He threw them back into the box, unformed curses moving his lips. "I ain't cut out for this kinda tinkerin'." He looked both ruddier and more tired than usual.

Damrick took a deep breath. "You think we should give it up?"

The question seemed to stun him. "Quit? Just when I'm about to get 'er all figured out?"

"Then you're making progress."

"You just go back to your ship, sonny. I'll come get you when I've got somethin' to show."

Damrick's eyes widened. "Then you think it may work."

"Oh, it'll work," Lye said. "And when it does, them pirates better turn and run."

Damrick allowed himself half a smile. He reserved the other half for when and if he saw his idea in action.

Inside the shot tower, red drops of hot iron fell in rapid succession from two hundred feet up, cooling only slightly before they splashed with a complaining hiss into a pool of water at its base. Damrick knelt beside the pool, reached in and picked up a cool outlier. It was perfectly round, black iron shot, barely a pock in its surface. Much smoother than the molded variety, and they would shoot straighter and farther. Assuming they were matched appropriately with a good musket.

"Who's down there?" the echoing voice boomed from above. The drops of molten iron ceased.

"Damrick Fellows."

"These are yours, then."

"Mine?" The echo of his own words died away. "Who ordered them?"

"Your man outside!"

"What size are they?"

The drops began falling again. "Either come up and talk or go away!"

Damrick climbed the wooden stairs that spiraled up the insides of the round brick tower. From the outside, this structure could have been mistaken for a giant tapered chimney or a castle tower, but there was no fireplace and no fortification in Nearing Vast that required anything nearly so tall. The inside was like an enormous musket barrel pointed toward the heavens. The wooden stairs winding around it were built into the brick, and reinforcement beams were few. There was no handrail, and the stairs grew narrower as they went up. The last sixty feet were an interesting climb. The stairs were no wider than a man's shoulders, and the walls actually angled in, as though pressing the climber toward the abyss. This, along with the constant dripping of white-hot metal mere inches away, turning red as it hurtled down into a hissing, panting darkness, gave the knees a mind of their own.

The top was not much better. The sudden realization of extreme height was a shock to the senses. But it was the intense heat and brutal sunlight that hammered Damrick's head. He felt like he was breathing the molten liquid that dripped from the cauldron just off the center of the round floor. Heat roiled from it visibly. The thick wooden decking under his feet was marked with grooves, concentric rings like a target, the bulls-eye being the hole through which the hot pellets dropped. The flooring was warped and charred, and it creaked as Damrick stepped carefully across it toward John Muzzleman.

The ordnance-maker hummed softly, oblivious to both heat and height. He wore no protection other than a heavy leather apron and thick, padded mittens. Short and stocky, built close to the ground like a tree stump, he was dark, with wild black hair that grew only on the back of his head, from ear to ear and nape to crown. Damrick would have assumed that the heat had singed the rest away were it not for the man's heavy, thick eyebrows. His round face looked like it was made of shiny new leather, and though he was clean-shaven, the dark stubble made it evident that he employed his razor in a losing battle with his beard.

Muzzleman looked up, nodded once, removed a glove, and extended a sweaty, stubby hand. When it met Damrick's, it squeezed like a steel vise. The tradesman immediately put his big glove back on and turned away. "I got to finish before this cools."

That anything up here might cool anytime soon seemed unlikely to Damrick. He watched as the munitions maker opened a small valve at the side of the cauldron. This allowed a trickle of the molten iron to flow down a narrow chute, not much more than a half-inch-wide groove in a thick steel plate. When it reached the end of the flume it hit a smaller, upright iron plate that stopped the flow, which then backed up and widened out until a puddle of hot iron formed, about the size of a large cherry. This put pressure on the iron plate until it overcame the resistance of a small counterweight, and the bottom of the plate opened suddenly, like a trap door sprung. A white droplet fell, and the little door snapped closed. The process began again, all under the watchful eye of John Muzzleman, who stood with one hand on the valve that regulated the flow. He was lost in concentration, increasing the flow gradually until the little door was ticking off drops at the rate of almost one per second.

Damrick waited, looking around him. There was no furnace here, nothing to keep the iron in the big kettle hot. It was brought up hot, then. Now he noticed the pulley suspended above them for that purpose. It hung from a tripod of iron beams that met about ten feet above their heads. A small, sturdy chain ran through the pulley and led down to a large winch positioned near the head of the stairs. But the hole in the floor was not nearly wide enough to allow up a cauldron of that size. Damrick looked again at the concentric rings in the floor, which he had until now taken to be no more than a grooved pattern. He saw hinges protruding at each ring, and he realized that the hole in the floor could be opened to almost any size, depending on which of these round doors John chose to open. With a bit of queasiness, Damrick realized he was standing inside the largest ring, meaning he was actually on top of a trap door himself. He took a small step backward, until he was convinced he was standing on a permanent floorboard.

He turned and looked over the parapet. The city stretched out for miles. To the west he could see the top of the royal palace, off in the distance. It was not substantially different than the other homes and buildings, but it was substantially larger. To the east he could see the docks, the ships lined along the prongs of the piers, their sails struck, and the ships moving in and out and around the bay, their sails catching the wind and gleaming white in the sun. And in between the docks and the palace, zigzagging streets, multicolored buildings of all different shapes and sizes, smoke rising from chimneys, horses and carriages and people with packages, in and out of shops.

"Three-fifths of an inch," Muzzleman said without looking up.

"Pardon me?"

"The answer to your question. Three-fifths of an inch."

It was not a standard shot size. "That's what Lye ordered?"

"Yes."

"How many?"

"One thousand."

"A thousand?" Damrick blinked. He heard the report of a musket, looked down over the edge of the parapet. Lye Mogene stood in the yard by his table. He lowered a long rifle and examined it. "He didn't seem that confident."

Now Muzzleman looked up and grinned. "Oh, these'll do."

"You've seen them work?"

"I made sure they worked." He turned back to his cauldron.

But before Damrick could ask more, the faint but frantic clamor of a fire bell rose up from below. He looked over the edge again and traced it to its source, maybe two miles to the north. He could see black smoke rising. Fire in the city. He could see people and horses suddenly in action, moving quickly toward the bell, a surge of energy engulfing them. More bells clanged, closer now. Men, women, and children began pouring into the streets, many carrying buckets. Damrick had been part of this before, but from above it was extraordinary, an entire city set in motion in an instant, reacting to a danger that threatened them all. He looked back to the source of the smoke. That was a part of town with which he was very familiar. It was near Fellows Dry-Goods store. Damrick felt a moment's thankfulness that his father had closed that shop and sold off most of the goods already. His parents, though, still lived above it.

Suddenly a thrill of fear went through him. "I'll come back," he said, his foot already on the top stair.

"I'll be here," Muzzleman answered.

The dark of the stairs left Damrick utterly blinded. He kept both hands on the wall, and moved his feet carefully down one step at a time, cursing his eyes for their inability to adjust more quickly. His mind whirled. He had taken great precautions to protect the *Calliope*, stationing his new recruits around it day and night. But he had not done the same with his father's store, his parents' home—and now he berated himself for it. He had set himself up against pirates and their partners, without protecting his parents. If anything happened to them…

"Wait, Mr. Hambone," Dallis Trum interrupted. "I don't get it. Ain't you going to tell what Damrick's idea is?"

"Aye," another chimed in. "He's testin' out guns and ammunition and all-like, but even with iron shot, how's he supposin' he'll take on cannons? He's just got them piles a' pistols and rifles."

"And them two swivel cannon," a third added.

After a few more similar questions, the storyteller let the dust settle. "First, Mr. Trum, my name is Drumbone. Ham Drumbone. Please do not truncate it into 'Hambone.' I heard enough of that when I was a boy."

"Sorry, sir."

"Apology accepted. And second, do any of you men remember when the Gatemen first took to the seas?"

There was silence. "Sure," said a voice.

"They was like ghosts," said another.

"That's right," Ham answered. "Pirate ships would just vanish without a trace. Some said it was magic. Some said the Firefish ate 'em. Some said it was the devil. Others said miracles of God. Some even did say it was ghosts that traveled the seas in the form of men. But I'm telling the story so you'll know that it weren't any of those."

"Then what was it?" Dallis asked. "What was it Damrick done?"

"I'm building up to that, young sir."

"You boys ain't figured it out already?" asked a crotchety voice. It was Sleeve. "Add it up. Iron musket balls. Problems with the waddin'. Furnaces ever' which where. Think back to that first fight Ham told, when the *Defender* attacked the *Savage Grace*. He's given ye about a thousand hints."

There was silence. Then another said, "But it ain't fair talkin' all around it, and not just sayin' when he knows exactly."

"Fair?" Ham asked. "What's fair got to do with it? It's a story, gents, not a contest."

"And that's all it is," Mutter Cabe now contributed, his baritone ominous. "Nothin' but guessin'. No one knows what happened to all them ships, and no one's left who'll tell. It's the Firefish got 'em."

"Yer a crazy old fool, Mutter," Sleeve countered. "Damrick Fellows got 'em. He's a smart man and was a hero fer a while, until people figured out he was no better than a murderer, a man who found out he liked killin' and went and found a way to get paid to do it. And who paid him the most, that's who he killed for. And that's why he ended up pirate, and no one sings songs to him no more."

In the silence, eyes and ears sought Ham's thoughts on the matter.

Ham just sighed. "I can see you're all gettin' riled. That's all for tonight, gents. More tomorrow, if I've a mind and you've the time."

On this night, no one complained.

Delaney remembered it as he sat there above his lagoon. When Hell's

Gatemen started sailing the seas, everything changed. There was a different spirit around, and while many ashore cheered and made out like the Gatemen were just local boys who'd had enough and stepped up to the challenge of pirates, there was a darkness that grew up around the whole venture. Many of the men who joined up were known criminals, or bounty hunters, or mercenaries—even assassins who would make little distinction between shooting one man or shooting another, so long as the result was gold.

Maybe Ham had the story right, and maybe he didn't, Delaney thought. But whether Ham made it up or Damrick actually thought the idea up and used it, there could be no doubt that someone had had an idea that could put a heavy cargo ship with a merchant crew and a couple of small cannon on an even footing with pirates.

Delaney swatted lazily at a swarm of insects that suddenly surrounded him.

Everybody seemed to have ideas. Everyone but Delaney.

Something bit him on the forearm. He whacked it. It was a tiny thing, but it left a big splot of blood where he'd mashed it. Then they were everywhere, a swarm of the bloodsucking bugs on his arms, his face, his shoulders, his back, biting like tiny little *Chompers* of the air. He breathed them in, coughed once, then turned in anger on the cloud and swatted and waved and whacked and blew until finally they moved off, leaving him covered with little red spots that quickly became welts. But at least they didn't itch.

Suddenly, as soon as he'd had the thought, he had an itch in the center of his back, a bad itch, a deep, biting itch just where he couldn't reach it. He dug his fingernails into his spine above the itch, then into his shoulder blade beside it, then scratched his thumbnail along his spine just below it. That only made it worse. He stripped off his shirt and batted himself on the back with it a few times, to no effect. Finally he tied a knot into the worn garment and, using it like a towel, he rubbed the center of his back vigorously.

"Now that's nearly worth the whole agony that went before," he announced, with a contented sigh. He wiped the traces of blood from his arms and face with his shirt. He glanced down at the pond, saw that his audience had returned. The *Chompers* were agitated again, rippling the surface of the pond. He watched for a while longer. Then he said, "Don't suppose you lot ever get an itch ye can't scratch?"

They didn't answer. And as they didn't, the image of a fish trying to scratch itself flitted into his head. He saw in his mind a saltwater swigget rubbing its inadequate little dorsal fin on a piece of colored coral, under the clear waters near the shores of some island in the Warm Climes. He laughed at the picture—a little fish just sawing away, stern expression on its little face giving way to a great, happy sigh.

Suddenly he sobered. His eyes went wide. "Wait, wait!" He swallowed hard, very serious now. That picture, that image, that idea…he had never seen it before. He had never even heard of anything like it. That was his mind wandering off on its own. It was like…like a play-pretend. An imagination.

An *idea!*

He looked at the knotted shirt in his hand with fear and wonder, as though it might somehow have caused this hallucination. But no. It had come from within him. From inside his own head. Excited now, he hunkered down to the task at hand. Lowering his head, he closed his eyes and puckered his brow into a deep furrow. "Idea, idea, idea," he repeated, hoping to cash in on the sudden fertility of his mind. When nothing more came, he began banging his forehead with his palm. "Think it up now!" he told himself.

Then he saw tomatoes. Ripe, red, juicy tomatoes. He shook his head… no, he'd already thought of those. He didn't need more tomatoes, he needed what was inside the tomatoes, the ideas that would come out of them. He didn't need regular, real tomatoes.

And then his eyes popped wide open.

Idea tomatoes were imagined, too. Why, an idea tomato…that, too, was an idea! He'd had that idea a while back, and hadn't even recognized it. Had he been having ideas all along, and not known it? Could that be true? He shook his head. No, no, it wasn't true. An idea tomato without an idea was just a tomato.

Or was it? He puzzled on that for a while. It was just a tomato, but it wasn't a real tomato. It was an imagined, play-pretend tomato. A tomato that was only in the mind. But what exactly was a tomato that was only in his mind, if it wasn't an idea? He closed his eyes again, feeling somehow he was on a path to places he'd never before been, big places, important places. Places he didn't belong. But he couldn't help himself, he just kept thinking.

Mind tomatoes.

What were they? Were they real, or were they not? No, they weren't real. They couldn't be touched or smelt or tasted. But still, that tomato was there in his head. And his head was real. So something about it was real. He could think up that tomato any time he wanted.

And there it was again. Big, red, bulbous, shiny…

He opened his eyes. It was gone. He felt oddly relieved. If it hadn't gone away, that would have worried him. If there was a mind tomato he couldn't make go away, what might it do? It might do anything. Instead of you eating it, it might eat you. At least, in your mind. Like things happen in dreams when you can't control them.

And now even with his eyes open he could still see it. Sort of. Not as clear. But he knew that the idea of an idea tomato was there in his head, and it would stay. It would never go away, somehow, but would show up whenever he thought about it. Same with the itchy fish.

He now had idea tomatoes and itchy fish inside his head forever, and no man had put them there. They'd grown there.

He struggled to come to grips with this new fact, this somber reality. Here was something he'd thought up, and now it would stay inside his skull for as long as he had a skull. Which meant, at least until nightfall. He looked up to the open circle of sky above him, and a new sense of wonder stole over him. The world was a different place than he had thought it was. It wasn't just a world of things, and people doing things. It was a world of ideas.

And now, some of those ideas were his.

"You goin' to tell us the idea tonight, Mr. Drumbone?" Dallis Trum asked.

"The idea?" Ham asked, shaking the flame from a match as the smoke rose from his pipe.

"You know. What Damrick was up to with all the muskets and pistols."

"Ah, that's still burning you, is it?"

"Thought about it all day."

"Couldn't shut up about it, more like," Sleeve answered. "You better tell us or the little twerp will drive the whole ship bats."

"It's an odd thing how a thought or a question can get inside you and make you miserable. There was much I was going to tell about how Damrick found the burning ruin of his parents' home and the shop beneath it, how he come too late to help douse the flame but not too late to find the charred remains within it. But we won't go into that. I will only say that it was the death of his mother and the grief of his father, many folks said, that drove Damrick Fellows from that moment on, turning him from a man with a new business to a man with a mission. A mission of vengeance, for how could he help but think this was more than a coincidence, happening as it did just after he'd announced to the world that he would 'safeguard the seas' and protect men, women, and children from the ways of the buccaneer? Others believed, as has been pointed out in these very quarters, that Damrick was no more than a ruthless killer before, so he couldn't have been much more ruthless after. But we know this. If it was done by those who thought to drive him from his plans by burning his parents' home to the ground, then they misjudged him by a wide ways."

"Let's hear the fight, Mr. Drumbone." The words silenced the entire forecastle, even as heads turned to the source.

"Aye, Captain," Ham said easily. "It's not often we are graced with your presence here in the nether regions of your fine ship."

Belisar the Whale leaned against the ship's bulkhead, his own bulk taking up the entire passageway, blocking entrance and exit both. "Just tell on, sir."

Ham paused but a moment. The men in the forecastle worried for their storyteller. The easy tone of Belisar's voice, the calm look in his eye, the casual posture, all spoke of coming cruelty. With Belisar, the calmer and more pleasant he became, the more likely it was that someone's blood would be spilled shortly.

"We were just at a critical juncture in our story," Ham explained, and now a trace of nervousness hung about his words. "For here is where Hell's Gatemen first took to the seas."

"I know all about your juncture, Mr. Drumbone. Word on board is, you've got the explanation of a mystery all worked out. I'd like to hear how you manage the tale of Damrick Fellows, our great enemy, and the legends he sparked. I'd like to know how you think he did all that is claimed of him. I'd like to know *whether* you think he did all that is claimed. Call it a personal interest of mine. Tell on."

"Aye, sir." Ham cleared his throat. "Let's see. Well, the *Calliope* left harbor on a summer's morn. Haze hung over the City of Mann. It was one of those hot days where everything not only looked gray, but it felt colorless as well. The heat was already pressing down hard at nine; by noon it would be driving the good citizens to the alehouses for a cider, or to the backyards for a sweet lemonade in a shady spot. Captain Didrick, as they called him, so as not to confuse him with Damrick Fellows his son, had buried his wife but three days before. He'd have set sail immediately, his grief still full, for he had dedicated the voyage to her, but there was nary a breath of wind. On this particular morning there was hardly enough to fill a spritsail, but it was wind, and it was from the south, and so they were bound away."

"Are you always so long getting to the point?" Belisar asked.

"Aye" and "Always" and "That he is, sir" filled the space. Respect-fully.

"Well you see, sir," Ham explained, "a story is a bit of a delicate thing. Too straight to the point and there's no, what you might call, building up. Jumping straight to the fight, as the men quite often prefer, is not so fulfilling as they would believe. Rather you need the feel of the times, so to speak, to experience it fully. Knowing what moves the characters, what they have at stake. See, it just takes a bit of setting the stage, as it were—"

"All right, all right," Belisar interrupted. "The question wasn't meant to slow things even further. On with it."

"Aye, sir. The ship *Calliope* was loaded to the gills and ready to sail. She sat heavy and low, full as she was of a precious cargo. Some of the best ale of the Nearing Plains was being shipped from Mann to Candon, to prepare for the Fall Festival there. Aboard was a crew of twenty souls, plus a full complement of merchant marines, Hell's Gatemen—another forty souls. These last were girded about in military fashion, with pistols and muskets, and had a straight and level bearing about them. They had everything to make them seem military, save for uniforms. So in place of the regal blue that was worn top to bottom by the Royal Navy, these men wore civilian clothes, but tied a braided leather lash around the arm above the biceps, and stuck a red feather plume in their hats. Any hat would do, or just tuck it behind an ear; it was the bright red feather that made the wearer a Gateman."

"What kind of bird has a red feather?" Dallis Trum whispered, imagining he wasn't overheard.

"They dyed it, ye ninny. Shut up."

"Oh."

"And above them all flew the banner of the Gatemen, a blood-red standard with crossed swords in a V-shape, tips down. A vision that was soon to signal doom for many pirates up and down the coast."

An awkward silence followed, in which eyes cut to the captain and the ship seemed to creak more than usual.

Ham cleared his throat and continued. "It was not long before they met resistance. Early the next morning, not one full day asea, they were overtaken by a vessel flying a crude skull and bones, and boasting the name *Tranquility* across her stern."

"Skeel Barris," said more than one sailor.

"Aye. It was Skeel Barris, the very one. A bawd and a ribald, here was a man who took to piracy for the sheer joy of it. Nothing made him happier than a joke and a pistol duel, preferably at the same time. His very standard was a grinning skull wearing a cocked fool's cap. But when he came upon the waddling, plodding *Calliope*, he found her not so comical as he might have hoped. For Damrick Fellows was about to test his new idea."

CHAPTER EIGHT

TRANQUILITY

WITHIN A DAY, the becalmed haze of the Bay of Mann had given way to strong westerly winds on the open sea. But *Calliope* seemed to be standing still as the much faster ship came upon her from behind.

"Battle stations, men!" Damrick called. He needn't have. His troops were already there, ready for any engagement. One of three riflemen who stood at the prow was none other than the muttonchopped Hale Starpus, formerly Damrick's commanding officer when they both sailed aboard *Defender*. Hale had meant to make a career of sailoring, but his brief engagement with Sharkbit Sutter, and then news of Damrick's crusade had changed his mind. Hale had a cutthroat's eagerness for the fight and felt compelled to go where he was most likely to fire and be fired upon. He requested and received his release. Now, all the Gatemen but Lye Mogene and Damrick himself served under Hale, who brought a coarse but commanding presence to the Gatemen, along with his wild, windblown sideburns.

Three additional riflemen stood at the ship's stern. Three manned each cannon. Ten more lined each gunwale, port and starboard, long rifles in hand. Amidships, two sweat-drenched men held glowing iron pokers that were thrust into the midst of a small blacksmith's forge set in the middle of the main deck, glowing red and throwing off heat like it was apprenticed to the sun itself. Five more men stood alongside these two, waiting, their hands covered in the thick leather mittens of the smith's trade. Lye Mogene stood and sweated beside them, the leader of this makeshift blacksmith brigade.

"Put some more water on that decking there," Lye instructed. "Keep 'er drenched or we're done, forget the pirates." One of the mittened men picked up a large pail and sloshed the deck and the wooden blocks under the oven's feet. Steam hissed and beads danced where water hit hot iron. Where it didn't, it ran quickly toward the starboard rail, the direction in which the ship was now heeled.

"He's got the weather gauge, Damrick," Captain Didrick said. "He'll take us from port astern. And in this wind, it won't take him long."

"Hard to port, then," Damrick answered. "Let's engage."

Didrick saw cold fire in his son's eyes. "He may ram us."

"He won't."

Captain Didrick shouted out the orders. The helmsman spun his wheel, and sailors loosed the sheets, swiveling the great sails, adjusting the angle to take advantage of the stiff wind under a new heading. The captain of the *Tranquility* saw, turned his ship likewise to port to maintain the upwind advantage.

"Range?" Damrick called out.

"Four hundred yards and closin' fast!" came the call from the crow's nest.

Damrick watched in silence, standing beside his father on the quarterdeck.

A cannon shot flashed from *Tranquility*, fire and smoke visible first, then the whistle and splash of the projectile not ten yards forward of the prow, and then finally the boom from across the waters.

"Hold steady, men!" Hale Starpus called out. "You know your orders!" He walked amidships, inspecting his men.

"Strike the sails," Damrick instructed his father.

"They'll think we want parley."

"They can think what they want. We're going to burn them to the waterline. Strike the sails, Captain."

Didrick took a deep breath, watching his son. There was anger in him. But he turned away and cupped his hands around his mouth. "Heave to! Strike the main, the fore, the mizzen!"

Hale Starpus ambled up, his short legs and long torso making his gait seem more waddle than walk. "Time to move the starboard cannon, don't ye think, sir?"

"Do it, Lieutenant."

Blaggard's Moon

"Gatemen! Starboard cannon to port!" Hale bellowed.

The three men at the starboard cannon were ready for the order. They had already loosened the bolts that held it to the iron deck plate as they watched the enemy approach. Within minutes, they had it bolted to an additional plate on the port side, installed for just this purpose.

"Let's line the rails," Damrick said to Hale.

"All muskets, port rail!" Sixteen more men joined the ten stationed there. The entire fighting force and both cannon were now positioned to oppose *Tranquility*.

A sound like distant thunder came from the pirate vessel. Had the ship been at a greater distance, they might have taken it for cannon fire. But no cannonballs flew.

"They're what, cheering?" Lye Mogene asked, joining Damrick from his position at the stove.

"No. Them are drums," Hale answered.

And shortly after, music drifted across the closing distance, not just drums but a pipe and an accordion as well.

"They're celebrating already?" Captain Didrick asked, amazed. "They must think we've surrendered."

"No," Damrick assured him. "Our flag is red, not white. And theirs is black."

"Skeel Barris likes a bit a' music with his savagery," Hale informed them. "He'd rather kill than dance, what they say. But to him, there ain't much difference 'tween the two."

"Can hardly wait to meet him," Captain Didrick said.

"With a little luck and a little marksmanship, we won't have to," Hale assured them all.

Didrick fingered the cross around his neck.

Damrick saw. The cold fire in his eyes now blazed hot. "Let's burn them down. Range?" he called.

"Three-hundred-fifty yards!"

The music could be heard clearly now, carried on the wind. It was a lively jig, a merry tune all out of place here. Damrick looked around at his own men. They all watched him, waiting. "Load up, sir?" Lye asked. Sweat dripped from under his cap.

"Not yet. But get ready."

Lye moved back to his position by the stove.

"Two-hundred-fifty yards!" came the call from above.

Damrick said nothing. All the Gatemen watched him, waiting.

"Steady!" Lieutenant Starpus called out sharply. But he, too, kept his eyes on Damrick.

"Two-hundred-and-twenty yards!" came the call from above.

"All right, Mr. Starpus," Damrick said softly. "Let's open the gates of hell."

"Hot loads!" Hale sang out.

Suddenly the decks were a beehive. The two men at the stove removed their pokers from the glowing oven, now revealed to be not pokers at all but something like long-handled ladles. They weren't iron, but steel, forged and tempered, and the bucket at the end glowed red. The Gatemen gathered in a rough semicircle around the small forge. The men in the mitts reached into the hot baskets and pulled out iron musket balls, glowing red, a fistful at a time. Then they dropped a hot ball into each of the upturned muskets. In minutes, with only a couple of mishaps requiring that a loose musket ball be kicked under a rail where it could hiss into the sea, the men had loaded and tamped down the shot.

Across the water on the approaching ship, sailors watched, happily guessing what the opposing crew was doing. They saw smoke from the oven, assumed it was no more than a hot lunch. They saw the armed men with the leather lashes and red feathers. They knew what that uniform meant, but they saw only two cannon. The ship's sails were reefed, she had slowed and then right herself. As they flew up from port astern, they saw a gathering amidships. None of this seemed particularly ominous.

Captain Skeel Barris himself, a grinning and pockmarked face atop a long and loose-limbed body, paused in his clapping and dancing. "Look, a prayer meetin'!" he said pointing, to general laughter. He folded his hands and put them under his chin. "Dear Lord, please let our leather garters and red feathers save us from the bad cannon of these ruthless scalawags!" His men roared their approval.

As the pirates made merry, the Gatemen aboard the *Calliope* returned to the rail and raised their rifles.

"Range?" Hale shouted.

"Two-hundred yards!" came the answer.

"Aim true, lads! For yer lives, yer wives, yer king, and yer country!" he cried.

"Looks like they gonna take us down with pop sticks," the big captain said with glee. "Go ahead and put some more cannon fire down on 'em, but be careful. The *Calliope*'s full o' good ale, and I'm thirsty!" His men had their main cannon primed and ready, but with little ability to aim they could only wait for their ship to come broadside. That turn to port was underway. The fore swivel gun, meanwhile, boomed again, launching its smaller round shot from amid a belch of fire and smoke.

This time the *Calliope* was struck square, the projectile smacking into the ship's topside hull near the midline. But the hole it created was not close enough to the water to be an immediate threat.

Hale eyed Damrick, his teeth clenched in impatience. "Them loads ain't gettin' hotter," he said. Then he added, "sir."

"Let's do it, Mr. Starpus," Damrick said with a nod.

"Cannon, fire!" Hale shouted.

Both cannon aboard the *Calliope* barked now in sharp, crisp booms. Two holes opened in the approaching ship's starboard hull. Though they struck at a glancing angle, these were long-range guns fired at close range, and both shots penetrated amidships.

As soon as he saw the results, Hale shouted, "Muskets now, hot fire!" Thirty long rifles erupted in a tight patter, sending tracers across the water. Gray smoke billowed around them, acrid in their nostrils, their eyes, and then it quickly blew away behind. Hale shouldered his own musket, letting it drift down onto the target, holding steady until it locked on. He, too, fired.

"Hot shots and bad aim," Skeel Barris said with contempt from the rail of *Tranquility*. "That's what they're bringin', is it?" Not one man aboard his ship had been hit. All the musket balls had hit the hull or nothing at all. "Raise your sights a bit, gents!" he called out to his enemies. His own men laughed. "All right, fire in return, boys!" he ordered. "Show 'em how it's done." And the pirates did.

Rifles and pistols cracked around him, putting smoke into the air. With the wind at his back, the cloud drifted toward the *Calliope*, obscuring his vision of his enemy. The captain took the opportunity to lean over the rail to see where in fact the hot iron had hit him. A bucket or two of water would douse any fire started by a musket ball. It had seemed as though the Gatemen's rounds had been aimed for a particular spot on the hull, but he couldn't imagine what.

Skeel could see where the cannon shot had penetrated his ship, two clean holes well above the waterline. No danger there. There were a few smaller, smoldering holes around it from embedded musket balls. But not many. Not nearly as many as had been fired. He squinted down at his hull for a moment longer, working it out. Then he stood up straight.

Suddenly, Captain Barris was no longer laughing. "Fire! Fire!" he sang

Blaggard's Moon

out. His cannon boomed and gray smoke billowed. Skeel shook his head in obvious frustration. "No," he corrected. "Water! Water!"

After the volley, when they could hear him again, Skeel's men grinned at their captain as he jumped up and down, running and shouting something about both fire and water. They didn't get the joke but were sure he must be making one. After all, the sorry marksmen aboard the *Calliope* hadn't managed to hit a single sailor on the *Tranquility*. Their cannoneers weren't close to a sinking shot, either, putting their rounds high up into the hull. And the Gatemen had retreated from the rails immediately, back toward the center of the deck, gathering around that little cookstove.

Aboard the *Calliope*, the dual cannon fired again. The crew had survived the return fire from *Tranquility*, mostly intact, their retreat to the stove for second helpings of hot iron keeping most of them from harm's way. The freighter had weathered the storm of *Tranquility*'s cannon fire, too, with chunks of hull and deck and masts flying, but light casualties. Now back at the rails, they fired again. All had been instructed where to aim and why, and all were following orders. Many of these were marksmen trained at sea as Damrick, Lye, and Hale had been, and so a good percentage of the musket balls found their way through the holes created by the cannon shells, and were now burning were they struck, deep inside *Tranquility*'s belly.

"We're afire, ye dimwitted swabs!" Skeel finally managed to say, with a full complement of pirates paying attention. "They've shot our hold full of fire!"

No one moved for a moment, and then, together, they realized the implications. The hold, of course, was where the gunpowder was stored.

"Fire in the hold!" the bosun sang out. "Fire in the hold!" *Tranquility* erupted into chaos, as men rushed to find and fill buckets, and get them below decks.

"Fresh out, boys," Lye told the gunmen who came back for thirds. "It's back to cold lead." Relieved, the sweating smithies cast off their big mittens and picked up their rifles. The *Calliope*'s regular sailors, having struck their canvas and tied off their sheets, also picked up rifles and pistols and joined the Gatemen. Lye Mogene gladly took his own musket to the rail with the rest of the crew, and stood beside Damrick Fellows. Every soul aboard now aimed at any pirate in sight, and together they poured out a merciless barrage of small arms fire that very quickly added a distinct crimson hue to the chaos.

Tranquility was disorder in motion as she drifted past, unhelmed. Men who went below found the hold ablaze. Most of them hadn't brought any water. Smoke and confusion and an excess of personnel kept even those with buckets in hand from any organized effort to douse the flames. Men who stayed up top were starting to choke on smoke as well as it poured up from below. Red-hot rounds that had not been aimed true burned where they struck. The high winds fanned the flames, spreading them rapidly. Those who tried to put them out were easy targets for the marksmen aboard the *Calliope*. As would-be firemen fell, the only men left alive on deck were those firing from protected positions, and unable to attend to the fire as it threatened to engulf them.

"Don't they ever reload?" Skeel Barris asked his accordion player. The Captain was seated behind the gunwale, his back to the fray, reloading his own pistol. The musician to whom he spoke lay sprawled on the deck, his head propped up by a bulkhead wall, his forehead shot through by a stray musket ball. It had been a hot iron ball, too, and so it had left a bloodless, cauterized gray tunnel as it passed through the man's brain.

"I can see what you're thinkin'," Barris said to the unlucky minstrel. Then he chuckled at his own joke. "You're thinkin' Conch'll have my hide. But Conch'll get the last laugh."

Now an explosion from below rocked the *Tranquility*.

"Then again, he may not be pleased," he said, less sanguine. "Me losin' a good ship to a bunch a' dandies like these." But he cheered up almost immediately. "Gimme that dance box, will ye?" Skeel pried the accordion from the lifeless hand of its proprietor and began squeezing out a tune. "I know ye can't sing no more," he told the man, "but if the wind kicks up just a tad, ye might find ye can whistle." He laughed again, and kept playing. "No? Well, keep an open mind about it." Then he laughed some more.

Another explosion followed, and he raised his head. Then in quick succession three more, the last one ripping through the decking not twenty feet from him, an enormous fiery fist punching upward into the air. He could hear men screaming below. Skeel dropped the accordion. He looked down at his own chest to find what he figured to be an eight-inch wooden splinter sticking out about three inches, just below the center line. "'Bout time I danced wi' the devil," he said. "Hope he can take a joke." He slumped over.

And then, with an enormous roar and a sudden bonfire of flame, the ship came apart from the middle, strewing deck and timbers, mast and sail, pirate captain and crew across the seas.

Cheering erupted aboard the *Calliope*.

"Keep firing!" Damrick's order was terse and uncomplicated.

Many looked at their commander. "Ye heard 'im!" Hale Starpus bellowed. "Fire on!" The men went back to work.

Only a few seemed to have a problem with the order, and Lye Mogene was one of them. He lowered his musket, checked the flint absently. He watched as the others searched for targets. Live, conscious pirates were rare now, but the men fired on anything that looked like it might have once been alive.

"We takin' no prisoners, then?" Lye asked. "Is that how we're runnin' this outfit?"

Damrick did not look away from the onslaught. He aimed, paused, fired. "That's how I'm running it. You have your orders."

"Then Lord have mercy," Lye said, aiming an unloaded weapon. "'Cause it appears Mr. Damrick Fellows won't." He clicked the trigger.

Delaney's fingers strained at the knot in his shirt, the one he'd used to scratch his back. He marveled now, as he had many times before, at how easy a knot was to tie and how hard it was to untie again. By the time he finally got it undone his fingertips felt like hot stubs. He put the shirt back on. It was still damp from his swim of…how long ago? An hour? More? But nothing ever really dried in this jungle. He watched the *Chompers* circle. They seemed playful with one another now. Just regular little fish in a pond, even if they were flat in the wrong way. They didn't look like killers at all.

But they were.

Delaney sighed. Dying and killing. He'd lived a life too full of both, around men who didn't all look like killers, didn't act like it always, but who were. He'd made his decisions, and he'd become one of them. Those decisions were like tying knots, he realized, knots that were just plain hard to untie. Damrick Fellows had made hard decisions, too. But it seemed to Delaney that Damrick had only given back to pirate captains what they'd done for ages, grimly refusing to give quarter even to those who begged for their lives.

If in fact Ham had told it right.

Delaney didn't usually doubt the truth of Ham's tales. Not that he believed there were no fabrications in them, but usually he had no reason to question one particular over another. But that night and that story, with Belisar the Whale listening, Delaney had to wonder. Pirates were not above pleading for their lives. They feared death as much as anyone, when it came right down to it. Many had become pirates for fear of dying, just as Delaney and his lot had done at Castle Mum. That not a one of Skeel's crew had swum for safety toward the *Calliope*, or waved a white rag, or begged or pleaded, that wasn't usual. That seemed like something Ham had left out. Telling it the way Ham did made the pirates seem braver. No sniveling or crying at the end. But the other way, the more likely way, that would be more like Damrick Fellows as he was known to pirates. He was no Avery Wittle. No, not at all.

One thing was sure and known to be a fact, and that was that Damrick's men had fished the body of Skeel Barris out of the drink. No sense leaving valuable goods to rot. That man had had a price on his head; he'd make the Gatemen as much money as the shares for the cargo would. And either way, returning to port with the corpse of Skeel Barris aboard would be sure to rile up Conch Imbry even more.

And that could only help Ham build that dramatic tension he liked so much.

"What say ye now, Mr. Mazeley? Ye still say I shouldn't a' gone after this wretch myself?"

The pair stood on the docks of Mann late in the afternoon, watching the *Calliope* sail toward them, lazy and golden in the slanting light. Mart Mazeley had no immediate answer for his boss.

They'd been in port for ten days now, enjoying the pleasures of the greatest city in Nearing Vast. The *Shalamon* had arrived here two days after the *Calliope* had set sail. Conch had been itching to pursue. But Mazeley had pointed out that *Shalamon* made port with a partial crew, and the lack of hands had created difficulties just managing the high winds. It would be a far greater liability in a real fight.

Besides, the news of the Gatemen's challenge had drawn other captains from nearer ports, including Skeel Barris, Braid Delacrew, and Shipwreck Morrow. Conch had arrived to find that Skeel had already sailed in pursuit, but he found Braid and Shipwreck loaded and ready. Each assured the Conch that they would happily clean up whatever little was left of the Gatemen after *Tranquility* had had her turn. There seemed no need for the *Shalamon* to set sail as well.

But now, against all odds, like something out of a bad dream, they stood on the docks and watched that fat freighter pull in. She seemed unscathed, and sat high in the water, having emptied her cargo at her appointed port. None of Conch's three ships had yet returned. None were visible all the way to the horizon behind her. There could be but one conclusion, and the two men drew it correctly. She'd bested the pirates.

"I shoulda gone myself," Conch Imbry repeated. "Ain't that right, Mr. Mazeley?"

The unimpressive man knew he needed to answer carefully. In plain fact, the return of the Gatemen only proved that Mazeley had judged aright. Somehow Damrick Fellows and company had survived attacks by three ships sent to take her prize, or scuttle her. Had Conch pursued them himself, as he had planned, the end would very likely have been the same. Factual as that may be, it was still not a truth he would like to claim as his own.

"Clearly," he said after much thought, "it takes more than what those captains had to defeat the Gatemen."

"The Gatemen." Conch said it with disdain. But he said it. He could no longer deny that they existed. "Maybe I'll just stand here till he disembarks that sea cow he's sailin'. Introduce myself by way a' slittin' him ear to ear and chin to navel. Be done wif it."

"Let's think about this," Mazeley offered. "If he's met even one of our three ships, he's not likely to come to port unprepared for a scuffle."

Conch contemplated, twirled a moustache end.

"Which means, it will be the two of us against a ship of Gatemen, fresh from the kill."

Conch sighed. "I hate 'im."

"Yes. As do I. But I recommend an ambush."

"Ambush, eh?" The more Conch contemplated, the more that seemed like reasonable advice.

Mr. Mazeley watched carefully but discreetly as the *Calliope* docked and the sailors made her fast. He was just another unimpressive Vast citizen watching the ships at harbor. True to his prediction, the merchant marines with their leather armbands and red feathers stood with pistols and muskets in hand, watchful, fully prepared for an attack from either sea or shore. None seemed anxious to disembark, either. When they did, they came in packs, guarding the valuable cargo acquired in their merchant voyage: Two biers carried up from the hold and then down the gangway, each pall managed by four men who were surrounded by seven others, all under watchful eyes of sharpshooters stationed above, at the gunwales of the *Calliope*. Even before the prizes were loaded into a one-horse dray, the gangway was pulled. More than thirty men followed the wagon to the sheriff's office, where the Gatemen would collect their reward for the capture of two wanted outlaws: Skeel Barris and Shipwreck Morrow.

"Hold on, now, Ham," a sailor sang out. "Three went after the *Calliope*. Barris, Morrow, and Braid Delacrew. Ain't that what ye said?"

"I did."

"But only two came back dead. What happened to Delacrew?"

Ham puffed his pipe.

"The Gatemen kilt 'im," another pirate offered. "Ham got it wrong. Ain't that so, Cap'n?"

Belisar the Whale had been silent. "Braid Delacrew was never heard from again," he intoned. "The subject of much speculation, as Mr. Drumbone well knows."

All eyes turned back to their reclining storyteller. "True enough, Captain. What is known for sure is that Damrick Fellows claimed reward only for two of the three, and the fate of Captain Delacrew was never resolved. Some say Damrick sunk him like the others, but his body was not recovered. This seems most likely, though Damrick swore he never saw a trace of the *Yellowbone*. But others say Braid fled to the Warm Climes and gave up pirating, like Fishbait McGee and Skewer Uttley. But unlike those two, he could not be found playing cards and drinking in any known spot down south. Yet others say it was the dark magic of Damrick Fellows, that drew pirates to their deaths like a flame draws a moth, and that he sails the ocean still in a ghost ship. Still others tell it as the hand of God Himself, who sunk the *Yellowbone* without a shot fired. A few have made it out to be just a storm, a sudden squall that rose up and swallowed her. And while that seems an easy explanation to us after all this time, those on the seas that day know that no such weather was in play. Then of course, there's those who say it was the Firefish."

A few grunts of agreement floated around the deck.

"Sea monsters," Belisar snorted. "A handy explanation for anything odd that happens at sea. But I'm interested in knowing what you believe, Mr. Drumbone."

Now the forecastle went silent, waiting. "Well, sir, I must admit that I don't have any special knowledge of it. But were I to guess, I'd say Damrick took that ship down with his hot-shot musketeers, too. And likely, the end was too bloody and gruesome to be reported."

The crewmen's heads swiveled in their hammocks, back to their captain. He nodded. "A likely scenario, I would agree. You tell a good tale, Mr. Drumbone. Tell on." And with that, he left them.

Taking a deep and relieved breath, Ham continued.

"Quite a feat," an old man standing at the docks beside Mazeley offered out of the blue.

"Really? What feat is that?"

"Why, what the Gatemen done. They took down three pirate ships in nothin' but that tub, and her all full a' ale, sloshin' around in her hold."

"The Gatemen?" Mazeley said, feigning ignorance. "Oh, yes, I heard about them. A man named...what...Fellows?"

"Oh yes. Damrick Fellows. He's from right here. I know his daddy. I run a saloon just around the corner."

"So which one is Damrick?" Mazeley asked, as though suddenly curious.

"None of them boys," responded the old innkeeper. "The short one near the back is Lye Mogene, I believe. He served with Fellows. He was the second man when Damrick boarded *Savage Grace* and kilt that crazy priest they called Sharkbit."

"Doesn't look like much, does he?"

"Nope. He was never much account before, what I hear."

"So you know Damrick, do you?"

"Sure. He was always a quiet lad. Serious boy. He wasn't ever a fighter. More studious, y'know. Brainy sort. Funny how he turned out."

Mazeley looked at the man's apron, the food stains on it. There was a faint odor of ale about him. "Which one's your tavern?"

"Slow Slim's Pub." He put out a hand. "I'm Slim Dubbin." Mazeley shook it. "Pub is just around the corner."

"I suspect there'll be some celebrating at Slow Slim's tonight."

Dubbin beamed, leaned in, spoke softly. "Damrick and his men are comin' around later. He wants it a secret, so don't tell. But stop by. I'll introduce ye."

"Thank you. I may just do that. But did Damrick get off the ship? Or is he still aboard?"

"Oh, he got off first, dressed as a plain sailor, helped tie her off." Slow Slim tapped his head. "He's a smart one, that boy. Pirates around, they say, and he's not makin' many friends with that bunch. Can't be too careful."

"I guess that's right."

"Hey, you be careful now yourself. And don't tell anyone what I told you. You never know who's listenin'."

"No, you don't. But you can count on me. Thanks for the invitation."

"You're welcome."

And he wandered off before Slow Slim thought to ask his name.

That evening, Slow Slim's was anything but. Everyone in the city knew by now that the *Calliope* had returned victorious, and even without knowing their whereabouts, people came to the docks to celebrate with the now-fabled Gatemen. Many found their way to Slow Slim's by accident. Many more had heard rumors.

Damrick and his men entered the pub from the back alley, in secret, and by nine o'clock braided leather armbands and red feathers filled the back room. Toasts were made and drunk in private, and it was meant to end that way. But by ten Slim's place was jammed with chanting, hollering patrons who banged on the doors to the back room, wanting to offer their congratulations. Alarmed, Damrick ordered his men to take off their armbands and remove their feathers, and head back to the ship a few at a time. He led the way, disappearing into the night. But fewer than half the Gatemen followed.

"Them's all friendlies, Damrick. What're ye worried about?" Lye asked, looking back longingly over his shoulder.

"I gave my orders."

"Aw, don't be too hard on 'em. They ain't used to bein' praised to kingdom come. And this ain't exactly a regular military outfit."

"They have their orders," he repeated. He looked to Hale Starpus, lumbering along with the pair. "Isn't that right, Mr. Starpus?"

"That's right, sir."

"Well they ain't gonna be happy with ye, not lettin' 'em celebrate what they done."

"Their happiness is not my concern. I'd like to keep them alive."

Lye went quiet. Finally, he muttered, "Well, ye'll have to patch things up in the morning with 'em, that's all."

But by morning there would be little left to patch up.

Slow Slim flung wide the doors to the back room well before eleven, and well-wishers flowed in to toast the Gatemen. Among them were friends and relatives, delighted citizens, the curious, and a quiet handful that fit into none of those categories. Rum and ale flowed. Gatemen tied their armbands back on, or had them tied on by admirers, and they replaced their red feathers, many with the single goal of assuring they could drink for free.

The quiet few grew into a dozen. And then a score. And suddenly, with no warning, the gunfire began. It lasted less than a minute, a sudden storm of black powder roaring red, yellow fire belching from under coats, under tables, gray smoke in sudden clouds, choking the room. Men cried out, swore. Bodies crashed through tables, chairs, windows. Women screamed, ran, fell to their knees with their hands over their ears. When the echoes died away and the bystanders had evaporated into the night, a haze that smelled of sulfur drifted across the bodies of twenty-two Gatemen lying in pools of their own blood. Slow Slim lay dead on the floor, musket at his side—the price paid for attempting to stop the onslaught. A dozen of Conch's men looked for signs of life among their enemies, and extinguished it wherever they found it.

"Come quick!" a voice shouted up from the dock beside the *Calliope*. "There's shooting! The Gatemen are under fire. Come help! Quick!"

Fifteen Gatemen grabbed their pistols and headed toward the gangway. Damrick stood in their path. "Your orders are to stay aboard," he told them. His eyes were dull and lifeless.

"You gonna sit up here and let your own men die?" one of them asked, incredulous.

"Slow Slim's was a trap. And so is this."

"Trap or not, we gotta help."

The others called out agreement.

Damrick looked from face to angry face. "Your orders are to stay here," he said quietly. "This ship needs protecting." And then he walked back to his cabin.

Lye Mogene and Hale Starpus followed Damrick, trying to talk sense into him. The rest clattered down the gangway, headed back to the pub.

Inside Damrick's cabin, the two men spoke as their leader checked his loaded pistols. "This is wrong, Damrick." Hale was angry. "They stood by you, you gotta stand by them. You're the leader a' this outfit. You got a reputation."

"And you've got two minutes," he told them. "Put the cannon overboard. We're leaving the ship."

"Yer runnin'?" Lye asked, blinking widely.

"It was a mistake to gather the men together." He looked up at them, sadness deep in his eyes. "We outfoxed the pirates at sea, but they've beaten us badly here in port. It won't happen again." He stood. "Conch and his men will be here in force in less than five minutes." He tucked his pistols into his belt; one in the front, one in the back. "After they've murdered all the men who just took their bait, they'll come here."

"Bait?" asked Starpus. "What bait?"

"Who do you think that was shouting up from the docks? One of ours? Ours were already dead."

"How do you know that?"

"Get your things, gentlemen. Throw the cannon overboard. Then get to the ship's boat, seaward side. We've got maybe four minutes. And those are orders I suggest you obey." He walked out the door, his duffel over his shoulder.

It was more than five minutes later, but not much more, when a sailor climbed the mooring lines of the *Calliope* and lowered the gangway so that Conch Imbry and his pirates could pour up, searching for Damrick Fellows.

"He ran, then," Conch said. "He din't fight. He ran."

"It would appear so." Mart Mazeley was looking at the vacant metal plates where the cannon were. His eyes moved to the iron furnace. A plate of beans sat atop it. Then he scanned the empty davit arms that had lowered the ship's boat into the sea. He scanned the darkness of the harbor, but could see nothing.

Suddenly Conch had Mazeley by the throat. He slammed the smaller man into the bulkhead. "Ye said he'd come. Ye said he'd fight."

"I was wrong about him," Mazeley managed, his throat gurgling.

"Now he's got away!"

Mazeley watched Conch's angry pupils work back and forth under the slits of his eyelids. But the unimpressive man said nothing more.

Finally Conch released him. "He *ran*. Like a coward. He let his men be slaughtered."

"And that's where I misjudged him." Mazeley rubbed his neck. "I took him for a man of vanity. The sort who couldn't bear the idea of losing a bar fight. But he's more dangerous than that."

"How?"

"He's righteous."

"What, ye mean he prays?"

"I mean he won't come to the aid of the unrighteous. Even if they're his own men. It means he has no loyalty, except to his vision of who he is, and what he's supposed to do."

Blaggard's Moon

"No loyalty? He can't lead men, then. He's disgraced himself."

"I don't think so."

Conch's ire was rising again. "What is it yer thinkin' now?"

Mazeley continued to massage his own throat. Red fingerprints were now visible under one ear, a red thumbprint under the other.

"Speak away, I ain't gonna kill ye fer bein' wrong, or ye'd a been dead long ago."

"I believe Damrick Fellows will rebuild the Gatemen. He'll find men who'll obey him. Men who'll share this righteous mission. Hell's Gatemen will be back, I'm afraid. And next time they won't be so easy to trap."

"Ye shoulda shot 'im when ye had the chance."

Mazeley looked surprised. "As far as I know, I have never seen him."

Damrick watched the fire from across the harbor. All three men sat still in the ship's boat; none made a move to leave even though they'd already tied up to a pier in front of a darkened cottage.

"Looks like a ship," Lye pointed out. "Don't it."

"It's the *Calliope*," Damrick affirmed.

"There goes yer daddy's ship, then," Hale added. Then he looked to Damrick. "Where's yer daddy?"

"I sent him away."

"When?"

"Soon as we moored. I figured he'd be an easier target than the Gatemen."

"Where'd you send him?"

"Somewhere safe."

All three were silent a moment.

"Is there such a place now?" Lye asked.

Damrick just shook his head.

"I got a question, Mr. Drumbone." It was Dallis Trum.

"Just one?"

He spoke very slowly, as if reaching for something just out of his grasp. "If it's three men sittin' in a boat, talkin' to each other, how do you know what it is they're sayin'?"

"Now there's an odd question. You just listen to them, like anywhere else."

"No, I mean, who listened?"

"They listened to one another."

"Aye, but...how did you know to tell us what they said?"

Ham laughed low. It was a rolling, rumbling, pleasant sound, like thunder when the crops need rain. "Ah, now you're sneaking in on the storyteller's art. Let me ask you a question. Do you know which of them three men I've ever met?"

"No."

"Do you know who it was told me the story, so I'd know to tell it to you?"

There was a pause. "No."

"Then are you saying you can't believe that one of those men would say such a thing as he said, to any of the other two?"

"No."

"Then all I have to say to you, Mr. Trum, is if you want to hear the tale, then lie your head back and hear the tale, and quit your worrying about where it comes from. That's my worry, and mine alone."

"Aye, sir." He seemed happy to oblige.

Delaney tugged at his wrinkled shirt. He didn't know where Ham had gotten all his particulars from, either, but he didn't give it much thought. He'd sat in boats, or at least on ships, and watched ships burn. He'd seen too often the remnants of a battle, where all the anger and sweat and energy of a fight and a plunder gave way to drying blood and corpses and smoldering ruins. Those were hollow, ugly times, and if a man didn't get a little bit thoughtful, why, he likely had no head with which to think. Death always caused Delaney to do at least a bit of pondering. Much like he was doing now.

He had seen men get themselves killed a lot of different ways. But unless they didn't see it coming, which was a mercy, they all died alike in one way. They died scared. Delaney had never really thought about it, but now his mind went there, and he followed right along after. He couldn't help but know the panic in the eyes of the Gatemen, there in the pub, as they realized too slowly they were under attack, as they tried to pull their pistols, time slowing to a crawl, reactions slowed by alcohol and surprise, knowing as curses left their lips and gun barrels filled their vision that they couldn't save themselves. It was that same terror that took the pirates on the *Tranquility*. The terror he'd seen before, with men weeping, crying, even calling out for their mamas in the most piteous way. Strong men, hard men. He'd seen some go crazy with rage, which wasn't anything at all but a whole lot of panic and a whole lot of pain all mixed together. Pirates were supposed to be rough men who laughed in the face of death like Skeel Barris did. But they were just men, at the bottom. And men were just boys who grew up some.

Delaney wiped and patted at the front of his shirt. It looked like it had been at the bottom of his locker for a year. Thing was, he thought, the longer a knot stayed tied, the harder it was to untie it, and the more kinked or wrinkled the rope or the rag became. Maybe it was the shadow of his own death approaching, and he was starting to get scared, but he felt he was about ready to try to untie a few knots. Thing was, he didn't really know how.

He looked around, wishing there was another rustle in the reeds, or maybe the *Chompers* would disappear again, and he'd have something else to think about. But all was quiet, and his mind went back where it wanted to go—where it needed to go, it seemed—but where he didn't want it to go.

One of the priests who had caught him once as a boy had read to him from a big, dark book of Scriptures. He'd spoken in a somber voice that sounded like it came from the inside of a barrel, and it had filled the room and his head at the same time. Delaney didn't remember the exact words, but he remembered enough.

Hell, the priest had read, was a place of eternal fire, where souls burned forever and ached for even the simplest pleasure. One old fellow that Delaney never forgot had even cried out, there in hell, for a drop of water. Not a cup, just a single drop of water to be put on his tongue. But those souls in torment, they could never get even that. If that book was right, then Skeel wasn't doing any dancing with the devil. He wasn't telling any jokes. He was sorry to the core he'd only, all his life, laughed and killed people.

Skeel's life was sort of like Delaney's, but with more jokes.

Heaven, though, that was different. The priests talked about that, too, and now that it came into his mind, Delaney felt a great sense of gladness just thinking that there was such a place, even if he'd never get there. Heaven was light, like dawn on summer days, with big mansions made by God just for the good people. Men and women didn't turn into angels when they died, which was what Delaney had been told by Yer Poor Ma. No, the priests said, angels were a whole different kind of being, and God used them to send messages to the earth, and to pour out judgment on the bad people. Whenever someone went to heaven, that person was happier than ever he'd been on earth. All the crying and hurting was over, and all was peaceful. No jokes, maybe, but also no pain, no wishing you hadn't left your girl behind all those years ago.

There was love there, too, they said. Not the kind of love between a man and a woman that got all fouled up back on earth, what with turning of heels and batting of eyelashes. No, not that. Just deep, deep, serene sort of love. All bound up in what the priests called *joy*.

Delaney hadn't believed it then. He figured if he believed heaven he'd also have to believe hell, and he didn't want any part of that. But now, now he felt different for some reason. He thought he'd very much like to believe some of that about heaven, even if he had to believe some of hell to do it. He'd like to have some of that joy they talked about, particularly with Maybelle Cuddy. Even though she would never ever be his wife in this world or the next. The more he thought on it, the more he was sure he would like it. A kiss on the cheek. A hug around the neck. And a knowing, deep down, that there's no way you could love anyone more, and no way you could ever hurt them again, and what you share is forever and no one can take it away.

Maybe there was some good in him not marrying Maybelle, now that he thought it out. He'd have probably made a mess of that, too, and made her miserable. Sure he would have. And maybe even she him. Most men he knew did that to their wives, and it worked the other way around just as often. Men and women tied those knots hard, and yanked them tight for a long, long time, and when they untied, if they ever did, they left bad kinks and wrinkles. Wrinkles that ran real deep.

Poor Jenta Stillmithers had gone through a lot of that. That was pretty much her story, now that he thought about it. Knots tied and untied, and kinks and wrinkles, all in her soul.

"How should I put this?" Ham began the very next night. "Let's us just say that no one could fairly accuse Wentworth Ryland of being tempted to stray in the early days of his marriage to Jenta. For temptation is known only in the resisting. No, sadly, Jenta quickly learned that her dear Wentworth gathered bad habits and bad company like a hunting dog gathers burrs. His secret marriage proved to be a poor windbreak against the gales of humiliation that blew his social sails to tatters."

"What gales and what sails?" Dallis Trum asked.

"Just tell the devil blasted story, will ye, and leave off with the poesy," Sleeve added. "The boy's right."

Blaggard's Moon

Dallis looked at Sleeve in shock, and then a great, proud grin spread across his face. Mr. Sleeve had agreed with him.

"Sleeve, you are a man of many surprises," Ham answered. "I was unaware you were acquainted with the concept of poetry, much less capable of recognizing it. But apologies. Perhaps I grow giddy with the praise from our captain of yesternight. I shall drop the language a notch or two, that the simpler souls among you might not miss the point."

"And keep it dropped," Sleeve said firmly, taking no apparent offense.

"Let me try again. Marrying Jenta had no effect on Wentworth. He chased women and drank, and stayed about as pure and wholesome as the inside of a spittoon. Everyone with me?"

The "ayes" carried the floor.

"Jenta, however, was a good wife. That is, a good fiancée. The need for secrecy, for keeping up the appearance of a respectable engagement, gave her all the reason she needed to avoid Wentworth in private, and that's what made her life bearable. Though just barely."

While Jenta and her mother lived in a stone cottage just at the edge of the Ryland estate, propriety demanded that Wentworth visit only with an invitation from Shayla, and then only when chaperoned by her, or by someone of her choosing. Whenever Wentworth was sober, he was content with this arrangement. At these times, he walked with Jenta in the garden, or spoke with her with grace and decorum over dinner at the Stillmithers' table. And of course, he was heartily apologetic for any previous bouts of boorish behavior. He grew practiced at thanking Jenta for not judging him according to his baser impulses, but rather forgiving him and helping him to become a better man.

When he wasn't sober, he was tolerable because she could lock him out. During these times, so long as the locks and the hinges and shutters held, he could be safely ignored. There were no neighbors near enough, or perhaps indiscreet enough, to complain about his raging tantrums. And so within a few months Jenta and her mother became accustomed to the banging on the front door, the demanding through locked shutters that she let him in. Jenta only needed to wait until he gave up or passed out, knowing that once sober, he would again become the repentant gentleman.

"How do you put up with it?" Shayla asked her one midsummer evening when Wentworth had finally gone quiet. For nearly an hour he had alternated between piteous begging and horrendous cursing. Mother and daughter had not heard him walk away, but neither could they hear the heavy breathing that signaled sleep. At the moment, they were unsure of his whereabouts.

Jenta looked hard at her mother, who was pushing a needle up through a piece of fine silk, pulling the thread high and tight, then driving the point back down through the cloth. They rarely spoke about Wentworth now. In the two months since that shipboard wedding they had tiptoed around the hideousness of the situation, the wreckage of what had been Shayla's headlong quest for respectability in a far southern port.

"Mother. Do I really have a choice?"

"Of course," she answered. But she did not look up from her needle-point. "Of course you do. We always have choices."

She stared. "I'm married to him, Mother. Even if we could run, which we can't because we have no money, Mr. Ryland would find us and ruin us. You know this. Why bring it up?"

Shayla stabbed the needle into the cloth. "Let's not fight, girl."

"He'd have his pirate friends hunt us, no doubt." A gray tomcat jumped up into her lap. She ignored it. "In fact," Jenta pressed, realizing suddenly that she wanted a fight, "maybe I should run to Captain Imbry for protection. He doesn't seem to care much for Wentworth or Runsford Ryland. Or for the law that scared us into compliance."

"That's no way to talk."

"But if we're to be treated as outlaws, why not simply join up and help scuttle a few Ryland ships?"

Shayla glared at her daughter. "I know you're not serious, but—"

"Why shouldn't I be serious? Conch is the wealthiest man in town, the richest pirate in the world. They say he has enormous troves of treasure hidden all over the world. And he's the toast of society! Just what you always wanted for me."

"That is not what I've always wanted."

"But we always have choices, don't we, Mother? Seems to me that's one of the few I have left."

Shayla lowered the needlepoint, her words sharp and angry. "Men like Conch Imbry never help anyone but themselves."

"Really? And how many men like Conch Imbry have you known, Mother?" The cat jumped from her lap, in search of a quieter place of rest.

But Shayla said nothing in response. She looked down, jabbed the needle into the fabric.

Now they heard a snore outside.

"Shall I go fetch a servant to collect him?" Shayla asked, mostly to change the subject.

"Mr. Ryland will send someone," Jenta answered. "He always does."

"I think he watches."

"No doubt."

Jenta let the argument drift off as she listened to the loud sawing on her front porch. What men ever helped anyone but themselves? Not Wentworth. He didn't love her, Jenta was sure, though he swore to the heavens he did. His jealous rages proved he had some sort of deep feelings, but when proclamations of undying love came laced with curses and threats of suicide, it just seemed all about Wentworth, not about Jenta. She thought again of the young man, dark and mysterious, at the punch bowl at the cotillion. Strolling down the gangway, in from his naval adventures. But even that private little dream was thrown into shadow now. Certainly at the bottom of his deep sense of purpose was something selfish as well. He was but a man.

A knock on the door jarred them both. It was quick and precise, four raps in rapid succession. Not Wentworth. Ryland servants? But they had never made their presence known before. Shayla stood. "Who is it?" she called.

"A wayfarin' sailor, ma'am. Come to ask about yer daughter's health."

"Captain Imbry," Jenta whispered into her mother's affirming eyes.

"What could he want?" Shayla asked in a whisper. But she knew. Jenta had already put her hands to her own hair, straightening it, trying to determine if she was presentable. Unfortunately, she looked stunning. "Step into the back," Shayla ordered her daughter, "and do not come out unless I ask you. Much is at stake here."

"Mother, I can—"

"Do not argue with me, girl. Not now!" she hissed.

Jenta set her jaw, but turned and left the room, closing the bedroom door behind her.

"Why, Captain Imbry," Shayla said to the Conch as he filled her doorway. "This is a surprise. I had not been given notice you would be visiting."

Chapter Nine

PIRACY, INCORPORATED

Conch stood straddling the fallen, snoring Wentworth. He looked down at the young man, one cheek bunched up where it pressed against the gray paint of the wooden porch, mouth open and drooling. "Beggin' yer pardon fer droppin' by wif no notice. Jus' got in from Nearin' Vast, where I been dealin' wif some scalawags…"

"Successfully, I hope?"

"Oh, we settled 'em down some. Caught all but the one I most wanted, is the pity. So I was up visitin' the old man," he nodded in the direction of the Ryland mansion, "and I saw the body lyin' here. Feared foul play. But looks like young Wentworth jus' took an odd spot fer his evenin' nap."

Shayla nodded her thanks. The pirate had a hat in his hands, but he hadn't worn it anytime lately. His golden tresses were perfectly combed out, falling down to his shoulders in waves. He wasn't wearing his usual yellow vest, but a gold-colored one, fine satin trimmed in maroon, with fine piping at the seams. He smelled of expensive cologne and the open sea. The contrast between the confident, courteous captain and the slobbering, whiskey-sodden Wentworth could not have been more pronounced. Shayla hoped her daughter would not see it.

"Why, Captain, do come in!" Jenta said from behind her. Shayla felt the voice like a cold knife between her shoulder blades.

"Ah, Miss Jenta!" The Conch's smile was crooked, but no less sincere for that. He stepped forward, and Shayla had little choice but to back away and let him enter. He took Jenta's hand in his and kissed it gently.

Shayla warned Jenta with her eyes.

"My health is fine, Captain," she said. "I see you're in better spirits than when we last met." She had not forgotten his rudeness at her wedding, and she was not prepared to let him forget it, either. "Now, we're quite busy with plans for the evening. Was there something else you wanted?"

He pulled his head back, and a grin spread across his wide face, causing the tips of his moustache to angle upward. "Might be indeed, miss. Or rather, I suppose it's ma'am now. The three of us…" he glanced at the open door behind him, "…the four of us all know what's what, don't we?"

"We do. If there's nothing else, then thank you for stopping by." She said it with finality.

A shadow crossed his face. "Ah, yer a hard one since yer marriage, then. I remember ye a bit more lively."

"And I remember you to be more of a gentleman than you showed last time we met."

"Jenta!" But Shayla could say no more than that, nor did she have the desire to say more, for her daughter was quite correct.

Conch's look grew hard, but it was not without interest. "If it's a gentleman yer wantin', then what's that lyin' at yer doorstep?"

"It is a gentleman, upon which I insist. Anyone else shall be locked out of my house and my heart, and may well die on my doorstep. That includes you, Captain."

The silence was highly charged.

"Perhaps we should all take some tea," Shayla said brightly, "before the conversation grows altogether honest."

They both looked at her. Conch's hard look softened. He chuckled.

"Tea?" Shayla offered again.

Conch looked like a man who suddenly remembered why he had come. "Thank ye, Mrs. Stillmithers. It's right kind a' ye to take pity on a poor pirate without much manners. I won't be takin' tea wif ye today, but I do have somefin' to ask yer daughter."

"Yes, and what is that?" Jenta answered, her voice again melodious.

"I made a wager wif yer…" he swung a thumb in Wentworth's direction, "…laughable wedded husband. On yer weddin' night. And I'm wonderin' if he's seen fit to mention it to ye."

"There were many wagers made that night, I'm sure."

"Oh you'd a' remembered this one. It had somewhat to do wif you."

She looked at him blankly. "What kind of wager?"

"Hmm. Thought he might a' mentioned it. Thing is, it was done wif so many witnesses."

"What kind of wager?"

"Not fer me to say, if he's not seen fit to tell it. I jus' come by to ask, is all. And so I'll say my good days. Miss." He touched his forehead. He turned to Shayla. "Ma'am." He bowed. And he walked out the door, stepping over Wentworth, avoiding the cat now seated at the snoring man's shoulder.

"Captain Imbry!" Jenta called. She stepped over Wentworth as well, looking down to manage her skirts. But Conch turned back suddenly, and when she looked up she stopped short, but not short enough. She was standing too close to him.

"Miss?" he said softly.

"You are no gentleman," she said. But there was too much breath in her voice now, and she knew it. She took a step back, careful not to step on Wentworth's feet.

"How disappointin' fer me. I would not like to be locked out here wif the likes a' him." Then Conch fished in his vest pocket. "Oh, I almost forgot." He pulled out a delicate wedding band. "I thought you might like to have this. It's yers. Won it off yer droolin' gentleman."

Her eyes went wide. Wentworth had said he was holding the bands until their public wedding day.

"Take it. Got the writin' on the inside and all. Go ahead, take a look." He held it out on his palm.

She reached for it carefully.

Wentworth groaned.

She turned back with a start, facing Wentworth. "No," she said simply.

But Wentworth sat up.

Jenta looked past Wentworth at her mother, who met her eyes. "Come inside, Jenta. Come inside."

Conch took Jenta's hand from behind, put the ring into it, and closed it. She let him. She looked up at him, now standing to her left. He smiled down at her.

She thought he was going to kiss her. But he tapped his forehead again in a casual salute, and walked away. She swallowed hard, watching him. Her heart raced.

It took Wentworth a few seconds for it all to register, to remember where he was, what he was doing, what it meant to see Conch Imbry standing beside his wife, holding her hand. And then what her look meant, the shocked look, the warning, as though she didn't want him to wake up, as though she didn't want him to see.

"Conch Imbry!" he shouted, and staggered to his feet. He lurched forward. "Conch Imbry! I challenge you! I challenge your honor, though you have none! A duel! A duel!"

Jenta slapped him hard across the face. "He's done nothing!"

Wentworth tottered for a moment, then collapsed, falling down onto his hindquarters with a thud.

Conch looked back and laughed.

Jenta ran into the house, where her mother slammed and locked the door behind her.

"I want a duel!" Wentworth screamed at the departing figure.

"You'll have what you want, sonny!" he called cheerily with the wave of a hand. "And after ye don't want it no more, it's mine!" He turned again, and kept walking.

The gray tomcat escaped up a nearby tree.

Wentworth sobered up, eventually. He came around again the next day, meek and apologetic, asking for entry. Shayla invited him around to the back porch for lemonade with shaved ice.

"Might I see Jenta?" he asked, glancing through the back window. He looked pale. His hands shook. He eyed the cold drink in his hand, then set it on the glass tabletop beside him.

"Of course. But I thought you and I might have a little talk first."

"Look, I know I made a fool of myself again. But ma'am, that was Conch Imbry I saw leaving your home. He held my wife's hand. I didn't dream that." He looked unsure, however.

"No. You didn't. You also challenged him to a duel."

"I do recall that, yes."

"My advice is, you should retract the challenge as soon as it is practical."

"And I will, if Jenta can satisfy me that his intentions here were good."

"What sort of proof would you need?" Her tone was cold.

"Not proof, I didn't mean it that way." He was very nervous now. "I'm curious what he wanted. What he may have…said."

"I see." She studied him. "How is your lemonade?"

"Excellent, thank you." He wiped a water bead from the glass with his thumb. But he still didn't drink.

"I cannot vouch for his intentions, though if he has any that are… poor…he did not make them known to us. But he did leave us with a question."

He didn't look her in the eye, but watched the water trickle down the outside of his glass. "And what sort of question was it?"

"He mentioned an unusual wager."

Wentworth nodded. He picked up the glass now and drank it down. He closed his eyes, struggling, as though he feared it might come back up. Then he looked at her. "What sort of bargain?"

"I believe I said 'wager.' Was there a bargain, too, Mr. Ryland?"

He shook his head. "No. No bargain. I misspoke."

"But there was a wager. One that involved my daughter."

"I am uncomfortable speaking to you about it, if you'll forgive me. It's between the Captain and me."

"And Jenta, it would seem."

"Yes. It does have something to do with her."

"The Captain's words, almost exactly. Was this bargain known to all the men at that table?"

"Yes. It was a bet, and it was coerced. I felt in danger of my life."

"Quite understandable. My advice to you, Wentworth, is this. Come clean with Jenta. Hold nothing back. Don't expect it to go well. But come clean anyway. More lemonade?"

"No. Thank you."

"I'll go get Jenta." She stood.

Suddenly, Wentworth was no longer anxious to see her.

"Why don't the Conch just go fer the mother, that's what I'm wonderin'," a sailor offered. "She's beautiful and strong and more closer to his age." It was Lemmer Harps, who still had both of his hands at this time in his life. One was behind his head at the moment, the other gestured thoughtfully, palm open to the ceiling.

Delaney, usually silent during these stories, this time piped up. "She's married, Lemmer."

"No she ain't!"

"I mean they think she is. She's from a good family in Mann, remember?"

"No, she ain't!"

"I don't *mean* she is! I mean she *wants* it that way. To be thunk that." Delaney wished he hadn't said anything.

"The Conch don't care what anyone thinks. He takes what he wants."

"Well, then, I guess he wants the girl and not the mother," Sleeve answered. "Let's get on with the story."

"I think he should like the mother, is all," Lemmer said by way of defense. "That'd clear it all up easy."

"I think it's *you* likes the mother," Sleeve scoffed. "Now shut up."

"There's no call fer sayin' that!" Lemmer retorted. "What I want's got nothin' to say about it."

"Well, I'll be. Ye really are sweet on her!" Sleeve's delight was cruel. "Next time we're in Skaelington, why don't ye get yerself all fussied up and pay her a visit? Maybe she'll like ye back."

The other men crowed, and Lemmer threw his hat at Sleeve. "You shut it now, Spinner! All of ye's, just shut it right up!"

"You brought it on, fawnin' over her. 'She's beautiful! She's strong!'"

Lemmer rolled out of his hammock, pushed his way toward Sleeve. "I'll take yer old bones apart fer ye, say one more word!" The other men, lying in their closely arranged hammocks about belt-high to Lemmer, smacked him on the head and the shoulders and pushed him as he bulled through, their hammocks rocking crazily. "I ain't fawnin', ye blowhard old coot!"

"All right, I'm shuttin' up," Sleeve offered, hands up, as Lemmer approached. "I know better than to get between a man and his one true love."

Lemmer came at Sleeve now, fists flying. Sleeve just laughed as the other men grabbed, shoved, and pushed Lemmer so that he fell to the floor before he got there. The men hooted and clapped like it was midnight at a barn dance.

"Well, that's all for tonight!" Ham shouted above the din. Then he added quickly, "More tomorrow if I've a mind and you've the time!"

"Men get real antsy about their women," Delaney told the fish. He'd seen it too many times not to notice. It didn't matter if they were good wives or bad mothers or even bad women. If there was a fight among the men, most likely there was some woman at the root of it. Or if it wasn't a woman, it was a gold coin. Often it was both combined.

"Aye," he instructed. "Women and money. That's pretty much the full range of topics that'll cause a fight between grown men."

"Tell me what you bet," Jenta demanded.

Wentworth's eyes were all over the back porch and the backyard, from the hibiscus to the ferns, the stone birdbath to the lattice and climbing ivy. Then they went down to his hands. "I'd been drinking. And he had a threatening way."

"Wentworth. Look at me."

He did. She did not seem angry.

"Don't hide," she told him. "You always hide."

"What do you mean? I don't hide." But he looked down. He couldn't help it.

"You're doing it now. You hide from me. You hide from yourself. If you want my help, you will need to quit hiding."

He forced himself to look her in the eye. "Your help?" The idea that she could help, that she would want to help, had never occurred to him. "Why…would you want to help me?"

She gave him a puzzled look. "We're married. You're in trouble. Why wouldn't I want to help?"

He could think of a thousand reasons. He was the man—he was supposed to be the strong one. But he wasn't strong. He was pathetic. He'd blackmailed her, he and his father. She married him against her will. He'd bet her in a card game with a pirate. He'd hidden that from her. She'd found out about it from the same pirate. What had he ever done to earn her help? Nothing. But she offered it anyway.

And suddenly, he was overcome by a great rush of strong affection, devotion toward her. "I will duel Conch Imbry," he declared. "I will prove my love to you."

She sighed. "You're hiding again."

He was crushed. "What? I'm doing nothing of the sort. I'm…taking my obligations seriously."

She just shook her head. "Tell me the wager."

This deflated him further. He looked at his hands. "I'm ashamed of it."

"Well, that's a start."

"What are you talking about?"

"You weren't hiding when you said that." She marveled. "Have you never been schooled in anything that matters? Every child in Mann knows that confessing and admitting the source of your shame is far more honorable than taking some sort of revenge because of it. It takes courage to face your own weakness. Any idiot with a pistol can die charging into a den of pirates vowing vengeance."

He wanted to ask her where on earth such things were common knowledge. And then, how could this horrible feeling of exposure ever, by any stretch of the imagination, be called courage? But he said nothing. He just watched her eyes. They were sincere.

"Wentworth." When she was sure he was there, listening, she said, "I know all about shame."

He saw a genuine, earnest, gentle person, who cared for him and was willing to share something deep and painful. She didn't want to be his wife, or desire him in any romantic way. He was sure of that—it was what tormented him. But despite those hard facts, he couldn't shake the idea that somehow, right now, she truly cared. And this in turn created in him a feeling quite new to him. But he recognized it for what it was.

It was hope.

"Now wait!" Sleeve complained. "Yer not goin' to make this Wentworth slug into some sort of a hero, are ye? Just when ye got us ready for the Conch to knock the stuffin's out of him fer a dandy, droolin' scum?"

"You know the story already?" Ham asked easily. "Why don't you tell it?"

"Jus' save us all the weepin' and repentin', will ye? Get on with it. Get to the fights!"

"Aye, the *fights*!" others agreed, though not quite wholeheartedly.

"Well, I suppose some of this may be a bit over some of your heads. But there's a story to tell here. Truth is, gents, Damrick needs time to rebuild the Gatemen. It'll be months before we see the battle that settles for all time the row between Conch and his pirates and Damrick and his Gatemen."

Moaning and other sounds of distress rose from around the room. "Months?" and "You gotta be kiddin'!" and "Just forget the whole fire-blasted story, then, and tell us somethin' else."

"Whoa, now. I'm not saying it'll take that long to tell it. Why, all I have to say is, 'It was nearly a year later, when…' and then we're there. What I'm saying is there's some story left between here and there. If I just jumped forward to the fight, how could others know the roles some of you men played there on the island of Cabeeb when it all happened? Delaney. Mutter. Spinner. Even Mr. Trum, and the younger Mr. Trum. You all played your parts."

"I'll tell that!" Dallis Trum suggested.

"Tell a word and I'll pickle yer hind end and leave ye to rot in the larder!" Sleeve roared.

"Okay then, I won't," Dallis Trum pouted.

"Now gents." Smoke mingled with Ham's words, and both drifted lazily through the forecastle. "You can't dock a ship afore arriving to harbor, can you? No, you can't," he answered himself. His voice kept rhythm with the creaking of the timber, the rocking of the ship. "For you need to sail the whole journey, one league after the next, and arrive to port at the end."

A confused silence followed. Then Sleeve said, "Aye, but we want to hear the fight."

Ham was patient. "A story is a journey, Spinner. That's what I'm saying. You can look at the chart of the seas and plot a course, but that ain't the same as actually sailing, is it? Just so, saying there's a fight coming is like looking at the charts and planning the voyage all the way to the destined harbor. Don't mean you're there yet."

"But there ain't no charts and no seas," Sleeve complained. "There's jus' you tellin' us a story. And we want to hear the *fight*."

The others now agreed.

"Think about it. In sailing, you have a big sheet of canvas, thick and heavy, and you catch something invisible, naught but air, and it moves your ship. In storytelling, it's memories and fantasies you catch in an invisible sail, and they push your imaginary ship right along. Too much canvas in a stiff wind, and you'll lay her on her beam-ends, and there goes the ship. Too much canvas in a light wind and your sails luff and flap, and you go nowhere. Same with a story. And gents, you're simply asking me for too much sail."

"That's 'cause yer givin' us nothin' but wind!"

Laughter.

"All right then. I can't tell the fight just yet, but I can tell you how it smoldered, and what all was at stake, which will make for a bigger, better fight when it comes. For this was a fight started long before Jenta could be persuaded to say 'I do' for a second time." Ham watched the smoke from his pipe rise as the questions came fast and furious.

"Wait! Jenta gets married again?"

"To who?"

"She marries Damrick, ye oaf! Right, Ham?"

"Damrick? Yer crazy. It's the Conch gets her!"

"Aye, Conch gets her next, ain't that right?"

"Hold on, what happens to Wentworth?"

"Wentworth's a wetmop! Conch's got her in his aim, Wentworth's good as gone!"

When they finally calmed, Ham said, "Well, if you'll all see fit to let me tell it, we'll all find out together, now, won't we?"

"And so I went all in," Wentworth concluded. "Both our wedding rings on the table. And this absurd proposition, that he could have you whenever I no longer wanted you, that was there in the bargain as well." As he unburdened the truth, amazingly, he began to feel somehow stronger. Not in a proud way, not at all. He knew the damage being done even as he spoke, and every word hurt him as it hurt her. But he felt like he was facing something that had cowed him and strangled him, but that was losing its power over him now.

"You told my mother that it wasn't a bargain."

"Were you listening?"

"Yes, from inside." She didn't seem the least bit embarrassed by it.

He nodded. He could not fault her for it. "It was a bargain as much as a bet. I lied to your mother about that."

"You were hiding."

He thought about that. "Jenta, I know I'm not the man you want me to be. I'm not even the man I want to be."

"Then be that man. Become what you want to be."

"It's not that simple."

"Why not?"

"Because I don't know how!" he snapped.

She watched him, not backing off, waiting.

He sighed. He looked away, off into a distance only he could see. Then he looked down at his hands. "I tell myself I won't, but I do it anyway."

"Have you ever prayed?" she asked.

The forecastle filled with grumbling again.

"Now you lot," Ham told them, "you don't know much about this sort of thing, and I can tell you don't want to hear about it from me. But such things happen in this world. People don't only turn to doing bad, you know. They also turn to doing good. And here's the part of our story where a man tries going the other way. My own daddy was a priest on the Nearing Plains, and so I've seen it happen more than once. I know how it goes."

There was silence.

"All right, I won't give you the particulars. You want to hear it, you come to me sometime and ask. But I'll tell all you this much, there was prayers involved, and there was readings from the Holy Scriptures. For our girl Jenta had been raised right in that regard. Shayla, her mother, didn't abide by such things, having been treated unkindly by church-people her whole life. Still, she sent Jenta off to Church School every Sunday. Because that's what the fine people did. And there, Jenta learned a thing or two she never did forget."

"Like what?" young Dallis asked.

Ham paused. "If I was to wager that the Trum brothers saw the inside of a church many a Sunday morning, would I win that bet?"

Dallis glanced over at Kreg. Kreg shrugged. "Sure. But we didn't learn nothin' we didn't never did forget. Did we, Kreg?"

"Nothin'."

"Ah. I see. Well, you might be surprised at the sort of things get tucked into the nooks and crannies of a young person's mind at church. Big things, stuck in there good and tight, just waiting for a moment when they might work their way out again."

The boys were silent, roaming their own nooks and crannies, wondering what might pop out.

"We get it." Sleeve sighed. "She talked religion. Then what?"

"Well, what happened was, Wentworth began to change. He quit his drinking."

"I knowed it! That's always the first step on the road to righteous ruin!"

Laughter.

"Wentworth stayed home," Ham continued, "since pubs and dance halls tend to appeal most to those who imbibe most, and tend to lose their appeal most for those who imbibe least. So he and Jenta had their quiet time of courtship after all, just as was planned.

"At first no one quite believed that Wentworth had changed for the better, and then that he'd changed for the better for good. But after a while, when he kept on staying sober, when a new thoughtfulness crept into his ways, when he not only went to church, but to Prayer Meeting of a Wednesday, and then to Men's Breakfast of a Friday morning, and as weeks turned to months and a kind of gentleman began to emerge from the wreckage of a squandered youth, well, the whole city began to marvel. And they rightly gave full credit to Jenta Stillmithers. She had been the toast of the Summer's Eve Ball, but now as autumn approached, she was the toast of the town. Even Shayla was amazed. But then again, so was Jenta, for while she had opened up the Scriptures for Wentworth because she knew them, and she knew he needed them, truly she had not expected anything like this result. So pretty much everyone was just pleased as punch. Everyone, that is, but the Conch."

"Here we go," Sleeve sniffed. "Finally!"

"Indeed. And the Conch had good reason to be displeased. Not only did Wentworth's turnaround threaten what was a very good hand of pirate's poker, it very quickly became a threat to his livelihood as well."

"I don't understand this column, Father," Wentworth said, looking at the ledger open before him. "What are all these payments to an entity called 'Protection Fund'?"

Runsford Ryland looked up from his papers, peered over his eyeglasses. His son stood at the other side of his huge desk, paging through a thick book of accounts. "It's a hedge against trouble," he told his son. "An account to defray the risks of business on the high seas, particularly in these perilous times."

"It's an extraordinary amount. Let's see...ten percent. Ten percent..." He did the calculations in his head, his finger running down the numbers. "Almost fifteen percent on this one." Then he looked up. "You're setting aside over ten percent of your revenues from every cargo contract. Not profits, but revenues. This must be one of our largest categories of cost."

"It is."

"Who manages this fund? How is it drawn down?"

Runsford took off his glasses and leaned back. "You're eager to learn all about the business. I'm glad to see it, finally."

"You've given me a fleet to manage, and I intend to do it well."

An accountant entered quietly, handing Runsford Ryland a sheaf of paper. "That pleases me greatly," the father said to his son. "It's only three ships, but I think it will give you every experience you'll face managing all seventy-four of them one day." He glanced at the paper. "Oops, I misspoke. It's now seventy-five!"

"Congratulations." Wentworth looked pleased, but then a sudden sadness crossed his face.

"What is it, son?"

"I've wasted so much time, and caused so much harm to so many. You the most. I want to make up for that now."

Now the father rose and walked around the desk, put a hand on his son's shoulder. "You're a Ryland. I knew one day you'd come around.

There's no sense looking back." He closed the ledger with his other hand. "All these details will be understood soon enough." He tucked the book under his arm as he steered Wentworth toward the door. "To understand them aright, though, you must see them in the broadest possible context. How a business wins its permits from the government, and how the government keeps the peace. Only by understanding the large levers that are pulled by those with power can you begin to realize all that must be done to ensure that the stream of gold coins continues to find its way into these Ryland accounts." He held up the ledger. "Let's meet at lunch, and we'll talk about these larger things."

"I'd like that very much."

Runsford patted his son's shoulder.

"May I take that, please? I'd like to study it further."

"Oh, yes." He handed it to his son slowly. "We'll talk at noon."

Runsford Ryland went back to his work. Five minutes later he looked up and saw, through the glass window of his private office, his son deep in conversation with an accountant. The two of them were studying a column of figures. The accountant was jabbering on, looking somewhat frightened, somewhat apologetic. Wentworth's brow was furrowed. Then the son raised his head, a faraway look in his eye. He turned as though drawn, and met the gaze of his father.

Wentworth's look was blank. Runsford's look was grim. Then Wentworth lowered his eyes back to the book. He thanked the chattering accountant, and walked out of the office building, carrying the book with him.

"He's doing what?" Jenta asked him that evening, pouring warm tea over shaved ice.

Wentworth was downcast. The book of accounts was open on the side table next to the small sofa in the cottage. "Paying pirates. Father told me at lunch that all the shipping lines do it."

"But I don't understand. Paying them for what?"

"Protection, is what they call it."

"Protection from what?"

"Pirates."

"Paying pirates to protect them from pirates?"

"Yes."

She finished pouring. "Then it's blackmail."

Wentworth felt a pang. He knew all about his father's propensity for blackmail. "Technically, it's extortion. But it's even worse than that. We're paying them so that they raid the other lines instead."

"But you said all the lines do it." She set the pitcher on the table beside the book.

"Yes, and whoever pays the most gets raided the least."

"That's…crazy." She sat beside him. "Your father approves of this?"

"Not at the core of it—he hates it. But he does it. And the story gets worse. Conch Imbry has reinvested his share."

"What are you saying?"

"I'm saying that the most famous pirate on the seas is a partner in the family business."

"Then your father must want it this way."

"Of course not. He says he doesn't like it any more than anyone else. But what can be done? He has merchant ships, not a navy. And there's no government force here that can or will stop Conch Imbry."

"Why not appeal to the King of Nearing Vast? Don't all these lines do business there?"

"I asked the same question. But the answer, apparently, is uglier still."

She looked at him in silence. "The king already knows about it."

He nodded. "And his ministers profit by it."

She furrowed her brow. "You mean pirates pay taxes?"

"I mean those who should be stopping it take bribes. Conch Imbry is apparently not just the wealthiest pirate on the seas, but one of the wealthiest men on earth. He has a cache of hidden gold that would make the king's exchequer look paltry."

She just shook her head. "What will you do?"

He looked at her with astonished eyes. "Me? How am I to know what to do? In the last weeks I've found my feet, thanks to you. I've stood up, for the first time in my life. I've been able to feel what it might be like to be a good man, a good husband, a good businessman. I've left behind me all the shame of my own indiscretions. But now, with clear eyes and a clear mind, I find I am part of a vast, bloody enterprise that profits by terrorizing the innocent. Ryland Shipping & Freight is apparently one small arm of Piracy, Incorporated."

She put a hand on his hand, and he immediately turned his palm up and grasped hers. He squeezed, looked into her eyes with a frightening urgency. "It's nothing but deceit and conniving, with murder and robbery all mixed in, rising up to the highest levels."

"And so," she asked again, more firmly, "what will you do?"

He let go of her hand and looked out the window, down the length of the manicured, rolling lawn, seeing nothing. "I have no earthly idea. I was better off drunk."

"Don't ever say that."

"But I feel it." He looked back at her. "And I'm not hiding. What answers does your Scripture book have?" He said it in resignation, not expecting an answer.

"It's not my book," she answered darkly. "Though I'm pleased to lay some claim to it."

"I'm sorry. I just doubt there's a chapter in there headed, 'When Daddy Is a Pirate.'"

"Maybe not. But we could go see someone who knows the book better than I do."

"Who?"

"A priest, of course."

"You know any?"

"Of course. And so do you."

"Yes. But not any I'd trust with this bit of news."

"You think that even the priests in this town—"

"Wait. There is one. One I've heard about, who has a history with pirates."

"What sort of history?"

"Just the right sort, I think."

Chapter Ten

SKAELINGTON CITY

"Nothing but rogues here," Lye Mogene whispered. He held his pistol just beside his cheek, pointed upward. He was standing still, leaning against the bulkhead, listening to the creak and patter of footsteps on the wooden decking above him. *"Waste a' time comin' here, if yer askin' me."*

"Shh." Damrick held a pistol in each hand. He sat on the small bunk beside the table, which was strewn with playing cards. His eyes swept the ceiling, as the intruders walked about above.

"Two of 'em," Hale Starpus whispered. *"One fore, one aft."*

Damrick nodded. The three had sailed as passengers and deckhands aboard this elegant yacht, owned and captained by a wealthy Vast merchant who had taken an interest in their new recruiting efforts in Mann. The vessel had been a good choice. It was fast, and not nearly big enough to be mistaken for a freighter. But its owner had gone into town to make some discreet inquiries, leaving the three of them to while away the time. The day had passed; it was deep dusk now, and as darkness descended, the vermin of Skaelington, apparently, grew bolder.

Now a hand jiggled the door handle on the hatch leading down into their cabin. "It's locked," a voice said.

"Break it."

"What if someone's in there?"

"You'd rather knock first?"

"I'd rather not get shot."

"We been watchin' for hours. There's no one. Come on, 'fore someone comes. Kick it in."

Damrick clicked back both hammers.

"Did you hear somethin'?" one of the voices asked.

"No."

"Listen."

Suddenly, Hale Starpus snored loudly. Damrick and Lye both swung their pistols toward him instinctively. His eyes were wide open.

Silence above.

Hale made the snoring sound again.

"You said there was no one!"

"It may just be one."

Now Damrick smiled. He made a snoring sound as well. Then so did Lye.

"Let's get!"

And they heard the footsteps retreat, felt the boat rock as the intruders jumped to the dock.

Damrick eased his hammer down. "Good thinking."

"Thieves and cowards," Lye muttered.

"Skaelington," Hale agreed.

Lye frowned. "We come here lookin' for people to fight pirates, when there ain't no one here *but* pirates."

"Where do you suppose the bitterest enemies of a villain would be found, Lye?" Damrick asked. "Far away from him, where people hardly give him a thought? No, his enemies will be nearby, among those he's hurt the worst."

"And they'll all be scared witless."

Hale Starpus snorted. "Or dead."

"Well, we weren't having much success restocking in Mann."

That was true. News of the defeat of the Gatemen at Slow Slim's had spread quickly, even more quickly than news of their success at sea against the pirates. Damrick's escape was not universally viewed as a sign of strong leadership, either, since most of the stories being told in pubs now featured him slipping out the back just as the gunplay began.

It didn't help his efforts that Damrick had raised his standards—he was no longer taking any man who could shoot and was willing to get paid for it. Just as Mr. Mazeley had predicted, he now wanted men of integrity, men who would give the Gatemen their allegiance, heart and soul. This seriously limited the pool of potentials. Occasionally some decent recruits, military or law-enforcement types, would talk to Damrick. Most of these didn't want to be seen with him. And so far, none had enrolled. Lye had counseled Damrick to give it up, or at least give it a few years before trying it again. But Damrick was undeterred.

Now more footsteps could be heard along the dock, coming closer. These were the confident sounds of one man, each pace accompanied by a familiar thump. By the time the gold head of the cane rapped on the hatch door, all three men were certain of its owner. Damrick slid the bolt back, and let the yacht's owner in. He climbed down the steep ladder with little trouble.

"I have set up a meeting," the white-haired gentleman said with an air of unexpected success. "Midnight, just a few blocks from here." Windall Frost's slightly bent posture, his permanent partial bow, was not from age but from rheumatism. But he employed his cane with such vigor that it did not seem like the crutch it actually was.

Damrick's brow furrowed. "A meeting with recruits?"

Windall laughed as he turned and locked the door above him. "I can do much with little, but not that much. No, this is a man who can help. He has knowledge of the city, and has connections among those who would likely be willing to help you with your mission."

"What kind of man is he?" Damrick asked. "Military? Business?"

Windall looked at Damrick thoughtfully. "Neither. But I think it best not to say anything that may prejudice you in advance. I would rather you draw your conclusions based on the man himself."

"How do you know this man?"

"You mean, why do I trust him?"

"Exactly."

"He is a friend of many, many years. There is no more trustworthy man on earth."

Damrick was satisfied.

But Lye said, "If he's so trustworthy, what's he doin' in this town?"

"It's a quarter to twelve, gentlemen," Windall Frost announced, looking at the ship's clock.

"Well then, let's go!" Lye breathed, throwing his cards onto the table and standing up. "I'm ready to get off this tub." He caught his patron's eye. "Not meanin' nothin' by it."

"No offense taken."

Hale stood as well, patted his pistols, prominent in holsters on either hip. "I'm more than ready myself."

The old gentleman was thoughtful. "Yes, well…about that. I have been hesitant to bring it up, but you should know there have been some changes since I was here last. It seems those weapons are not allowed in the city."

All three looked at Windall Frost in stunned silence. Then they looked at their own weaponry. Then they looked back at him with questions written deep on their faces. But he seemed completely serious.

"What on earth you talkin' about?" Lye asked.

"Not allowed by who?" Hale added, gripping his pistol hilts tightly.

"I didn't suppose you'd take the news well. But it seems there's a new law in Skaelington. No weapons are to be carried on the streets."

"You're kiddin'!" Lye blurted.

"I'm not, I'm afraid."

"Mr. Frost, we are in Skaelington City, aren't we?" Damrick asked, perplexed. "Every outlaw here is armed to the chin. You can't mean they've managed to disarm the entire city."

"No they haven't, and apparently, that's the whole point. The Gatemen may be old news in Mann, but you put a good scare into them here. The mayor and his council passed this law about two months ago. Seems that certain powerful elements want to be sure that law-abiding citizens are no threat to them."

Damrick digested that for a moment. "So, what are you saying, that brigands and pirates are still carrying weapons? Openly?"

"Of course they are. But then you see, they're outlaws. They don't obey the laws anyway."

Lye dropped his mouth open, dumbfounded by the simple brilliance of it. Citizens either had to declare themselves criminals or go around unarmed, submissive as puppy dogs. He turned to Damrick. "What are we goin' to do, Damrick? Are we outlaws, or not?"

"We are not outlaws."

Lye and Hale both started complaining at once.

He held up a hand, waiting for them to go silent. When they finally did, he said, "We are not outlaws. But in this town, I'm afraid we may be mistaken for them."

Skaelington City had never been a port of call while Damrick, Lye, and Hale served in His Majesty's Navy, and they were soon thankful for it. It was a deadly place, at least near the docks, and death seemed to hang in the air. Here, nationality mattered little. In their short walk the men saw Drammune, Cabeeb, Vast, Sandavallian, Urlish, and many others, most in their native dress. But that was not the source of the danger. Had this been the City of Mann near the docks at this same hour, taverns would be alight, music and laughter and the occasional gunshot would be heard, drunken sailors would stagger through the streets, many clinging to women of apparently indiscriminate taste. The feel would be one of hazardous frivolity.

But Skaelington had twice the hazards, none of the frivolity.

Armed men moved in and out of shadows with their heads down, their eyes furtively watching everything around them. They looked hard and scarred, abused and disheveled. And angry. When they spoke to one another, they whispered. Saloons were dark and quiet within, the occasional music that could be heard from the street was low and slow. Women were scarce, and were not draped around men but behaving much like them, fully armed, suspicious of all around them, careful, hard, and angry.

As the four men walked away from the docks and into the streets of Skaelington proper, a gunshot rang out. Everyone on the street turned to look, hands moving to weapons. The toes of a man's boots pointed upward, and another man went through his pockets, the haze of gray pistol smoke hanging over him. Everyone looked away, appraised one another, then went about their own business.

Damrick, Lye, and Hale grew quickly self-conscious. As rough as these Gatemen may have appeared back home, they could not match the general level of disrepute that shrouded these streets. It wasn't just the people, either. The buildings were shoddy and worn, the windows small and painted or boarded or broken, the boardwalks mangled and worn and warped. Horses were few; carriages fewer. The Gatemen looked and felt like choirboys at a dogfight. Having a well-dressed businessmen at their side did not help. They attracted stares almost every step of the way.

After a block or two, Damrick put a hand on the back of their cheerful patron's neck. "Try to look a little bit scared to be walking with us, will you?" he whispered.

"If everyone don't know who we are by morning," Hale muttered to Lye, "I'll lower my opinion of the riffraff in this place."

"Don't know how my own opinion could get lower," Lye answered, a hand on each of his pistol butts.

They turned from a dark side street down a darker one. Their boots echoed through deepened shadows. Here the danger seemed to hover over them, to crowd in on them from above.

"Ah, this is it!" Still cheerful, Windall Frost rapped twice with his cane on a small, heavy oaken door fitted into a brick wall. Both door and wall were badly in need of a new coat of brown paint. The slat of a peephole slid open. Windall Frost spoke, identifying himself, and the slat slid shut. Several clicks and a jangle of chains later, and the door swung inward. They entered.

The man who closed the door behind them and locked it back up tight wore the gray robes of a priest of Nearing Vast. When he turned back toward them into the lamplight, they saw a thin man of medium height with a thin face, scarred on one side from a bad burn. His head jutted forward, and a prominent Adams apple made his neck appear to have a crook in it. His eyes seemed dim and distant, but his expression was one of great enjoyment. "So, Win, these are the hunters you've brought to the lion's lair." He opened his arms and embraced his friend.

"I suppose so," Frost answered. "But I hope to have your help keeping them from the lion himself."

"Until the time is right, I assume." The priest turned in the direction of the three men. "Carter Dent," he said, and put out a hand. Damrick reached for it, awkwardly, and shook it.

"Damrick Fellows."

"What, is he blind?" Lye asked bluntly.

"Yes," the priest answered easily. "He is blind, but he can still hear quite well. I don't believe we've met." He extended a hand toward Lye's voice.

The Gateman shook it dutifully, but quickly. "Lye Mogene," he mumbled.

"Pleased to meet you. Do you go by Lima, or Gene?"

Lye turned red. "Lye."

"I'm Hale Starpus," the third Gateman offered, putting a long pause between his first and last name. He leaned forward and found Father Dent's hand.

"Good to meet you, Hale. Come into my study, and we shall talk." But he didn't move.

"You said you'd have a guest for us…?" Windall asked.

"Yes. He's waiting. This way." Now he walked ahead of them.

The Gatemen followed, hands on the stocks of their pistols.

They climbed a narrow stairway and entered a small sitting room.

Waiting there was a young gentleman of obvious means. He stood as the priest and his four guests entered.

For the first time on the trip, Windall Frost seemed out of sorts. "Good Lord! Wentworth Ryland. What are you doing here?"

The Gatemen drew their guns.

Wentworth threw his hands in the air. "Steady now, gentlemen. Let's be cautious with the artillery. I'm a friend."

"You can put those away," Father Dent assured them. "You'll want to hear his story, of course, but I think you'll find this young man will be of great service."

"That will need to be one whale of a story," Windall said, when the pistols were holstered again. He did not look any less suspicious. "Gentlemen," he said to the Gatemen, "this is Wentworth Ryland, son of Runsford Ryland, heir to Ryland Shipping & Freight."

Damrick's eyes blazed, and he kept his palm close to his pistol. "Who knows you're here?"

Wentworth showed little concern. "No one. Well, my fiancée. You must be Damrick Fellows." He put out his hand. Damrick did not shake it. Wentworth lowered his hand, nodded at the other two men. "And you must be Hell's Gatemen."

"There would be no Gatemen, and you would not know my name, if it weren't for your father's signature on a letter to Sharkbit Sutter, giving that pirate a license to plunder."

"I'm sure I don't know what letter you mean. But I am not here on behalf of my father. Rather I hope to undo some of the wrongs forced upon him by Conch Imbry."

"Forced?"

"Why don't we sit?" Father Dent suggested when the silence grew too thick. "I believe we all have much in common. Shall we explore our areas of mutual interest?"

As a result of that nighttime meeting, and through the priests' complex communication network, often called the Church, a few solid souls began to learn that the Gatemen were more than stories. Then, maintaining a level of secrecy only possible when the alternative is explosively dangerous, the interested began to organize. Regular meetings of church elders suddenly swelled from a half a dozen to two dozen men. Potluck dinners that normally drew a dozen families, mostly women and children, now drew three or four dozen men, almost all of fighting age. One by one, the interested became the intrigued, and then the invited. These found their way to a tribunal of inquiry, and faced interrogation from unnamed men who sat in shadows and alternately prodded and provoked.

"Can ye shoot?" a voice asked from the darkness.

"I can. Was in the Forest Brigade for five years, back in Mann." The respondent sat in a bare room with one lantern for light, its hinged barn-door cover closed in the back. The voices who questioned him sat in the darkness beyond it.

"Forest Brigade," the voice said. "Shootin' what, bears?"

"Mostly."

"Ever shot at a man?" a second voice asked.

"Once or twice. Criminals that live in the Deep Woods."

"Hit any of 'em?"

"I hit what I aim at."

"Do you have family?" asked a third voice.

Pause. "A wife and a young son."

"And are you prepared to leave your wife a widow?"

"My parents are alive, if that's what you mean. They'll take her and the boy should anything happen to me."

"Thirty-seven Gatemen died this year. Are you prepared to join that number?"

Silence. "Didn't know it was so many. But I honor the memory of every last man."

"Rumors say Damrick Fellows ran scared, and that's what got his men killed at the pub in Mann."

"I don't believe that. He took down Skeel Barris and Sharkbit Sutter. Braid Delacrew and Shipwreck Moro, too. That's no coward. And I seen how that sent a spike of fear to the hearts of Conch Imbry and his like. They're gonna send around rumors; it's how they do."

"Four pirates and a spike of fear...is that worth leaving your boy father-less?"

A thoughtful pause, a wrinkled chin. "My son is six years old. He's a good boy. I want him to be a good man one day. If I don't fight what I know is wrong, and give it all I got to give, what kind of man am I? What kind of man could I ask him to be?"

"He may well grow up without you around to ask him anything."

Another pause. "If I fight against these thugs and die doing it, then at least I'll have left him a show of what's right. His mama can point him the way his daddy went, after that."

Papers shuffled. A pen scratched on parchment.

"Here is a folded slip of paper. Do not unfold it."

A blind priest walked from the darkness into the lamplight, and handed the paper to the man being questioned. "Don't open it," he said. "That paper has on it your calling. A black 'P' is your commission to pray for the Gatemen. They need those who will beg God earnestly for protection, and success. A black 'S' is your commission to work in the service of the Gatemen, in secret financial and organizational support against all those who would stand in their way. A red 'G' will tell you that you are to join with them on the seas, as a Gateman. All three are honorable paths, and any of the three will show your son how to do what is right. Do you understand?"

"I do understand that, yes."

"Good. Whichever letter you have been given, know that there are many out there, whether you see them or not, who pray and serve and fight. Do not unfold this scrap of parchment until you have thought this through one more time. Put it in your pocket, and go home. Consider your choice. If you feel for any reason you are not ready to take on a life devoted to this cause, whether in the open or in secret, then burn this note. No one will know but you. Continue on with your life as though this meeting never happened. Do you understand?"

"I guess I do."

The priest withdrew.

Now the third voice spoke from the darkness, the one that had asked about his family. "Understand this. We will never stop, never cease, until every last pirate is dead or in prison, along with every man who supports them. If you are prepared to dedicate yourself to this mission, regardless of what letter is written on that parchment, then, and only then, open it and learn your fate. Once you open that parchment, you are one of us. We expect equal devotion, whether in prayer, service, or as a Gateman on the seas. Do you understand?"

"I do. But how will I find where to go, should you want me sailing?"

"We will find you."

After a few moments of silence, the man spoke up. "Hello?"

There was no answer.

He stood and grasped the single lamp, and turned it around, squinting into the darkness. He walked over to a black sheet hanging from a stretched string, and looked behind it. A table and three empty chairs. He was alone in the room. He let himself out the door.

On the way home, he walked with his hand in his pocket, clutching that scrap of paper. And as he walked he hoped, and then he prayed, that written on it he would find the red letter that spelled the end of Conch Imbry's hold on Skaelington, and on the Vast Sea.

"What's that supposed to be?" Conch asked, irritated. He didn't like his evening cigar interrupted by business.

Mart Mazeley looked down at the scrap of folded parchment he had handed to the Conch, then up at the two serving girls. The captain liked to hire barmaids to work aboard when he was in port, turning his private saloon into something more like a public one. But Mazeley never trusted them.

"All right," Conch sighed. "Ladies, step outside." They set down their drinks and sashayed out. When the door clicked, Conch turned to Mazeley, his ire up. "Make it fast."

"It's a parchment—"

"I see it's a parchment. Someone wrote a 'S' on it. So what?"

"That someone was Damrick Fellows."

Conch looked at it more carefully. "How do ye know? Where'd it come from?"

"A citizen came looking for you. He wanted money. He gave me this and told me his story. He says Damrick Fellows is in Skaelington. He's been here for over a month."

"Here? No!"

"I followed up. There are a number of these parchments floating around town."

Conch sat up straight and peered at the paper again. "So. What's he doin'?"

"He's recruiting Gatemen."

"He's what?"

Mazeley told the story, all he'd been told…the churches, the interrogations, the scraps of paper.

Conch fed the small paper into the flame of a nearby lamp, then dropped the burning paper into the ashtray next to his cigar. "Find him."

"I've got men searching now. But he hasn't left many tracks."

"Well, clean some a' the boys up and send 'em to these priests for volunteers."

"We're trying. But the Gatemen are working through the church, and most of these congregations are very tight. Everyone knows everyone. And they're suspicious."

"They oughta be." Conch snarled. He thought a moment, and then said, "I always hated church."

The footsteps came running down the dock this time. There were a lot of them, maybe twenty or thirty by the sound. The small yacht rocked crazily as the men jumped aboard by twos and threes. There was no debate this time; the butt of a rifle slammed down on the handle. It slammed once more and the handle broke off. The door was flung open, and armed men poured down into the cabin.

A young couple sat up in the bed, covers to their chins, terrified.

Pistol hammers cocked back.

Mart Mazeley walked calmly down the stairs, ducking into the cabin. The men parted.

"Where's Windall Frost?" he asked the couple gently.

"Who?"

"Windall Frost. He owns this dinghy."

"That's the man sold it to us," the young woman said to her mate.

"Sold it to you?" Mazeley asked.

"We bought her cheap." The man pointed to his coat. "There's the papers over there. In the pocket."

Rough hands ripped the pocket open, passed the parchment to Mazeley.

"Was it stolen or something?" the man asked.

"I told you it was too cheap," she hissed at her partner.

Mazeley scowled. "Dated last week." He looked up. "Where'd he go?"

The young man shrugged. "Said he was shipping out to Nearing Vast."

Mazeley looked at the couple with calm, deadly eyes.

"We didn't know nothing, Mister," the young man pled. "We just bought a boat, that's all we did."

"You still don't know anything, do you?"

"No, sir."

Mazeley sighed. He turned to his men. "Take the boat and everything in it to Captain Imbry."

"What about them?"

"When you get two hundred yards out, toss them overboard."

"But I can't swim," the young man said, panicked.

He studied the two of them. "You should have thought about that before you bought a boat."

"I can get you out of Skaelington," Windall Frost told them. He was seated in Shayla's parlor, on the edge of his chair, cane in hand. He looked as though he was prepared to leave at a moment's notice. Which, of course, he was. "I can take you back to Mann. But you have to decide now. It's going to get very dicey here very soon. Conch's men are sniffing everywhere. There's no way our efforts will stay secret for long."

"That's kind of you, Mr. Frost," Jenta told him, "But I can't leave Wentworth."

"Why not?"

"Because I'm married to him."

His brow furrowed. He studied Jenta's face. Then he looked to Shayla, saw no denial. He looked back to Jenta. "Dear Lord."

After a pause, Shayla spoke. "Runsford has a warrant for our arrest in Mann. It was marriage, or prison."

"Prison? On what charge?"

"Something about swindling rich men."

"He's lying, of course. There could be no such warrant."

"I saw the document. He's a very powerful man."

"Yes, but…this can be sorted out. A marriage under such duress, why, there are ways…"

"None of that matters here," Shayla answered evenly.

"Then come back to Mann."

She said nothing for a moment. Then she asked, "Did you know, when your Gatemen made their pact with Wentworth, that he was engaged to Jenta?"

"Engaged, yes. I asked after the two of you, of course, and he told me that much. But I had no idea—"

"You had no idea about what, Mr. Frost? You came to this city knowing full well it was awash in pirates, knowing your actions would enrage them. You came into the bear's den to poke the bear with a stick. You made your pact with Wentworth Ryland, knowing he was betrothed to Jenta. You handed him your stick and showed him precisely where to poke. So what was it that evaded you, Mr. Frost? What didn't you understand?"

He stiffened. "Madam, I have come to offer you help, in good faith. As I ever have."

She returned a cold look. "You have put my daughter in lethal danger, a danger she could hardly imagine, for an errand with no chance of success. Now you come here to frighten us into fleeing with you from the very danger you've created. This is your idea of help, in good faith? Tell me, Mr. Frost, if we flee your nightmare with you, what would we find back in Mann? Prison?"

"No."

"Can you guarantee that?"

"I will do everything in my power—"

"Against Ryland? Against Conch? Against the king?"

He was silent.

"So we escape prison, then what? What do you have for us then? Endless piles of your dirty laundry?"

"Mother!"

Shayla's eyes went cold. "I shall see if the tea is ready." And she stood and left the room.

Windall looked at the rug, then to Jenta. He spoke softly. "Jenta, it has never been my intent to harm you. Neither you nor your mother."

"I know that."

"When Wentworth agreed to help Damrick Fellows, of course I had misgivings because of the two of you. But he was so earnest, and he could do so much good, so quickly. And you and your mother…"

"We had already made our choices. I know. And we had already refused your help. Really, sir, this is not your doing."

"Had I but known you were married to him…"

"I'm glad you didn't know. You did what you came to do, and what you came to do is honorable. Yes, it's dangerous. But you need not concern yourself with our choices, nor the result of them."

He sat back. "But of course I'm concerned."

Jenta stood and walked to the window. Outside the night was dark. The path to the road through the manicured lawn was lit for a dozen yards, festooned with flowers, and then it dropped suddenly into darkness. "It was not my desire to marry Wentworth," she told him. "But marry him I did." She turned back toward him. "Even so, had you come with this offer any time within those first, bitter weeks…I would have been packed before you finished asking. But things have changed. What we have started here, aligning citizens with the Gatemen, and against the pirates, *we* have started. It is as much my doing as Wentworth's. Perhaps more." She looked at him now with eyes that spoke of tragedies carefully considered.

"I do fear it will end badly. But I cannot run. Not now. Wentworth is not a strong man, but he is, or has become, a good man. And I cannot leave him to face alone the consequences of our actions together."

"Conch's revenge will be cruel. I don't think you can imagine how cruel."

"I don't fear what Captain Imbry will do to me."

"You should. It may be more terrible than anything you have dreamed."

"But I do not fear it. What I fear is what he may do to Wentworth without me to intervene. I know a bit about the Captain. I have met him. I have danced with him. I have…" she trailed off, a memory suddenly fresh, him at her side, looking down at her, pressing a ring into her hand. "He has taken an interest in me. I believe that I may be able to mitigate his wrath, should it come to that."

Windall shook his head. "You're a brave young lady. Brave, but foolish. He will have no mercy."

"But the battle is engaged. Whatever the result, I must stay and fight it."

"And that's your decision?"

"Yes."

"Then I wish you all the best." He stood. He pulled two coins from his pocket. He held them in an open hand. "Take these. Hide them. You may yet need them."

She accepted them. Then she kissed his cheek. "You have always been good to us. Thank you."

He smiled sadly. "Let's pray that we will meet again soon, under happier circumstances." He could not hide his lack of optimism.

A crowd of cutthroats leaned into the lamppost, pushed on it until it bent, then broke, spilling glass and flaming oil down the alleyway. A few heaves and a twist, and the rusted metal post jerked free of its base. They raised it, held it like a battering ram, and ran it into the small oaken door set in the brown brick wall. It left a puncture mark, but the door held. They rammed it again. Again the door held tight.

"Forget the door, ram the brick!" Mazeley called out.

They did. Five tries later, a hole in the wall was big enough for hands to pull the bricks out. Then big enough for a small man to squeeze through. A moment later, the door was open and they streamed into the priest's home.

Mazeley posted half a dozen men outside, and then went in himself.

"There's nothin' here, sir."

"Nothing and no one, is that it?" Dust covered the furniture.

"Aye, sir."

Mazeley walked through the home. In the priest's bedroom, the faint outline of a cross could be seen on the wall above the bed, where a crucifix had hung for many years. Mazeley's usual calm began to crack. "Where's the nearest church?" he growled.

Conch Imbry walked into the sanctuary and looked around. It was a small church, with a few high windows on either side, near the ceiling. Designed for defense, he thought. Or it would be if there was any way to climb up to those windows and shoot down on attackers. Just like churchmen to forget that small detail, and make useless an otherwise highly effective means of defense.

The altar at the front was adorned by a large wooden cross nailed into the wall. The dais, two steps high, was currently patrolled by pirates. One of them was sniffing a loaf of bread he'd found on the altar. He took a bite. Seated at the front of the steps, facing the Conch, was a priest. He was bowed down, hunched forward, and Conch couldn't see his face. Beside him, squatting with one knee on the first step, was Mart Mazeley. As Conch watched, Mazeley grasped the thin priest's hair and pulled his head back.

Blood trickled from the man's mouth and down his chin. A scar from a large burn nearly covered the left side of his face.

Taking another glance around the church, seeing nothing but empty pews, he walked forward. "This our man?" Conch asked.

Mazeley looked up. "Meet Carter Dent, priest of the Most High God. Seems to feel that this robe gives him the right to undermine the institutions God has put in place to rule the earth."

"Don't be talkin' that way," Conch hissed. "Let's get him outta here." He looked up at the cross, clearly uneasy.

Mazeley watched his boss, amused. "I'm only using words he'll understand."

"Ain't this place got a basement or somefin'?"

"Sure, Captain. Of course. We can take him into the basement."

In the darkness of the cellar, with three lamps burning, Conch was more himself. When Mazeley had tied the priest to a chair, Conch took a good look at him. He examined the prisoner's face, putting a finger under his chin and raising his head. He waved his other hand in front of Father Dent's distant, clouded eyes. "He's blind as a bat."

"Yes, he is," Father Dent said thickly, but with obvious practice. "But he can hear quite well."

Conch scowled. "And can talk, too. And that's what ye'll do now for us, won't ye?"

The priest sighed. "Your man has been beating me for an hour. I won't tell you anything I haven't already told him."

"What's he told ye?" Conch asked of Mazeley.

"Nothing."

"Nothing?" Carter Dent asked, surprised. "You want to keep secrets from your boss, that's your business."

Now Mazeley looked concerned. "He's said nothing. He's bluffing."

"Tell me what ye told him," Conch demanded, a knife suddenly at the priest's throat.

But Carter Dent had said all he was going to say.

Conch looked at Mazeley again. "What did he tell you?"

"Nothing of any value. He used to know Sharkbit Sutter, back in seminary. He met up with him later, here in Skaelington, after he turned pirate. The good father here wanted to turn him back to the light. Sutter gave him those scars for his trouble, and took away his eyesight."

Conch grinned. "What'd he burn ye wif?"

Father Dent said nothing.

"Lamp oil, I believe it was."

"That an' a match'll do it. That all he said?"

"Well, he did add that he'll gladly die in the effort to bring you down. But no information at all as to how he planned to do that."

Conch straightened up. "Torturin' priests. Nasty business." Then a thought occurred to him. "We should take him to the Hant."

Mazeley studied Conch's face. "You're serious?"

"Sure, why not? One priest to another."

Mazeley looked at Carter Dent. He leaned in close. "You might want to reconsider your silence, friend."

No response.

"All right," Mazeley sighed. "Have it your way. But I need to warn you, once the Hant gets started, no one can call him off."

Delaney grew restless. He hadn't liked this part of the story when Ham told it, and he liked it a lot less now. The Hant was one of the chieftains who came from these very jungles, the same sort Delaney had met just last night, with bones tattooed all over him. Conch's chieftain had been captured by the pirates and brought to Skaelington, where Conch set him up in the dungeon of a ruined fortress, way back in the wilds. There, the chieftain-priest practiced his dark arts, boiling potions and chanting and burning powders and whatever else, convinced he was moving the powers of earth around, directing wind and rain and tides. The way Ham told it, Conch gave the Hant everything, anything he wanted, except his freedom. Conch did it because he felt the old chieftain was useful in instances just like this.

Delaney looked up at the sky, its bright blue now dimming to gray. He didn't want the story to keep flowing through his mind, but the images came anyway. He saw the thin, blind priest chained to a wall, naked to the waist, smoke and steam filling the dungeon, pungent aromas that clogged the senses and then filled the mind. The Hant chanting and incanting, working on the poor man with sharp bones and whetted knives and long steel needles. The priest screaming.

Hour after hour.

Until finally all he knew came spilling out. Names, times, places.

Everything.

Delaney blinked away a sting in his right eye. Hants. As much as he didn't like priests, he'd take a boatload of them over a single chanting Hant.

Now Delaney looked down to the fish. The *Chompers* were almost invisible in the murk of the lagoon. "There's dark powers in the world," he told them. "Darker and more powerful than you." He thought of the mermonkeys. "'Bout as bad yer little friends under the water there."

How did people ever stand up to those powers?

"You cold?" Lye asked.

"It's a bit chilly." Wentworth Ryland tried to smile. He stood on the docks in the pre-dawn darkness, shivering. It was autumn, but here the winters were much like the summers. The slight chill in the air was not the cause of his trembling, and the Gateman sensed it. "I don't know why I feel like I'm the outlaw here," he added, more truthfully.

"I don't neither," Lye said. "Maybe it's that yer not used to what honest feels like," he suggested helpfully. "You about ready to load up the boys?"

"Mmm." Wentworth looked at his three ships, saw the sailors aboard, the cargo loaded, everything in place. Or almost everything. He looked behind him at his own carriage. The two horses were impatient. One stamped a hoof on the decking, another snorted and shook its withers. Jenta peered from the window. He couldn't judge from this distance, but she seemed impatient as well. The old driver, bundled in a heavy jacket, looked like he was sleeping.

Wentworth sighed. "I suppose it's now or never."

"If those are yer choices, then I recommend now."

"Do we have the all-clear from Damrick?"

"We do."

"All right. Load them up."

Lye turned and waved a hand. Nothing happened for a moment, and then men began to appear. They were dressed in dark clothing, carrying duffels and long rifles. In another minute a silent flow of merchant marines had covered the docks, ascending the three gangways. Crates appeared, some long and narrow, some square and fat, and were carried up with the flow.

Among these could be seen, if one looked carefully, an older man with white hair, leaning on a cane. He wore a dark suit and a black cloak, and he climbed, with a noticeable limp but no noticeable difficulty, up to the deck of the lead ship.

Also among these men was Damrick Fellows, dressed as the rest, walking with Hale Starpus, careful not to be seen as a commander. He walked past the carriage and caught a whiff of perfume. It was light and airy, and it spoke of honeysuckle. He walked past without looking. After a few more steps, he slowed. He kept walking, but he felt a strange draw, like a memory from long ago. A dance. A young girl looking for a promise. Finally he stopped. He turned back, saw a woman seated at the window. "That carriage has someone inside it," he told Hale.

"Aye. Many a carriages does." Then Hale saw Damrick's expression, his intensity—as though he were studying a portrait, or a battlefield. He saw the woman in the window. "Wentworth's gal, I'm guessin'?"

Damrick handed his lieutenant his duffel. "She's done more for us than anyone but maybe Wentworth and Windall Frost, and yet I've never met her. Carry this, will you? I'll catch up."

"She's spoke for, Damrick."

Hale watched him walk away, then easily shouldered the extra load and lumbered along with the others toward the gangway of the lead ship.

Ten yards from the carriage, Damrick stopped short. The hair, the eyes. He had not forgotten. He had put her image out of his mind too many times to forget her. Those were the eyes that had seen too much of the world as she climbed that gangway. Here was the face, the very same look that had stopped his world spinning at the cotillion, had told him plainly that he'd been watching her all evening and she had noticed. This was Wentworth's fiancée.

And suddenly he knew what she'd done. He knew what had happened to Wentworth Ryland. She had done it. She had inspired him. She'd changed him. All this, everything, had happened because of her.

And when Jenta looked at Damrick, she felt that she had awakened into a dream. She had carried his image also, the dangerous, distant, driven boy at the punch bowl, the young marine just in from the fight, eyes alight with purpose. She had equated him in her mind with her proper station, with no pretense. This was the sort of man she should know, could be with. Might have married. And now here he was, walking toward her. Coming to find her, at last.

Finally, he recovered enough to take ten more steps toward her. He fought a strong, strange impulse to open the carriage door and climb in beside her. But he stopped a safe distance, out of the reach of...what? He didn't know.

"We seem destined to meet going opposite ways," she said. Sadness and light.

The words seemed fraught with meaning to him. "Not always, I hope."

"I'm Jenta Stillmithers."

"I know who you are. I came to thank you."

"Thank me? For what?"

He felt adrift in her eyes. "You've helped us more than I can say." Then he said exactly what he was thinking. "You turned Wentworth's heart."

She felt a stab through her own. Her eyes widened. "You're Damrick Fellows."

"Yes." He felt inexplicably vulnerable, and glanced around him. The stream of sailors was dwindling. He needed to be aboard. "Thank you," he said. Then, "I have to go."

"Of course. But you will come back. Won't you? And you won't wait this time, you will come find me?" It was more than a question. She wanted that promise.

"Yes. Yes. Depend on it, Jenta." He didn't know why he used her first name. It was improper. But he said it, and waited for her reaction.

It was warm. "I will, Damrick. I will depend on it."

He intended to turn and walk away from her, but somehow he didn't.

Instead he took several steps backward, still looking at her. His heel hit a warped board, and he stumbled slightly, recovered quickly.

She laughed, remembering the reason why he wouldn't dance with her. Then she covered her mouth in apology. Then she waved.

Red-faced, he turned away, turned toward the ships and the men and the fight ahead. But his mind was filled with the echo of her laughter, and the image of her moving her hand from mouth to air.

As though blowing him a kiss.

Within five minutes of the time they had appeared, the Gatemen had disappeared once again. The three ships looked precisely as they had: quiet, serene, and ready to sail.

"They're very good, aren't they?" Wentworth asked Lye.

"They'll be all right, once we can drill a bit on the open seas. Some can shoot straight already. With the others, we got plenty a' ammo this time, thanks to you and yer friend Mr. Frost. And we got Hale Starpus to whip 'em into fightin' trim." He inhaled. "Well, Mr. Ryland, give the orders and we're off."

"Where's Damrick? I didn't see him."

"You weren't supposed to. But don't worry, he's aboard yer flagship."

Wentworth scanned his lead ship, the *Ayes of Destiny*, but saw nothing. Common sailors preparing to set sail, and the captain at the quarterdeck rail, awaiting a signal.

Wentworth waved his hand. The captain moved away from the rail. A bosun piped out orders. Sails dropped. Mooring ropes were loosed. Shoremen on the docks put sounding poles to the ship's hull, preparing to propel her seaward.

"Good day to ye then," Lye said, and hustled away, the last man up the flagship's gangway before it was pulled.

"Good day," Wentworth said softly. "I hope that it is." Then he turned quickly and walked back to his carriage.

"Well, it's done," he said as he climbed in.

"Yes, I suppose it is." Jenta had a faraway look in her eyes.

"Something feels very wrong to me," he said.

This brought her back. "What feels wrong?"

"I don't know. It's like…I can't explain it. I've spent my life being bullied by my father. Now that I've stood up to him, I can't shake this feeling…"

"What?"

He knew what the feeling was; it was just hard to say the words. Being honest with himself was still new to him. Being honest with someone else, even newer. "The feeling is…that now I've let myself be bullied by Damrick Fellows."

She nodded. "He has a powerful presence."

He squinted at her. "You've met him?"

For some reason she didn't understand, she lied. "No. I'm just saying, he seems to wield a powerful influence."

"That's true—he does." Wentworth knocked on the roof with a gloved hand. Then he looked out the window as the carriage moved off the docks.

She was glad he looked away. She could feel her face flush.

"Now I must tell my father," he said after a moment. Then he sighed.

"It's your fleet to manage. Didn't he say so?"

"Yes, but I'm sure he isn't expecting me to manage it quite this way."

"You said he doesn't want Conch Imbry's influence."

"He doesn't. But he'll be quite angry that I didn't consult him. I've put him in a very difficult spot."

Now Jenta put a hand on his sleeve. "Don't tell him. Not yet."

"What? But we agreed—"

"Why hurry? Let it play out a while."

"He'll find out soon enough, when I don't pay into Conch's little Protection Fund. Conch will come looking for him."

"Just give them a few days. Out at sea. What could it hurt?"

"Jenta, are you worried? I don't think I've ever seen you this way."

She smiled, and she knew it was a cover. She knew she was hiding. "So much is at risk, that's all." She turned to look out her own carriage window. The lead ship came back into view as they passed an open street. Its bow was a dozen yards from the dock now. "Just give him a few days to get away from Conch." The carriage moved on, and a building blocked the ship from her sight.

When the carriage stopped in front of the cottage, Wentworth jumped out and looked around him. The trees overhanging the street kept everything here in dark shadows. Twin lamps burned on either side of the cottage door thirty yards back from the road, and those lamps provided the only light. He turned, and put his hand into the cabin to help Jenta out. He heard a rustle from the woods, but had no time even to turn and look before he was slammed into the carriage, his shins and thighs banging painfully into the step and the lower doorframe. He was immediately manhandled back into the carriage, and two of Conch's men climbed in behind. Each carried a pistol. Both smelled of rye.

"The Conch's lookin' fer ye," one of them said, hauling Wentworth roughly into his seat. "Not happy!" He was tall and lanky with long red hair, and even in the dark they could see that the skin of his face was covered with big patches of brown on white. It was for this that Conch had nicknamed him "Motley."

The other, a low-slung man with a bad haircut, said nothing, but aimed his pistol at Wentworth.

Jenta clutched Wentworth's arm. Wentworth clutched back, ignoring his throbbing shins. Neither said a word. The carriage remained still and silent for another minute, until they heard the door of the cottage slam. The silhouette of Shayla, still in her nightgown and robe, could be seen between two men. Each had a firm grip on one of her arms.

"This is outrageous," they could hear her say. "Not allowing me time to dress." Even now, she didn't raise her voice. Her face was a perfect mask of calm. "You should be ashamed of yourselves," she told them.

"Aye, ma'am, we're sore ashamed," one of them told her. "Ain't we, Dack?" Dack just laughed.

Shayla said nothing to Jenta and Wentworth, once inside the carriage, until she had straightened her hair, adjusted her robe. Then she looked from one to the other. "Isn't this a pleasant surprise?"

"Quite," Wentworth said.

"I knew this would come to no good."

"Did you, Mother?" Jenta replied coldly. "Did you know exactly how things would turn out for us here in Skaelington? Did you really?"

"I suggest we wait to see what Conch actually wants," Wentworth interjected. But his confidence was more damaged than his shins.

"What he wants?" Motley crowed. "Why, he wants yer heads!" The carriage lurched forward. "Next stop, the Ryland mansion. One more passenger." The man's glee was evident.

Mazeley arrived with Conch's men in force at the south pier, pistols and muskets loaded and in hand. They streamed out onto the docks, and then stood quietly in the chill morning air.

"What did ye expect to find, Mr. Mazeley?" one of them asked.

"Ships. Three Ryland ships."

"Looks like they sailed," the man observed.

Mazeley looked at him blankly. "You're a clever one."

CHAPTER ELEVEN

PIRATE'S POKER

"WHO CAN SAIL?" Conch asked Mazeley. The two men stood on the deck of the *Shalamon*, looking out to the east. The moonlight was blunted and diffused through rain clouds that hung back on the horizon. Just under them, the dark shapes of three square-masted ships could be seen against the brighter gray. The trio of vessels was headed southward, around Noose Neck and toward the open sea.

"Other than the *Shalamon*?" Mazeley asked. But he did not wait for an answer. "Dancer Clang is in port, just arrived last night."

"Who else we got?"

"Lafe Larue has been here for weeks."

Conch scowled. "Lafe's a drunk. What about Scatter Wilkins? He's a bloody one."

"*Lantern Liege* sailed yesterday."

Conch thought a moment. Then he sighed. "Just spread the word. A gold piece for every sailor on any ship takes down one of them tubs. Twice that if it's done today."

"That's a rich bounty."

"I'm a rich pirate."

"*Shalamon* could be ready in less than—"

"*Shalamon* can't sail," Conch groused. "We got a rat's nest here in port. And I got four rats need my attention."

Mazeley paused.

"What?" Conch growled.

"The Gatemen. I'm thinking of their mode of attack. We should warn those who sail against them."

"What do ye suggest we tell 'em? Watch out, or they'll fling the fires of hell at ye from a thousand yards?"

"Your captains should know what we learned from the priest."

"The priest told us nothing. He knew nothing."

"We know that they fight with fire. Your captains should expect hot loads."

"So tell 'em to carry plenty a' water and plenty a' buckets, and shoot straight."

Mazeley nodded.

"You have somefin' else to say?" Conch prodded irritably.

"No. I think it's wise to send the other ships. Save the *Shalamon* for another day."

"Ye think I don't want to face 'em myself."

"No, sir. I think just what I said. Until we know exactly how he's using that heated ammunition to take out better armed and faster ships, I think it's a reasonable course."

Conch put a big hand on Mazeley's shoulder. "We got the Ryland rats to deal wif first."

Mazeley nodded. "I'll get word out to Dancer Clang and the rest."

"Do that. And then get back. After the rats've stewed a bit by theirselves, we'll bring 'em to a boil in the same pot." The captain winked. "And we'll need yer best deck a' cards."

It was almost dawn before Conch Imbry walked through the doorway of his Poker Deck. He looked around. Everyone was in place. Highly satisfactory. Mart Mazeley sat in his usual seat, shuffling a deck of cards with more dexterity than any man has a right to possess. To Mazeley's right was Conch's open seat. To his left sat Runsford Ryland, still in the smoking jacket he'd been wearing when taken from his home last night. He looked grim and tired and irritated. Across from him was Wentworth Ryland, his son, looking haggard but haughty. Unrepentant. Beside Runsford sat Shayla, wearing a dressing robe over a nightgown, expressionless, though drawn and pale from lack of sleep. Jenta Stillmithers sat beside Wentworth. Her hair was unkempt, but she appeared to be the only one to have slept at all. Her look was somewhere between defiance and impatience.

"Well, ain't this a glum bunch gathered fer a little sport. Last time I saw ye together aboard ship, ever'one was a bit merrier, seems to me. But then, ye've been a busy little bunch since then, ain't ye?"

"Captain Imbry," Ryland said, rising. "I demand to know the meaning of this. Why have you dragged us here in the middle of the night?"

"Sit down, Ryland," Conch said dismissively. "I don't wanna hear a bit of it." Now he grinned. "We're here to play cards." Still standing, he clapped, rubbed his hands, looked around the room. "So where's the drinks?"

As Runsford Ryland sat down slowly, Mart rang a small bell at his side. A barmaid entered with a tray of tumblers and cigars.

"Ah, that's more like it. Everyone takes a glass. Grab a cigar if ye want one."

One by one, each of those present, Mazeley excepted, took a tumbler of rum. No one took a cigar.

"No smokers, eh? Well, I'll pass then, too, on account of the women. Not usual to have two fine such ladies here in these quarters." He looked at Jenta, and held up his glass. "A toast! Here's to the gentlemen of means who grace this table…" he paused. "Hmm, my usual don't seem quite fittin'. How about this…Here's to those what will win this little game at cards. May ye live long and happy lives, and may ye remember the losers fondly!" He drank his rum down, and looked around at the silent stares. "Still a glum bunch. Well, drink up, it might cheer ye some anyways."

All present drank, at least a little, except for Wentworth.

Conch sat. "The game is two-card stud. Don't matter what's up or what's down. All right, Mr. Mazeley, deal the first hand."

Mart Mazeley put two cards face down in front of Runsford Ryland, who looked around the table, then at Conch. "What is this about, Captain? Am I the only one playing?"

"Shut up," Conch said evenly. "Ye got two cards, ye can only keep one. Turn 'em up."

Ryland did.

"Looky there. The ace a' diamonds, and the jack a' clubs." Conch nodded, seeming quite pleased. "Not bad. It's a simple game, Ryland. Now ye discard."

Runsford did not hide his irritation. "What are the stakes? What's the bet? Why am I playing alone? Come now, Captain, this is ridiculous."

"Is it?" He scratched behind an ear. "Well, I suppose I should say a bit more, then. You ain't in it alone. Wentworth here is in the game as well." But rather than instruct Mazeley to deal the young man in, Conch pulled a pistol, laid it on the table in front of him, with the barrel pointed directly at Wentworth. "As fer the stakes. I'm gettin' to that. But afore I do, Runsford, I got a question. How much did ye know about yer boy tryin' to ruin me behind my back?"

"What?" He glanced at Wentworth, then back to Conch. "What are you talking about?"

"Ye make a good show of it," Conch said. "I'll give ye that. But yer boy has banded together with the Gatemen. Recruited 'em under my very nose, loaded 'em aboard yer ships, and set 'em to sail."

"No! That's absurd. Tell him, Wentworth. Tell him you've done no such thing."

Wentworth raised his chin, spoke to the Conch. "My father knew nothing about it."

Ryland's mouth fell open. "Dear God."

"In yer next breath," Conch said to Ryland, "I suppose ye'll say that since he's yer son and all, ye beg me to show 'im mercy."

"I most certainly do." But the consequences of Wentworth's actions clicked through his mind like a key turning in a padlock.

"I s'pose I'm gettin' soft in my old age. I ought to just kill ye both and be done wif it, rather than sort out who knew what, and who did it why. But Runsford, ye've done me many a service over the years. So I'm doin' ye a favor back. Ye get to choose."

Ryland's mouth was still open, but no further words emerged.

"Here's the stakes. That ace ye got, that's yer business. That's Ryland Shippin' & freebootin' Freight. The jack, now, that card stands in for yer son. That's Wentworth. So ye got two cards. But ye got to discard one. So that means ye get to keep one, and ye lose the other."

Runsford swallowed hard. "Captain, I…"

"Maybe I ain't been plain enough." His voice and eyes went hard. "Ye can either keep yer business, and then yer son dies. Or, ye can keep yer son. And if ye do that, I take all ye have, Ryland. Ever'thin'. And the two of ye live out yer days in the old castle, sharin' space with the Hant. And I put a price on the head of any man who so much as thinks about helpin' ye make a brick out of a pile a' mud. There. That clear enough?"

Runsford's eyes were wide as dishpans. He looked at Wentworth. "Did you do this thing?" he asked.

Wentworth hung his head, but only for a moment. Then he looked back up. "I did. I was going to tell you about it."

"Why, son?"

Conch put a hand on the pistol. "Enough talk. Time to play. Pick up the cards, Mr. Ryland."

He did.

"Now. Discard one."

Ryland looked down at the two cards in his hand, both of which trembled. Slowly, he chose a card and laid it face down in front of him.

Conch reached over and swept it up. He looked at it, nodded. "Runsford, yer free to go. Thanks fer playin'."

With one last look at his son, a look that held both bitter accusation and overwhelming disappointment, the shipping magnate stood and walked, head high, shoulders back, out the door.

Conch tossed the card face up into the center of the table. Jenta gasped. Shayla closed her eyes. It was the jack of clubs.

"Looks like ye lose, Wentworth."

Wentworth seemed to shrivel before them.

"Ah, don't take it too hard, son," Conch said with a shrug. "Yer daddy never was much at cards."

Now Wentworth's eyes went to the pistol. His body began to shake uncontrollably. But Conch did not touch the weapon again. "Calm down, boy. Game ain't over yet. That was jus' the first hand. Deal the cards, Mr. Mazeley."

Mart Mazeley dealt one card face down in front of Wentworth, who stared at it like it was a viper.

"Pick it up."

Wentworth obeyed, though he had to claw at it several times before he could get his fingers under it.

"Hmm. Ye'll need two cards to play. So I guess ye better pick up the one yer daddy discarded."

Wentworth did, with slightly less effort.

"All right. What d'ye got?"

Wentworth laid down his two cards.

"Looky there. The queen a' hearts to go wif yer jack a' clubs. But in this game, ye can only keep one. Ye'll have to throw one away."

Wentworth's eyes searched Conch, looking for the meaning.

"That jack, that's still you. And that queen, why, that's yer fair bride here."

Wentworth looked at Jenta. His fear was so deep, his sorrow so tangible, that she reached out for him.

"Don't!" Conch roared. "Don't you touch him." Conch turned back to Wentworth. He calmed himself. "We still got a bet goin' from the last time you was here. Do ye recall it?"

"Yes."

"Ragged little weasel that ye are, I'm sure ye do. This here little game is part a' that one. I'm just raisin' the stakes a bit. It works like this. Keep the queen, that means yer keepin' the girl. It means ye still want her. And so ye'll have her, like I promised. Keep the queen, and she'll die right along wif ye."

Now Shayla lowered her head.

"Couldn't be otherwise, could it? I'm a man a' my word. And you, son, are surely bound to die. But ye got another choice. Ye can keep the jack and discard the queen. And that means ye don't want her no more. So then, she don't got to die wif ye." He paused. "But ye remember our bet. When ye don't want her no more, she's mine." He eyed Jenta, who met his gaze now with a steely look of her own. To Wentworth he said, "So, either she dies wif you, or she lives wif me. You decide. Do ye want her, or do ye not?"

Jenta shook her head. "Wentworth, don't—"

Conch snatched up the pistol and aimed it at Wentworth. He cocked back the trigger. "I'll kill 'im right here, little missy, you don't shut up. And wouldn't that be a pretty sight for pretty eyes to see?"

She sat still as a stone.

Conch sniffed. He set the pistol down. "What I mean is, this is his game to play, Miss Jenta. Yers is next." Then to Wentworth, "I believe it's yer turn, son. Pick up the cards."

He did.

"Now, discard one."

Wentworth laid down a card without hesitation. Mazeley stood, reached across the table, and swept it to the Conch.

Conch looked at it. "I'll be." He looked at Jenta. "Looks like he don't want ye no more." He flipped the card face up on the table. It was the queen.

"Next hand!" he announced. "Wentworth, ye can stay fer this if ye like, though yer a dead man watchin'. Might as well see the end, you bein' the cause of everythin'." He turned to Mazeley. "Deal."

Mazeley dealt one card down to Jenta. She looked at Conch sadly, shaking her head almost imperceptibly.

Then Conch slid the queen of hearts across the table toward her with a flick of his fingers. "Pick up yer husband's discard. Got to play the game right."

She did.

"Go ahead, take a look."

She looked.

"Now show 'em both."

She laid them faceup on the table.

"I'll be. The queen a' spades to go with yer heart. Pair a' ladies. Good hand. But yer gonna have to discard one of 'em. Would ye like to know the meanin' of 'em first?"

She raised her chin in defiance.

He laughed. "Sure ye would. So I'll tell ye. The queen a' hearts, that's still you. And the queen a' spades, that's yer mama here. Yer gonna need to discard one or the other."

She stared at him. "Captain. Please," she said gently, as though there might be a different man inside him somewhere, or a heart with which she could reason.

He ignored her. "First thing ye might do is discard the queen a' hearts. That means yer givin' yerself to me. I know yer husband already threw ye over. But you got a say in it still. Though ye may hear otherwise, I never have made a woman do what she don't want to do. Jus' not sportin'. And by way of makin' my case, I can tell ye right now that bein' the Conch's woman is good work, and many a lassie has wanted the position, though few has ever got it. So, ye got a choice. And that choice is the other card ye can lay down. Ye can give me yer mama."

Shayla cringed, a visceral flinch that she could not control.

Conch watched her. Then he said, "Discard mama, and yer free to go, just like Runsford did. Go do whatever ye please. Go back to Mann, marry some society tra-la-la, whatever comes into yer pretty head. But just like him savin' his own skin at the price of his son, why, you'll be savin' yerself on the back of yer mother."

There was a pause.

"Yer probably wonderin' what I'll do to her. Fact is, I ain't rightly decided. But I'll tell ye what, though. Jus' to make yer choice easier, I won't even kill her. There's a promise. But I will say that there's markets in this world where she'll fetch a gold coin or two." He looked at Shayla. "Maybe three." He looked back into the distant, depleted eyes of Jenta.

Jenta didn't look at her mother. She knew the dark emptiness that Shayla had become. "You know I'd never let that happen." Now she heard a catch in Shayla's breathing. But Jenta looked only at Conch. "So where's the choice here?"

He shrugged. "Jenta, ye threw in with the weasel," he nodded toward Wentworth, "bringin' my enemies right to my hometown. Don't ye see that there's a price to pay fer that? Sure ye do. Anyone else, and yer dead. But I'm not killin' ye—that ain't even on the table. I'm givin' ye a chance to walk, jus' up and walk away like nothin' ever happened. So don't be sayin' there's no choice in it." He paused, waiting to be sure she wouldn't argue with him.

She did not.

"Good," Conch said, almost gently. "Now, Miss Jenta, pick up yer cards."

She did.

"I know it's a hard choice, and I don't want any confusion. Give me the spade, that's yer mama, or give me the heart, which is yerself."

There was a request in it. Almost a plea. She shook her head. Here he was, promising to murder her husband and sell her mother, and yet in his mind, he was showing mercy.

"Discard me, Jenta," Shayla said suddenly. "I'll kill myself, and you'll be free."

"Mother!"

Furious, Conch snatched up the pistol. "Shut it!" he yelled. But he couldn't figure out at whom he should aim the weapon. "I'll kill the room of ye, and forget the game!" He calmed himself again, seeing that Shayla would speak no more. "What I'm tryin' to tell ye is, ma'am, that it's yer daughter's choice and not yers." Conch's voice was still ragged but now under better control.

"Don't worry, Captain," Jenta said, feeling a rush of cold strength from within. "I'll play your game."

She laid down a card.

A look of respect grew in Conch. "Well, good fer you. A card player."

When Mazeley swept the discard to Conch, the pirate left it on the table, facedown, and stared at the back of it for a long time. Then turned it over. He smiled. "The queen a' my heart." He stood, rubbing his hands together vigorously. "Well, our game's done! Mrs. Stillmithers, I had a game all set fer you, but we won't be needin' to play it now. Yer carriage awaits. I apologize fer gettin' ye outta bed fer nothin'. Jenta, on the outside chance ye'd make just the choice ye did make, I got a stateroom all decked out, right next to mine. I took the liberty to order ye up some widow's weeds. I think ye'll look fine in black. After ye cry yer eyes out a while, fer which I won't hold a thing against ye, then I think ye'll find yer quarters quite comfy. I'll take ye there now, if yer ready."

Conch stood. "Wentworth," he said with a sideways glance, "ye always were a wretched little puke. But I do feel a might sorry fer ye, losin' a woman like this to the likes a' me." He slid his pistol over one place. "Clean my pistol when yer done wif the boy, will ye, Mr. Mazeley?"

"Don't I always?"

"That ye do, Mr. Mazeley. That ye do."

Wentworth hung his head.

"Well, let's jus' skip over the sad goodbyes, shall we...?" He held out a hand to Jenta.

Jenta did not stand. She watched Wentworth for a moment, then looked at Conch. Her eyes were calm defiance. "One more hand," she said evenly.

"What?" Conch asked.

"I want to play one more hand."

"No, missy, my game's done."

"But mine's not." There was no anger, no animosity in her voice. In fact, she said it with perfect poise.

He stood in silence, looking around the room.

"Not a risk-taker then?" she asked. Her tone was light and there was a glint in her eye, as though he had done no more than to refuse to dance.

Shayla looked at her daughter in confusion.

"Well, what's the game?" Conch asked, amused.

"A cut of the cards."

"What's the stakes?"

"If I win, Wentworth lives." Wentworth's head came up.

"Yer a soft heart. But I cain't do it. He survives, and people will think I'm the soft one, and then they'll try to take me down. Makes fer all sorts a' trouble. Asides, if he lives, yer still married."

"My dear Captain," she said, pleased and surprised, "that matters to you?" Her look now was almost coy.

And now Shayla's confusion melted into recognition. Jenta had made a choice, but not the choice Conch gave her. She had decided to play a different game, one she'd been learning to play all her life. While Jenta didn't bat her eyes at him, a lady with less sophistication might have.

He shrugged a shoulder. "Well, no, to be frank. But it matters to you,

I reckon. And asides, I'm a society man in this town. What would people say?"

Mazeley smirked.

"My marriage can be annulled," Jenta told him, her eyes not leaving his.

He blanched. "Not if ye've ever—"

"The marriage can be annulled," she repeated easily.

"Even once—"

"Captain. My marriage—can be—annulled."

Conch looked at Wentworth and laughed, a low rumble. "I called ye a weasel. That was overgenerous. Yer naught but a mouse."

Wentworth closed his eyes. His chin sank to his chest again.

"And what if I win?" Conch asked. "Ye save the mouse if you win. What do I get if ye lose?"

"Then you take his life."

"I already got that. Give me somethin' I don't have." He watched her for a moment in silence, then said low, "And don't be sayin' it's you, 'cause I already won that game, girl."

Shayla closed her eyes, lowered her head.

Jenta paused a moment, but she didn't falter. She raised her chin. Her nostrils flared. And in a voice smooth as silk she said, "I'll bring you Damrick Fellows."

"Whoa! She'll trade Damrick for Wentworth?" Sleeve asked.

"Naw, bad choice, Jenta!" shouted another.

"See, Conch's already won her, and that's how he beat the Gatemen!"

Ham waited. "She's a woman of secrets, as I been telling you. You want to hear how it goes, or not?"

"Tell it!" and "Aye, we're shuttin' up!"

Conch leaned in toward her. "Yer sayin' you can give me Damrick Fellows. And how do ye propose to do that?"

She folded her hands on the table, and stared at him. "I will tell you, if you win."

The silence in the room was heavy. Mazeley began shuffling the cards. Wentworth looked at Jenta, his head shaking back and forth. Shayla watched in something close to awe, her mask in tatters. Jenta refused to look away from Conch.

Conch pondered. "You don't even know 'im," he said to her at last, watching her eyes.

She raised an eyebrow. "Are you playing, or not?"

"I'm thinkin'." He remained standing, studying her.

She watched his eyes as he watched hers.

Then he said, "Yer bluffin'."

Alarm went through her, but she just smiled. "Am I?" She knew he needed something more. So she gave it to him. "Damrick is in love with me."

Now Conch's head cocked to one side. "Ye knew him from before. In Mann."

She stared at Conch, raised one corner of her mouth just slightly. She felt the pained eyes of Wentworth, the emptiness of her mother. Neither of them, she realized, could know for certain if she was lying or telling the truth, any more than Conch could. Somehow, that fact gave her more confidence. "Are you in or are you out, Captain?"

Now his mind started turning. The possibilities clicked through his eyes where she could fairly see them. A beautiful woman…not highborn, she would have had many admirers. Damrick could easily have been among them. He might have been in love with her for years. He could have come to Skaelington just to find her. Jenta watched as the bitter sting of jealousy took root. She did not know what he would do with it, however, until he said, "Mr. Mazeley, cut the cards."

"No," Jenta said easily. "This is my game. My deal." She held out her hand to Mazeley. "Unless you don't trust me."

"I don't trust you," Mazeley offered easily, continuing to shuffle.

"Give her the cards," Conch ordered. He watched Jenta, but now she wouldn't meet his gaze. He looked at her differently; she could feel it. She was no longer the sweet young prize, but a crafty doe in a dense, craggy forest. Worthy prey. Maybe even dangerous prey. Maybe a lioness, and not a doe at all.

Mazeley gave the cards one last sorting, and handed the deck to Jenta. She fanned them in her hand, turned them over, examined them. Then she began to shuffle. She had some skill.

"Where'd you learn that?" Conch asked.

"From my mother."

"You learned a lot from her."

"I learned everything from her. Are you in?" she asked.

"I'm in. Mr. Mazeley, pick a good card for me."

She put her hand on top of the deck to prevent Mazeley from touching it. She looked at Conch. "Am I your woman, or am I his?" Her question mingled the pleasure of ownership with the sting of jealousy, and she knew it.

He put both hands on the red felt and leaned across the table toward her. "You cut for me," he said to her.

She picked up the top third of the deck. The card was the jack of hearts.

"Nice cut."

She shuffled the cards, laid the deck down again. When she cut the deck this time, she showed him the king of clubs. The corner of her lip rose.

"I win!" Conch barked, standing up straight.

"But Captain!" Jenta rose quickly now. "I believe your card was the jack. The king is mine."

"No, he ain't!" His blood rose to a boil. "Nothin' on board this ship is yers, missy! Nothin' unless I give it."

"But you did give it."

"Did I? Well I'm takin' it back. I don't like yer game. Mazeley, shoot the mouse. Hell, shoot the mother, too, I'm tired of 'em both." He held out a hand. "Now. Ye can come with me, or ye can die with them."

She paused for a moment, on the edge of a precipice. She had gambled big and thought she'd won, but suddenly she had lost everything. She had angered the Conch, and now he would do whatever he wanted. And what he wanted was to kill. Mazeley already had the pistol in his hand. His finger was on the trigger. His thumb was on the hammer. In a moment it would be over; her mother and her husband would be dead.

She could not let this happen. She walked straight to the Conch.

She wasn't sure what she would do when she reached him, but she knew she must stop him. And in those few steps, it came to her. By the time she reached him, by the end of the four quick steps it took her to round the table, it was over and done, her future settled. Another woman might have gone at him with fists flying or nails scratching, but Jenta was not that woman. All her schooling, all her graces, all her charm came to her now in a single moment, as a single whole. She felt in control. And so in those few steps, with Wentworth reaching out to stop her, with Shayla pulling back, withdrawing yet further into herself, with Conch watching, waiting, eyes cold, right arm outstretched and waiting for her to take his hand…she stood tall, squared her shoulders, met his gaze, and walked past his open hand, inside his arm, and stopped before him. "I didn't mean to anger you. You always win, of course. That game was just my foolish way of telling you that I dearly love my mother, and I've grown so fond of Wentworth. He's like a brother to me."

He dropped his hand. She put hers into it.

"Brother, is it?" Conch pondered the idea, eyeing Wentworth over her shoulder. "Black sheep a' the family, ye ask me."

She nodded her agreement.

His eyes narrowed. Hers were disarming, but he was not disarmed. "What's all this about Damrick Fellows? That all a bluff, was it?"

"Oh, no. That was no bluff at all. I can give you Damrick Fellows." She swallowed, but her poise remained.

"Ye can. But will ye?"

She raised her eyebrows.

Conch sniffed, assessing his options. Then he raised her hand and kissed the back of it. He winked at her. "Look, ye want a real man to take care a' ye, I get that. It's what a real woman needs. And ye want yer mama and the mouse alive, I get that, too." He looked around the room again, as though considering the possible consequences of a moment of mercy. "All right then. As a gift to ye, I won't be killin' 'em. But ye gotta make me some promises now. Ye got a bad and rocky past, sidin' with the likes a' the Gatemen. Ye got to leave that all behind."

"I will."

"Swear it?"

"I do—I swear it."

"And no secrets from me. Not about Damrick Fellows, or the Gatemen, nor nothin'. Understand?"

"No secrets."

"Ever. I need yer word on that, too. Do ye swear it on yer life, and the life of yer mama and yer…?" He hooked a thumb toward Wentworth, but couldn't find the word that would finish the question.

"I do."

Conch watched her eyes for a long while, and then he sighed, content. He looked down at Mazeley, still seated with the pistol in his hand. "Ye won't be needin' that after all." Mazeley eased the hammer back down, handed over the gun. Conch tucked it into his belt. "Get Mrs. Stillmithers back to her carriage, Mr. Mazeley. Send her on home. Then find a suitable spot fer Mr. Wentworth Ryland, somewhere no one'll ever know that he lives on. Especially not his daddy. And then, fetch me a priest, or a judge, or whoever can undo the joke that this pair been callin' a marriage." He looked at Jenta, saw her gratitude. "On second thought," Conch added, "do that last little job first."

"Yes, sir."

Jenta would not look at her mother, nor at Wentworth. She had shamed herself, she knew, but she had already fled from that shame. She simply left it behind. She looked only at the Conch, willing him to believe that he was all she thought about, all she would ever think about again; he was the sun in her day and the moon in her night. She willed herself to believe it, too. Everything depended on that now.

And underneath that mask, in the deepest pocket of her heart, she tucked herself away. She secluded herself, shrouded herself, buried herself in a place where she wouldn't feel the sting of conscience or the burn of humiliation, a place where she could await some moment far in the future when she might perhaps come out again, and determine just how much damage she had done.

"I *knew* the Conch'd get 'er!" Sleeve crowed. "Now she's seen reason."

"I don't know, Sleeve," another sailor countered slowly. "Ham said she hid herself away. That don't sound like seein' reason."

"Oh, come on. That's just her talkin' herself outta her old ways. Ain't it, Ham?"

Ham puffed his pipe.

"See, boys," Sleeve explained, "all that nonsense about religion and doin' good, and listenin' to conscience and all, like there's some kinda God lookin' down on everyone and shakin' His finger, all that does is, it just keeps ye from doin' what ye got to do to get by in this world. It gets deep under the skin, and it's hard to shed it all, even once ye have a mind to do it. But Jenta did it. See, now she can do what's necessary to make her way in the world. She jus' grew up, there at the table, that's all."

"But she hid herself away fer a time," the other sailor countered.

"Aw, that's just the way ye get shed of it. After a few months, years maybe, why, she'll forget she's hidin' anything. She'll realize one day, hey, I'm free of it, I don't feel no guilt about anythin' at all. I don't need never to go back. Conscience is gone, and I can do what I want without it draggin' on me. Trust me, boys, I know. That's how I done it."

There was silence in the room.

"Me, too," a voice said.

"Yeah, and me. Sorta," said another.

Delaney had to admit that was his path, too. He'd made a lot of little choices to run from conscience and all such things. But then when he swore to follow the Conch, both to kill and die, he told himself it was just because he had to, not forever, and later he could go back on it if he wanted. But he never did. And the longer he went, the less he ever wanted to.

"There's other ways," Sleeve continued, encouraged by the agreement in the room. "Some people, they just get real mad at God, or at the Church, and so whenever they feel that old stab a' guilt, they just get mad all over again. And pretty soon, after they been cussin' God long enough, the mad jus' sorta goes away, and so does the conscience, and then, why, one day they find they're shed of it and don't care a whit no more."

"That's me," another voice announced.

"I done it that way," yet another confessed.

"There ye go," Sleeve continued. "And there's other people who find other ways, like I heard an ol' boy said he was readin' and studyin' all sorts of arguments, like how it makes no sense for there to be a God, how it's all made up in people's minds and not real at all. He got to thinkin' that only the stupidest folk on the face a' the earth could ever think it was so. He jus' laughed at all the poor idiots runnin' around tryin' to make some invisible nothin' happy, and that took away its power, see, and pretty soon there was no way he could ever think a' bein' religious again, on account of it bein' so far beneath 'im."

Silence.

"No one here never did that?"

More silence.

"Well, I suppose that's fer a crowd with more schoolin' than us lot. But anyways, it don't matter which way ye choose so long as ye get it done somehow, and then live a fine old life doin' just as ye please, and not ever worryin' about it, whatever ye do. And so that's how I know Jenta's on the right path, havin' let all that go. Now she's picked out a real man, like Conch says, one with power and money, lots a' gold...so she'll get his power and his money, or at least all she needs of it. And after a while she'll forget all about her little hideaway self, and there's yer happy endin'."

After a silence, Dallis Trum said, "Don't seem like she got power. Seemed...like a bad thing, somehow."

"Ah, what do you know, ye little scrub? Ballast is all ye are, and all ye'll be if that's the way ye look at things. Take it from me, son. You give one a' those ways a try; ye'll see how it works."

"So which is it, Ham?" Dallis asked. "Did she do right? Or not?"

Ham sighed. "That's all for tonight, lads…"

There was another rustle in the reeds, this time to Delaney's left. The light was dimming on the pond now, and the shadows deepening, but that same something lurked again. Or perhaps, a different something.

"Surroundin' me, are ye?" Delaney asked. There was no answer, and he expected none. "Probably just gettin' a good seat for the show," he muttered.

The air seemed cooler now, though it was far from cool. He looked up at the sky again, and tried to guess how much time he had before dark. How much time he had left. A couple of hours, anyway. Then he'd be going on to the next life, and he'd find out if there was something over there on the other side, like Avery and the priests said, or if there was nothing but a big nothing out there, like Sleeve said. Delaney sure didn't know, and he didn't know how anyone could find out, other than going on ahead and dying.

It didn't really seem fair. It was hard enough for a man to guess what the future would bring to him on the earth—and that's where he could make all the plans he wanted, and try to bring a particular thing about. How was he supposed to guess what happened after, where no one could see and no word ever came back from?

And if a man's supposed to do good on the earth, why is the doing of it so hard? Like pushing a sledge up a hill, and not an empty one, either, but one full of all kinds of the heavy goods of life, and it keeps sliding back on top of him. The plain fact is, it's hard to do good. And then when you do good, it hurts more often than it helps. Look at Wentworth. He turned good, and what happened? Wham! Took it square in the kisser. Jenta tried to do good, too, helping Wentworth, and then helping the Gatemen. What did she get for her trouble? Wham! Shayla tried all her life for a better place for her daughter. Wham! Avery Wittle? Wham! Father Dent? Wham! And Delaney. One good deed, saving a little girl, and—Wham! *Onka Din Botlay.*

Mermonkeys.

The more Delaney puzzled, the darker his thoughts grew. What kind of world is it where the Conchs get rich and the Dents get whammed? It was enough to make a man angry. Enough to turn a man mean. Enough to make anyone want to throw the whole thing overboard, turn pirate, and have done with it. Like Sleeve said.

And not only that, why was it easy to turn bad and hard to turn back good again? How did that make any sense? Like gravity isn't enough, everyone else has got to go and lean on the sledge from the other side, pushing it back toward the pit, back on top of the poor man trying to move it up the hill. Whatever it was that Jenta did to make Wentworth turn good, there with the Scriptures and the prayers and all, it must have been like pulling teeth. Delaney never did learn what it was. But he got some clues when he'd heard Ham talking about it to one of the men on deck, while the three of them were cleaning their pistols after a little target practice on some sea turtles.

"How did he do it?" the young sailor asked. "How did Wentworth turn all good like he done?"

"Now son," Ham started. "You know this is dangerous territory. You sure you want to hear about it?"

"Aye. I'm not scared."

"You hear it, though, you might just start heading in that direction. The Whale catches wind, and you might want to reconsider getting scared."

The sailor shrugged. "Just want to know, that's all. Not sayin' I'll do a thing with it."

"I don't know if I ought." Ham looked down the barrel of his pistol, then rammed a rag down it with a cleaning rod. "Tell you what, I'll tell you a part of the story I didn't tell the others, if you want to hear it. You do what you will with it."

"Sure!"

"Okay. Well, this was back when Wentworth first started visiting Father Dent."

"The scarred-up priest?"

"Aye, the very one. You remember how Wentworth complained to Jenta about how hard it was that, when he tried to turn and do what's right, suddenly he's face-to-face with so much more that's wrong, which he never did see before?"

"He was talkin' about his daddy's agreement with the Conch, which he never knew about whilst drinkin' his life away. Sure, I remember."

"So he tells Carter Dent the same thing, and the priest just nods. Then he explains. 'The holy Scriptures,' he says, 'tell us that good men and women will have three enemies, and each one is worse than the next. They are your own flesh, then the world around you, and lastly the devil below. Wentworth, you overcame the first one. With the help of Jenta and by the grace of God, you beat back the flesh, which is your desire for drinking and gambling and womanizing. But with that one managed, you then came face-to-face with the world. It came dressed as your father, but it was really all the business that's done in this world that needs a heavy dose of evil to keep it going. To keep all the money rolling in. And I can warn you, too, that once you stand against the world, the world will turn you straight over to the devil.'"

"You mean the Conch?" the young sailor asked.

Ham shrugged. "Are you sure you want to know more about this?"

The sailor swallowed hard. "Jenta saved him, though, right? There at the poker table? So it didn't go all bad for him. And then there's Damrick. What about him? He licked all his enemies, didn't he?"

"Ah, but you haven't heard the end of their stories yet."

"No, I guess not." He thought a moment longer, scratched a patchy beard. "Still, I'd like to know how it works. How a man turns good. But just to know," he repeated.

"Okay, then." Ham took a deep breath. Then he spoke low, in a whisper so quiet that Delaney had to lean in close to overhear. "There's passages of Scripture that are straight about it. Tell you plainly what you must do to be saved."

"What do they say?" the sailor asked, also in a whisper, eyes wide.

"They say it's all about believing. It happens inside." Ham tapped his chest.

"Oh." The sailor seemed disappointed. "'Cause I thought it had to do with priests. You know, wavin' their hands and chantin' certain things over you."

"I'm not saying that can't help. But here's the thing. There are certain particulars that if you agree with them, even once, just one time in the secrecy of your own heart, why, you'll cross over from darkness to light. And there's no turning back neither, because once you do that, you've handed your very soul over to God. And He don't ever forget. And He don't ever let go. Now. Do you want to know what those things are, those things you got to agree with and believe?" Ham asked.

"Aye," the sailor nodded, his mouth open, his eyes wide.

Then Ham looked over toward Delaney, who had stopped cleaning his pistol and was hanging on every word, his heart in his throat. "How about you?" Ham asked him. "You want to know what those things are?"

"No sir!" Delaney said, shooting to his feet, heart hammering his chest like a drum. "No, I was just needin' to go get some more oil!"

Ham pointed to the can of gun oil at his feet.

Delaney looked at that can like it would grab his ankle. "No, not that oil. Some other oil," he explained, and he collected up his pistol parts and got out of there as quick as he could.

But now he kind of wished he'd stayed. Just to know. Whatever it was, it must be a very hard thing to agree with, Delaney figured, because so few turned good. Those Scriptures must say that you have to believe something that's almost impossible to believe. Otherwise more would believe it, some maybe even accidentally, and then they'd end up turning good in spite of themselves.

Delaney watched that sailor close, from then on. He wanted to see if he ever went good, and then if he got whammed. But there was never anything to notice. Maybe he'd hang back a bit from a plunder, where jumping in would have got him some nice silverware or a brooch or something. But that could have been caused by indigestion, or any other little thing. It was hard to say there was a change. Until one day in port, he didn't come back to the ship. Maybe he'd got killed or jailed. Or maybe he just didn't feel like pirating anymore. If that was the case, then the next time the Whale saw him, he'd get whammed for sure. Pirate captains put up with a lot of strange behaviors, but one thing that they could not tolerate was disloyalty.

Another was cowardice. Delaney sighed. He could feel a great, dark fear creeping up on him; a dark tide of gloom rolling in with the gloaming.

Chapter Twelve

WIDOWS MIGHT

Dancer Clang received the news at about two in the morning. The captain of the *Widows Might* set down her mug, folded her hand, rose from the card table and collected her winnings. Then she went about the task of rounding up her crew. The *Widow* had hit port just about dinner-time, and so the crew had been ashore just long enough to hurt them-selves in the usual ways in the usual taverns and inns. But Dancer Clang understood the lure of gold.

By six in the morning almost all of her sailors had shuffled, staggered, or been carried aboard. Those that weren't retching over the gunwales were standing, sitting, or reclining on the main deck, where they found gallons of hot coffee steaming in an open pot, and a table laid out with pounds of sausages and sliced smoked hams, dozens of boiled eggs, and a vat of porridge.

By ten, they were under sail.

By three, they had caught the much slower freighters.

Damrick Fellows watched the ship through a spyglass. This was the latest of half-a-dozen gray shadows that had lurked on one horizon or another since they left port. But unlike the others, this one had sailed close enough to see and be seen clearly, close enough that the Gatemen recognized her black standard, and the white skull emblazoned on it. Close enough that she in turn was sure to have seen the blood-red flags of the Gatemen, one flying over each of the three rogue Ryland ships as they sailed north in tight formation. But Damrick was watching the curious ship's stern now. She had turned away, apparently content to sail on like the rest.

"That's pirates," Lye said with a nod. "They fight those who'll run, and run from those who'll fight."

"*Widows Might*," Damrick told him. "That's Dancer Clang's ship."

"Dancer Clang? Here, let me look." Damrick gave up the telescope to his friend and partner. "She's really a woman, ye think?" Lye asked.

"That's what they say. But woman or man, if the *Widow* comes in range we'll take her down."

Lye adjusted the barrels, trying to make the ship come into focus. "I never fought no woman before." After a few moments he lowered the apparatus, disappointed. He could see nothing particularly feminine about the cutter. "Just feels wrong, don't it? Fightin' a woman."

"Do you suppose she'll have pity on you because you're a man?"

"The opposite, what I hear."

Damrick took the telescope back. After a moment, he said, "She's not retreating. She's coming about." The ship had approached from starboard astern, on the same northerly heading as their own *Ayes of Destiny*. The wind was from the southeast, and all fours ships were on a starboard tack. Though she kept her distance, Clang had brought the *Widow* up almost even with the Gatemen, just a couple of points abaft the beam, before turning hard to starboard, showing them her stern as if in retreat. But now it was clear she wasn't running; she held her starboard turn until she was beating to windward, and past. Now she was coming across the wind facing southeast, in irons, but only for the moment. As Damrick watched, her crew brought the boom of the mainsail across the ship's stern. The sail luffed momentarily, then caught full. Now she was on a port tack that would take her directly behind all three freighters, and quickly.

"That cutter is fast," Damrick reported. "Better call the men to stations. Rather it be too early than too late."

The cry went up, and the *Ayes of Destiny* and her two sister ships, *Blue Horizon* and *Lion's Pride*, burst into activity. Sailors scrambled into the rigging, sharpshooters collected their long guns and positioned themselves at the rails, and smithies stoked up their stoves. For this voyage, each ship had not one, but three small furnaces, one positioned near each mast. And this time they were not manned by novices like Lye Mogene, but by blacksmiths and ironwrights who'd been selected from the recruits in

Skaelington for just this purpose. The marksmen would not run low on hot loads again.

But while the smiths were more experienced, the shooters were less so. With all the volunteers to choose from, Damrick had found many with sailing experience, and many more crack shots. But finding men who had sea legs and dead eyes, both, was a challenge. Generally, Damrick had chosen in favor of those who could shoot. But he knew that the skill required to account for the motion of a ship on the waves was not one that could be acquired in a day, nor in a week, nor even in a month. He hoped that the sheer numbers of hot iron musket balls from a dozen more shooters would help to balance out the experience and the precision he'd lost.

And, he had one new idea he was anxious to try.

"Let's make quick work of these tubs," Dancer Clang sang out. "There's a heap a' gold on every one of 'em. It's two coins apiece if we can show we took 'em down today."

Her crew, mostly recovered from their intemperate night, shouted out their support.

The *Widows Might* was a small ship, and the crew was a small outfit, just twenty-five souls. But they were among the most successful pirates on the seas, and every hand aboard was rich by almost any count. Clang was not the cruelest, nor the most colorful, nor the greediest, nor even the most cunning of pirate captains. But no one could deny that she was among the most successful.

She had never been a dancer. That was a myth. Dancer was her given name, bestowed by parents who expected somewhat more delicate graces. "Clang" was the nickname. It replaced her married name, which she'd quit using shortly after her first husband died of severe gastric distress, a disorder commonly assumed to have been brought on by a generous dash of arsenic in his evening stew. Running from the law, she dropped her last name altogether, disguised herself as a man, and joined the first cutthroat crew she found sailing from port. As a pirate, she was known simply as Dancer. By the time her secret was known, it didn't much matter. She'd already proven herself with a sword and a pistol and a dirk—not the greatest technique but as bloodthirsty as any. The revelation of her gender caused slackened jaws and amazed oaths and whispered comments, but then she settled right back into the work.

Her new last name came years later, when she struck out on her own.

She found a ship she fancied and commandeered it, stealing it from the harbor of a southern port with the help of a handful of accomplices. She quickly proved to be an excellent captain. She knew how to sail, and she understood strategy. And she knew how to motivate her men. It was her habit, after a successful raid, to dole out shares in gold coin while sitting at a tin-covered table.

"Love that clang," she'd say.

Pretty soon her crew took to the term. "Let's go collect our clang." And, "I reckon that ship's carrying a whole lotta clang." Once the term came to mean plunder, it was only a matter of time before they hung it on the captain herself, who kept them knee-deep in it and, more importantly, kept them alive to enjoy it. They in turn happily took and kept their oaths of allegiance. Clang's crew developed a reputation. They took a vicious, carnivorous pride in their work. They were good at it, and they knew it.

The woman who could inspire such fierce loyalty in two-dozen brutes stood five-feet-four-inches tall, and weighed one hundred and forty pounds. She was no beauty, but neither was she the hag that rumors would have her be. Now at almost forty years of age, her round face was lined but not wrinkled. Her skin was weathered but not leathered. She wore a black bandana tied tight around her skull, from under which tufts of stringy blond hair escaped. Her only adornment was a thin gold coin, an ostentatious bit of clang garnered from some tropical kingdom. She wore it as an earring.

But those who met her rarely remarked about her appearance. They always commented on her tenacity, her drive. "That's one tough woman," they'd say. Or "I'd hate to be the man standing in her way when she wants something."

Right now, the man standing in her way was Damrick Fellows.

"Stand by hot loads," Hale Starpus called out. The orders were relayed not just to the crew of the *Destiny*, but through a flagman to the *Horizon* and the *Pride* as well. The smiths were already busy. "Hot shot coming!" one of the men with the mitts shouted, sweat pouring from him.

"Don't get anxious on me!" Hale called back. "Hold for my order!"

"That thing is fast," Damrick repeated, as the cutter raced toward them.

"They ain't turnin', Captain," Dancer Clang's first mate told her. He was six-feet-four, slouched, scarred, rumpled, calm as sunset. "They gonna let us run up on 'em?"

"They may," she answered.

"That's a lot a' smoke. Maybe they're burnin', is why they take no notice."

"They're heating their cannon shot," she said, watching the smoke rise from the decks of all three ships.

The mate looked with renewed respect on their prey. "The Gatemen," was all he said.

"Aye, the Gatemen. Let's fly by, and see what they've got. What do you guess is their range?" She handed the first mate her telescope.

"As far as cannon, it looks like swivel guns is all. Four I can see on the starboard rails. None fore, none aft. All small bore. Maybe four-pounders. Range…three-hundred yards, I'd say. If they can shoot."

"They can shoot." She took back the scope, studied a while longer. "Don't recognize the make of cannon. Plenty of musketeers, for what good that'll do 'em." She lowered the spyglass. "They all say this Damrick Fellows is cagey. I don't see it. He looks like a duck on our pond."

"Then let's kill 'im and roast 'im."

"Pass the stern of the laggard ship at about two-and-a-half-hundred yards. See what they do. In and out quick as you please."

"Aye, aye." The mate gave the orders.

"They're in range, Damrick," Hale told him. "Give the order and we fire."

Damrick leaned on the starboard rail of the quarterdeck. Lye Mogene eyed the approaching ship through a spyglass. "They got six guns to a side. Half of 'em smashers."

"Smashers? Lemme see," Hale said. Lye gladly handed off the scope, and the responsibility.

Damrick was thoughtful for a moment. "Carronades on a sloop like that. Why?"

"They're smaller and lighter?" Lye suggested.

"That's a close-range, high-impact cannon," Hale said. "They look to be forty-pounders. Like dropping rocks onto a paper boat. But their range can't be a hundred yards."

"They mean to get close, then," Lye stated.

Damrick nodded. "She can fly loops around us. She expects us to turn to her, to give her a broadside. Then she'll use her speed to stay astern, get in close, where most ships have only a swivel gun."

"Like we did to *Savage Grace*."

Hale sniffed. "Only it'll be us this time chasin' our tail around till we're in irons and she's got us from the rear."

A corner of Damrick's lip rose. "So she's a dancer after all. And she wants to lead. Let's see what she does if we decline the offer. Hold all fire. Steady as she goes."

"They ain't turnin'," the first mate said.

"I can see that," Dancer Clang answered. "So what's our range now, two-fifty?"

"Mebbe a little more."

"What have they got? They're baiting us. Why?"

The first mate had the telescope. "Nothin' aft but a lot a men with rifles lined up across the stern. Four swivel cannon to starboard." A pause. "That's it, Captain."

"What about the other two ships?"

"Same thing."

"Let's pull out, make a run right at the laggard. This time from dead astern."

"Aye, aye, Captain. That oughta spook 'em."

Damrick watched the little cutter turn away to port, retreating once again. "She's circling away."

Just then the captain of the *Ayes of Destiny* walked up. "You know your business, Mr. Fellows. But I know mine, too. If that ship runs at us again, we'll need evasive maneuvers. We can't let her have our stern."

"Yes we can," Damrick countered evenly. "She wants our stern, we'll give it to her. Furl some of the jib and ease the mainsheet. Let's make sure we're in the rearmost position."

He stared at Damrick.

"So she'll attack us."

"Yes, sir."

The captain, a distinguished man of sixty-two, stood dumbfounded. "You want her to attack our stern? She'll take out our rudder."

"We need her in range of our small arms."

"I thought your cannon were long-range weapons."

"They're also small bore. We need close range to pour fire into her. Give her our stern, Captain, and we'll take care of the rest."

"Like I say, you know your business, but—"

"If that's all, Captain, I've got a battle to fight here." Damrick didn't look at the officer he'd just dismissed.

"I hope you know what you're doing," he said with a snarl, and then turned stiffly and walked away.

"She's comin' about again," Lye noted. Then, "She's a quick one, that *Widow*."

"Directly astern," Damrick noted. "Good. Go get the guns."

"Now?" Hale asked.

"Keep the men astern, so they block her vision. Make sure the other ships do the same." Lye saw the fire in his eyes now. "Come on, Dancer," he said to her. "Let's dance."

"They still ain't turnin', Captain," the first mate said.

Dancer shook her head. "They're fools. I expected more. Bring all the buckets to the main deck, and fill them. We'll take some fire. But so will they."

The first mate went off to make it so.

"Cannon ready?" Damrick asked, tension in his voice.

"Almost, sir," one of the sailors said, turning a wrench as he spoke. Damrick had four cannon per ship, thanks to the generosity of his patron. But he had sixteen mounting plates: four per side, four astern, four on the bows. When the *Widow* first appeared on the horizon, Damrick had ordered all four cannon mounted on the starboard side. Now, on Damrick's order, all four were moved to the stern. Sailors and riflemen stood clustered around the guns at the weather deck rail, blocking all view of the activity. The cutter was coming up dead astern, with no visibility to the starboard rail. On the *Blue Horizon* and the *Lion's Pride*, men clustered on the starboard rails as well, disguising both the removal of cannon there and the remounting astern.

In all, sixteen long-range guns were being prepared, all aimed at one sixty-foot cutter.

"Range?" Hale shouted.

"Two-fifty!" came the call from the lookout.

"And closing," Lye offered.

"Hard aport, *Horizon* and *Pride*," Damrick called to Lye. "Let's give them clear shots."

The message was relayed, and the two sister ships, both downwind from the *Destiny*, began to drift away from formation. As they did, their sterns faced directly at the *Widows Might*.

"Let's load them up," Damrick said to Hale.

"Hot loads!" Hale Starpus yelled, and he rumbled off to supervise, his long side-whiskers blowing in the breeze.

Dozens of shooters now left the rails, joining those already standing at the ovens. Smithies began dropping bright-red musket balls down barrels. As soon as a man had his load, he rushed to the stern rail.

"We're closing in on one-fifty, Captain."

Dancer Clang said nothing, but peered through her spyglass.

"What's happening?" the first mate asked his mistress. "Them ships leavin' formation?"

She lowered the telescope. Doubt floated up behind her eyes. She had been watching the activity at the stern, but there were too many men crowded at the rails for her to fathom what it meant. None of the three vessels had stern cannon. Why would they separate now, and expose themselves even more? She looked through her telescope again. Then the crowd of sailors at *Destiny*'s rail suddenly parted, revealing four guns where none had been.

"Retreat," she said.

"What?" the mate asked.

"Pull out! Hard to starboard! Now!"

Damrick gave the order. On Hale Starpus's command, all stern swivel guns fired: sixteen cannon blasts came in the space of a few seconds. Every one of them found a target. These long-range cannon were fired at short range. Each missile penetrated the hull twice: once entering, once exiting. Sixteen cannon rounds opened thirty-two holes in the little cutter. And since the angle of the guns was steep, firing down on the smaller ship, the cutter's exit wounds were all under water.

The fury of the blasts jarred the ship; the deck shuddered violently, knocking pirates off their feet. Four of the twenty-five souls aboard were knocked into the ocean. The *Widow*'s efforts to turn and flee were slowed as sailors regained their feet, and moved back to the rigging amid flying debris and fallen comrades.

And then came the rain of fire.

Hundreds of bright-red musket balls traced paths through the air, all drawn, it seemed, to the *Widow*. Men staggered, cried out, fell. The boom of the mainmast came free, then swept across the stern, battering two more sailors into the ocean.

The array of tin and wooden buckets set out on deck to prepare for fires, those that weren't already toppled by cannon fire, now collected some of the errant shot. Musket balls plinking through metal pails made a sound oddly like a coin hitting a tin table. Dancer Clang heard it. She saw and heard it all, the red tracers, the slap of iron into wood, the flying splinters, the steam and sizzle of hot iron into water. The steam and sizzle of hot iron into flesh. Smoke rising where heated shot struck wood. Then the flames. Men crying out in pain. Gasps, bodies thudding to the decks. And the endless, nonstop crack, crack, crack of rifle fire like a drumroll, all from the weather decks of three slow, lightly armed, heavily laden freighters. And in her grew the realization that this voyage was over. There would be no gold coins today.

And then came a second round of cannon fire. Large chunks of the small ship flew into the air. The deck shuddered, cracked. The cutter listed hard to starboard. The *Widow* was sinking fast, and burning as she went down.

And then suddenly it stopped. The rain of fire ended. The smoke drifted clear of the stern of all three ships. And the three ships sailed on silently, somber men watching as though at attention.

Dancer Clang stood at a shattered rail, now angled severely as the ship began to heel over. The mast, cut almost in half by a shell from the second volley, now cracked, then broke just above her head. It groaned and splintered like a tree falling. Canvas floated down from the sky and rested in the sea. Her instinct was to assess the damage, to count the casualties. But she couldn't bring her mind to the task. The losses were total. Instead, she watched the three ships sailing under red flags as they left her behind, just so much wreckage in their wake. And a bitter truth rose in her. They hadn't slowed. They'd lost no time. She'd been no more than a minor inconvenience.

"Hey! Come back!" a pirate called out. And then another shouted, "We surrender!"

"Buck up, men!" Dancer bellowed at them. All heads turned to her. "They beat us. They're leaving us here. Grab something that floats, and abandon ship."

But then, one of the ships, the laggard they had tried to attack, began a turn to starboard.

"They're comin' back!" one man cried out. Other men cheered.

But Dancer Clang just watched, recognizing a maneuver she herself had performed more than once.

"You're circling back for survivors?" The speaker was Windall Frost. The old gentleman clung to the starboard rail of the quarterdeck as the ship shuddered through the surf.

Damrick lowered the spyglass. He wasn't looking at what he'd left behind, but what might be yet to come, scanning the horizon in all directions. "I'm circling back. But not to pick up survivors."

The old man seemed agitated. But he said no more.

Damrick looked down at his boots, then back up to the sky. "Should we leave them to tell the Conch and his hordes how we win our victories?"

"I see." Windall Frost sighed. "Nasty business, isn't it?"

"Yes." Damrick showed no patience. "If you're having trouble with it, sir, perhaps you should go back to your cabin. I suspect there'll be more of the same soon."

Frost just sighed. He looked old. "I own much responsibility," he said, "for the outcome of this voyage."

"Then I suggest you shoulder it, and carry it. Sir." Damrick meant the statement to have a knife's edge, to cut short the conversation.

But Frost just nodded and looked out over the ocean. "I wonder... how does one develop a fist of iron, to hammer back at injustice, without developing a heart to match?"

Now Damrick said nothing.

"I paid a visit to Runsford Ryland," Frost suddenly confessed.

"Ryland? When?"

"Two nights back. I called on him late, hoping to find out whether there was any chance he'd align himself with us. I couldn't even get to the subject, because of his anger at, well, at you."

"That was a big risk. You might have told me."

"You might have stopped me. I needed to visit a former employee of mine. She lives on Ryland's estate with her daughter, Wentworth's fiancée."

Damrick's eyes flashed.

"Well," Windall explained, reacting to the look, "It might have been quite awkward to be spotted on his grounds late at night, if I hadn't bothered to announce myself to him. So I had to stop in."

But that's not why Damrick's pulse had quickened. "Jenta's mother... worked for you?"

"Yes. For many years."

"Doing what?"

"Shayla was a household servant."

"A household..." he shook his head, as though trying to clear it. "I thought she was...you know. Born noble, or something."

"Who, Jenta?" Windall eyed Damrick carefully. "I didn't realize you'd met."

"We've met."

"Well, the royalty rumor has been going around in Skaelington. Runsford may have started it, actually. Wouldn't put it past him. But no. I can assure you that Jenta grew up in the cellar of my home. Her mother had a bit of bad luck with the girl's father, and found herself with few choices. It was Ryland moved them both to Skaelington, promising a better life."

Damrick turned to look out over the sea. He saw nothing but Jenta, ascending a gangway, waving from a carriage. Those eyes, so sad and worldly, now meant something completely different. The girl was not at all what she seemed. Even at that first dance.

But then, perhaps that meant she was not out of reach, either. He raised his telescope, scanned the horizon. Wind flapped at the canvas and the bosun called out orders. Timbers creaked and waves dashed themselves against the hull. The burning wreckage of the *Widows Might* grew larger as they approached. But Damrick saw only Jenta's face; heard only Jenta's voice.

...This time, you will come find me?

Runsford Ryland's desk was covered with ungainly piles of books of accounts, contracts, and notes. He had pored over the history of the small fleet he'd entrusted to his son, and now he stood, leaning heavily on the dark, polished walnut. He hung his head.

"Sir? Is there something I can do?"

Runsford raised his head slowly, looked at his assistant. "Yes." He looked with empty eyes at the bustle of his office through the plate-glass windows that surrounded him.

"Sir?"

Ryland nodded. "Have my yacht made ready. I'm sailing to Oster."

"When, sir?"

He turned on the man. "Just as soon as my yacht is ready! Now, go!"

It was one week later when the three rogue Ryland ships unloaded their goods in the Port of Oster, south of Mann. Though they'd seen many ships on the horizon, some certainly pirates, and several followed at a safe distance, no more had attacked Damrick and the Gatemen. Wentworth's little fleet arrived intact, and without another shot fired.

Now sugar, tea, and coffee were hoisted up from the holds, swung out onto the docks, accompanied by the grinding of chains, the screech of gulls, and the shouts of deckhands and shoremen. Chests of gold coin were carried under heavy arms to the local bank, where it would be divvied up among merchants whose goods had been sold in other ports.

News about who had accompanied and protected these ships, and what famous pirate they had defeated, spread quickly. Within hours, the piers and docks were filled with citizens come to welcome conquering heroes just in from glorious victories at sea.

"I guess they've heard of the Gatemen up here in Oster," Hale Starpus commented, looking down from the quarterdeck onto the crowd. People held up the flags of Nearing Vast, and even a few crudely made, crimson-stained flags of the Gatemen, swords crossed in a ragged "V." The people waved, they clapped, they chanted.

"Damrick should see all this," Lye marveled.

"Aye," Hale answered. "But the boss don't like to come out much."

Lye watched Hale, saw no apprehension. His eyes drifted back over the crowds. "You know he don't like a fuss. Makes 'im nervous the pirates'll come after us in port again, I reckon."

"I reckon he's right about that." Hale rubbed his hairy cheek with a knuckle. "What do you s'pose he does in there by hisself?"

Lye shrugged. "He thinks."

"About what?"

"About plannin'."

Hale considered that, looking back toward the cabin. "That's a whole lot a' plannin', then."

A fiddle player jumped up onto a dock post below them, facing the crowd. A smattering of applause met his short effort to tune up.

"He gonna sing one of them songs about the Gatemen?" Lye asked.

"Maybe. There's some still spreadin' around, I hear."

"I think Slow Slim's kinda squashed most a' that."

The fiddler tapped his toe, nodded his head, sawed his bow, and began singing. Very soon the crowd was clapping along with the lively rhythm, some even singing snatches of the words.

Young Damrick, he got angry
When they let ol' Sharkbit be,
So he took a pint of whiskey
And some pistols out to sea,
And he boarded Savage Grace
Just as pleasant as you please,
Said right to that pirate's face,
"You're a comin' back with me!"

Here the crowd cheered as the fiddler played a tuneful bridge. Then he began another verse:

Ol' Sharkbit shook his fist now
And he told his men to shoot,
But Damrick had four pistols
And a fifth one in his boot.
Four pirates fell in order,
Then he made the others dance;
And Sharkbit, he boiled over
When his cutthroats soiled their pants!

The crowd crowed their pleasure.

"He didn't make no one dance," Lye informed Starpus. "No one messed his britches neither, that I saw. That's all made up."

"Folks seem to like it, though," Hale noted.

Sharkbit pulled a knife to slit him,
But young Damrick pulled his gun;
Those pirates all yelled "Get him!"
But ol' Sharkbit was outdone.
Yes sir, Damrick pulled the trigger,
And there's no need to explain
What happens to a blaggard
When a Gateman takes his aim!

A great cheer arose, and then a smattering of calls for Damrick himself.

"Not much mention a' yours truly," Lye muttered.

"I thought you fell into the drink and missed it anyways," Hale offered.

"Most of it. So maybe it's better this way."

Very quickly the entire throng began chanting Damrick's name, demanding he come forth.

"I'm not going out there," the head Gateman told his two lieutenants, as they stood in his cabin. He was lying on his bunk, head and shoulders against the bulkhead. He needed a shave and his hair was mussed. He looked like he hadn't slept. Books were scattered about, some open. A quill stood up in an open inkwell beside several sheaves of foolscap covered with a careful, precise hand. A lamp and two candles burned, adding a soft haze to the direct light from the single open porthole.

"Listen to 'em!" Lye pleaded. "They started out happy, but you keep not showin' up. Now they sound about to turn mean."

"So are they for us, or against us?" Damrick asked.

"For us, a' course," Hale answered.

"Then why would they turn mean?"

Hale shrugged. "They just need someone to cheer on, I guess."

"Well, I don't feel like being the man they cheer on today."

"Ye don't care what they think?" Lye asked, stumped.

"No. And I don't know why you do. They left you out of their song completely."

"You heard it?"

"I heard it." He glanced up at the porthole.

"Well. That's true, they did. It was a good song, though. Spite a' that."

"I'll tell you what I care about, gentlemen. I care about those in the crowd who won't get angry just because I don't come take a bow. I care about those who believe in what we're doing, and will back us no matter what happens. I wouldn't give a chewed plug for a thousand crowds who cheer and sing songs when we're successful, and then disappear when we need them."

"But Damrick," Lye tried. "That was Mann. This is Oster. These are simpler folk. They only want to thank ye."

The crowd's restlessness grew into another chant. *Damrick! Dam-rick! DAM-rick! DAM-RICK!*

"If you won't go, then I'll go wave at 'em," Lye said. "Maybe they'll think I'm you, and go home."

"Go, then."

Damrick listened from inside his cabin as the chant turned to a great, raucous cheer. Then it suddenly died down amid calls of "Speech! Speech!"

"This won't go well," Damrick predicted.

Hale nodded. "Lye gets flustered, people lookin' at him."

After a moment's pause, they heard a faint voice, followed immediately by cries of "Louder!" and "We can't hear!"

The brief silence that followed ended with a shout from Lye Mogene. "I ain't Damrick, blame it all!"

Boos rained.

"He's an honest man," Damrick said pleasantly.

The chant was gone, but the rhythm returned. They stamped their feet and clapped in unison. It was a threatening cadence.

Lye burst back into Damrick's cabin as the cadence on the docks grew darker.

"How did it go?" Damrick asked, unable to keep the corner of his lip from rising.

"Not so good," he panted. "I think they still want you."

"All right, go give them this message. Tell them it's from me. Say, 'Damrick sends his thanks to you all. He will meet each one of you, one by one, as you either swear allegiance to the Gatemen's cause, or come against him in battle.'"

Lye's eyes went wide. "I can't say that."

"Why not?"

"It ain't what they wanna hear. They don't wanna swear nothin'. They just want to cheer ye."

"Tell them I'll meet them, one at a time, as they either swear to follow the Gatemen or meet us in battle. If they don't want to do either, then I'm sure they'll never see me. Now go. Do it." Damrick's eyes were hard.

Lye's shoulders slumped as he left the room.

Hale and Damrick heard boos, then heard the boos die down, and then heard Lye's voice.

"Damrick says thank ye!"

A smattering of applause.

"He says he'll see most of ye face-to-face sooner or later, if ye want to foller him, or if ye decide to fight against him. But that's it. He ain't comin' out, so quit yer bellyachin'!'"

Boos and threats rose again. Then they died down as Lye shouted, "Wait! Wait!" Amid mostly silence, Lye shouted, "That last bit about the bellyachin', that was from me, not him!"

And then the boos began again, but halfheartedly. They died away into grumbling. And by the time Lye returned to Damrick's cabin, his face redder than usual, the docks were quiet.

"Nice work," Damrick told him.

"Ahhhh," was his only reply.

At the back of the throng were six men who had not joined in the rhythmic demand for a glimpse of Damrick Fellows. They stood on the ragged stoop of the harbormaster's office as the crowd thinned. Two of them were deep in conversation. One of them, tall, gray at the temples, slightly round at the middle, spectacles pinched onto his nose, faced the other. It was Runsford Ryland, dressed in the white slacks and blue jacket of a captain. He made his points into the shorter man's ear. The shorter man stood with thick arms crossed, facing the crowd, watching the ship, apparently ignoring the harangue. This one wore no hat, and under his short-cropped hair could be seen several washboard rows of wrinkles that ran across the back of his scalp, behind his ears, above his neck. These wrinkles were not from age, just a healthy excess of flesh, both fat and muscle. He appeared to be somewhat less than persuaded. Flanking these two were four more men, four well-dressed and well-armed bodyguards. They also ignored Ryland's lecture.

"It's my ship," Ryland insisted. "He's a dangerous man. I demand that you come aboard with me."

Finally, the shorter man replied. "Demand all you want. You want him arrested, you need a warrant."

"I don't want him arrested. Not yet, anyway. Have you heard nothing I've been saying? I…want…your…protection! I need to speak to him, to find out whether he needs to be arrested. You can go aboard without a warrant, Sheriff, to protect citizens and their property," Ryland insisted. "That's what lawmen do."

"Thank you for telling me my business. You got your own bodyguards. Use them."

"I don't want a shoot-out. I want my ship. My ship. Ryland Shipping & Freight. I'm Ryland. Do you see the insignia on the stern?" He took off his cap. "Do you see the insignia here? I don't want a fight, I want your protection. As a citizen of Nearing Vast, I demand your protection."

"We can protect you, Mr. Ryland," one of the four men standing by said. He was tall, with long red hair, and his skin was blotched. Motley. "We don't need no lawmen." His look was a confident sneer.

Ryland ran an exasperated hand through his hair. "Thank you, Motley. I'm sure Fellows will respect your authority here."

Now the thick Sheriff spoke. "How do I know it's your ship? You got papers on it?"

"Papers?" The taller man grew apoplectic. "You want me to show you my papers? He's the one you need to ask about papers!"

The Sheriff spat.

Ryland stepped in front of him, locked eyes. "What was your name again?"

"Haggarty."

"Haggarty. Don't think I'll forget it. If my men are required to engage in gunplay to capture back my own ship, their blood will be on your hands."

"You got papers prove you own that ship, then we can talk."

"The *papers* are on the *ship*!"

The Sheriff was silent. He rubbed the bristles at the back of his neck with a big hand. Then he crossed his arms again, saying nothing.

Ryland looked upward, grinding his teeth. "I pity the people of Oster. What kind of law must this town have?"

At this point the shorter man turned to the taller one. Arms still crossed, he squinted up at the bitter face. "The kind of law that don't much like pirates."

Chapter Thirteen

SLOW SLIM'S REVENGE

"Runsford?" Damrick asked calmly. "Runsford Ryland?"

Lye Mogene nodded. "He's on deck, dressin' down the Captain, askin' after you."

Damrick, still lying on his bunk, now with his hands laced behind his head, just stared up at the ceiling. Word was out then, in Skaelington. Word had gotten to Ryland almost immediately. "Is Wentworth with him?"

"Didn't see the son."

Damrick sat up on the bunk. "Well, show him in."

"He ain't happy."

"Show him in."

"He's got goons with 'im."

Damrick shook his head. "Just Ryland."

"Aye." His lieutenant gone, Damrick stood slowly, then carefully picked up a pistol from the small table beside the bed. It was one of two new ones he'd purchased in Skaelington, as part of the refit of the Gatemen. It had two barrels, side by side. He turned it over, checked the loads. It felt good in his hand. He tucked it into his belt behind his back.

The door burst open. Damrick expected Runsford Ryland to come in like a hornet's nest rolling down a hill. But he didn't. He walked straight to Damrick, stood before him. "Damrick Fellows, at last. What an honor." He put out a hand.

Damrick watched him carefully, declining to shake. Runsford wore a silk shirt under his blue jacket. He was awash in cologne. "Close the door," Damrick said quietly, but not to Ryland.

The door closed.

Ryland didn't turn away. "Well. I would say we have much to discuss."

"Do we?"

"I think so, yes. You are illegally in possession of my ships."

"I have a contract with Wentworth Ryland."

"Let's see it."

Damrick glanced down at the writing desk. He pulled a folded parchment from the bottom of the pile, and handed it to Runsford.

Runsford tore it in half and tossed both pieces back onto the desk. "You have nothing."

"I have your three ships full of my armed men."

Ryland sighed, and turned away. "I'm not afraid of you, Fellows. Obviously you are not afraid of me." He turned back. "That's good. We can speak as equals. But I'm here to tell you that you and your men are hanging upside down over an alligator pit. You need a new contract, a new deal. I have come here to offer you the terms."

"What happened to Wentworth?"

"He's no longer in charge. You need to deal with me, and I'll tell you why."

Damrick waited.

Ryland stepped in close, rising to his full height, his hands folded behind his back. "I'll speak in a language I know you'll understand. I can have the Royal Navy hunt you down on the sea. I can have the Royal Dragoons hunt you down on land. I can put a price on your head in every port in every country on the ocean, a price so high mothers will be begging their sons to kill you. You will have nowhere to turn, nowhere to run. Do I have your attention?"

Damrick studied him. "You won't do any of that."

Runsford lowered his eyebrows. "My dear sir, I didn't get where I am by making idle threats. I run the largest shipping line in the world. Perhaps you've heard."

Damrick's hand came up like a viper striking, grabbing Ryland at the neck. He shoved the older man backward, three quick steps across the cabin, and pinned him roughly and painfully to the wall with a thud—Ryland's skull cracking on wood. His boatman's cap fell to the floor.

"You're a pirate, Ryland," Damrick breathed. Now his pistol flashed, in an instant its cold barrels were pressed to Ryland's cheek. "I shoot pirates." He cocked a hammer back, and raised an eyebrow. "Perhaps you've heard."

Ryland's head spun and his throat gurgled. He grabbed at Damrick's hands, but they were like rocks, like oaks. "You can't kill me," he croaked.

"Can't I?"

"That would be murder."

"Yes. Murder. Just the way you and your pirates do it. You think honest men and women will never cross that line? You pay pirates; you bribe governments; you play all sides. And you think you're safe. You think you can come in here and threaten me and never worry what I might do. Not because of your strength or your wits or your money or your deals, but because you're sure decent people won't murder you. You're protected by the goodwill of the very people you cheat and rape and slaughter, because you know they won't quit being good just because you're evil. They won't become like you, just to destroy you. And you count on that. But give simple men and women hope that someone who holds their principles will fight you, let them believe there's one of their own who'll stand up for once, toe to toe, and they'll rise up. And you'll be gone. That's why I scare you and Conch and every other pirate. And that's why I'll kill you."

Finally, doubt drifted through Ryland's eyes. "We can talk about this."

"No, we can't." Damrick moved the pistol's double barrels from Ryland's cheek to his temple, pressed hard. Ryland tried to turn his head away, but the pistol pinned it to the wall. "I'm not a complex man, Mr. Ryland. I see a rat, and I kill it."

"Please." He let go of Damrick's hands, brought his own up, palms forward. "Please. Let's just talk about this. We can come to an arrangement."

Damrick shook his head. He cocked back the other hammer. "I don't make deals with pirates. Goodbye, Mr. Ryland."

"I can give you Conch Imbry."

Damrick hesitated. "And why would you do that?"

Runsford Ryland closed his eyes. "Because he killed my son."

Damrick lowered the pistol. He watched Ryland until he was convinced he saw truth, then turned away. He sat on the bed. He crossed his arms, pistol in his right hand. He studied the old man before him, who now looked weak and spent. "What happened?"

"I tried to stop him," Ryland said, rubbing his temple. "But there was nothing I could do. It caught me by surprise. If I had known of your deal with Wentworth, I could have saved him."

"By double-crossing me, no doubt."

"Yes. Maybe. I don't know. But I could have planned something to stem Conch's vengeance. He felt betrayed. He *was* betrayed."

"Wentworth was a good man."

"He was a fool." Now he looked hard at Damrick. "He hired the Gatemen, signed a contract, helped you recruit all those members right under Conch's nose, and then had you sail out of his home port, flags flying, without so much as a way to explain any of it."

"How much do you know?"

"I know everything. Wentworth kept books on everything."

"What does Conch know?"

"He found out before I did."

"From Wentworth?"

"No."

"How, then?"

"How would I know? He has ways."

"Guess."

He took a deep breath. "I'd guess it was Jenta who told him."

"Jenta? Why would she do that?"

He shrugged. "She's a woman. I saw her dance with Captain Imbry. I've seen them…together…a couple of times. There is a spark there. He's a persuasive man. Wentworth was extremely jealous. She never actually liked Wentworth very much."

"But she was engaged to him."

"Engaged! That little arrangement was between her mother and me. Jenta's heart was elsewhere."

Damrick's darkness turned foul. "Where is Jenta now?"

"With Conch Imbry aboard the *Shalamon*, as far as I know. Look, Mr. Fellows, I didn't come here to threaten you. I blustered a bit, no harm in that…I like to negotiate from strength. But I'm not so foolish, whatever you may think, as to come in here unarmed expecting a fight. Ryland Shipping & Freight needs you. Wentworth was right to believe I would favor your help. He was only wrong to hide it from me. And of course, to reveal all his plans to that lowbrow little girl."

Damrick's jaw tightened. "So." He looked hard at Ryland. "Tell me how you're going to get me the Conch."

"Yer all dead men," the goon said, raising the tension level to one notch below fisticuffs. "Ye know that, don't ye?" There were only four of them, and they were surrounded by some twenty Gatemen. But they had no intention of being intimidated. Rather, their leader seemed eager to provoke. "Conch Imbry'll see to that," Motley said.

"I swear, if Damrick wasn't talkin' to yer boss right now," Lye Mogene told him, "you four'd a' been bled out like slit pigs long before ye got one fancy boot heel aboard this ship." He didn't take his eyes off the long-haired villain in cut coat and vest. By trade, Ryland's goons were sailors, though they adapted easily enough to the role of bodyguards and mercenaries in the employ of a shipping magnate. By dress they might have been confused with high-ranking dignitaries of some foreign city. But by action and habit, they were easily identified as pirates. Conch Imbry, after all, supplied Ryland with his muscle.

Motley just laughed. "All talk. Why not shoot me now? Afraid to pull that little popper at yer belt?"

"I'd like nothin' better. Looks to me like ye come aboard dressed for burial anyways."

The Gatemen laughed.

Motley took it, then said, "Sorry we ain't got the style to suit you boys. I'm sure the ladies in these backwater towns go all atwitter when they see ye wearin' them stirrup straps on yer arms, and them plucked chicken feathers in yer hats."

Motley's fellow goons now laughed. "Red chicken feathers!" one of them said with dull glee. "That's fancy, all right!"

Lye thought a moment, then said, "Well, I'm sure yer women think yer just the king's britches in them boots and vests. Course, when yer payin' 'em, I reckon they'll say about anything you want."

Now the Gatemen crowed. But Lye watched the goon's eyes, and saw he was ready to draw.

"Do it," Lye dared him, his hand on his pistol hilt. "A dash a' red will look good with that shiny white shirt."

"You first," Motley answered. "Or maybe ye want to dye them feathers yellow?"

Lye held his tongue but kept his hand on his pistol hilt.

At that moment, Damrick and Ryland walked out onto the main

deck together, and all eyes turned. When their two leaders turned to one another and shook hands, the goons and the Gatemen looked equally bewildered.

"Good doing business with you," Ryland said.

"We sail in three days. For Skaelington," Damrick told him. There was a warning in the words.

"Three days. I'll be ready." Ryland nodded. He turned to his men. "Let's go."

"What the…" Lye began, watching the five men depart the ship. "What happened in there, Damrick?"

Damrick took a deep breath. "I made a deal."

"With the devil."

"Maybe."

"What's the deal?"

"If he can be trusted, he'll give us Conch Imbry."

"And if he can't be trusted?"

"He'll give us hell."

At the bottom of the gangway, Motley stopped Ryland, stood in front of him. "You made a deal with them squid?" Motley's loyalty to Conch clearly ran deeper than his loyalty to Ryland.

"I did indeed," Ryland confirmed.

"What kind a' deal?"

"The kind that buys us three days." He glanced around. "Keep walking." Motley fell in next to Ryland. "I've got a job for you men. Go round up every gun hand you can find. Every pirate, bounty hunter, outlaw, and misfit that can pull a trigger. Get them down here from Mann if you can. Sober up the drunks. Empty the jails. Bribe the jailors if you have to. But try not to kill anyone. Keep it quiet; the citizens think these men are heroes, and will sound an alarm. But get me an army here. I'll round up all the weapons and ammunition you need."

Motley looked energized. "What's the plan, boss?"

"I just told you the plan! We're going to kill off the Gatemen. Right here in port, before they ever set sail."

The next day, the activity was intense in the small section of the docks where Ryland's three ships were moored. In these close quarters goods for the three ships were hauled in and unloaded from wagons and carts. Crates and sacks and boxes filled with linens and hardware, nails and gunpowder had to be checked and weighed, then netted and loaded on pallets, then hoisted up and over the rails into the holds. There was so much happening that some of the Gatemen were assigned to do nothing but block access from the street. With a tight cordon in place, they turned back all well-wishers and onlookers, assuring that only those with legitimate business could pass.

The shoremen and the crewmen were efficient. What usually took three hours took two. What generally took a day took little more than half. By nightfall on the second day, the activity had thinned and the docks returned to their usual level of bustle. There was little left to be done now but to load the crew's rations and wait for one last wagonload of ammunition. Despite the return of a more leisurely pace, the checkpoints scattered around the docks remained. No one got near a Ryland ship without showing proof of official business.

Runsford Ryland was not seen. His men reported to him from the docks, but he conducted most of his business for those three days from an elegant hotel room in the heart of the city. All sorts of characters came and went, bearing messages in and out. During the day, he saw businessmen and merchants. At night his guests grew rougher; late at night, they grew seedy.

But one nighttime visitor stood out. He wore robes, and not the simple gray of a common priest, but the white and yellow of high office. He entered Ryland's suite with a letter in his hand, a parchment bearing the seal of the High Holy Reverend and Supreme Elder of the Church of Nearing Vast.

A few minutes later, he left Ryland's quarters without it.

Sheriff George "Grub" Haggarty tapped his badge as he passed the checkpoint, then wandered onto the docks below the *Ayes of Destiny*. He stood for a moment, looking her up and down. Two Gatemen, braided leather armbands in place, stood at the foot of the gangway. Haggarty sauntered up to them, touched his badge again.

"Need to talk to your man Damrick Fellows."

They looked at one another. "We'll call him out."

"Mind if I go up?" he asked.

The two guards looked at one another again. Then one said, "I'll go with you."

Haggarty gestured with an open hand, inviting the Gateman to go first.

The guard shook his head. "You go."

The Sheriff climbed the gangway.

"Excuse me," he said to a sailor who brushed past him, carrying a duffel up. Haggarty flattened himself against the gangway rail, looking behind him to be sure he wasn't in anyone else's way. Then he hiked the rest of the way up onto the deck.

"The Sheriff here," the Gateman said to the three men stationed at the top of the rail, "wants to see Damrick."

"I'll go get him," one of them answered. But instead he went up the stairs to Lye Mogene, who stood on the quarterdeck. They spoke. Both men turned and looked at the Sheriff. Then Lye came down the stairs. The Sheriff put his hand out as Lye approached.

"I'm not Damrick," Lye told him. "I just work for him."

"I know who you are." He smiled and shook Lye's hand. "You were with Damrick on the *Savage Grace*."

Lye straightened a bit. "That's right."

"I saw your speech. I'm Grub Haggarty, the Sheriff here. Nice ship."

Lye looked around as though he'd never really noticed it. "She'll float."

"Pulling out in the morning, are you?"

"Early as the weather allows. Damrick's a might busy right now. Can I get 'im a message?"

"Oh, just tell him I'm here. We can talk whenever he finishes what he's doing. I'll wait."

Lye studied him. "Is there some kinda trouble?"

"I'd just like to speak with Damrick about a few items might be of interest to him."

"Oh."

Grub Haggarty's expression said he would look Lye square in the eye for as long as Lye cared to look back.

"I'll go see if he can talk."

"That would be kind of you." Grub smiled.

In a few moments Lye returned. "He wants to talk in his cabin, if ye don't mind."

"I don't mind." And he followed Lye below decks.

"I'm in favor of what you're doing," Grub told him. "I want you to know that."

"Thank you."

Grub sat in the one small chair by the one small table. Damrick sat on the bed. Both men leaned forward slightly, attentive to one another, as though each expected important news from the other.

"It's not that way in every town."

"I know."

The Sheriff watched Damrick's eyes for a while. "Mr. Ryland, now, he's a powerful man."

"So they say."

"He didn't seem happy when he came to me yesterday. Said you might be in possession of his ships illegally."

"We got that worked out. You can speak to him, if you want."

He waved a hand, dismissing the thought. There was a pause while Grub Haggarty looked around the small room. "You spend a lot of time in here." There were books, a meal tray, various papers, the pen and ink. The candleholders now held large melted globs of wax at the base.

"I attract attention when I'm out there. Not good for our cause."

"Ryland...word is he's not too happy with your deal."

"What deal is that?"

"Whatever deal got you and him on the same side."

"What are you hearing?"

"Just bits and catches. Like maybe there's something brewing against you. And there are drifters in town. A good number of them I don't know and never heard of. Some bounty hunters I do know. Lots of armed men. A number of them coming and going at the hotel where Ryland stays. People seem to think it's the same bunch bushwhacked you at Slow Slim's in Mann."

"You're worried there might be a war in your town."

"The thought occurred to me."

"I wouldn't fret about it. We'll be gone in the morning."

A pause. "Ryland stands with Conch Imbry. Doesn't he." It wasn't a question.

"Ryland stands with Ryland."

"Harbormaster reports a ship anchored just inside the breakwater. *Lantern Liege.* You heard of it?"

"Scatter Wilkins's ship."

"I'm told that a pair of his pirates, one of them a woman, came ashore for a while. They were seen at Ryland's hotel."

"Runsford Ryland has many friends."

"You don't seem surprised."

"I'm not. And I won't be, Sheriff. Not tonight and not tomorrow, if that's what's bothering you."

The Sheriff watched him closely. "I've got some men. We can help."

"How?"

"Round up some of these gun hands now, get them off the streets."

"On what charge?"

Haggarty smiled sadly. "There was a time when I would have...when I wouldn't have made any such offer. Not for any reason. Not for any man. 'The law is the law,' I would say. 'It's not my job to separate the good from the bad, but the law-abiding from the law-breaking.' But...too many good people end up in jail, or dead; and too many bad people end up walking around breathing free air, and it makes a man think. So I've come to a conclusion." He paused. "You want to hear it?"

"Yes," Damrick said. "Yes, I do."

"It's just this. Sometimes it isn't about good people breaking the law. Sometimes it's about the law breaking good people. And when it gets to that, a man has to make his own choices, no matter who he is or what's his job."

"I agree with you there."

"I don't know if you're good people or not, Mr. Fellows. What I hear, you probably are. But I know you're trying to do a good thing. If you want me to make the sweep, I'll make it."

"And if I don't want you to make that sweep...what would you think then?"

"Then I suppose I'd think you and your boys are prepared to relieve me from the need of it. Maybe for a long time to come."

"You're the Sheriff. You round up who you want. But my opinion is, it's not necessary. You and your boys can sweep up after. If there's anything left to sweep."

"That's all I needed to hear." He stood.

"Sheriff."

"Yeah?"

"You know the shopkeepers around here?"

"Around where? The docks?"

"Yes."

"Sure, I know 'em."

"Can they be trusted?"

"They're good men and women. Family businesses mostly." He eyed Damrick. "Trusted with what?"

"I'd like to talk to them. You think you could arrange that?"

"Depends. You bringing them into danger, or sending them away from it?"

"That would be their choice, wouldn't it?"

At six in the morning, the light of the gray sky softened the docks, the piers, the posts, the moorings, outlining all in a gauzy haze. The sun had not risen, but the darkness had faded. Echoing footsteps preceded more than a hundred gunmen as they emerged from shadows, flowing down gray streets toward the masts that poked up skeleton-like above the buildings. As they moved, their long rifles, pistols, muskets, blunderbusses came out from beneath riding coats and jackets.

The *Ayes of Destiny*, the *Blue Horizon*, and the *Lion's Pride* sat still and silent, moored in a row, tethered to shore. Out in the harbor, the fading darkness revealed the outline of the shadowy ship that had arrived in the night. On board that ship, dozens of pirates stood ready and waiting, leaning over rails and loading small arms, or tending to cannon. The *Lantern Liege* floated silently at anchor several hundred yards from the docks, blocking the path of Ryland's rogues to the sea.

Runsford Ryland stood on the front stoop of the Harbormaster's office. The docks were filled with gray shapes, and now the air filled with the clicking of hammers. Ryland's goons, his lieutenants, watched him, awaiting a sign. But he stood silently, looking up at the *Ayes of Destiny*, and his men saw a doubt in him. "Where are they?" he asked.

No one answered.

"Damrick Fellows!" he shouted. His voice echoed. There was no movement aboard. No Gatemen stood on guard. None lined the gunwales.

Ryland's mouth worked and his eyes flitted around his ships. "Get up the gangway," he ordered Motley, again well-dressed, now anxious for orders. "Go find them. Take half the men with you, I don't care. Just get up there." Then more loudly, more generally, Ryland said, "Fire on any Gateman shows his face!"

A dozen men followed Motley up the unguarded gangway. The ship was silent for a minute or two, and then the goon came to the rail. He shrugged. "Nobody here!"

"Check the other ships," Ryland said angrily. He didn't move from the stoop.

But soon enough, others confirmed it. There wasn't a soul on board any of the three ships. Every cabin was cleaned out. The anchor plates remained, but the cannon were gone.

"What now, Boss?"

Ryland sighed. "Comb the harbor. Find the Gatemen."

"You think they ran?" Motley asked.

"I doubt it. They're somewhere."

The Gatemen were indeed somewhere. On top of the buildings, on the roofs of the nearby pubs and warehouses and small businesses, on any structure that overlooked the three ships, new gray shapes now emerged. Men in leather armbands, guns in hand. And then on street level, from within those buildings, from within the houses, the offices, the stores, the pubs, yet more silhouettes began to emerge, flowing now out onto the cobblestones. They wore red feathers in their hats, or tucked behind their ears.

The Gatemen closed in on Ryland's army.

"Now we got a fight!" Sleeve crowed. The rest of the forecastle rumbled its agreement.

"Aye, it's a fight," Ham Drumbone confirmed. "And no one-sided ambush this time. A full-on brawl between a hundred outlaws and a hundred Gatemen, evenly matched in weapons and in the ability and the desire to use them."

"Who won?" Dallis Trum asked.

"Who do ye think?" Sleeve answered scornfully.

"I don't know," Dallis replied truthfully. "Is this the big fight that ends it all?"

"Naw, how could it be?" another sailor called. "Conch's a thousand miles away."

"Shut up and let Ham tell it!" another sailor yelled, and others agreed.

They quieted almost instantly, and Ham began again.

"Hold!" Motley said, standing by his boss. "What's that?" He was looking up at his men along the rails of the ships, most of them milling about on deck. But Motley was listening to the creak of footsteps above his head. "Did you put men on the roof?" he asked Ryland.

"Me? You're the one organizing this."

"They *tricked* us," Motley said angrily, as if somehow the Gatemen had cheated. "The rooftops, boys!" he shouted. "They're on the roofs!"

That's when the shooting started. First, a single crack, fired from a ship. Then that shot was answered from a rooftop. Two more shots, then three more at once. Then Motley shouted, "Fire, ye blaggards!"

And then there was a countering call from above: "Remember Slow Slim's!"

And suddenly the docks were a match struck in the dark. Flashes of fire and plumes of smoke crisscrossed the docks, lacing the air with musket balls that ripped through anything in their path. Pirates and brigands on the decks of Ryland's ships found plenty of cover, and shot across or up at the rooftops. Those still on the docks below aimed upward as best they could, but the Gatemen were well concealed, and they rained gunfire down onto the docks and the decks at will.

It was equal give and take for a minute or two, until the second wave of Gatemen arrived on foot. Then, under cover of heavy fire from above, they started a bloody push, moving the pirates across and down the docks, toward the ships, toward the end of the pier. Muskets and pistols fired, swords came out of scabbards and plunged into enemies, knives flashed and disappeared, reappeared red. And then they were upon one another with fists, teeth, knees, elbows. The Gatemen moved forward yard by yard, foot by bloody foot. The outlaws did not retreat; the Gatemen simply moved them backward. Men fought, and stumbled, and fell. Had the outlaws had any protecting fire from above, they might have prevailed. But Damrick's men had the higher ground. Ship-bound brigands who tried to shoot down on their attackers left themselves exposed to fire from the rooftops.

Finally, all engaged on the docks saw the end coming. Several of the outlaw horde broke, trying to flee up the gangways. They were cut down with swords and pistols. The Gatemen kept driving, those in the fore fighting hand to hand, those in the back using the fallen—their own and their enemy's—as cover as they reloaded.

Damrick pulled his knife from a fallen enemy, and sheathed it. Blood-spattered, he called out. "Lye!"

Lye's pistol, pressed close to a pirate's belly, fired. He looked at Damrick as his opponent fell. "What?"

"Follow me." He gestured with a nod toward the Harbormaster's front stoop. "Grab a couple of men!" Without waiting for an answer or watching Lye's reaction, Damrick moved back the way he'd come, down the alley, circling around behind the buildings.

As the bloody advance inched forward, Motley and his three lieutenants fired from the Harbormaster's stoop, kneeling behind the low, loosely spindled rail. They were protecting Runsford Ryland, who was seated behind the four men with his arms around his knees, his back pressed against the door of the Harbormaster's office, as low and as invisible and as out of the line of fire as possible.

Suddenly, the lock behind Ryland clicked, and the door at his back opened. He was jerked inside. Then a Gateman with two double-barreled pistols stepped out and fired three shots, killing three of Ryland's goons. Motley turned and aimed, but he had not finished reloading. Damrick Fellows's eyes were hard and shimmered like crystal. His hands were bloody, and red spatters covered his face. He shook his head, and droplets of sweat fell from wet hair. "Put it down, and get inside," he ordered. With a sour look, Motley obliged. Lye Mogene and his two companions tied the two new prisoners securely, while Damrick joined his Gatemen in pressing the attack once again.

The smell of gunpowder was heavy when Lye rejoined the fray; a low cloud of pungent gray mist swirling across the docks as men moved through it, fought in it, added to it with every shot fired. At the front of the line was Hale Starpus, leading his men. He and the Gatemen shot when they could, cut and slashed when they couldn't reload, punched and kicked and bit when they couldn't even move or remove a blade—always pushing toward the ships. Now several of the last brigands standing on the wooden decking splashed into the water, trying to swim for safety. They were shot by Gatemen.

"Charge 'em!" Hale shouted. And with one final push, the dock was theirs.

"Up the gangways!" Damrick ordered. The pirates and brigands on the decks of Ryland's ships now rose, risking exposure to turn their weapons on the three narrow gangways. Hale took the lead and began ascending the *Destiny* under heavy fire. He stopped, pinned down from above, and took cover behind the bodies of those pirates shot and hacked while attempting to flee from the docks.

Then the cannon fire began. Hale was not one to shrink from any attack, but he froze now. He heard cannon shot shatter wood. He looked to his right, saw the source, saw more flashes from a dark ship not a hundred yards away. "Back down! Back to the docks!" he shouted behind him. And as the Gatemen retreated, two explosions rocked the *Ayes of Destiny*.

Fire from above dwindled.

"We just hold still, them pirates on that ship'll kill off their own kind!" Hale marveled.

More cannon fire rocked the *Destiny*. Now panic swept the decks of Ryland's ships as brigands raced to the far port rails and waved their arms, shouting for their allies to cease fire. For their trouble, they were picked off like so many pigeons on a fence. Cannon shot hit the *Lion's Pride*, and then the *Blue Horizon*. Debris and splinters leapt from all three ships, and the entire dock shuddered.

The chaos on board gave the Gatemen sharpshooters on the rooftops every advantage. Within two minutes, the small arms fire declined. Inside one more, it stopped altogether. Shortly after, the cannons ceased to roar. Acrid smoke drifted across the entire scene. Surviving Gatemen stormed up the gangways, finding the dead everywhere, assuring that the wounded joined them.

"Fire into the air, boys!" Hale called out. "Those pirates expect a pirate's celebration!"

Several of the Gatemen whooped and fired off their pistols. Many more would not waste the ammunition or the energy, just to fool a shipful of enemies. But the meager effort did the trick. The pirates out in the harbor joined the celebration. Pistol fire answered back, and an echoing roar rose from that distant deck. The pirates put up their guns.

Hale Starpus, dripping sweat and blood and nursing a badly cut shoulder, stood at the prow of the *Destiny*, and waved at them. "Our thanks, until we meet again…" he said softly, through a smile, "…and we shoot ever' last condemned man of ye dead between the eyes."

"That may be sooner than you think," Damrick told him. He was watching a ship's boat being lowered from the davits of the pirate vessel. "Let's go change the outcome of this fight. Now."

"Yer sure this is the right thing—"

"You have your orders! Get that armband off." Damrick handed him a fat wad of braided leather lashes. "We don't have much time."

"Aye, sir."

"And find Lye. He left our pair of prize prisoners alone, and we need them gone."

Hale looked down at the docks. "Looks like he's already doin' it."

A battle-weary Lye Mogene was headed back into the Harbormaster's ofice, two men with him.

"All right, you two. Get up and let's go!" Ryland and Motley were lying on

Blaggard's Moon

their sides trussed like hogs, hands tied behind them, feet bound together, hands lashed to feet by a short length of rope. They were gagged.

The two Gatemen with Lye, one young and stocky, one weathered and thin with a drooping, clouded eye, cut loose the men's feet and stood them up.

"Take a look out there," Lye said, pointing out a broken window at the docks, which were now littered with the dead. "What happens when ye go up against Gatemen. Got a good look?"

Ryland nodded, his gag tied tight and deep. Motley narrowed his eyes with hatred.

"Let's have them sacks." Lye pointed to burlap bags behind the counter. He put one over each man's head. "We're takin' you two out the back way."

The jolly boat sent from the pirate's ship docked just in front of the prow of the *Ayes of Destiny*. Two sailors climbed up onto the dock and began picking their way through the dead. One of them was a big man with dark teeth and a lumpy skull, clearly visible under a thin stubble of hair. He held an enormous pistol in his right hand. The other was a woman, dark, wearing black forester's leathers. The woman's pistol was in her left hand. She held a sword, a fine and polished rapier, in her right.

Damrick and Hale Starpus watched them from the rail of the *Destiny*.

"Who's the woman?" Hale asked. "She looks foreign."

"She's Drammune. I've heard of her. She sails with Scatter Wilkins."

Hale's mouth opened. He spun to look at the pirate ship anchored in the harbor. "That's the *Lantern Liege*?" Her markings were still not visible at this distance, in this light. She was silhouetted against the rising sun.

"I'd say so."

Hale looked back to the dock. The big man kicked the shoulder of a lifeless body, his toe at the leather armband tied above the bicep. "That's Scatter hisself, then?"

Damrick shook his head. "Not unless Captain Wilkins is taking orders from a woman." The woman pointed with her sword at the gangway, and the big man walked toward it. Then she looked up at the rail, caught Damrick's eye. Even at this distance he felt a chill, as though he were prey measured by a predator.

"You really think we can make 'em believe we're the pirates?" Hale asked.

"We'd better, if we want to get to the Conch."

The woman moved like a cat up the gangway, her eyes constantly scanning. When she reached the deck she glanced calmly around at the faces that watched her, and then she walked straight to Damrick. Without any hints or help, signs of office or insignia, with little more than a sideways glance from a Gateman or two, she had determined that Damrick was in charge. He felt the chill grow as she approached. This woman was not only cunning, but clearly in her element, energized by the bloodshed and the danger around her.

"Where is your captain?" she asked. Her accent was thick, with heavy rolling R's. Her dark hair was braided tight against her head at one ear. A heavy scar ran down a cheek.

"Who wants to know?"

"I am Talon. Captain Scatter Wilkins wants to know." She held her sword at an angle to the deck. Her pistol was pointed downward as well.

"Then your captain can talk to me."

"*I* will talk to you." Her sword twitched, but did not come up. Still, it struck Damrick as a warning.

"This ship is mine now," Damrick said flatly. "We thank you for your help, but we didn't need it. Me and my men, we're claiming Conch Imbry's reward. So you can tell that to Scatter Wilkins."

She looked Damrick up and down, her eyes pausing on the bloodstains, the spatter. Then she looked around at Damrick's men, seeming none too impressed. She scanned the bodies along the decks, most of them wearing leather armbands. "Where is Damrick Fellows?" Now her eyes came back to him.

He felt she was probing him, and had the sense that she knew he was concealing something. "No idea. Maybe one of these dead. Then again, maybe he ran."

"And who are you?"

"I'm the man who's through answering your questions." He drew his pistol. But before he could bring the barrel up, well before it was aimed in her direction, the tip of her sword moved, and his weapon dropped to the floorboards. A gash along the back of his right hand began bleeding. He covered the wound with his left hand as more than fifty weapons came up, and dozens of hammers cocked back all across the deck.

"Move that sword again, woman, and there'll be two more dead on this deck."

"Put it up, ye stupid witch," the big man hissed at her. "Get us both killed fer nothin'." He showed brown teeth and a bad disposition. To Damrick, he said, "I'm Jonas Deal, Cap'n Wilkins's first mate. He didn't send us to fight," he glanced at Talon with contempt. "Just to see what's what. Cap'n Wilkins ain't after no reward. He wants to know the Gatemen are dead, is all."

Damrick nodded, but didn't take his eyes from Talon. He looked her in the eye for a moment longer, then said. "You've seen. Now go."

"How many escaped?" Talon asked, apparently oblivious to the threat, or to any other part of the conversation of the last few moments. Jonas Deal rolled his eyes.

"Not many," Damrick answered.

"What is your name?" she asked. There was accusation in her tone, somehow made more ominous by the thick accent.

Damrick studied her but didn't answer.

The big man spoke instead. "We're headed to Skaelington, is why she asks. Cap'n Wilkins, he'll tell the Conch about ye, make sure it's you gets the reward."

"I'll tell the Conch myself." He leaned down and picked up his pistol, keeping an eye on Talon's sword. Then he stared hard at the woman. "Maybe I didn't make it plain enough. You aren't welcome here anymore."

"You have something to hide," she told him. And her eyes flashed. "I would dearly love to make you reveal it."

"A charming proposal. But no."

She smirked. Then she sheathed her sword, looked around at the men on deck. They did not lower their weapons. She turned as if to leave, but instead walked up to Hale Starpus. "You fought the Gatemen?" she asked him, looking at the blood on his shoulder.

His jaw was set, his pistol aimed at her heart, but looking into her cold, piercing eyes, he felt off his guard. "Aye." His chin came up in defiance.

"A hard morning's work. This wound will heal." She reached up with her right hand, as if to touch the gash on his right shoulder. But instead she grasped his pistol hand, a movement so quick and agile that it did not seem threatening until she had already twisted his thumb up and away from the pistol grip, causing a sharp, popping pain that levered the gun from his hand. It fell harmlessly to the deck. Gatemen surrounding her gripped weapons more tightly as a murmur rose and faded. But Damrick just shook his head. The moment of danger had already come and gone. She did not raise her weapon. They all watched, riveted.

Without acknowledging any enemy, without a change of expression, as though she and Hale were the only two people in the world, Talon cocked her head, let her eyes fall on Hale's good shoulder. She moved her pistol barrel to his left upper arm, pushed it at the cloth there. "But what would cause a ring of sweat, right here…I wonder?"

Hale recoiled, then looked down at the obvious sweat line, the wrinkled cloth, evidence of the armband that had been there during his exertions. He looked back up at her, his mind reeling. She had caught them; she had figured it out. She'd disarmed him without any effort, and now she could see right through him. She could see through all of them. He could think of nothing to say, and there was nothing he could do. His eyes reached out to Damrick, pleading for help.

"He was one of our infiltrators," Damrick said easily. "You and Scatter Wilkins might attack the Gatemen head on, and beat them. But we're not that good. We needed men on the inside."

She scanned the deck again, looking for similar signs. "You had many infiltrators." Then she locked onto Damrick once more. "My proposal stands."

"I'll try to remember."

They all watched as Talon descended the gangway.

Jonas Deal hung back.

"Is she always like that?" Damrick asked him.

"No. Sometimes she's worse. She suspects everyone of everythin'. But don't worry, I'll give the Captain a good report."

"Thank you."

Damrick watched as he followed down the gangway, caught up with Talon.

"That was good thinkin', that about me bein' a spy."

Damrick didn't respond. He watched Talon and Deal pick their way through the dead. Finally, they climbed back into their jolly boat.

"Let's get these ships ready," he sighed. "Seal off the docks again—no one in or out. When the Sheriff arrives, bring him straight to me." He raised his voice, making sure all his men heard it. "You're mercenaries and bounty men now. Spread the word that all the Gatemen are either dead or joined up and turned pirate. And if anyone asks, tell them Damrick ran again."

"I don't know, Damrick," Hale said, when only his boss could hear. "Seems like a real bad idea. We won't get recruits again, they think we all got kilt."

"We don't need recruits."

"You'll get a reputation won't help us."

"I don't care about reputations. I care about killing pirates."

"Seems like we just let two bad ones go. And there's a whole ship full of 'em about to sail off."

"Yes. I would have liked to have killed Talon. But I have to get to the Conch while I have this chance. After that, we can kill all the Scatters and Talons and Jonas Deals we want."

"You don't need to tie me," Ryland tried again. It came out a muffled mess, much like all his previous attempts.

The rough sack was now off his head, but his hands were bound behind him, pressed hard against the wooden seat of the carriage. His gag had not been removed, and he faced an insistent pistol barrel. The bumps and jolts of the ride caused Lye Mogene's weapon to rise and fall and swing to and fro like some bizarre churchman's blessing.

Beside Lye sat the droop-eyed Gateman, pistol in hand, though his was pointed at the bound and gagged Motley. Next to Ryland on the other side was another Gateman, the solid young man.

"Oo hoh hee hoo hi hee," Ryland told Lye once again.

"All right," Lye said with a sigh, admitting defeat. "Get the gag off 'im. I'm tired of all this hummin' and mumblin'."

"Thank you." Runsford said when he could, wiping spittle from his cheek onto his shoulder. "All I was saying is, you don't need to tie me. I'm not dangerous."

"Yeah, well," Lye answered.

"I'm no threat to you," Ryland insisted, hoping to make his point clearer.

"Unh hi hee, hoo!" Motley raged.

"Yer both stayin' trussed," Lye told them. Then to the goon, "And yer mouth's stayin' stuffed, so might just as well shut it."

Ryland took a deep breath. Unlike Motley and himself, the three Gatemen in the coach were stained and spattered and smelled of drying sweat and blood. Little about his current situation appealed to him. "Where are you taking me?" Ryland asked.

Lye said nothing.

Ryland tried the stern young man at his elbow. "Where are you taking us? Can't you give me the least idea?"

Nothing.

He looked at the Gateman across the carriage, seated next to Lye—haggard, scraggly, with protruding eye misted over with cataract. Runsford opened his mouth to ask him the same question, but he hissed. He actually made a sound like an angry cat, revealing as he did a gold tooth and several gaps where teeth should be.

"Unpleasant fellow," Ryland murmured.

"I wouldn't cross ol' Murk-Eye," Lye counseled.

"I'll take it under advisement."

Murk-Eye glared from his one good eye, and hissed again.

Ryland focused back on Lye Mogene. "I want to speak to Damrick Fellows."

"Hee hoo!" Motley demanded through the gag.

"Shut up, Motley," Ryland told him.

"I need to see Damrick."

"Oh, you'll see him all right. I wouldn't be so anxious, though, I was you."

It was all the information Ryland needed. He was content to remain silent the rest of the trip, as they stopped in the middle of a dense wood, and walked through a narrow path past a rotting cabin and toward an inlet that might have been a lake. While Motley kept up a stream of muffled curses and required rough treatment to keep him moving, certain that he would be shot at any moment, Ryland did not suspect Lye Mogene's comment was anything but sincere, nor did he suspect the Gateman was misinformed.

The party found a rowboat moored to a pine at the water's edge. Lye gestured for the prisoners to get in. But Motley pulled back, and refused to move further.

"Oo hahn uh hoo huh, hoo huh hee."

"Jus' shut up and get in the boat." Lye smacked Motley in the back of the head with his fist, then poked the pistol hard into his back.

But Motley planted his feet. He shook his head. "Oo hahn uh hoo huh, hoo huh hee."

"What's a' matter with him?" Lye asked Runsford.

"Remove the gag, and I'm sure he'll tell you."

Lye nodded toward the solid young man, the one they called Stock, who belted his pistol and untied the rag.

"You wanna shoot us, shoot us here!" Motley repeated, glaring his defiance.

Ryland sighed. "He speaks for himself only," he informed his captors, then stepped awkwardly into the rowboat. It rocked back and forth like a hobbyhorse until he managed to position himself in the stern seat.

Lye climbed in and sat beside Runsford. "Comin' alive, or stayin' dead?" he asked Motley. "You choose, but make it quicklike. Murk's itchin' to shoot ye." The red-haired goon frowned at Murk, pursed his lips tightly, eyed Ryland suspiciously, and then stepped into the prow.

When they rounded a small finger of land, Ryland saw his own sloop, *Success*, anchored about twenty yards from shore. Standing on the deck was Damrick Fellows.

"Hello, Mr. Fellows," Ryland called out as they drew close. "I hope you've made yourself comfortable."

Damrick didn't answer.

When the prow of the rowboat banged into the hull of *Success*, Damrick spoke softly. "Mr. Ryland goes below. Tie the other one to the mast." And he disappeared from the rail.

Murk and Stock took care of securing Motley while Lye kept a firm grip on Ryland's elbow, maneuvering him toward the tight stairway that led below deck.

"I'll take him," Damrick said.

Seeing he was dismissed, Lye nodded, and let Damrick steer the prisoner below.

Runsford Ryland found a familiar face waiting for him in the saloon. "Hello, Mr. Ryland," the old gentleman said. "Prisoner on your own ship, are you?" Windall Frost stood and put out a hand.

"Quite true, Mr. Frost," Ryland answered dutifully. "But for that fact, I'd shake your hand." Damrick, standing behind Ryland, pulled his knife and sliced the bonds. Ryland rubbed his wrists briefly, then shook hands with Frost.

Lye yanked on the knots. Motley was seated with his back to the mast, his wrists bound behind him. Then he checked the gag. Satisfied, he joined Stock at the rail.

"Nice boat," Stock said appreciatively.

Lye looked around him and grunted. It was larger than Windall Frost's, and except for the ostentation of its multi-colored woods and polished brass accoutrements, it was of the same class. "Looks like we're the crew, though," he sulked. Three Gatemen who had sailed here with Damrick now pulled on the oars of the rowboat, back toward shore. "I ain't much a sailor, comes down to it."

"Them boys said we're half a league from the ocean, just up around that point," Stock told him.

Lye nodded. "I thought it was a lake."

"Nah. An inlet."

"What're they doin' with Ryland down there?" Murk asked. His one good eye was focused on the small door.

"How do I know?"

"Oughta be shootin' 'im, ask me," Murk brooded. "Don't know why we started takin' prisoners all a' sudden."

"Ain't arguin'. It's Damrick's business, though. He's got some plan he's cookin' up, just wait."

"So you've underwritten the return of the Gatemen." Ryland, Damrick, and Frost stood in the saloon. "A rather expensive hobby to take up so late in life, isn't it, Windall?"

Frost was sunny. "Not nearly so expensive for me as it will be for you, if you're willing to lead us to the Conch."

"I am quite willing." Ryland looked at Damrick, who as yet had not spoken a word to him. "That was a nice little strategy, Mr. Fellows, moving your men to the rooftops."

Damrick's eyes were blank. "You came with three times the numbers we expected, two hours earlier than planned."

"And yet you were ready, thank God. I wanted to warn you, of course. But I was unable to find a way, surrounded as I was with that army of hooligans."

Damrick's eyes only grew colder.

"Dear man, I hope that is not accusation I read in your eyes. Once you light a fire in the woods, it's very hard to control what burns."

"So!" Windall Frost offered into the icy air, "Something to calm the nerves, gentlemen?" He gestured toward the saloon's bar, which he had arrayed with brandy, rum, and several liqueurs. "Ryland keeps his boat well-stocked."

Damrick and Ryland disengaged their mutual stares.

"Splendid," Ryland agreed with a sigh. "A cordial would be perfect, Mr. Frost."

"Nothing for me," Damrick said. "We have some rather detailed plans to make. I'd like to keep a clear head."

The forecastle echoed with "Whoa, whoa!" and "Hang on!" and "Wait!"

"Are you sayin' that fight was rigged? Ryland, he crossed Damrick, right?"

"Sure he did," Sleeve answered. "Ryland wouldn't lead Conch's men to get slaughtered a' purpose."

"Those weren't Conch's men fightin' Damrick," another countered. "Other than the three goons with Motley. The rest was signed on fer a fee."

"Ryland's a slink," Mutter Cabe intoned. "He gave 'em all up to die."

"He's a slink all right," Sleeve insisted, "but he did his best to double-cross Damrick, bringin' all them extras. He just got outfoxed when Damrick put his men on the rooftops. Otherwise, Ryland's men would a' won the day. Ryland is Conch's man still. You'll see."

"So which side is Mr. Ryland really on?" Dallis Trum asked Ham.

Ham puffed his pipe calmly. "You gents done talking? I'd like to go ahead on with the tale, if you don't mind too terribly."

They all agreed he should.

"All right. So the *Success* set sail, headed back to Skaelington and Conch Imbry, staying well ahead of the three rogue Ryland ships, which now also claimed that port as their destination. While all the Gatemen sailed southward, there in the city of pirates our Miss Jenta has had herself a difficult time. True to her word, she had concealed nothing from Conch Imbry. Or should I say, almost nothing."

"Hold on now! You ain't gonna tell us where Ryland stands? You ain't gonna say what was what, with the fight in Oster?"

"Or what they're plannin' against the Conch now?"

Ham puffed his pipe again. "Gentlemen. Have I been with you so long, and you don't understand yet how this works? Maybe that's enough for tonight…"

But the pirates wanted more. So Ham, seeming somehow both reluctant and satisfied at once, continued.

Chapter Fourteen

THE CLEAVER AND FORK

CAPTAIN CARNSFORD BLOODSTONE "Conch" Imbry entered his pub with a swagger. The saloon doors popped, and all eyes turned toward him. He stood tall, arms outstretched, hands holding the doors wide.

"Captain Imbry!" and "The Conch!" and "Hello, Captain!" greeted him from behind raised mugs and glasses. Two men stood immediately, one at the bar, one in a front corner, and drew their pistols. They did not look at the Conch, however, but watched the patrons with anxious eyes, should there be any of their boss's enemies among them.

A great, proud grin spread across the Captain's face. The Cleaver and Fork wasn't big, but it was his. It shone with silver and gold trim, dark walnut and fine red cherrywood. The patrons were equally well-adorned, in silk and satin and gold brocade. They were seated at linen-covered tables, mostly, though a few leaned on the enormous bar that ran three-quarters of the length of the main room, left to right, then made a hard turn away into the back room and continued on as a heavy burgundy and gold velvet curtain separated the main room from the private dining and gambling area.

"Good day to ye all!" the pirate called out in a booming voice. "How's the ale?"

"Excellent!" and "Perfection!" Mugs were held high in delight. Many of those here today came on the outside chance they might catch a glimpse of the celebrated pirate, knowing he sometimes made appearances just like this.

"Ought to be at these prices!" he told them.

They laughed.

"And how's the grub?"

"Splendid!" and "Couldn't be better!" Hunks of meat on the bone were raised in toast.

"And the service?"

The patrons nodded and mumbled. There were a few whistles.

Conch scowled. "Somethin' wrong wif the service?"

"No!" one answered. "Not at all!"

"It's...gorgeous!" another shouted. And then the rest laughed.

Conch's good humor returned. "And where is that splendid servin' wench?"

The curtain parted, and Jenta Stillmithers emerged. Lithe and tall, she flowed when she walked, her hair tied loosely behind her neck from where it cascaded in soft waves down her back. Her bright blue eyes fixed Conch Imbry steadily as she approached him.

"Ah, there's my Jenta," he said with a depth of satisfaction few had seen in him before. He took her in his arms to kiss her, but she gave him only a peck on the cheek.

"Hello, Captain," she said. "Your table is ready for you in the back."

"Ah, but I cain't stay to enjoy it, more's the pity," he said. "Just stoppin' in to see the fine, fine fruits of all my labors."

"Not even time for a pint?" she asked. Her voice betrayed disappointment, laced with the faintest hint of need.

"Ah, maybe just a pint, then..."

The patrons laughed and clapped as the two walked arm in arm behind the curtain. A whistle or two sang out. And then the pub returned to its business, buzzing a bit louder than it had before.

There were no others here, as Conch had signaled ahead his intention to pay a visit. "Ye sure yer well?" he asked her, when she brought his mug to the table.

"Do I look well?"

"Aye." He chuckled. "Ye look very well."

She sat beside him, watched him drink. "What's the news from the Church? Has the annulment come through?"

"Girl, ye'll be the first to know." The pleasure ran away from his face.

"What's the delay?"

"Papers gotta come from Mann. Their high holy priest is takin' a unholy long time to put a scratch on a piece a' parchment, ye ask me. 'Specially since his men didn't even do the marryin'."

"You're a gentleman, Conch. I knew that. You are patient, too." Her eyes drew him in. She put her hand on his hard knuckles. "It's a worthy trait."

"Aaaah," he brushed off her compliment, but not her hand. "And yer still all right wif all the work yer doin' here?"

"I prefer it. It keeps my mind occupied. And here, I feel a connection with you."

"Ye do?"

"Of course. Everyone comes in looking for you, asking about you. They hold you in such high esteem."

"Wouldn't put much stock in that. They're mostly crooks and villains." But he beamed.

"Oh, but they're not. The mayor comes in often. Bankers, businessmen. They all talk of you."

"I bet they do." Conch took a drink. He watched her eyes, then nodded once, satisfied. "I'm still waitin' on word a' that Gateman."

Her heart beat faster. She picked up the pitcher and topped off his mug. "What word is that?"

"I want to hear he's dead and hung and quartered and fed to sharks. But I ain't hearin' none of it yet. He's still causin' me mischief. So I want ye to be careful."

"Do you think he may be headed back here?"

"I ain't heard he is. But I ain't heard he ain't. That one, he slips in and out like a...shadow or somefin'."

"I'll keep a close eye out."

"Ye know what to do, when he shows."

She looked him deep in the eye. "I know your men, Conch. They're always here."

"Ain't many ever set eyes on the Gateman. So it'd be hard for 'em to spot 'im. But you, ye've seen 'im four times, so ye know 'im."

"Three times, Conch. The dance, the docks in Mann, and the docks here."

He nodded. "That's right. I ferget."

"I've told you only the truth, Conch. Always, and no secrets. He promised to find me."

The pirate captain grinned. "That's my girl. Ye see 'im, ye jus' say. A nod or a wink is all it takes."

"What will they do?"

"Why, they'll kill 'im."

"Right here?"

Conch shrugged.

"But your guests…"

Conch looked thoughtful. "Yer worried it might take 'em off their feed?"

"Most of them aren't used to such things." She paused. "Nor am I."

"Ah, well. Fer you then. I'll have a word with the boys. They'll be sure to take 'im out to the street first if they can."

"Thank you."

Conch took another drink. "Ye don't mind bein' bait, then?"

She stroked the back of his hand. "Why should I mind? It was my idea."

He took a deep breath. "Yer my kind a' woman, Jenta Stillmithers. And I'm proud to have all the folks of Skaelington know it."

"So am I, Captain."

"You can call me Conch. I told ye that."

Her eyes went soft. "But you are my captain."

His chest swelled. He stood. "Well! Got business to attend. Give us a kiss, and we're off."

She brushed her lips against his cheek again. He held her tightly around the waist.

"Not yet," she said into his ear, in a whisper. "Not yet, Captain. But soon."

"Ye drive me crazy, woman!" But he didn't seem to mind it. He turned her loose, turned away, and left her in the private dining room. She could hear the patrons calling out to him as his proud boots struck the polished planking, and she heard him calling right back to them. She walked behind the bar, but stayed behind the curtain. She didn't want to face the customers out front right now; she knew the sort of looks she'd get. She put her apron back on and looked down at the dishes in the washbasin. A small pile of steak knives lay drying on a towel.

It crossed her mind that any one of them could end her misery.

"Misery!" Sleeve called out. "See, I told you boys she had it bad for the Conch! He'll get everythin' in the end!"

"Aw, shut it, Sleeve," one of them answered. "She don't want to kill herself 'cause she can't marry the Conch yet. She wants to die 'cause she hates her life!"

"Well," Sleeve offered sullenly, "she'll get over that in time."

And that was at the heart of it, Delaney thought as he glanced at the line of shadow on the lagoon, just what Sleeve said. Sleeve hadn't known it when he said it; he hadn't known he was saying the whole secret of things. But he was. Life is about what things you can get over, and what things you can't, in time. And the trouble is, you really don't know which are which when they're happening. It takes years, maybe all your life, to figure out what you can't run away from no matter how hard you try, and what will dim and go away, if you just let it be. It's almost like people don't really know who they are, not completely. It's like they're all taking a guess, until they can sort out what's there, inside them, built in. And that can only be sorted out with time.

He looked up from the water to the sky. Evening wasn't here yet, but it was slowly coming on. Just a shade darker, a shade gloomier. He looked around at the reeds and marsh grasses at the edge of the pond. Rustling seemed to be everywhere now. The Hants were coming to watch him die—he had no doubt of it. "Get a good seat, now!" he called.

He straightened his back, and it sang out in pain. He stretched, arching it, until he felt it *pop-pop-pop* right down the middle. Then it felt better.

And it seemed to Delaney like it was usually women that made up those things a man couldn't ever get over. Like Yer Poor Ma, who he could never forget. She'd been his whole world once, though she was in fact just a small, no-account woman who got herself married to a drunk, and had a kid. She wasn't any kind of special person in any way. But she was still his Poor Ma. She still had magic in her songs, and a heart that blazed like a cookstove in his memory, and she was all inside him and would never leave him. She would always be singing him lullabies as the dark waves rose.

And Maybelle Cuddy. Just a barmaid, a plain barmaid, not like Jenta, but a regular girl serving up ale and getting pinched and slapping away rude hands and counting her tips at the end of a day. But oh, those eyes. That voice. Those things she said to him. He thought he could leave her behind, but he couldn't. She'd always be in his heart now, always promising she'd love him forever. Didn't matter it didn't prove out that way. She was there for good and all, and she was still making him that promise.

And the little girl. *Autumn* was her name. Same deep blue eyes as Jenta.

But her sweet song was so pure, and her little heart was so big, as big as the ocean and the night sky above it. He wondered now whether she'd be the same, whether that song and that heart would just rip him up inside, always. He supposed it would. But he wouldn't know for years.

And he didn't have years. He took a deep breath. He let it out. He watched the reeds rustle, and wondered if Hants had the same trouble with their women.

Probably. It was as though men just couldn't help themselves. Look at Conch Imbry, as fierce a man as ever was, and yet Jenta Stillmithers had softened him all up. She was stroking his hand, and he was a puppy dog. It was like…it was like women were made to do that to men. Like men were made with a big soft spot, and no matter how tough they got they couldn't protect themselves there. Like maybe, when God took that rib from the man to make the woman, the way the priests told it from their Scripture books, He left a hole in the man. One that she could always slide into. And the man couldn't stop her doing it, either.

Why were men made that way? If the priests and the holy books were right, then it was all on Him. He made it all. He didn't seem to care much about changing things, either. He just let it all roll on. He let people who did good get whammed down, and people who did bad get rich. And He would let Delaney get eaten by *Onka Din Botlay*, just for helping Autumn go free.

One thing he was sure of now, now that he'd had time think. There was a strong pull in men to do good in the world. Even inside Smith Delaney. He had a great desire to protect that little girl, to do right by Maybelle Cuddy, to be loved by Yer Poor Ma…nothing he knew in life was stronger. Even though doing good was hard and often got you hurt, and even though doing wrong was easy and hurt only other people, leaving you be, doing right was still better. He'd have made that choice all day long if he could just be by himself, without having the need to make some money, without having to run from pirates or do what captains said and whatnot. If there was a straight choice to be made between good and evil, forget the consequences, why good was just better, no matter what Sleeve said. A man's conscience was there to drive him to do good, not to drive him to shut the thing down so it wouldn't bother him anymore. Good had to be chosen, or the choice was, well, just bad.

Delaney felt a sense of being clean, thinking that way. Like a dip in a clear pond. Yes, choosing good was *right*.

Then he sighed. It was *after* choosing to be good that the problems came. That's where it got complicated. He could see that, even just looking at the men he knew who chose to be good. Avery took one way, and Damrick took another. Where Damrick seemed to turn bad in order to do good, or least he seemed to turn almost bad, why, Avery seemed to turn good and just let bad go on its merry way. Which was better?

After a short ponder he concluded that if a man had to stick around in the world a while, putting up with pirates and brigands and who-have-you, then Damrick made the better choice: clean up the mess. But if a man's time was already up, and he was about to stand before God Almighty, then Avery's choice seemed a whole lot safer. He felt he'd much rather be Avery standing at the Judgment, having just said no to pirates and got himself shot, then to be Damrick, having just said no to pirates and shot one of them himself.

But he wasn't sure why he felt that way.

Jenta put the key into the lock and turned it around once, feeling the heavy deadbolt slide into the wooden frame. The back door of the Cleaver and Fork was locked tight.

"I'll take that, ma'am," a stoop-shouldered pirate told her. She handed him the key, then walked between him and his hulking partner as the two pirates escorted her back to the *Shalamon*.

The sun's light was creeping upward from the eastern sky. For most of her life she had loved the morning time, loved being awake to hear the call of the songbirds. They always seemed to be laughing the world to life, announcing that a new day had dawned and all who slept were missing out. But these walks back to Conch Imbry's dark ship every morning had cured her of that. The sun's light seemed harsh and unwelcome; the bird's trills were brash and tactless, even mocking. She found herself relieved on those nights when the regulars left early and the pub shut down before dawn. Then she could walk the eight blocks to the wharf in the still, silent shroud of night, the streets lit only by meager lamplight, and perhaps a cold and distant moon.

Reaching the ship, she climbed the gangway and thanked her escorts, inwardly grateful that they had been instructed not to speak to her. She climbed from the main deck to the quarterdeck and fished her own key from her pocket. But she stopped short outside the door to her cabin. It was ajar. She leaned in close and heard the hard, heavy breathing within. Conch Imbry was not quite snoring, but was definitely asleep.

She blew out her cheeks and swept a wisp of hair from her forehead.

She hated when he did this. Though he had thus far been true to his word, making no effort to force her affections, he was quite consistent about arranging little events like this, opportunities for her to change her mind. She turned her back to the door, looking around, wondering where else she could go, even for a few minutes. The galley? Yes, the cook would have made coffee by now. He would give her a cup. But then he wouldn't stay. No sailor cared to answer the Conch's inevitable questions about how he came to be alone with Jenta, and what, exactly, transpired between them.

Now she heard footsteps down on the main deck. She didn't want to be observed standing outside her own door, hesitating. But she didn't want to enter, either. She looked at the large double doors of Conch's cabin and suddenly wondered...were they locked? She crossed the four steps in a silent hurry, turned the knob, and the door opened inward. Instantly, she was inside and the door was closed behind her.

She stood in the dark for a moment, listening. The footsteps did not approach. She turned around. A lamp burned low on the table before her. She walked to it, turned the flame up. Then she sat quietly on the bench of the captain's saloon and looked around at the familiar space. She took most of her meals here, with Conch and Mr. Mazeley and sometimes others of the crew. She had also spent many evenings here alone with the Captain, talking to him as he drank and told his stories, as he eyed her approvingly or teased her. Testing her. Wooing her. The space was not plush, nothing like Runsford Ryland's accommodations. But it was the sort of place he found most comfortable—worn, smoke-stained, smelling of lye and rye and old tobacco. It was the bear's den.

The bear. She and Wentworth had poked him with a stick, and he had snapped it in half, cornered her, devoured him. She hung her head. Poor Wentworth. Slipping her hand into her dress pocket, she fingered the delicate gold band she kept on a chain there. She pulled it out and looked at it. Her wedding ring.

Suddenly she stood, snatched up the lantern, and walked boldly into Conch Imbry's private quarters. She had not been within these walls, had not desired to see them, but now she had a mission. Starting with Conch's dresser drawers, she began looking through all his things. She went through drawers of clothing, finding nothing. Moving to his nightstand, she pulled on the one small drawer. It stuck. Pulling harder, it came out in her hands, and she nearly dumped its contents onto the floor. Instead, she dumped it all on his bed. Setting the lantern on the bed as well, she poked through the items: sealing wax, various brass seals and signets, matches, gold coins, silver coins, a bosun's whistle, two pocket-knives, various beads and carved ivory trinkets, all prized and kept for one reason or another. But no gold wedding band. She scooped the contents back into the drawer with two hands, carefully sweeping the dust from the bedclothes.

The ship creaked loudly.

She froze, listening. Her heart beat quickly, insistently. But she heard nothing more. She picked up the drawer to put it back into the nightstand, and her hand came to rest on a piece of parchment affixed to the outside of it at the back. She looked at it in the lamplight. It was folded, aged, covered with dust, tacked at its four corners. It was something important, something he kept secret. But it wasn't a wedding band, so she returned the drawer to its rightful place.

Then she went to his wardrobe. She looked around the base, his shiny boots and his buckled shoes. Then she went through his hanging clothes, the jackets, vests, shirts, checking all the pockets. At the far end of the rod, she found a small velvet bag hanging from a braided silk cord. She set the lantern on the floor and opened the drawstrings of the pouch, then poured the contents into her hand. Rings, diamonds, gold earrings, even a few gold teeth. Holding them down by the light, she found what she was looking for. A gold band, inscribed on the inside with the single word, "Jenta."

A pang shot through her. It was such a simple inscription, almost childlike. Certainly more innocent than any of the circumstances surrounding it. She slipped it into her pocket and scooped the remaining valuables back into the pouch. She drew the drawstring tight, closed the doors, looked around her. Everything was as it was—undisturbed. She took the lantern and left the room.

Seconds later, she returned, an unnamed anger driving her, a bitterness not aimed at the Conch, particularly, but at the world, at the ways in which good things were twisted and manipulated, in which hearts were wrung and cheated, lied to and coerced. She set the lantern on the bed, and yanked the small drawer from the lampstand. Using the blade of one of the pocketknives, she prised the tacks from the corners. She pocketed the tacks and the parchment, and returned the drawer to its place.

Assessing the cabin one more time, sure she had left no traces of her visit, she drew the door closed behind her, replaced the lantern on the table, and turned the light down low. She listened at the door for any telltale sound. She heard footsteps, waited until they faded away in the distance. She straightened her dress, then her hair. She raised her chin. And she stepped back out the door, closing it quickly behind her. She looked around. No one.

She walked boldly into her own cabin, leaving the door open behind her. "Why, Captain Imbry!" she exclaimed cheerfully. "What a pleasant surprise! Can I get you some coffee?"

"Those knots holding tight?" Runsford Ryland asked Motley.

"No thanks to you, ye traitor!" Motley growled. Night had fallen, and the small ship was anchored in a silent, craggy, wooded cove several miles from Skaelington. The red-haired goon was still tied at the base of the mast. His fine clothes were soiled; his long red hair greasy. He smelled bad.

"Let me check those," Ryland said, leaning down as though to test the knots. He glanced up at Murk-Eye, who stood at the rail, back turned. Then in a whisper he said to the prisoner, "Damrick's gone on a raid. Just me and that Murk fellow are left here to guard you." He put a small knife into Motley's upturned palm, then dropped a derringer into his front pocket. "You shoot him. I can't be the one to do it."

"Hey, keep away from him!" Murk-Eye ordered. "Damrick says!"

"Damrick says!" Motley mocked. "Ye disgust me."

Murk sighed. "Now that's gonna keep me up all night." He turned away again, watching the woods along the shoreline. His pistol remained in his belt.

"The Cleaver and Fork," Ryland said in a whisper. "Tell Conch it's the Cleaver and Fork. Damrick's going to raid the pub tonight, steal his woman."

Motley nodded. "Cleaver and Fork," he whispered back.

"Tonight!" Ryland emphasized. Then he left the prisoner at the mast and stood next to Murk at the rail. The two men spoke softly to one another.

"You give 'im the pistol?" Murk asked, now whispering himself.

"And the knife," Ryland nodded. "I can't believe I agreed to do this."

"Ye've agreed to a whole lot worse, I reckon."

"Well, I can't argue that." Ryland heaved a sigh. He turned his head until he could just see Motley out of the corner of an eye. Then he faced away again and whispered, "He's free."

"Ready, then?"

"You're sure the pistols were loaded properly?" Ryland looked nervous.

"Loaded 'em myself," Murk assured him.

"That doesn't give me a warm feeling."

Murk turned to Ryland and gave him a grin that was more gaps than teeth. "Well," he said in a voice plenty loud enough to be overheard, "since everyone else is gone and left us, think I'll just check on the prisoner!" He stretched. "Then maybe get some shut-eye." He turned from the rail and walked toward Motley.

With a leer that spoke of great satisfaction, Motley raised the small pistol, aimed it at Murk, and fired. The Gateman clutched his chest and went to his knees as the crack of the derringer echoed around the rocky cove. Then he fell forward onto the deck and lay still.

Ryland ran to him, knelt beside him, put a hand on his neck. "Dead!" He looked up at Motley, who stood at the mast with a haze of gray smoke hanging in a small cloud before him. Ryland took the pistol from Murk's belt, stood, and held it out toward Motley. "Take this." But behind him Murk moved. And then a second small pistol cracked. Now Ryland dropped to his knees. "I'm shot!" he announced.

Motley cursed, took the weapon from Ryland's hand, and fired at the wounded Gateman. This pistol boomed, throwing out a blinding yellow flash. The echo was like a roll of thunder. Murk jerked, and lay still.

Ryland slumped backward now, and stretched out on the deck. "The blaggard's killed me!" He seemed more surprised than angry. "Go! Tell Conch." He squeezed his eyes shut in a grimace. "There's no time to waste."

Motley watched for a moment longer, his own eyes wide. He looked once more at Murk-Eye, who lay still. When he looked back down at Ryland, the businessman was also silent and still. Motley knelt beside him. There was no breath in him. He stood up again, looking into the darkness of the woods, listening. Finally he took two steps and leaped over the rail, splashed into the water, and swam for all he was worth toward shore.

When the splashing turned to crashing through the woods, Ryland raised his head. Murk winked his good eye. Stock came up from below. "Lotta ruckus," he said with a grin.

Damrick's calm eyes peered out from under a broad-brimmed hat as he walked in the shadows of the side streets of Skaelington. He wore a full-length riding coat and kept his hands in its pockets, fingers wrapped tightly around two loaded pistols. Beside him was Lye Mogene, wearing a shorter coat and no hat. The two finally stopped in a pool of darkness at the foot of a small church. Damrick glanced once at its towering spire, then looked back down the street.

Satisfied they were not followed, and had drawn no one's attention, he motioned to Lye with a nod. Damrick climbed the seven steps to its red front door, Lye Mogene right behind him. He didn't knock, but turned the large brass handle and both men entered.

"Wait here," Damrick told his lieutenant.

Lye nodded, and positioned himself in front of one of the two small windows of the dark foyer. Damrick went through the door into the sanctuary.

It was black dark within, as though the shadows here cast shadows, and it smelled of must and dust. But it was not unpleasant. In fact, Damrick breathed it in deeply, finding its silence and the feeling of remoteness comforting. He sat in the back pew until his eyes grew accustomed to what starlight came from the few high windows above. He could just make out the shimmering outline of a cross on the wall above the altar.

A door creaked. A shaft of light fell on the cross, and the altar. Then a thin, frail priest in a hooded gray robe shuffled down the center aisle. He was little more than a shadow himself, with only the dim light from the doorway behind him to outline his robes. Damrick slid over, making room, and the priest sat. He was breathing heavily, like a rasp on wood, as though the trek had taken all his strength. He kept his head bowed. The hood shrouded his face.

Damrick waited for him to regain his breath. Then he said, "I have a question to ask you, Father."

"And I have a message for you."

Damrick took a folded, sealed parchment from his pocket. "Is this legitimate?"

"What is it?" The priest reached out for it. Damrick could see that his left hand was badly scarred, front and back. Not burns or ragged cuts, but concentric and interlocking patterns, as though his skin had been carved very carefully but very deeply with tiny knives. His hand trembled as though with great age. Damrick placed the parchment in the priest's palm. He felt it, turned it over, examined the broken seal and the ribbon with the fingers of his right hand, the skin of which was similarly patterned.

"This is an official letter from the Church," the priest said.

"Are you sure?"

"The size, the weight, the paper, the seal. Or it's a very good imitation."

"We found it hidden on Runsford Ryland's boat."

"Unopened."

"It's addressed to Conch Imbry."

There was a pause. "You want me to open it?"

"I didn't feel it right…" He trailed off.

With one trembling hand the priest lowered his hood, revealing a face covered with the same patterned scars that tattooed his hands and arms. His skin was sallow and jaundiced everywhere except where the reddened scar of an old burn marred and puckered his cheek. "I can do little with the short time left me." He raised his head, turned it toward Damrick. Father Carter Dent's eye sockets were empty. "But I will do anything I can do to bring down Conch Imbry."

Damrick swallowed his revulsion until it turned to bitterness in his belly. "Did he do this to you?"

"His Hant chieftain, yes."

"I'm sorry."

"You didn't do it. He did." The priest's carved fingers fumbled, and the seal broke. He unfolded the parchment, and handed it back.

Damrick read it silently. He stared at it a long time. Then he said, "It grants an annulment of marriage to Jenta and Wentworth Ryland."

"I didn't know they were married."

"Nor did I. Why would it be addressed to Conch Imbry?"

"Only if he was the one who made the formal request. And I can think of only one reason he would do so."

Damrick set his jaw. "Yes. It is signed by Jenta also."

"Coerced?"

Damrick didn't answer. He wasn't sure he wanted to know the answer. "But why all this effort? Ryland says Conch killed Wentworth. That's a much quicker annulment, and much more Conch's style."

"Maybe she believes Wentworth is still alive. Maybe Imbry lied to her."

"Or maybe Wentworth actually is alive, and Ryland lied to me."

"But why?"

"So I would believe he has motive to kill the Conch. So I would believe I should trust him."

"I hope you don't. Now I have a message for you from the Gatemen."

He cocked his head. "What is it?"

"It comes from those who call themselves 'The Black S.'"

Damrick nodded, waited. The priest referred to the scrap of parchment that designated some Gatemen as those who Serve.

"They want you to know that Conch has put Jenta to work at the Cleaver and Fork."

"I've heard she works there."

"He's given her the pub, to run. Their message is this: Conch expects you will try to rescue her. He is sure you will at least attempt to contact her. But do not go there. It's a trap."

Damrick bowed his head, rubbed his eyebrows.

After a pause, the priest asked, "What will you do?"

He sighed. "What I must do. If that's what Conch expects, so be it."

"What you must do to get the Conch? Or to get the girl?"

Damrick squinted at the priest. "She and Wentworth stood up to Conch Imbry. They did it by throwing in with me. They're both paying for that decision. Don't you think I owe them?"

"Whatever they have done, they have chosen to do."

"Thanks for the message, Father."

"I have another message. This one from a higher power."

A tingle went down Damrick's spine. "What is it?"

"I don't hear voices as a rule. I believe people know what is right, and are expected to do it. But this...this was different. I don't have much time left here. And I have been given a word of knowledge to pass on to you."

Damrick waited.

"You will bring down Conch Imbry."

The message seemed to deflate Damrick, and he put a hand to his forehead. And then, just as quickly, he sat up straight, his shoulders back, and seemed to grow stronger. "Thank you," he said. And in his voice was a world of gratitude that reached out far beyond a marred and mangled priest in a dark, quiet church.

"It's the pirate's pub!" Lye said urgently. "We don't know who's in there."

Damrick eyed the Cleaver and Fork from across the street. Like most Skaelington pubs, it was quiet and dark from the outside. But this one was distinctive, painted black with crimson and gold trim, with rich velvet curtains visible through big, wide windows. People inside were visible from the street.

"It's just you and me here," Lye tried again. "Two men, four pistols. If this is yer plan, Damrick, I got to say it ain't much a' one."

Damrick still said nothing.

"That priest," Lye tried, "said it's a trap. Right?"

"He said that's what people believe. He said a lot of other things besides." He did not take his eyes from the big windows of the pub.

"It's a pretty fancy place," Lye offered, changing his tack. "We ain't dressed. Prob'ly throw us right out, soon as we set foot in. Don't ye reckon?"

"They might."

"Asides, Conch's prob'ly got people watchin'. Could be watchin' us right now for all we know," Lye suggested, looking up and down the street, up to the rooftops. "Makes sense to just keep on walkin'. Come back with three ships full a' Gatemen, when they arrive. Right?"

Suddenly, Damrick pulled his wide-brimmed hat down over his eyes and stepped out into the street.

"Hey, ye ain't goin' in there, really. Are ye?"

But Damrick didn't turn back.

After a few muttered curses, Lye said, "Whoa, wait up!"

Damrick chose a table in a dark corner to the right, at the front, and put his back to the wall. Lye sat opposite, but turned his chair so he could not be blindsided. Jenta served tables across the room, near the bar. Damrick watched her as though in a trance. She moved like a vision, smiling in that sad, deep way he had first seen in Mann. And then suddenly, she laughed.

Another barmaid broke his line of sight, asked what he wanted. Lye spoke up for an ale, but Damrick said nothing, so Lye put up two fingers and gave her a wink.

"What're we doin' here, Damrick?" Lye leaned in when she had gone. "Here I thought you been cookin' up all sorts a' fancy plans. What with kidnappin' Ryland and capturin' and then lettin' Motley go, I been worried we're gettin' to where there's more plannin' than straight fightin'. I regret that now, sincerely. I'm tellin' ye, I'd rather we worked out a plan afore we get ourselves into a straight fight in this place. And I mean it."

"Who says I don't have a plan?"

"Well, me, fer one." Then after a pause, "Okay, ye seen Jenta. She's fine. She's laughin' and happy. Conch Imbry ain't here. Let's get, and figure out how we can catch 'im."

Damrick watched Jenta, and Lye watched Damrick.

The barmaid returned with two mugs. "Who is that?" Damrick asked her, nodding toward Jenta. Lye lowered his eyes.

"Who's that?" she repeated in disbelief, hands on hips. "Where you two from, anyways? That's Conch Imbry's woman. Best leave her alone, if you're thinking what I think you're thinking."

"I'm sure I know her from somewhere."

"Yeah, that's one I hear a lot."

"Could you ask her to stop by?"

The girl shook her head. But when she left, she spoke to Jenta. After a few minutes, Jenta glided over to the table. She wore a long crimson gown that somehow matched the draperies, though it was smoother, softer. It was cinched at the waist and cut in a V at the neck, where she was draped in pearls. Her only accommodation to her profession seemed to be a white bar towel that she carried in her hand. As she approached, her expression did not change. She might have been coming to check on any two customers.

"Can I help you gentlemen?" She threw the bar towel over her shoulder and crossed her arms. She looked at Damrick as though from far away.

Damrick said nothing.

Jenta spoke again. "Sal says you recognize me from somewhere. Must have been a very long time ago."

"Not so long," Damrick said.

"Long enough," she answered. "Did you need anything from the kitchen?"

"Jenta." Damrick's voice was low and urgent. "What are you doing here?"

"Why, I run this place. Haven't you heard? I'm Conch Imbry's woman. Everyone in town knows that."

"Do they?"

"Everyone." Now he saw a deep stab of pain within her.

And he felt the same within himself. "What happened? What happened to Wentworth?"

She brightened. It was forced. "Now you're prying." She quickly brushed something from the corner of her eye, a movement hidden inside the sweeping back of a wisp of hair. "You two gentlemen are welcome to drink and eat, but I won't gossip with you about private matters." She put a hand on her hip. "Now, can I get you something to eat? We have a fresh meat-and-potato pie, still hot. Guaranteed to fortify."

"What kind a' meat?" Lye asked.

Damrick stared at him.

"Mutton and lamb," Jenta replied.

"Either one, or mixed together?"

"Mixed. It's a pie."

"Well, them's two a' my favorites." He cut a glance at Damrick. "But no thanks, ma'am." There was a trace of sorrow in his voice.

"Enjoy your ale, then," she said. And she left them.

"I was curious, is all," Lye explained. Then when Damrick said nothing, he took a deep breath. "So she's Conch's woman. If she sold out Wentworth, she'll sell us out just as quick. We better get goin'." He took a big sip of ale, sighed conclusively. "Ready?"

Damrick shook his head. "She's trapped here. Conch has put her up to this."

"No, we're the ones trapped here. Let's go."

"Go if you want. But I don't think she's going to reveal us."

"Why?"

"Because she hasn't done it already. And Conch's men are watching."

"What? Where?"

"The big man at the bar facing us, and the one slouching at the table by the window in the far corner, his back to the wall."

Lye started to turn around to look, then caught Damrick's scowl. "You mean them cutthroats been watching us this whole time?"

"Relax. They don't know us from the Crown Prince and his brother." Now Damrick's eyes drifted back to Jenta. She approached the slouching man. The two spoke briefly, and the man cut his eyes to Damrick. Damrick did not look away, and the man glanced back down to his dinner. Jenta left him, and worked her way back to the bar. The slouching man made no further moves.

"Finish your ale," Damrick said to Lye. "I've got some business to take care of. But be ready."

"What business... Wait, be ready for what?"

Damrick stood.

"Ye cain't!" Lye whispered.

But Damrick took his mug with him and walked to the bar. He nodded at the man he'd just identified as Conch's spy, then settled in four places away, putting his mug on the polished mahogany.

Lye Mogene stood, grim-faced, and took Damrick's place on the far side of the table. From this seat in the corner, he could see the whole pub. He put a foot up on the chair across from him. Under the white linen tablecloth he pulled his pistol and rested it in his lap. He took a long drink, thinking about the meat pie he hadn't ordered, wishing he'd ordered it.

Damrick faced toward the bar, his eyes never leaving Jenta as she pulled on the spigot of a barrel of ale, pulling mug after mug. Eventually she set the tray on the bar for the other barmaids, and came to wait on him.

"How did you hurt your hand?" she asked, sliding a leather coaster under his mug of ale.

He looked down at the stitched gash, Talon's handiwork. "Oh, the usual. Pirates."

"They'll do that, I hear. Did you decide you wanted the meat-and-potato pie after all?"

"No. But there is something I want."

Her eyes caught his fire. She looked away, toward Conch's spy. She shook her head just slightly, signaling that this customer wasn't any trouble—no need to intervene.

"I've come to find you, Jenta. As I promised."

"So you've found me." Her look was distant, waiting. "This is what you've found."

"I asked you about Wentworth," Damrick said softly. "But I don't believe you've answered me yet."

"I did, though. I told you that my business is my business, and none of yours."

He saw no way in. "Jenta. There must be some of your business that could yet be some of mine."

Now she laughed. "I run a public house." She put one hand on a hip. "You want some of this business? If so, I've got dishes you can wash."

Damrick glanced at the big spy, who was eyeing him carefully. "I have no fear of dishes." He looked back at Jenta. "Seems to me you could use some help." He said it urgently.

"Really? Do I appear helpless to you?"

"How do you move that ale from your storeroom to the bar?" He gestured at the rows of oaken barrels behind her. "I'm guessing the Conch doesn't haul it for you."

She took the towel from her shoulder and began wiping the top of the bar in front of him. After a moment she said, "You think I can't get a man to roll a barrel for me?"

"I think you could get a man to do pretty well what you please."

"Any man?"

"Not just any man."

She watched his eyes, said nothing.

He watched hers. "You know who I am, Jenta." His voice was barely a whisper, but his eyes flamed.

"Yes," she said in rhythm, too low to be overheard. "You guard the gates of hell. Protecting men from pirates." He did not miss the slight emphasis she placed on the word *men*.

"I can protect anyone from pirates."

"Can you?"

"Yes. Even from Conch Imbry."

Her look grew distant. "If you're paid to."

"If I've a mind to."

She stopped wiping, straightened up. "What is it you want from me? Tell me. I'll answer, and you can go your way."

Now his eyes were hard as diamonds. "I want to know where your heart lies."

She shook her head. "That's just it. My heart lies. I don't trust it, and neither should you."

"But I will trust it. If you will let me."

Her lower lip trembled once. She set her jaw. "You don't know me."

"I know you have many secrets. I don't know them all. But I know some."

"Do you?"

"I know the cellar where you grew up." She said nothing. "I know the bargain you made with Runsford Ryland. I know about Wentworth. I know about Conch."

She shrugged. "You still don't know me."

"I know you've been waiting for an answer from the Church of Nearing Vast."

Now her face dropped. "You'd better go."

The man four stools down saw Jenta's eyes flash, heard her tone change. He stood.

Across the pub Lye Mogene grew alarmed, and also stood.

"I know what the Church's answer is," Damrick told her.

"Problem here, ma'am?" Conch's man was much bigger than Damrick, several years older, with blunted features pocked and lined with the scars of multiple fights.

"This one is getting a bit personal. Perhaps you could see him out."

"Looks like you got a habit a' gettin' in trouble," he said, noting

Damrick's wounded hand. "Let's not have any of it in here, son, and they won't be stitchin' you anywheres else." The big man's demeanor was surprisingly gentle as he raised his left hand to clamp it down on Damrick's shoulder.

Damrick caught the big hand at the wrist and spun its owner around, pinning him against the bar so that his arm was bent up behind him like a turkey trussed for cooking. Pressing up with one hand, Damrick drew the man's pistol and pushed the barrel of it against the back of his skull.

Across the room, Conch's slouching spy now stood and drew, wiping his mouth as he rushed the bar. But Lye Mogene was already standing in the center of the room. He put his foot out, and the slouching man went sprawling between the tables, his pistol clattering away. As his head came up, Lye's pistol butt came down. The pirate's spy lay still, fully slouched now, and Lye picked up the weapon.

"Nobody move!" he shouted, now brandishing two pistols. When no one did, he said, "I don't wanna hurt nobody, but I will, if ye make one move I don't like!"

Damrick didn't bother to look behind him. He whispered into the big spy's ear. "Tell your boss that Damrick Fellows is back in town. Tell him the gates of hell are open for business."

"Are you him?" the man asked. "Are you Fellows?"

"Are you going to give Conch that message, or not?"

"No, I ain't."

Damrick pulled back the hammer.

"Shoot me if ye want, mister, but I ain't sayin' nothin' about no gates a' hell. Not to the Conch."

Damrick sighed. Then he raised the pistol and cold-cocked the pirate with it, hitting him hard at the base of the neck. The man shuddered, but stood. Damrick scowled, then took another swipe at him with the pistol butt, this time across the back of the head. The man wobbled, teetered, and fell.

"That man's got a thick skull," Lye noted.

Damrick turned to Jenta. She was far away, detached. "Come with me now," he said urgently. He put out his hand.

She looked at it, but shook her head. Her eyes were cold.

Damrick felt like he'd had the wind kicked out of him. "Why not?"

She spoke slowly, to make sure he understood her. "Because I belong to Conch Imbry."

Lye blew out his cheeks. "Reckon she's got a thick skull, too, Dam—"

he caught himself halfway through the name, and looked around him. "—it all," he concluded loudly. "Come on, let's get, afore some real trouble comes along."

Damrick refused to move. He kept the spy's pistol in one hand, pulled the sealed envelope from his pocket with the other. He laid it in front of Jenta. She stared at it.

"Sit back down!" Lye barked at a gentleman who was making a move for the door. The man sat. But others were at the window, outside looking in. He couldn't stop them from leaving, from going to report all this to Conch Imbry. "Let's get!" he barked, though it came out more like begging.

"Go ahead, open it," Damrick directed Jenta.

"It's not addressed to me."

"But it's about you."

She opened it, and read. When she looked back up, she was far away. She tossed the paper back onto the bar.

"Wentworth is alive," Damrick said. "Isn't he?" She did not respond, and he knew it was true.

"Now I will marry Conch Imbry."

"But why?"

"Because I choose to." Her demeanor grew urgent. "Now. Will—you—leave me—alone?"

The muscles of his jaw tightened. "No."

"Oh, boy," Lye said with a heave of his chest.

She stared at Damrick, then turned and walked away, toward the private room. When she came out from behind the curtain she had a pistol in her hand. She saw Damrick, shook her head as if to say, *You're still here?* Then she raised the pistol, and aimed it at him.

Damrick shook his head. His mind turned. She was a pirate, then. She had a gun. So did he. The oaths he'd made others take, his calling, his mission, justice, the law, even his instincts...all led him to one single conclusion. She should die.

Jenta clicked back the pistol's hammer. Her eyes were empty and dark.

How does one develop a fist of iron, Winall Frost had asked, *without developing a heart to match?* Damrick heard the words in his head.

He made his choice. Without taking his eyes off her, he set his pistol on the bar.

"I'm not leaving you to him," he told her. And this time his low voice

was sharp enough to split an oak. "And I'm not leaving here without you."
His next words were spoken with the same intensity, but a softer edge:
"Jenta, I want to marry you."

The immediate result was a sharp, collective inward breath, a room
full of gasps followed by a long stretch of no breathing at all.

The pirates in the forecastle reacted the same way, and then were quiet
for a long time. Finally, Sleeve broke the silence. "Well I'll just say this
and then shut up. If I went out searchin' the world over fer the very best
way to make smack solid sure I wouldn't never live a life that was long
and happy...why, I believe I'd stop right there on that one."

He found no disagreement.

CHAPTER FIFTEEN

SUCCESS

"HE'S SHOT DEAD," Motley insisted glumly. "I saw it with my eyes." He was covered in mud and dried blood. His long hair was matted with burrs and his clothes reeked of swamp muck. The dappled marks on his face were hidden under mud and blood and welts from thorns and briars. He sat on the deck of the *Shalamon*, and Mart Mazeley knelt on one knee beside him.

"Did you kill Runsford Ryland?" Conch's unimpressive card dealer asked calmly.

"No! No sir. I shot the Gateman! I told you that. It was the Gateman shot Ryland."

"Why would they shoot him if they believed he was on their side?"

"It happened real fast. Ryland was checkin' on one of 'em, a man with a popped-out eye. Mr. Ryland thought he was dead, but he wasn't."

"The Gatemen shot Ryland, but they let you escape."

"No one let me! I told ye, I'm the one shot the Gateman." Motley was glum. He could tell that this was not going well, but he couldn't tell why.

"How many did you shoot?"

"Just the one."

"And where were the rest of the crew?" Mazeley asked.

"On the raid."

"They left you with one guard, whom you managed to shoot, while he shot one of his own. Did the Gatemen strike you as inept?"

He looked confused. "They didn't strike me at all."

Mazeley blinked. "Did they come across as incompetent?"

"Incom…"

"I'll ask a different question. Why did you and Ryland run from the fight in Oster?"

"We didn't run. Me and Mr. Ryland got captured while still fightin', and was lucky to live."

"Captured while fighting. Yet the Gatemen were overrun and killed."

"Naw, not in Oster. They beat us real bad. Kilt everyone but me and Ryland."

Mazeley just blinked again. Then, "Did you see Scatter Wilkins there?"

"Oh, yeah. He brought the *Lantern Liege* into the harbor to block the way. Fired with his cannon."

"Do you know that he's here, in Skaelington?"

"Well, I seen his ship." He threw a thumb over his shoulder.

"Your men were 'beat real bad.' Yet Wilkins and his crew came through with no casualties at all."

Motley looked suddenly thoughtful. "That's kinda funny, then."

"Hmm. Why did Damrick Fellows believe that Mr. Ryland was working with him?"

"I guess Ryland fooled 'im?" Doubt began to gather like a mist.

"But now Ryland's dead."

"That's right."

"So…all of Ryland's men died, and so did Ryland, and you are the only one left alive to tell the tale. Except for Wilkins's entire ship, who tell the opposite tale…that the Gatemen were slaughtered in Oster."

"They do?"

"Yes."

Motley swallowed hard. "Sounds kinda funny, then."

"That is not the word I would choose, Mr. Motley. What makes you think that Ryland isn't actually working for them, against us? What makes you think he didn't let you go, to bring Conch Imbry false information?"

Motley's eye twitched as he thought hard about the question, and felt the gaping maw of its implications as they opened under him. "'Cause he was shot tryin' to help the Conch."

"Was Ryland shot trying to *help* your captain? Or was he shot trying to *hurt* him? Or are you just a liar?"

"I ain't no liar, Mr. Mazeley!" It was a plea. "I swear I'm honest."

"You're honest? Well, that won't endear you to many pirate captains."

"I mean, no…I'm jus' honest about what I'm sayin' to ye now. I can lie good when I need to."

"I'm quite sure of it. What exactly did Mr. Ryland instruct you to tell the Captain?"

"He said Damrick's goin' to the Cleaver and Fork tonight on a raid, and ye can catch 'im there."

Mazeley rubbed his chin. "Ryland told you that Damrick could be captured at the Cleaver and Fork."

"Aye."

"And then he cut you loose so you could come tell the Captain."

"Aye."

"Isn't that something, then." Mazeley was silent, thinking. Then he stood up and beckoned two sailors over. "I need you to go find Captain Imbry, below. Tell him—"

"Conch! Conch Imbry!" The cry came from the dock.

Pirates rushed to the rail. A well-dressed gentlemen stood below. "There's a fight at the Cleaver and Fork! There's someone come after Jenta Stillmithers!"

Jenta stared hard at Damrick. She did not lower her pistol. Then the corner of her lip rose. "So that's what this is about? You came here to marry me?"

"No." Then he thought better of it. "Yes. That's why I came here, though I didn't know it until just now."

Her expression did not change.

Damrick's face went slack with fear—fear that she would yet turn him down. He took three long strides and stood before her, the pistol now pressed into his chest. He looked down at it, then up into her blue eyes, then he stepped forward into the pistol and put a hand on her waist, as though he was prepared, finally, to dance with her. He stepped closer. The pistol slid away. He kissed her. She let him. But she did not embrace him in return. He pulled away, took her left hand in his right. Her pistol pointed at the floor.

"You're the pirate's woman," he told her. "But you are no man's wife. You are free to choose your husband."

She stared up at him, stunned, searching. "I can't. He'll kill…"

"He'll kill who? You? No, you'll be with me. Your mother? I've already sent a carriage for her. She'll be safe."

Jenta blinked. Then she said, "He'll kill Wentworth."

Damrick studied her eyes until the realization dawned within him. "You convinced Conch to spare Wentworth. That's what all this is about. This is how you saved Wentworth."

She closed her eyes. "You have to go. Don't you see that?"

"No, I don't. It's too late." He took her by the shoulders. "I'm not going anywhere. Not ever. I will stay here and fight for you."

"You'll die."

"Then I'll die."

"I..." She looked into his eyes, searching.

He saw light there. He saw a spark. He dropped to a knee, took her left hand in both of his. "Marry me, Jenta. Marry *me*."

Her look was longing.

"Tell me how that would be a worse fate than marrying the Conch."

"But Wentworth—"

"We will go find him, together. I will save him, if it's in the power God gives me; if any man can save him, I will."

"You would do that?" And suddenly her eyes were awash in an unexpected hope.

"That, and more. Will you marry me, Jenta?"

Her search suddenly ended, she absorbed the light she saw, the hope she felt rising in her, rising up from him, carrying her somewhere she had not imagined she could go. "Damrick Fellows." She said the two words as though they were an incantation, as though the name itself would ward off unseen evils.

The guests gasped in sudden recognition, repeating the incantation to one another.

And then Jenta said two more words in reply, in rebuke of the storms that raged around them, in defiance of the dark waves that rose to crush them, in agreement with and submission to this new, sudden promise of hope. "I will," she said. A tear rolled down her cheek. From the midst of the reckless light and warmth that washed through her, she said it again. "I will."

He stood and kissed her again. Her right hand, still holding the pistol, wrapped around him, pressed into him, and she kissed him back.

The room stirred, chairs creaked, and a low whistle rose from the back.

"Can we get now?" Lye asked. He wiped at the corner of his own eye. "I can't take no more a' this."

The pirates listening to Ham expressed wholehearted agreement with Lye Mogene…though in most cases for quite a different reason.

"Battle stations, everyone!" Mart Mazeley called, rising to his feet. "I expect an attack on this ship at any moment!"

"What?" Motley asked, still seated on the decking. "Damrick's at the Cleaver and Fork, jus' like I said!"

"It's a diversion, you idiot."

"It's a what?"

"The fight is coming here."

"Ye still don't believe me!"

"No, I still—" Mazeley paused, looked to the stairway, recognizing the booted footfalls approaching.

Conch Imbry climbed up from below. "Who's that hollerin'?"

"Them Gatemen's down at the pub, Captain!" Motley blurted. "Mr. Mazeley won't—"

Mazeley kicked him in the jaw, a quick, savage thrust with the sole and heel of his shoe. Motley's head snapped back, and then his skull hit the decking. He rolled over on his side, holding his mouth with both hands. He groaned.

Conch's eyes widened, impressed.

"Apologies, Captain. But Motley here has just escaped from Runsford Ryland's boat. He claims Ryland told him that the Gatemen plan to raid your pub and steal your girl."

"Who's that yellin' below?"

"Not one of ours, though he is providing the same report."

Conch drew his pistol. His eyes took in Motley, who lay on his side with his eyes closed, probing a loosened tooth with a bloody finger. Conch turned back to Mazeley. "Explain yerself, Mr. Mazeley, why ye ain't moved to save Jenta. And be quick."

"The last thing you want to do, sir, is move your men off this ship." Mazeley calmly ticked through the list on his fingers. "First, Motley claims that the Gatemen won the fight in Oster, and completely overran Ryland's men."

"That wasn't Talon's report."

"Indeed. Second, he says that he and Ryland were taken prisoner during the fight."

Conch now eyed Motley with suspicion, as the ragged man struggled back to a seated position. "The Gatemen have never left a man alive."

"My thoughts as well. Third, he claims that the Gatemen all believed Ryland was working with them, and against us. Yet when Motley made his daring escape, they somehow shot Ryland and let our Motley get away."

"Ryland's shot?"

Still dazed, Motley stared at the blood on his fingers.

"And finally, the urgent message that Ryland gave Motley, for your ears only, was that you should send all your men to the Cleaver and Fork, where you'll be sure to capture Damrick Fellows."

Conch took two steps, squatted in front of the miserable Motley. "Did he say all that right?"

Motley blinked several times, his mouth drawn down, his eyes focused on Conch's pistol. "I don' know. Wasn't really listenin'. Cap'n, I'm jus' tryin' to do ye right, sir."

"Ryland said we'd best catch Damrick at the Cleaver and Fork, did he?"

"He said it. Aye, sir."

Conch chewed a lip. "What d'ye make of it, Mr. Mazeley?"

"Either Motley's a lying traitor, or he's a complete, witless fool who can't see when he's being used to trick his own captain."

"I'm a fool, then," Motley managed thickly. He spat blood. " 'Cause I sure ain't no traitor."

Conch stared hard at Motley one more time, then stood. "I believe ye." His eyes drifted over the docks, across town. "Maybe he got the rest of it wrong, but for Ryland's message."

"The only message I'm hearing is, don't trust Runsford Ryland," urged Mazeley. "Why would Damrick Fellows risk everything for a woman? He wants you."

"Aye. He wants me. But not in the same way." Conch walked to the rail, leaned on it. "Yer not the sort to understand such things, Mr. Mazeley. But sometimes smart men get foolish over women."

"Then they're not smart men."

Conch turned his head, his narrow eyes cornering Mazeley. Then he walked back to Motley, loomed over him. "Ye saw Ryland take a musket ball, did ye?"

"In the back. Shot dead!" Motley couldn't have opened his eyes any wider. "Breathed them words a' warnin', and never again moved after that."

Conch stood. "I hate to ignore a man's dyin' words." He sighed. "Make yer recommendation, Mr. Mazeley."

"I recommend we strip Motley to the waist and tie him to the grate. Then I recommend battle stations. Should there be a fight here at the *Shalamon*, and should Motley survive it, then I'd like permission to take the skin off his back until we learn what he's made of underneath."

"Very reasonable, as usual. All right. Prepare this ship to fight, Mr. Mazeley." But he spoke without his usual bluster, and his eyes were drawn again toward the lamp-lit streets of Skaelington.

The couple left the pub through the front door, Jenta under Damrick's left arm, her pistol still in her right hand. Damrick now held his own pistol in his hand as well, once again ready to face any opposition. Lye Mogene followed them, walking backward, the barrel of his weapon swinging back and forth in a wide arc to take in the entire room.

"Nobody moves, hear me?" he said as he pushed through the doors. As they closed he turned and saw for the first time the size of the crowd now gathered on the streets. "Damrick!" he called. "I hope ye know where yer goin'!"

"Follow me, and keep your eyes open."

"Oh, they're open."

But though the crowd was large, it was quiet, and did not seem hostile. No one reached for a weapon before the trio ducked up a dark alley. Then the gathered citizens dispersed. The pub emptied, too, leaving two downed pirates to come to their senses in their own time.

Minutes later in a small church with a red door, down the alley and up two blocks, a broken, scarred, blinded priest with barely the strength to stand, voice rasping but assured, stood before them in the glow of a single candle. He led them through their vows.

Though he was but the witness, Lye was more nervous than the groom. He kept his back to the ceremony and his gun in his hand, watching the doors.

"We can skip the rings, if you like," the priest asked at the appropriate point.

"I'm afraid we don't have any—" Damrick began, but stopped when he saw Jenta's eyes widen in something that looked much like amazement.

"I have these," she said, and produced two gold bands from her pocket. "Wentworth bought them and had them inscribed," she explained, as he took them from her open palm. "But we never said vows over them, and never wore them."

Damrick read the inscription inside the larger one. "'Jenta.'" He shook his head. "I'm not sure…"

She looked at him. "But I am. He and I were never married in the eyes of the Church. If he were here, and I do wish he were, he would bless this. I want to honor him, Damrick. I want to honor his highest, best intentions. With this gift, he is here, and a part of us for as long as we live."

Damrick nodded. "For Wentworth, then." And he closed his hand around the rings.

"Let us continue," the priest urged. "Time is short."

When Father Dent closed with a prayer, he drew the sign of the cross in the air above the couple's bowed heads.

"May God have mercy on your souls," he said in benediction.

Damrick looked up at him sharply.

The priest coughed once. "I'm sorry. I meant to say, you may now kiss the bride.'"

As Damrick complied, Lye muttered under his breath. "Got it right the first time."

"So where's the attack, Mr. Mazeley?" Conch asked. His gruff voice was calm, but a storm brewed behind it.

Mazeley stood beside him at the ship's stern, scanning both the city and the seas. "Motley likely got everything wrong."

Conch put a hand on his sword hilt, belted around his waist in preparation for a fight that now did not seem inevitable. "I'm thinkin' it was you got everythin' wrong."

"Wait," Mazeley said, pointing.

"Those are our men!" Conch's tone was a threat, his teeth bared. "Ain't them the two was guardin' Jenta?"

The pair approached the docks, walking unsteadily. One was a big man with a scarred face, the other was thin, and slouched. Both looked haggard. Each had a bottle in his hand.

"Doesn't look like good news, does it?" Mazeley asked serenely.

Conch did not answer, nor did he wait for the two men to reach the ship. He ordered the gangway lowered and walked out to meet them. Mazeley followed Conch. Half a dozen cutthroats, obeying silent gestures from Mazeley, followed both of them. Threescore more lined the rails of the *Shalamon*, watching.

These sailors had seen Conch Imbry's wrath before. They stood stonily, watching it again, grateful to be at a distance. They saw their

Captain begin the grilling even as he strode up to the pair. Both men hung their heads. Then they shook them, each in turn. A few words, no more than a sentence or two, passed their lips in their own defense. The big man held up his right hand, pointed at the back of it, demonstrating for his captain the distinguishing mark of a stitched scar carried by the perpetrator. Then Conch Imbry took the bottle from the big man's hand, held it up to the light, smelled it, and gave it back. He stood inches away, and the sailors could hear his voice, ragged and commanding. They saw the big man raise the bottle to his lips, obediently. Then the sailor put his head back, drinking down the contents in long pulls. They watched as the Captain put his pistol's barrel under the big man's chin, and fired. They saw the flash, heard the report, saw the man's body go suddenly stiff, as though a bolt of lightning had run through him, and then collapse backward onto the wooden slats of the dock. The bottle shattered on the planking.

They watched as Imbry held out his left hand, and Mazeley put a pistol into it. They saw the slouching man cringe, trying vainly to duck even as his feet were planted and unmoving, as though unable to decide whether to flee or stand. Conch pressed the barrel into the back of his neck. The man's bottle hit the deck, rolled away. He made his decision, bolted for the water at the edge of the dock. Conch raised the pistol, fired. They all saw the man fall forward, as though diving too soon for the safety of the sea. He hit the dock with his knees, then his stomach; then he flipped forward into the water. From the ship, the splash sounded like a single, solid thud. He floated on his back for only a moment, unmoving, and then he rolled over as he sank, bubbles gurgling upward.

They all watched as Conch strode away, headed toward the Cleaver and Fork, his sword swinging at his side.

"First watch!" Mazeley cried, turning back to the ship. "First watch, follow me!"

And one third of the ship scrambled to obey.

"Not again." Shayla squinted past the driver, trying to identify the carriage parked out in front of her cottage. It looked like one of Ryland's, but in the darkness it was hard to tell. She pulled her robe up around her neck against the chill. "It's two o'clock in the morning."

"And my apologies for that, ma'am," He was not one of Runsford's regular drivers; at least not one Shayla recognized. He was stiff and formal, dressed more like a businessman than a coachman.

"And you can't tell me who insists on seeing me at this hour?"

"Only that he is a person of some note, with questions bearing on your daughter's well-being. That is all he has instructed to me to say. Forgive me."

"Well, you're polite about it anyway. I'll need time to dress."

"The issue is rather urgent. How much time will you need?"

"An hour would be sufficient."

He blanched.

"But ten minutes will do."

He bowed. "We shall wait."

Fifteen minutes later, Shayla swept down the front steps of her house in a cream-colored gown, matching gloves to her elbows, a stole around her shoulders. Her hair was down—imperfectly brushed but perfectly disheveled, as if in defiance.

There was only one person waiting in the carriage, and she recognized him as soon as the door was opened for her. "Oh," she said with disappointment. Then lifting her chin, she said with perfect grace, "To what do I owe this honor, Mr. Frost?"

"Please join me, and I shall tell you."

The driver held her hand and helped her up into the cab. When the door was shut and locked, and the dark carriage lurched forward, Windall said, "Damrick Fellows sends you his greetings, and his apologies. As do I. But this is not a social visit."

"Really? How surprising."

"Last time I visited you and Jenta, I asked you both to leave Skaelington. This time, it's not a request. I'm afraid your time in Skaelington has come to an end."

She hesitated. Then she said, "I see. Poked the bear but good this time, did we? Where is Jenta?"

"She's fine. She's with Damrick."

Shayla took a deep breath, then put her head back against the seat. "She's with Damrick." She let thoughts flow through her mind. "I suppose that's where she wants to be?"

He said nothing.

"Are we going there, too?"

"Where is that, ma'am?"

"Wherever they are."

"No. With any luck, they are already sailing away from this island."

"Headed where?"

"I do not know. It's safer for them that way. I have arranged another boat to take you back to Mann."

"With you, I suppose?"

"Yes, ma'am. I hope that's acceptable."

After another long moment's reflection, she looked down at her hands, then up at Windall Frost. Her eyes were clear, her expression open. "I have done all I could. I tried to break the rules, but they have broken me." She spoke with no bitterness, but as someone who had thought it all through over a long period of time. "Jenta is with Damrick Fellows, a person of her own social stratum. And I am going back to Mann with no place, no position, no possessions, no family." She rubbed a thumb along her fingertips. She smiled. "And the calluses were finally gone."

His look was compassion laced with regret. "You don't need to believe this, Shayla. But I admire you more than I can say."

"Thank you for giving me permission to doubt." Then after another moment, her head held high, she said, "Sir, I have treated you poorly. I have made…serious errors of judgment. But I ask you, if you could see fit, would you allow me to return to my old position? I promise that I will cause you no more trouble." A tear welled in the corner of one eye, and she made no move to hide it, or to wipe it away.

He shook his head. "Mrs. Stillmithers, I have no idea what you're talking about. I understand that you are fleeing Skaelington with only the clothes on your back, having faced up to the pirates here and thus put yourself in peril. You not only have my protection, you also have the thanks of all those who work to rid the seas of the scourge of piracy. I would be honored if you would stay in my guesthouse. It isn't much, but it's yours for as long as you wish it. I can only hope you will not find the accommodations too modest for a lady of your stature."

Shayla remained silent as they rode through the darkness.

Conch stood in the streets outside the Cleaver and Fork, a loose ring of men around him. Six bodies lay strewn at his feet. Two were shot with spent pistols now lying on the paving stones, four were run through with the bloody sword he still held in his hand. He looked around, caught Mazeley's eye.

"Who else helped 'im?" He raged.

Mazeley shook his head. "I can give you more citizens, Captain, but I doubt they'll know any more than these whom you've already…

questioned." He gestured with an open palm toward the corpses of the random, unlucky dead.

Conch bared his teeth. Then he raised his face to the heavens. He held his arms out to his sides, dropped the sword. It clattered onto the stones. "Ye'll pay fer this, Damrick Fellows! Ye'll pay with blood! Ever last man, woman, and child that sides wif ye, I'll quarter and burn 'em! I'll see yer head on a pike! Ye stole my woman, and if ye harm one hair on her head, I'll ram ye—"

"He won't harm her, Captain."

Conch stopped, stunned by the interruption, the gall of it, the confident tone of it. He turned slowly and looked behind him. It was the skinny priest, the one the Hant had cut up. The robed figure walked forward. Conch's men moved aside, aghast at what they saw.

"What'd ye say to me?" Conch asked him.

The hollow, empty eyes seemed to bore in on Conch Imbry. Yet the scarred, marred face, yellow with jaundice, carried no expression. "He married her. I officiated as they pledged their lives to one another. Damrick and Jenta Fellows are man and wife." He held out the letter from the Church, which had been left with him by the fleeing couple.

Conch walked up to him, grimaced at the disfigured face. He grabbed the letter, read it, threw it aside. "He forced her."

"No, Captain. You did. All your life you've set yourself against man and God, forcing your will on those around you. 'But do not be deceived. God is not mocked; for whatsoever a man soweth, that shall he reap.' Your time is at hand, Carnsford Bloodstone Imbry. Repent while you still can."

Conch looked at him as a king might look at a jester who has made a joke at his lord's expense. "Repent?"

"Yes. I can forgive you for all you've done to me. If a man like me can do that, then certainly God can forgive the rest."

Conch laughed. He looked around at his men. They did not seem to share the joke. He turned, walked back to his bloody sword, picked it up. He hefted it in his hand, feeling its weight and balance as he returned to where the priest stood. "The Hant's poison been addlin' yer brain."

"No. It's been killing my body. My mind is clear."

"And so yer sayin' straight? Ye can forgive me?"

"I'm saying I will forgive you. And so will God. But you must repent."

Conch thought a moment. "Ye married my woman off to my enemy. Way I see it, ain't me needs forgivin'. It's you what's done me wrong. The question ye should be askin' is, will I forgive *you*?"

Blaggard's Moon

288

As Conch drew back his sword, Father Dent bowed his head. The sword tip penetrated the priest's robes just above the rope of his belt. The hilt struck his belly so hard that it doubled him over, forcing wind from his lungs in a great, sudden rush. Then Conch's sudden jerk upward forced blood from the priest's mouth and nose. He choked on it, his body trembling, and he coughed up more blood.

Conch pulled the sword free. Father Dent was still on his feet, but doubled over. With his left hand, Conch raised the man's chin with two fingers, an almost gentle move, straightening him upright. He watched the priest's face flush as he struggled to breathe. Then Conch put a hand on the back of the priest's head, and bent him over again. Raising the sword high, its point aimed downward, he drove it with both hands hard into the priest's back, through his ribs, piercing his heart. The priest fell to his knees dead. Conch left the sword there, a foot of blade visible between the hilt and the robe.

"I forgive ye," Conch said to the lifeless, kneeling body. He leaned down. "Ye see, sir, I would a' held a grudge had ye lived. Now yer dead, and yer deed is punished, I can see fit to let it pass."

He stood up straight and grinned a crooked grin. Now his men laughed out loud, in solidarity, obedience, and relief. Conch pulled the sword free from the priest's back and tossed it, clattering, onto the street. He then grabbed the dead man's elbow with two hands, and pulled him upright, turning into him, twisting the limp arm across his shoulder, and stood up straight. The bloody priest now dangled like a gruesome rucksack. The pirate captain carried his burden to the Cleaver and Fork and kicked the doors open. Inside, he laid the body on the bar, and walked back out.

"Burn that place to the ground," he ordered. "I never want to see it again."

"Why, Damrick! Welcome back!" Ryland stood from his desk as Damrick entered his cabin.

"You seem surprised to see me."

"Not at all," the smooth businessman answered. "Why should I be surprised? Did all go as planned?"

"No, actually. It did not."

"No? What happened? All went as planned on this end."

"Someone told Conch Imbry that our target was the Cleaver and Fork."

"Really? How could that be?"

"Hard to know. Unless it was Motley."

They heard footsteps above on deck. The anchor winch clinked in a metallic staccato.

"But I gave Motley the information we agreed upon. I told him you were planning an attack on the *Shalamon*."

"Did you?"

"Of course!" Ryland was indignant. "I'm sure he believed me. I was shot dead on account if it, for all he knew. Of what do you accuse me?"

Damrick looked away, shook his head, looked upward, looked back. "You make me tired, Ryland."

"Tell me what happened!"

They felt the ship heel gently to port. They were under sail.

Damrick walked to the bunk and sat heavily. "I really should shoot you."

Now Ryland was alarmed. "Shoot me? But what on earth—?"

"Just shut up. I don't want to hear it. I know about the letter."

"What letter?"

"Stop. Please. The letter from the Church to Conch Imbry. The one you were carrying to him in secret, to tell him he could marry your son's wife."

Ryland glanced at the floor panels.

"Yes, the one you hid here." Damrick scuffled the rug away from the floorboards with a boot. An iron ring was fitted flush with the floor. He grasped the ring and pulled it open. "Are you smuggling, too, Ryland?"

"No. That's…for personal protection."

"To hide yourself. From whom? Pirates? Or from me?"

"Look, I don't even know what that letter said. A churchman gave it to me. It was addressed to him. What was I supposed to do?"

"You were supposed to tell me about it. But you didn't, because you've been doing Conch's bidding. You told Motley we would attempt to rescue Jenta at the Cleaver and Fork. Admit it."

Ryland blew out his cheeks. "I didn't," he lied. "Maybe Conch was there in force by coincidence, I don't know. I'm just glad you survived."

Damrick stared at him.

"I've risked everything to side with you. Don't you see that? I feigned my own death for you!"

"You did that because you can't resist playing both sides. Dying for his cause, you'd be beyond suspicion. Doing what I asked, you'd convince me of your loyalty. Conch wouldn't hunt you down, and neither would I.

Once there was a clear victor you could proclaim your loyalty to whichever one of us was left alive."

"I'm sorry your plans were foiled, Mr. Fellows. But I could never have planned all that out in advance. You have a very devious mind."

"It comes of following a rat down a rat hole." Damrick stood slowly, then grabbed Ryland by the collar at the back of the neck, and propelled him roughly up the stairs.

"What are you going to do to me?"

"I'm not going to do anything to you. Conch may not be able to say the same." Damrick shoved him out onto the dark deck. The ship was already out of the cove, nearly to open waters. The moon was rising, huge and golden, on the horizon.

"You didn't think this one through carefully enough, Ryland. Can you swim?"

"You're putting me off my own boat?"

"Yes. Can you swim? Now would be the time to tell me, if you can't."

Ryland raised his chin and tried to straighten his shirt and jacket, but Lye Mogene and Murk grabbed him, held his arms tight. "I have been loyal to you."

"No," Stock said, walking up to Ryland, putting his young face into the older man's. "I wasn't hidin' below deck, but was just inside the door. You tol' Motley the truth. I heard it. You was supposed to lie."

Ryland sneered at his captors, but did not struggle against them. "The boy lies. But it doesn't matter. I'll have no problems with the Conch."

"Won't you?" A woman's voice.

Ryland's head spun around, and his eyes strained into the dim light. But he recognized the source. "How did you…?"

Jenta stood at the rail, leaning back against it, both hands on the polished wood. "Hello, Mr. Ryland. Please give Conch Imbry my regards when you see him. I'm afraid he won't be very pleased."

"Dear Lord."

"He might even be a bit angry," Damrick added.

"But not with me! I tried to help him outwit the lot of you rabble," he added, defiant now in defeat.

"Yet he was outwitted in the end. And so were you. You helped us, rather than him."

"I did no such thing."

"But you did. If someone as cunning and disloyal as you told me I should go to a pub and leave my ship unprotected, do you know what I'd do? I'd do just what Conch did. He doesn't trust you, Ryland. He thinks you're working with me." Damrick walked over and stood beside Jenta. She put her arm through his.

Ryland could not hide his disgust. "So it's Damrick now? Why you worthless little lowborn—"

He was stopped by Lye Mogene's fist, which struck him squarely in the mouth. His head snapped back, his hair flopping into his face.

"Sorry, ma'am," Lye said to Jenta. "Din't know he was gonna say that, or I'd a hit 'im sooner."

"It's quite all right," Jenta said. "He's said worse things to my mother and me."

"He has?" Lye asked, astonished. So Lye hit him again. Runsford's knees trembled as quivering hands came up to fend off further blows.

"That's enough!" Damrick ordered. He pulled Ryland's hands away from his face, looked into his eyes. "Are you all right, Mr. Ryland?"

"Yes," he said with disdain, jerking his hands free of Damrick's. "Leave me be."

"As you wish."

And Damrick leaned down, wrapped his arms around Runsford Ryland's waist, stood suddenly, and tossed the shipping mogul over the rail.

Jenta took in a sharp breath; Stock, Lye, and Murk all laughed aloud as the splash rose, white in the dark night, and disappeared.

"Will he be all right?" Jenta asked, looking after him.

"He won't drown, if that's what you mean." They were but a hundred yards past the beach. Ryland sputtered to the surface behind them. Then he swore. Lye Mogene swore back.

Then Ryland turned and swam for shore, as *Success* sailed without him.

Ham's pirate audience cheered and laughed, pleased with the trouble Ryland had in store.

When they calmed, Dallis Trum spoke up. "But I don't get it. How did Damrick know Conch wouldn't go to the pub, when that's where Motley told him to go?"

"Well, it's like this," Ham answered. "Damrick had worked it out so that Motley would not be trusted." The rest were quietly amazed. Ham seemed actually to be answering the boy's plain question, and giving a plain answer.

"But wasn't Ryland really working for Conch all the time?"

"He was and he wasn't. There are men in the world, young pup, who won't choose a side. Which is why your pirate captains all require a blood oath, so's no man will be tempted. It's why the Gatemen did the same. Mr. Ryland, though, he never swore such an oath. But let me tell you what's happening in Ryland's head as he sits on that sandy beach all by himself, his nose and mouth bleeding and stinging from the salt water, his own ship sailing away into the night. He's got the whole ocean spreading out before him, and the moon coming up bigger than the sun, bigger than anything on earth, and that ship, his own ship, *Success*, just dwarfed by it, swallowed up in it, floating black like a shadow, impossible to tell if she's coming or going. And he's thinking about all his choices. He's contemplating how he might have made a different choice at that card table, and thrown everything away to save his son, and be sitting on a beach beside Wentworth watching that dazzling moon, but able to appreciate it, to enjoy it, because he did what he should have done. And though he'd be poor and living on coconuts, he'd be in better shape than he is now. Because now, he's trying to figure out how he's going to ever get his business back when Conch thinks he's dead.

"And the more he thinks about how he can explain it all to the Conch, the less he likes his story. He can't claim that he'd been straight with Motley, because then he can't explain why he isn't shot dead, or at least got a hole the size of a musket ball square in his back. No matter what he says to the Conch, professing how true he is, the very fact that he's still alive tends to argue against him. To prove himself trustworthy, you see, Ryland has to actually be dead. And no matter how he works it around, it always comes back to that. Only a dead Runsford Ryland can be trusted. So it's not a happy stretch of beach on which he sits."

Ham stopped and puffed, his pipe crackling. He waited as his listeners thought through that little conundrum.

"What does he do?" someone finally asked.

"He can see only one way out. Runsford Ryland then and there makes a very grave decision." Ham puffed his pipe again, the draw crackling the tobacco again.

"What'd he decide?" another asked, practically pleading.

"For that answer, you need to hear the rest of the story."

When the groans died away, he continued.

Delaney ran a hand over his head, and it came back to him wet with sweat. He wasn't sure why he'd started sweating; it hadn't gotten any hotter. Cooler if anything. The reeds were quiet now. If his audience of Hants were there, they were being particularly polite. The *Chompers*, too, were quiet, swimming easily. Hovering. Waiting. Nothing much had changed at the pond, except for the shadows that kept deepening. There were just the last little rays of sun lighting up the forest canopy now, way at the tops of the trees. Maybe it was that the air had gotten more dense or something.

Or maybe, maybe it wasn't the air at all, or anything in the world here, but rather something in that story that got into him and made him sweat from the inside out. Maybe what Ham said about Ryland, sitting on that beach regretting. Watching his ship sail off into a full moon.

Delaney felt for him, all of a sudden, even though he'd been a blaggard right along, and even though when he'd heard Ham tell the story the first time, he'd felt nothing but glee. But now it seemed…Ryland seemed…a whole lot like Delaney. He didn't feel scorn or contempt now, didn't feel at all superior. He felt just the same. Ryland had a full moon, and Delaney had a new moon. Ryland had a beach and an ocean, and Delaney had a post and pond. Ryland was trying to figure out how to keep from getting dead because of Conch, and Delaney was trying to keep from getting dead on account of mermonkeys. But how did that make him different? Both of them were blaggards.

Delaney had only turned his back on his girl, while Ryland had turned his back on his son. That was true. Ryland was worse there. Delaney took a deep breath. So maybe they weren't the same after all.

But then, Ryland had a reason for what he did. Wentworth had crossed him and had made his own bed, so to speak. And Wentworth was a grown man, besides, who could do as he pleased. Delaney couldn't even remember why he'd done what he'd done, walking out on Maybelle Cuddy like he did, and leaving behind their own son or daughter they might have had one day. Little babies, who couldn't even care for themselves, and he'd left them without a father. Or a mother, for that matter. He thought of Maybelle now, with another man's little boy on her knee. Delaney had left his own child there, for another man to have with her. Somehow.

The sweat returned. And now he knew what it was. It was shame. He felt ashamed. And that sweat, that was just the shame needing to come out of him because it filled up all that was inside, and had nowhere else to go. So it just oozed out of every pore.

CHAPTER SIXTEEN

SHALAMON

THE *SHALAMON* WAS A CUTTER, larger than most pirate vessels, but still fast and highly maneuverable. She was dark, made of night-oak, a wood both prized and rare that came from the Forests of Sule—the sacred grounds of the Hants. The wood was supple and lightweight when cut, but when cured it turned almost black, hard as the knots of other oaks. If it wasn't cut and drilled and nailed green, there was no way to cut or drill or nail it.

Now the *Shalamon*'s sails were trimmed for hull speed, all ahead flank, and the black ship raced south and east behind the *Success*. Conch Imbry stood on the quarterdeck under the full moon, which was not giant anymore, but still bright where it had risen overhead. The wind whipped his perfect hair into a wild mop. He looked over the ocean, saw a low wall of darkness far off in the east. He scanned his own ship, the main deck, and his eyes locked onto the great iron grate, the one that generally covered the hold but was now lashed open. He watched for a time the man who hung there, stripped to the waist and tied by his wrists. A bloody series of stripes crisscrossed his back. Blood stained the top of his trousers, where it had run down and dried. His head lolled back and forth with the rhythm of the ship on the billows. Conch felt the waxed tips of his moustache, just to be satisfied the wind hadn't mussed them. Then he walked down the stairs to the main deck, crossed over to the grate.

"Rain's comin'!" Conch shouted over the wind at the bloody figure. "Clean them wounds some!"

The dark-headed man's head lolled.

Conch grabbed his hair, twisted his head around so he could look him in the face. "What's a' matter, Mr. Mazeley? Got nothin' to say to yer Cap'n?"

Mazeley opened one eye. "What's our heading?" he managed.

"Mumtown! Have ye forgot? I saved Ryland's son alive, just fer that wicked woman who done me so bad wrong. But I've repented of it now! And I mean to correct the error of my ways!"

"I'll kill him for you." It was an offer. A request.

"A' course ye will, Mr. Mazeley."

Mazeley closed his eyes, grateful.

Conch patted the back of his head. "A' course ye will."

"Ships! Starboard bow, hull down!" shouted one of the hands aboard *Success*.

Damrick was on deck for the first time this morning. He opened his telescope and watched three sets of masts, sails unfurled, angled away from the wind. "I believe those are ours. Change course to intercept."

As *Success* moved in closer, they could see smoke from the furnaces rising on deck. A cannon boomed from the *Destiny*.

"It's a salute," Damrick said to Lye. "Hale recognizes us."

"Good thing."

Then he and Lye exchanged glances. "Couldn't hurt to run up the white flag, though."

Lye agreed fully, and complied immediately.

The sloop's port gunwale banged and knocked against the starboard hull of the *Destiny* before Damrick was able to grasp the rope ladder and climb. The two ships parted ways as he topped the main deck's gunwale. He embraced Hale Starpus, and shouted into his ear, "Good to see you, friend!"

"Aye, likewise!" But the big man seemed a bit uneasy with the uncharacteristic show of affection.

"We haven't much time!" Damrick called. "Change course, to Mumtown!"

"Mumtown? The Cabeebs?"

"Yes!"

"What happened?"

"Too much to tell!" Damrick turned to the rail, waved for *Success* to come back for him. "Skaelington isn't safe…Wentworth's alive, and being held in Castle Mum. We need the Gatemen to break him free!"

"Wentworth? How'd ye learn that?"

"Jenta!"

Hale nodded, though he looked confused. His muttonchop sideburns blew in the wind. "Wentworth's Jenta?"

"Mine now. I got her!" Then he pointed to *Success*.

"You *got* her?"

"I got her!" Now he pointed to his ring finger. "Jenta Fellows!"

"*You* got her?"

"Long story!"

"Ain't been long enough fer a long story!"

"I'll tell it in Mumtown! We'll fly ahead, you anchor in the bay—don't moor at the docks until I give the all-clear!"

"Aye, aye!"

"Watch for Conch and the *Shalamon!*"

"Don't I always?" His eyes were alight.

Damrick grabbed the rope ladder and swung over the edge.

"You *got* her!" Hale shook his head.

"Now let's get Wentworth!" he shouted.

Hale nodded, watching him descend.

But Damrick stopped. He climbed back up a few rungs, leaned in to Hale. "Is there a brush aboard?"

Hale looked like he'd just gone hard of hearing. "A brush?"

"A hairbrush…for a lady."

"Oh…so she got *you*, too!"

"You have one or not?"

Four minutes later, Hale Starpus came back with a piece of canvas wrapped and tied around Damrick knew not what. "Take this to yer…yer missus! The boys collected up some things!"

Damrick nodded. "Thanks!" Now he climbed down the rope, leaped to the deck of *Success*.

Ryland sat on that beach the rest of the night, untrustworthy in life, faithful only in death, until the moon rose high and sank again and the sun began peeking up over the horizon down the beach. And then, suddenly, he stood. His eyes went wide. A grin came over his face. Energized, he began walking up the beach and toward the rising sun, toward daylight. Toward Skaelington.

Oblivious to questions and second glances, he walked through the back streets to his home. He cleaned himself up, shaved, dressed, and walked to the cottage of Shayla Stillmithers. Finding her gone, he sought instead the burned and tortured priest. Finding him unavailable for services, at least on this earth, he paused outside the church. He walked past the burned-out remains of the Cleaver and Fork. He found there a handful of citizens determined to clean up its charred remains. He saw the flowers laid out in the street, marking the places where loved ones had departed this world. He rolled up his sleeves, picked up a shovel, and began working alongside them. He said not a word about why, introduced himself to not a soul, just went to work, speaking only enough to be sure his efforts were somewhat coordinated with those of the citizens around him.

He heard their whispers, felt their looks, the glares, and he ignored them. When lemonade was brought out, and all the others stopped to drink and wipe their brows, he kept at it, hands filthy and blistered, shoveling wet black coals and soot into creaking wooden wheelbarrows.

Finally, one of the men walked up to him, carrying an extra glass. He watched a while, then said, "Don't you want a little somethin' for your thirst?"

And Runsford said, "My thirst is a bit deeper than what squeezed lemons can quench." And he kept on working.

After another moment, the man said, "You're Runsford Ryland, ain't you?"

"I am." He kept shoveling.

"Then what in the entire nation are you doin' this for?"

"Conch Imbry killed my son," he said. "And I've vowed not to rest until every patch of green earth he's scorched in his evil life has been cleaned up, restored, and grows freely again." He didn't look up. It was a fair piece of speech. It should have been; he'd been working on it all morning. He kept shoveling, and the man walked away. But pretty soon another came up to him, an older man who hadn't been digging and carting and cleaning.

"What you said earlier, about going after Conch. Did you mean that?"

Now Runsford ceased his labors, and leaned, panting, on his shovel. "I've said a lot of things in my life I didn't mean. That's to my shame. But I meant that, and will mean it until Conch is dead and gone, or I draw my last breath and join my son."

The older man was earnest, intelligent, his brown eyes piercing. "I don't trust you, Runsford Ryland. You're known to be Conch Imbry's man."

"I don't blame you for that. But I'm his sworn enemy now." He went back to digging.

The man nodded. "I want to believe you."

"Believe whatever you will."

After a while, the man said, "Follow me. I know a way you can take a big step toward redemption. If that's what you want."

"It's what I want." Runsford gladly dropped the shovel.

The man took him inside a nearby general store, then into the back room. He directed Runsford to sit at a worktable, where he lit a lamp. He left the room, came back with a small scrap of folded parchment. He put it on the scarred table in front of Runsford, who picked it up and turned it over in his hand.

"Open it," the man said.

Ryland did, and saw a handwritten "S," its only marking.

"Ever seen anything like that?"

"No. But I've heard about the Black S. Is it yours?"

The man nodded.

"You're a Gateman."

"I am. Sworn to be such until my own dying breath."

Ryland nodded, set the paper down. "Your people helped Damrick get Jenta Stillmithers out of town."

"Your son's fiancée. Taken by the Conch."

He nodded. After a long pause he said, "I guess I owe you for that."

"You owe for a lot more than that."

"What can I do to repay?"

"You can join us."

"How would I do that?"

"You'd take the oath. In front of witnesses. Other Gatemen."

"I'll do it. Then what?"

"Then we'll talk."

And Ryland did.

"Where are we headed?" Jenta asked. She was seated at the writing desk, working a small comb through her hair, rather unsuccessfully. She'd found one of Ryland's robes and was wearing it over one of Damrick's shirts. His duffel lay open on the floor by the bed. Her dress hung on a hook beside the table. Damrick stood silently, leaning back against the closed door, just watching her.

She smiled at him shyly. "Damrick."

"Yes?"

"Are we headed for Mumtown yet?"

"Oh. Yes, Mumtown." Then he remembered the package in his hands. "Here, I brought you this." He held out the canvas, tied with twine.

"What is it?"

"I have no idea."

She laughed.

Now so did he. "Well, it's from Hale and the boys aboard the *Destiny*."

She untied the twine and opened the package. In it were four men's combs of various sizes and shapes, most missing several teeth, a small, petite pair of scissors with a cracked handle, a length of faded, frayed ribbon that at one time had been crushed velvet, a large brass button with a curlicue pattern on it, two small hairbrushes, one of which was cracked with its bristles askew, and a half a bottle of sweet toilet water. All things that the men thought were ladylike. "That was sweet of them," she said. "Truly." She picked up the second hairbrush, looked at the greasy gray hairs wound all through the bristles.

"Wedding presents," Damrick said with a shrug.

"It was wonderful of them." She set the brush down. "And of you." She grew thoughtful. "I have something to show you."

"What is it?"

She reached over to the dress hanging beside her, picked up the hem, held it out between her hands. "Go ahead."

"What?" He took the hem, felt something inside it, sewn into it.

"It's a map," she said. She did not look away from his eyes.

"What kind of map?"

"It's Conch's. I found it when I was looking for Wentworth's wedding ring."

"So you took it."

She nodded.

A corner of his lip rose. "He never noticed?"

"It didn't look like it had been disturbed in a long while."

"What does it show?"

"It's a drawing. With instructions. Very detailed instructions. It tells where he keeps his gold, and how to get it out."

300

"How to get it out?"

"When you see it, you'll understand."

He felt the object again. It was about six inches wide and three inches tall, just a half an inch thick. He bent it. It didn't crinkle or rattle.

"I wrapped it in oilcloth," she explained. She held out the little pair of scissors to him, so he could cut open the hem.

He watched her eyes. "To keep water out. So you meant to escape. You planned to swim from the *Shalamon*."

She lowered the scissors. Her eyes grew distant. "I don't know what I meant. It was more an act of rebellion, I think. I could have tried to escape several times, but didn't."

Damrick returned his attention to the map. He felt further down the hem. "What's this? Are these coins?"

"Yes. Given me by Windall Frost."

He nodded. "Maybe it's better to leave this sewn in here, where it is."

She looked at the dress, then at him. "You're worried about what may happen in Mumtown."

"We'll get Wentworth out."

She looked away. "I keep thinking he's in that dungeon, paying the price for what I've done."

"He did what he chose to do."

"But I encouraged him."

"You saved his life, Jenta."

Now she was very present, her eyes crisply focused on him. "I paid a high price to protect him. I don't want you to pay an even higher one."

He knelt down beside her, took her hand in his. He kissed it. "I don't want to pay that price, either." He touched her cheek. "After Mumtown, when Wentworth is safe and Conch Imbry is dead...then I'm finished."

Her eyes searched his. "Damrick. You expect to meet Conch in Mumtown?"

"Yes." He dropped his eyes. "He'll come."

"Why?"

Damrick stood, crossed to the bed, sat. "Because Conch will want to take his vengeance on Wentworth. So I have to go there to save him. He knows you will tell me where Wentworth is, and so he knows I will go there. I have to go try to save him, and Conch has to go try to kill him. Neither of us has a choice."

"We all have choices."

"I suppose so. And this is mine."

Delaney watched the reeds and grasses. Still quiet. He looked up into the sky. It was near dark now. Where last time he looked around it had been darkness coming to shade out the light, now it seemed the other way around, with just a little bit of light left to glow up what was pretty much darkness otherwise.

"Light's dyin' now, for sure," he said aloud. But he knew it wasn't dying. It was just going away overnight. It would be back, shining bright tomorrow, and every day, day after day, on the same trees, the same leaves. No, the light wasn't dying. Delaney was. The world turned on, not caring a whit who lived or died, just doing the same things it ever did. But there were some times, it seemed like, when the uncaring world caught people up in it as it turned, like when a man gets a foot caught in a loop of line when the windlass is whirring and he gets yanked overboard, busting up a bunch of bones. Which Delaney had seen once. The fellow lived, but broke his foot and leg up bad, and hobbled around ever after. But even when it wasn't a line or a rope or any other thing you could see or name, it seemed there were some things in the world that could catch people up and take them places they wouldn't go otherwise, but they had to go anyway. Seemed like there were some things that were going to happen to people, no matter what, no matter how much a person did or didn't want it, even when they saw it coming.

Like in Mumtown. Damrick had had to go there, and so had Conch, and both had to go because they figured the other one would, and neither wanted to get there second. So neither one could not go. They'd gotten caught in that loop of the world's line.

Like Damrick and Jenta aboard the *Success*. They couldn't just sail straight to Cabeeb Island, because they had to go intercept the three Ryland ships with all the Gatemen, because they needed the Gateman to fight the Conch. But because they had to go get those ships, they lost the time and the chance to get there first. Not that they knew that at the time. They didn't. They thought they'd got there first. But if they'd really got there first, they wouldn't have had to fight the Conch because he wouldn't have been there yet, so they wouldn't have needed the Gatemen. It was a little like that old story about Firefish, where you needed to eat its flesh to be strong enough to kill one so that you could eat its flesh. Except with Conch and Damrick and Mumtown, it all just sort of wound together, closer and closer, not in circles like a game of

Round-the-Monkey, but more like a whirlpool. Like a maelstrom that wound you in closer and closer until you just went down the hole and no one ever saw you again alive. Once you're in, there's no getting out again, either.

And like Delaney, who was just sitting on a post now, but who had nowhere to put his mind, nowhere for it to go but back to the story. He felt like a loop of line in the world was pulling him right down again, back to Mumtown. Ham would tell the story again, starting with that dream of the fast ship and the girl singing, and Delaney would wake up in that jail cell. And pretty soon there would be Conch Imbry again, standing next to Mart Mazeley, the unimpressive man, bleeding from Conch's whip. And there would be Dallis Trum, pleading for Delaney to save him, and Delaney would save him and Kreg both by swearing to follow the Conch, to kill when Conch said kill, and die when Conch said die. And then there'd be Avery, doing a good thing. Doing a right thing. A hard thing. Sent straight to heaven, all prepared and ready, by that single shot from Conch Imbry's pistol.

But that wouldn't be all.

No, there would be more. And Ham would tell it.

The next thing that he would tell, that's the part that always kept Delaney's mind running away, or his feet moving, so he wouldn't ever have to remember it, so he wouldn't ever have to face it. But Ham would tell it. Everyone didn't have to listen, but no one could stop the tale. That was the vortex, the dark maelstrom he could ignore for a time, but would always pull him back. It was the loop in the line of the world that caught his foot. It happened, true and certain, and it would be told. Ham only told what was.

"Called hisself a 'true hand,'" Conch Imbry intoned. Smoke rose from his pistol. "My own feelin' is somewhat different." He addressed an attentive, silent, dumbstruck audience. "True hands, ye see, are true only if they're true to *me*." Now he looked from eye to eye until he'd seen into every living captive soul whose body was tied to a cell bar in Castle Mum. Avery Wittle no longer fit that category. His wrists were still tied, and his body was captive, slumped back away, arms outstretched, head lolled back, mouth open. But it housed a living soul no more.

The gunshot still rang in Delaney's ears when he heard himself say, "Look away, now, youngster." He said this to the Trum boy, Dallis, who was standing there with his mouth dropped open, too.

Dallis tore his eyes away, blinking against the sting of a tear.

"You." Conch pointed at Delaney with the smoking pistol. "Ye got a soft spot fer the boy. It'll hurt ye."

"He's a bit young for such, is all," Delaney answered with a sniff.

"Aw, I shot my first man when I wasn't yet his age."

"Still…" Delaney started, but couldn't think of a way to finish.

"Seems to me," Conch said, walking to Delaney, "that all you men jus' swore to kill when I say kill and die when I say die. Ain't that right?"

There were nods all around, but no one spoke up. Other than Sleeve, who swore allegiance again on the spot without even being asked.

"Anyone wanna go back on that promise?" Conch asked, looking at Delaney.

Every man shook his head. Except Sleeve, who said, "No, sir!"

"Mr. Meeb, bring me my other prisoner."

Horkan Meeb nodded and left.

"Mr. Mazeley, would ye be so kind as to reload my pistol?"

"Gladly."

The jailor returned in less than a minute with a thin, sick-looking man in tow. The prisoner was tall, but hunched over. He dragged his feet and his ankle chains clattered. His wrists were manacled together and his arms hung straight down, like the chains were too heavy for him. His eyes were black and sunken. His clothes, which were clearly of a fancy make and design, were stained and matted, torn here and there. His eyes were dull. The skin of his face and hands was caked and cracked and blistered, so it was hard to tell what was dirt and what was canker. He smelled strongly of urine.

"Set him on the stump," Conch ordered.

Meeb helped the man sit on the wide, natural platform in the center of the courtyard. The prisoner slumped forward, shoulders sagging, head hung down weakly. Delaney thought he might fall over, but he stayed seated as the jailor stepped away.

"Ye crossed me," Conch said to the hunched man. "I shoulda stepped on ye then, like the mouse ye are. But yer woman, turns out she ain't a mouse. She's a rat."

Now the man's face came up. "She's escaped," he croaked. Then, as Conch's face went sour, the man's face went calm. A peacefulness stole over him. And he lowered his head again. That's when Delaney got the idea that maybe Wentworth wasn't just tired and sick, and hanging his head because of it, but maybe he was praying.

"This man crossed me," Conch announced, walking up and down in front of the prisoners. "I want him dead. Now, who will help me out?"

Sleeve said, "I will, Cap'n."

"Cut that man loose," Conch replied. *Horkan* Meeb obliged. "Stand over there," Conch said to Sleeve, pointing to a spot beside the tree-trunk platform. "Let's see who else is willin' and able."

No one else volunteered.

Then Conch walked up to Delaney again, and looked him in the eye. "You, sailor."

"So how was I supposed to know?" Delaney said aloud to the dank air of the pond, and to the invisible *Jom Perhoo* below the surface, and the invisible God above. "He was just a ragged prisoner, half-dead already. I figured he was a cutthroat who crossed the Conch."

But he didn't seem to be a cutthroat, did he?

"I guess not. But Conch, he woulda killed me if I hadn't done it, and then Sleeve or some other body woulda killed Wentworth anyways. And then I'd a' died for no reason."

Except for Avery's reason.

Delaney held his breath. That was the sticking point. That was the barb that hooked him every time. That was the pile of rocks at the bottom of the whirlpool. It was Avery's choice that made Delaney's look so poor. A good man dies before he'll do bad. It doesn't have anything to do with anything else. And there's no way around it, once you've seen it up close like that. Good men do good. And they pay whatever price is to be paid for doing it. Avery did. That priest did. And then Wentworth did.

And that's the way it works.

But Delaney did not do good. He did bad. He did it, and it was done, and it could never be undone.

The Trum boys, they never looked up to Delaney the same way again. It was like they were scared of him, and it seemed like they gave him a wide berth even when they were right nearby. And always, they gave him that look. Like he was dangerous. Like he was some sort of monster. Or at least, some sort of animal. And so Delaney knew he was truly a pirate. He'd turned.

And the worst of it was, killing Wentworth Ryland was not the end of Delaney's crimes that day.

Success sailed into Cabeeb Bay just ahead of the rain. It had been threatening all day, with that wall of dark clouds building up behind them like

Blaggard's Moon

305

some fell prophecy not yet fulfilled. Lightning could be seen jumping around within it, and an occasional low rumble reached out from it, reminding them of what was coming. Another five minutes and it would be on top of them.

Damrick scanned the bay carefully, ship to ship to ship, but did not see the *Shalamon*. He lowered his spyglass. "Conch isn't here. Head into port," he ordered. *Success* was already flying straight toward the inlet, where the docks were built deep into the city.

"Yer sure?" Lye asked. "What if he's moored up in there?"

"Not like Conch to corner himself. And if he is there, we have the faster ship. We'll have time to turn and run, wait for our Gatemen."

"But if not, we still got a castle to scale." He was gazing up at the blackened rock fortress above and behind the city.

"But that's where we're headed. No one knows this ship. Surprise is on our side."

Lye took a deep breath, let it out in an unduly drawn-out sigh.

"What?"

"Nothin'."

"What is it?"

"I'll get the boys ready fer a fight." But he didn't move.

"Lye, we've been through a lot. You've always trusted me before. What's bothering you this time?"

"Ye want me to say it?"

A pause. "Yes."

Lye took a deep breath. "All right then. I'll say it. What are we doin' here, Damrick?"

"You ask that every time."

"Well," he grumped. "Don't mean I don't want an answer. What are we doin' here?"

"Other than getting Wentworth out of that prison?"

"I'm sayin', why not let's moor up in some cove like we did in Skaelington. Go in quiet, find out what's what."

"Cabeeb Island has no coves like that."

"An inlet then."

"Once Conch gets here, he'll turn the town loose on us. Now's our chance to get in and get out. We don't have time."

"We cain't just walk in and pull our guns and say, 'Give us the skinny man with the crooked teeth.' This ain't a pub we're takin' over. It ain't even the *Savage Grace*. It's a castle. A fortress."

"You've always gone in with me before. And we've always come out."

"Aye, but it's always been about killin' pirates before." He said it darkly, almost under his breath.

"What is it about now, Lye?" Damrick's voice had an edge.

"I don't know, but it ain't about what it was about back when. Yer takin' crazy chances, and I don't know why."

"You said the same before we went after Sharkbit Sutter."

"But ye shot the pirate and shut me up. We were in Skaelington, *Skaelington*, fer two days. But we didn't shoot no pirates, Damrick. Not a one. Hit a couple of 'em in the head. Stole another one's woman. Then we ran. Din't even kill Ryland, who's as big a pirate as they come. Nor Motley. No one."

Damrick spoke calmly. "We didn't have the men take on Conch Imbry in a straight fight."

"Well, we didn't wait for 'em to show up, neither. Did we?"

Damrick turned hard eyes on his lieutenant. "Are you accusing me of something?" There was a threat in his voice.

Lye lowered his eyes, groused under his breath. "I din't think ye wanted to hear it."

"'I guess everyone dies somehow. Might as well cash out doing the world some good.' Those are your words."

"Well, if I do got to die, I want it to be while doin' the whole world some good. Not just…" he wagged his head toward the door leading downward, "*yer* whole world."

"We can't die," Damrick said. "We're going to take down Conch Imbry. The priest said so."

"Is that what he said? We cain't be kilt?"

Damrick watched the Mumtown harbor approach. The black clouds were almost overhead now. The temperature was dropping, carrying the scent of rain and the crackling air of the storm that would be upon them in minutes. Lightning fired now, and thunder pounded. Finally Damrick said, "You may be right. I'm getting tired of killing."

"Oh Lord, don't tell me that. Not now."

Damrick didn't look at him.

"Okay, here's what we do," Lye said earnestly, holding out a hand to demonstrate. "We go blast a few Cabeebs, break Wentworth out. Then we kill the Conch. Right? After that, why, ye can get tired a' whatever ye want."

Damrick smiled. "After." He pulled one pistol, checked the load, then pulled the other. Satisfied, he put them back in his belt and pulled his hat down snug. "Yes. After."

The docks were built close along either side of the inlet, so that they lined a long narrow path of water that led deep into town. At the end of that narrow path was a rocky cliff, and on top of that cliff was Castle Mum. And on the rampart of Castle Mum stood Conch Imbry. With him were his new recruits: Smith Delaney, Spinner Sleeve, Nil Corver, Mutter Cabe, the two Trum boys. All were there, fresh from their prison cell, along with a dozen crewmen the Captain had brought along just for this purpose. Each of the new men had been given their own pistols back, and a musket courtesy of *Horkan* Meeb. Conch also took his place, armed, on the parapet. Cabe, Corver, and the Trums manned a cannon. Four other cannons were manned by Conch's other men. Sleeve and Delaney stood side by side, muskets at the ready.

"The ship is called *Success*," Conch instructed. "She's a sweet little sloop. Woulda liked to own her myself. Shame to mangle 'er all up." He paused, staring down at the docks. "And that's her right there." He pointed. "When the shootin' starts, start firin' and don't quit 'til she's sunk."

"Who's aboard?" Sleeve asked with a hungry grin.

"Don't ye mind about that. You jes' sink 'er to the floor."

"Yer enemies are my enemies, Cap'n!" he exulted.

"Who's to start the shootin'?" Mutter asked.

"Ye'll see when ye see. Then commence to firin'."

"Not a berth to be had." Damrick noted.

"No," Lye agreed. Their mainsail was struck, and they were drifting slowly. A few rain drops spattered here and there on the decks. The end of the navigable water was in sight, and still they had found no place to moor the sloop. "Everyone's gettin' in out a' the storm, I reckon." He scanned the docks. "Sure a lot a' people watchin' us, though."

They were silent for a moment. From ships, from docks, from moored boats, from houses along the shore, many silent eyes followed them, and they seemed to be joined by many more even as they watched.

"Why are they standin' outside with the rain comin'? Ye think they recognize Ryland's ship?"

Damrick shook his head. "They aren't looking at the ship. They're looking at us. Conch's already here."

Blaggard's Moon

"Uh-oh," Lye said.

Damrick followed Lye's line of vision. The thunderstorm was upon them. Lightning flashed, and a crack of thunder rumbled down the little pathway from the bay. But Lye wasn't looking at the sky.

"*Shalamon*," Damrick said.

And so it was. Coming up from behind was the dark ship, still under sail, filling the inlet. Her canvas billowed, and she moved with amazing speed. And with her came the rain, as though she carried with her the wave of black clouds. Suddenly, the wind drove water horizontally at the sloop, and the drops came stinging.

"All hands, prepare to fire!" Damrick ordered. But not one of them needed to move in order to obey. Then to Lye he said, "How'd she hide from us?"

Lye was dumbfounded. "Rode the storm in."

Gunfire came now with the stinging rain, peppered from plumes of smoke and flashes of yellow fire. And all those faces, all those who lined the docks watching, now brought weapons up to squinting eyes. Pistols, muskets, rifles—small arms fire ripped from shore to ship, a thousand tongues of flame lashing, an echoing of thunder to match that of the storm, rolling back up the narrow valley.

The sloop was riddled in an instant.

Stock was at the helm, and he fell first, a thud of lead into flesh and bone, a rush of breath from his chest. Then Murk-Eye went down clutching his neck at the starboard rail, shot through the throat. Four more musket balls struck him where he lay. Stock raised his pistol, fired lying on his back, and then tried to reload. But now he was hit in the arm, the hand. He lay there, looking helplessly at his pistol, trying to determine how he might get a powder packet into its barrel with only one hand, when another musket ball ended his quandary.

"Devil blast that pirate, he owns this town, too!" Lye muttered. His pistol came up and cracked, but it was a paltry reply to the downpour now unleashed against him. He ducked behind a stern rail that provided the merest cover, squeezed off one more shot, and then fell to his backside, struck square between the ribs. He dropped his pistol and turned over, crawling for the small doorway to get below. He was hit three more times before his body lay still, face down across the reddening deck.

A double-barreled pistol in each hand, Damrick fired four times in rapid succession, moving backward, also trying to make his way to the door, but he too pinwheeled to the deck. He was shot through, just below the right shoulder. He crawled, and was hit again in the left side as he reached the open door mouth.

Now the whistle and sploosh of a cannonball drove a flume of water high into the air just off the bows. It was followed immediately by the bellow of a cannon. From the castle above, the musket shot was erratic. But the big round shot came in with deadly accuracy. A second effort exploded into the stern of *Success*, splintering it in an instant, bouncing the craft as though it had been tossed on a mammoth wave.

Damrick looked back, saw Lye Mogene's head move, and then his face turn toward him. He reached down with his left hand, grabbed Lye by the collar, and pulled. His boots scrabbled against the wet, slick wood beneath him. But Lye crawled forward until he was beside Damrick, looking at him through bloody, gritted teeth.

"Dropped my pistol," Lye groused.

"Get below," Damrick ordered. Then he sat up and grabbed Lye by his belt and pulled, slinging his lieutenant forward, propelling him through the open hatchway and down the stairs.

Another musket ball slammed into Damrick's right thigh. He cried out, turned over, and pulled himself forward, willing himself through the opening. He slid face-forward down the steep stairs, somersaulting onto his back near the bottom, landing on Lye Mogene.

Darkness rose as the pain overwhelmed him.

When it cleared, he saw her face.

She was heartbreakingly beautiful, dressed again in her serving gown, her hair hanging down toward him. She was not the cold barmaid of the Cleaver and Fork. She was the young woman at the docks, flowing up the gangway, rising above him, bearing the weight of the world. And now, there was something else in her. There was joy within the sadness. He reached up for her. She floated, smiling, as though under water. She took his hand, pressed it to her cheek. "Is it over already?" she whispered. "Tell me it's not over."

He felt her tears, warm on his hand.

The crashing of another cannonball rocked the sloop, and brought him to consciousness. The ship listed badly, toward starboard astern. Jenta was nowhere to be seen. He pulled himself up to one elbow, saw Lye Mogene lying beside him on his back.

"Ye coulda kilt me, landin' on me like that." Lye coughed softly.

"Where's Jenta?" Damrick asked. He looked into Ryland's cabin. The flooring was smooth and polished.

"She got outta that hole, and I told her to get back in or else I'd shoot her."

"Thank you." Damrick had shown her Ryland's secret compartment. He had made her swear she would get into it as soon as she heard gunfire. She had promised him, in front of Lye. But then, he had promised in return that he would survive, that he would come for her.

Musket balls continued to patter the hull, many now penetrating it.

"Blaggards ever' which where ye go," Lye complained. "Ye got another pistol on ye?"

"Where's the one you used to threaten Jenta?" Damrick asked.

"I was bluffin'. Ye got a pistol or ain't ye?"

"In my boot."

Both of them looked down at Damrick's boots. Neither made a move.

Lye coughed again, and spit out blood. "Well, one of us needs to shoot back soon, or they'll beat us sure."

Damrick was silent, listening to the steady crack and ping of firearms. "Lye, I may have taken one too many risks."

"Nah," the Gateman said, one cheek rising up under a tired eye. "We did the world some good. Right?" He winced suddenly in agony, and grabbed Damrick's left hand with his right. He squeezed it hard. "I'm okay," he said after a moment, breathing again, though heavily. But he did not let go of his friend's hand, and there was fear in his eyes.

Another cannonball smashed into the ship, down through the decking, crashing into the saloon where they lay. Debris and dust and splinters flew. The ship jarred, and listed suddenly, with a rush of air, almost a moan, accompanying it. The round had broken through the hull below. Damrick could feel the water before he saw it. He could smell it before he heard it gurgling up. Another explosion ripped through the cabin, and seawater poured in from the side of the hull.

"Can you swim?" Damrick asked. But when he looked back at Lye, his partner was silent, his eyes staring upward. A ragged piece of the ship's ribbing jutted up through his chest. "Lye Mogene," Damrick said quietly to his fallen comrade, still holding onto his hand. "You did some good in the world, sir. You sure did."

And then another cannonball crashed through the ceiling astern. Dust and smoke were everywhere, everywhere there wasn't already water.

Another explosion, and then another.

And then the ship's hull split open, and water poured in, a deluge now, pulling Lye away from him, driving Damrick backward, slamming him into a bulkhead that he felt give way behind him almost immediately. And then he was engulfed in a swirling torrent of water and debris.

Success was sunk.

Cheers rose from the freshly minted pirates on the parapet. Their first pirate battle had been a sudden and complete triumph.

"It ain't over," Conch told them. "See them three ships out in the bay?"

Delaney squinted through the rain into the dark shadows beyond the harbor. When the lightning flashed he could make out the blurred outlines of several ships, but wasn't sure which ones Conch meant.

"They come from Oster, I'll bet my life, followin' their leader who we jus' sunk. And like as may, they're all full a' enemies. Fat shares for all, if ye take 'em down. Now, follow me to the *Shalamon*."

"What about the sloop?" Dallis Trum asked. "Don't we get a share a' that?"

Conch turned on him. Dallis blanched, and recoiled. "Well, Mr. Ballast," Conch said evenly, "it appears ye got some vinegar after all. Ye'll make a fair pirate yet." He winked. "If there's anythin' left to share, then aye, ye earned it. But I doubt there's nothin' on board that sorry sack a' timbers worth half a minute's lookin'."

Success drifted downward in pieces. Damrick tried to propel himself in the direction of what was once Ryland's cabin. The ship's interior walls had come apart, and clothing, papers, splintered wood, swarms of unidentifiable pieces of junk floated in slow circles among the jagged edges and planes. He looked for Jenta's little steel-lined compartment. He found the flooring, but there was a hole where the box should be. It had come loose. That was good. It was designed to do that, then. Might actually float. He started to move in closer, but too much wreckage blocked his path. And he needed air. He would surface, see if the box had floated up. If not, he'd swim back down for her.

He clawed upward toward daylight, surrounded now by clouds of his own blood in the water. He found a space where the hull was gone and a ship's rib was missing; he tried to squeeze through. The wound in his right shoulder caught on a jagged splinter, which pushed into his flesh like a spike, hooking him like a fish, pulling him down with the sinking ship. He forced himself backward, downward, removing the splinter, then wriggled up between the ribs and out.

The surface above him was littered with flotsam as he kicked toward it. He saw musket balls tracing through the water. A cannonball entered near him, a flume of air following as it dove deep out of sight in an instant, creating a concussion he felt all the way through him. Using both legs, feeling only one, he kicked his way upward toward a large section of broken hull. He grasped it with his left hand and surfaced under it, pushing it up, using it for protection. He gasped and coughed for air. Musket balls plunked into the water around him. The rain was heavy and the wind kicked up the water; he hoped it would make it difficult to be seen. His right thigh burned. He felt as though his leg was missing below the knee. He looked around, trying to see anything like a trunk or a box, but saw nothing remotely similar. He took a hard, painful breath of air, and submerged. He meant to turn and swim back down to Jenta, but he couldn't. He had strength only on his left side. He couldn't even turn himself upside down.

Jenta was trapped under the water and he was now trapped above. He cursed himself as he peered down into darkness. He hadn't thought it through…he should have planned for her safety. He should not have put her in that box. He should have put her off the boat. He should never have sailed into the inlet. He shouldn't have brought her here at all.

He pushed up on the piece of wreckage again, breathed twice, and kicked for the docks. His right arm was completely useless. His right leg whipped crazily. Suddenly he felt a crack in his right thigh, and knew his leg bone had broken. He felt the ends of the fractured bones hammering one another, two clubs beating against each other within his flesh. But the docks were just a few yards away. Gunfire was rare now. He made it under the dock, and let go of the flotsam. He was hidden from view by the boardwalk above.

He grasped a support post, quieted himself and listened. The sound of cannon had ceased entirely.

"There's one!" a voice above him shouted. "He's alive!"

"Shoot him!" another voice instructed.

Damrick pulled his chin in, waiting. The musket exploded above his head. But the shot was aimed out toward the wreckage of *Success*.

"Got him!" the voice cried, triumphant.

"Ah, he was already dead," another voice intoned.

Damrick knew he had to get out of the water, had to get the bleeding stopped. He let go of the pier post and propelled himself further inward, further under the docks. But there was nowhere to get out. The docks were built out over water with nothing but a flat, straight seawall on its inner edge. The seawall was faced in rock, or stone, and where it wasn't, it was gravel behind iron bars and iron mesh. He pulled himself along the wall with his left hand, up the inlet in the direction of the castle, looking for some break. Almost forty yards later, he found one. A small crawl space between the top of the wall and the decking above; it was a shelf of rock that could support him, and hide him, if only he could get up onto it.

Rain was still pouring down between the slats as he tried to pull himself up. But with only one arm and one leg, he failed twice. Then he found a small support, a truss nailed at an angle, within the narrow space. By grasping it with his left hand and positioning his left foot on a pier post, and by making a huge and painful effort, almost a leap, he got his chest and shoulders up onto the shelf. He inched his way in until he was on his belly, then kicked his left foot up onto the shelf. He rolled himself in, turning over onto his back.

There he lay wincing, breathing the pain in, then exhaling it again. He tasted blood. He was facing up, his head toward the castle, his good leg nearer the water. His bad right leg was twisted around, and pounded with pain. He tried to realign it with his hands, but couldn't do it. He could barely reach it, and had no strength to move it.

The bleeding was his biggest concern. He knew he had already lost a lot of blood, but he hoped that the cloth of his pant leg, twisted tight against his wound, would help slow the bleeding there. His right shoulder pounded, but he could now use his left hand to compress that wound. The rib wound could not be addressed, but except for the pain it hadn't seemed to do much harm. With a little luck, the ball had not lodged within him. With just a little more luck, he thought, the bleeding would stop on its own before he passed out.

He struggled against the darkness as long as he could, but then he saw Jenta's face again, sad and beautiful, hovering above him. And then he saw that compartment like a coffin, her closed into it, sinking beneath the sea. The sorrow of loss stole over him.

He drifted into oblivion.

Jenta came awake in the small, dark box. She did not remember losing consciousness. She couldn't straighten up, or sit up. She felt for the handle, the ring on the door, but as soon as she moved pain raced through her from the neck up. She felt the back of her head. A great, painful lump had risen. She must have been slammed into the end of the compartment.

But now another great shock rocked her; it was earsplitting, and the box moved. The sound of something metal rasping against metal was deafening, even excruciating. She felt like every bone within her was being scraped by the sound. And then the box turned, and shifted suddenly, throwing her to one side. Her hip hit something hard, and she winced. She felt it with her hands. It was the ring. She had somehow turned around in this small space. And then she had the sensation she was rising.

A gentle rocking now replaced the sudden shifts. She heard a constant, gentle patter. She recognized it as rain. She heard gunfire, but muffled, as though from far away. That was good. If someone was firing, then someone was likely still firing back.

Damrick. He wouldn't die here. He said he'd come for her. But her heart felt stabbed within. If the ship had come apart, and she had floated up, then where was he? From where was he shooting back?

And where was she? Floating in a hostile harbor inside a watertight box. And someone, probably Conch Imbry, wanted them both dead.

But she felt peace, somehow. She had done the right thing, marrying Damrick, leaving Conch, no matter where it led. "Any end's a good end now," she said aloud. And she believed she meant it.

CHAPTER SEVENTEEN

MUMTOWN

THE RAIN HAD slacked off to a steady dripping. Conch Imbry walked past the bodies of his enemies, lined up now side-by-side on the dock. He held his hands behind him, examining each, as though paying respects. But he had no respect to pay. He toed a chin, turning a head. "Nothin' better than a deck full a' dead enemies, eh Mr. Mazeley? Warms a pirate's heart."

Mazeley said nothing.

"And what I'd like to see is jus' that. A deck full of 'em."

"These three are all we've recovered. Likely more sunk. If so, they'll be up in a couple of days."

"Unless they're trapped inside the hull." Conch squatted beside Lye Mogene. The Gateman's eyes were open; his expression seemed conscious and determined. "We think we got 'em, and then we ain't." Pulling a knife, he cut the leather lash from Lye's arm, rubbed it between his finger and thumb. "Damrick Fellows shoulda been aboard."

"And Jenta as well."

"Don't!" Conch snarled at Mazeley, pointing the knife up at him. "Don't ever say that name! Call her the wench, call her the wanton, call her any hard and evil thing ye please…but not that name."

"The wench then."

Conch stood. "So they ain't here, where are they?"

"They might have stayed in Skaelington. But I doubt it. It's pretty hot for them now."

"He outfoxed you there. He got away from me here. So what's he doin' now?"

At that moment, Damrick was lying just below the dock, listening. He had awakened as bodies were being dragged across the boards above him. He wasn't dead, but it seemed to him only a matter of time. He was in great pain. His shoulder throbbed. His leg was a useless lump. All his joints ached. But the worst was that every breath was a sharp pain, like a lance into his lungs. The shot to his ribs did that. Now he feared the wound that had seemed the least would end being the worst. And on top of it, he was cold. He could barely keep his teeth from chattering. A bad sign. The air could not be as cold as he felt.

"What're them three ships up to?" Conch asked, squinting against the rain into the harbor.

"Nothing. They've cast anchor in the bay. They seem to be waiting."

"On what?"

"Instructions, I'd guess."

"Them are Ryland's ships?"

"Yes. Wentworth's rogues."

"So. Who do ye think was wrong? Talon? Or Motley?"

"I don't know."

"The answer is kinda important. If they fooled Talon, then them ships are full a' Gatemen."

"I don't know how to guess on this one."

Conch looked at him askance. "Well, I'm glad to hear ye say that, Mr. Mazeley. Rankles me when ye always know. 'Specially when ye don't."

The patter of rain stopped, and a gentle scraping began. Either the rain had let up, or Jenta had floated under some sort of cover. The scraping and knocking were rhythmic now. Small waves, bumping her up against a wooden structure. A boat or a dock. The air inside had grown thick and close. She had to take her chances. She reached around for the handle, and tried to turn it. It didn't move. She pulled on it, but nothing happened. Nearing panic, she twisted it the other way. It turned. A crack of light appeared. Relieved, she pushed the door open. But water flowed in, pouring over her like a cold bath. It surprised her how cold it was. She pulled the door closed without thinking, and it latched. But now the water that sloshed around inside pooled at her feet, and the box began to tilt upright. She twisted the handle again, just as she had before, and it turned. But now the door wouldn't open. The water pressure from outside held it closed. Heart racing again, she pushed harder, with her shoulder. The door still didn't budge. Panicked, she pushed with everything she had, and it opened, first a little, with seawater rushing in, then filling the box in an instant, slamming her head back, filling up her nostrils. Then with a large slurping sound and a great glug, the container sank—faster than she would have imagined possible. She tried to pull herself out.

She was sinking with it. Twisting and churning, she found the rim of the door with her hands and propelled herself out. She felt her gown catch on something; the corner of the door, where it was hinged. It was pulling her down. With a huge effort she yanked on it with her hands, pressing against the box with her feet. She felt it rip; she was free. She swam upward, desperate for air. But she saw the tracer of a musket ball, which shot down into the water beside her, coming from a boat. She saw the shallow keels of small boats moored in a line, and angled for the darkness on the far side of them, hoping it was the shadow of the docks, and she broke the surface sputtering and gulping.

The air was clean and fresh and cool.

She had in fact come up under the dock, and was well out of sight. She grasped an upright support, heard approaching footsteps that passed over and moved on. She suddenly wished she had never gotten into that compartment; she wished she had stayed with Damrick. Then she'd know. If he was dead, then she would be, too. She didn't want to think about what had happened to him, but she knew the likelihood of her loss.

It had all gone to pieces so quickly.

But then, it had all come together so suddenly. And she had not one regret, not even now. She thought of her mother, and how terribly angry she'd be to see her daughter, the lady she'd raised so carefully, clinging to a post under a pier, with nowhere to go that didn't lead to pirates who wanted her dead, or worse. The thought was almost humorous, the contrast between the garden parties and balls that Shayla dreamed about for her, and a pirate's cruel revenge, to which that very dream had led. The society lady, that was Shayla's dream. Damrick was Jenta's. She hadn't even known what her dream was, until it saved her.

She began swimming under the docks as best she could. A large hunk of her dress had been torn away, mostly in the front and down one side, so her legs were free enough. Her shoes were gone; she had no recollection of when or where. The sodden material around her torso and her waist was heavy, and tended to catch small nails and slivers of wood, and the sleeves and shoulders of the wet garment constricted her movements. But she could swim.

She moved under the dock, past small boats moored one after the other on her right, a solid seawall on her left. She didn't know what she was looking for, except some way to get out of the water without being seen. She swam from post to post, listening, careful not to splash, careful not to cause a stir or make a sound greater than the drip of rain from the dock above, or the gentle slap of small waves against the hulls and walls and posts.

Then, as though from a nightmare, she heard the voice of Conch Imbry. It was muffled, quiet. But it could not be mistaken. She froze, listening. And then she heard him quite clearly.

"Don't!" he barked. "Don't ever say that name! Call her the wench, call her the wanton, call her any hard and evil thing ye please…but not that name."

"The wench then." That was Mazeley. His quiet, confident voice made her shudder. He seemed so rational, so…normal. And yet he did evil all day long, every day, every night.

The voices dropped away again, so that she couldn't make out the words. They kept talking, and they were talking about her. She wanted to get farther away, to turn and swim, but felt she should hear more. It would be important to know. Slowly and carefully, she moved in closer.

"Well, I'm glad to hear ye say that, Mr. Mazeley. Rankles me when ye always know. 'Specially when ye don't."

"I think we must assume that the Gatemen hold those ships. And even if they don't, if we take them down the message will be clear."

"So…attack the rogue tubs regardless, send 'em to the floor with whatever goods they got. Ask no questions; take no prisoners. That's what ye recommend?"

A pause. "Yes, sir."

"I like it. Wentworth's dead. So now we bury his ships under a few hundred feet a' water, Gatemen or no. We find Damrick and the wench, kill 'em ever' which way over two, three days' time, draw it out so there's plenty a' pain and cryin' and wailin', then we hang what's left of 'em up in Skaelington bay where all can see. And we're done! Then I can see fit to move on to more interestin' matters."

"Aye, sir."

The footsteps moved off, headed down the docks away from the castle, toward the *Shalamon*.

"What do we do now?" a voice above her asked. It was a young voice, its owner hardly more than a boy.

"You can do what ye want, but I'm followin' the Cap'n." That was an older man, who spoke with a sneer. A group of men shuffled off, their footsteps creaking in the direction of the bay.

Jenta felt she should follow, too, but by the time she made up her mind to do it, they were too far away. She'd never keep up. She looked up through the dock. The rain was still dripping down, but now she noticed something lying on the slats, blocking the light in regular intervals. Cargo, maybe. Boards laid side by side? As she swam underneath one of them, she saw a hand. Then she saw a leather lash around an arm. She gasped, and put a hand to her mouth. These were bodies. This was her crew, the Gatemen killed in the attack on *Success*.

Her heart pounding, she swam along under them, craning her neck painfully, searching one after the other, treading water, peering up, blinking into the dripping rain, trying to identify the one body that she prayed would not be here. She looked for the hair, the long dark hair that would identify him.

"Oh, Damrick," she pled aloud in a whisper. "Damrick, Damrick. Please don't be here."

"Sorry to disappoint," a ragged voice said from the seawall behind her.

She spun around, splashing, peering into the darkness. She saw a movement, a hand. Then she saw his face. She swam to him, tried to climb up where he was, taking his hand, his arm, but he winced and shut tight his eyes against the pain. She slid back down into the water. She gently took his left hand in hers. It felt cold and lifeless. She kissed it.

Then she saw his twisted leg. "Damrick, what happened?" She spoke softly, but urgently. She could see him clearly now. He was pale and his lips were blue. The moisture on his face was not all from the rain. She felt his cheeks, his forehead. He was cold. But his eyes were warm.

"Damrick, your leg…"

He shook his head. "I'm sorry. I meant…never to leave you."

"Oh, Damrick. You never left me." She looked around in desperation. "We need to get you out of here, get you some help—"

"No," he said. "We can't let them find me. It's better this way."

Fear grew in her, then anger. "You can't give up!"

"He got me, Jenta. The priest was wrong. Conch has won. It's over."

Her anger turned back to pain in an instant, a deep stab that shot through her body. She looked at him, watched his eyes. They were as calm as the sea. "Please," she begged him. "You can't go now. Not yet."

He swallowed. It was a painful effort. "I've been lying here," he said with difficulty, "praying. Like my mother did."

She wanted to say something, to do something. She wanted more than anything to climb up with him, and hold him. But all she could do was hold his hand while her soul was being rent in two.

"I prayed for you," he said. His breath caught. "And God brought you here." Light was in his eyes, but it was distant.

"I'm here. I'm here."

"He helps the helpless. That's what she always said." His eyes closed. Then he opened them again. "That's why He never helped me. Until now."

"Of course He's helped you."

Damrick just shook his head. "It's not so bad as I thought it would be." Then he coughed. "I have something to say."

"I'm listening, Damrick."

"I want you to live." He looked her in the eye. "Promise me."

It was a strange request. His mind was going. "I promise. Damrick, don't leave."

He shook his head. "Go back to Mann. My father is in hiding. I'll tell you where. Go to him." He coughed again. Blood came from his mouth. She wiped it away. "Do you promise?"

"Damrick…" Tears blinded her, and she cursed them silently. They kept her from seeing the only thing on earth she wanted to see.

He raised his head. "Do you promise?"

She bit her upper lip. The tears streamed now. She nodded. "I will."

He nodded, and relaxed.

"Damrick, you don't have to go. Listen, can you hear me?"

He nodded.

"You stay, all right? You just hang on. We'll both go home to your father. We'll build a cottage. A cabin. Okay? It'll be way up in the woods." She nodded, though he couldn't see her now. "Far away from the ocean. And we'll have chickens in the yard out front. Fresh eggs every morning. There'll be a cow in the pasture. We'll have milk and cheese. Won't that be wonderful?"

He smiled, his eyes still closed.

"The days will be warm, all summer long. You'll shoot squirrels, and deer." She put her hand against his cheek. "And in the winter, we'll have a fire in the fireplace, and a big yellow dog asleep in front of it. A lazy old thing that's good for nothing. And you'll go out in the snow to cut firewood. And our children will watch from the window." She paused, her voice cracking. "Our children, Damrick! You have to stay. You have to stay for them."

He opened his eyes and looked at her. He seemed nearer. Closer to her.

She felt hope. "You'll come back inside with the firewood in your arms, and they'll run to the door! You'll set down the wood and pick them up in your arms. Then they'll take your mittens and your scarf and hang them by the fire. Oh please don't go, Damrick. Stay with me. Stay with us!"

His smile faded. "Jenta," he said. He looked at her.

"I'm here."

"You saved me."

"No, Damrick. You saved me."

He shook his head. "I rescued you. But you saved me."

She couldn't understand. She'd gotten him killed. Then she realized he was talking about something more. He was talking about the next life. "Oh, God," she began. And she continued. She prayed aloud, a fierce and aching and damaged prayer, for him, for his soul, for his life…and then for his eternal rest. She hadn't meant to pray it, but the words just came.

She opened her eyes, and looked into his. She saw firelight there now. She saw it flickering. She felt the glow of a hearth. Great warmth flowed from him. And then she was there, inside that light, inside that warmth. It was the two of them, one flesh, one spirit, and they were home. His hand was warm, his cheeks were ruddy, his eye was sharp and full of mirth. She heard a child laughing. And then he sighed, and the light in his eyes receded. It just pulled back, slowly at first, like a lantern on a departing carriage. She thought, she believed, just for that moment, that she could go with him, that she could follow where he went. She tried to follow after him, in her heart, in her spirit. She called his name. But the lamplight dwindled quickly. And then it flickered out. His face was gray. His hand was cold. His eyes were silent.

Jenta stayed there in the water, holding her husband's hand for a very long time. People came and went above. She heard little. After a while she noticed the dock again, the people above, the coldness of the water.

A few comments filtered through, spoken about the Gatemen, spoken about Damrick Fellows, spoken about her husband.

"He keeps riling up all those who want to fight the pirates," one voice said, "and then he gets 'em killed."

"Yeah. Then he goes gets more."

"Seems he's helping the Conch more than anyone else."

A snort. "Conch's probably paying him a bundle."

A laugh, and the footsteps moved on.

The cold suddenly reached deep into Jenta's bones. She did not want to leave. She wanted to stay, and die with Damrick. More than anything else, she wanted to leave this wretched earth and be with Damrick, where there was light and warmth.

But she had made a promise. Now she knew why he had insisted. He had known. He knew what it would be like for her, when he was gone. And that gave her some comfort. Finally, she let go of his hand. She moved closer, and pulled herself out of the water until she could place her cold lips on his cold cheek. And then she slid back down, under the surface, under the water. Strange, distant echoes sounded, and she couldn't tell if they came from without, or if they were just the hollow places deep within her, echoes of what was no more. She surfaced.

And then she swam away, under the docks, in the direction of the castle.

"Any end's a good end," Delaney said out loud to the air, wiping away a tear. He hadn't cried listening to Ham, that night in the forecastle when he'd told that story. He'd only felt the sting of shame. Now he looked for his fish, suddenly wanting their company more than anything. But he could only see one or two, pale below the dark surface of the pond. He spoke to them anyway. "That's how it is when ye've made the right choices. Any end's good when ye've done right." He shook his head at their inattentiveness. "You little boys don't know about that. But it's true."

Delaney hadn't made the right choices. Not nearly. But he hoped he could make a few now, at least in his mind and his heart. He hoped he could face his end as Damrick had. He knew no one would hold his hand or spin him yarns of comfort or pray for his soul. But then, he deserved none of that, either. He'd done nothing in his life to earn such things.

Now that he was thinking on it, now that he was looking straight at it without flinching, Delaney knew exactly what he had done. And he knew what it meant. He had sworn allegiance to a pirate, and within minutes of the vow he had killed a good, good man. A weak man, to be sure. But one who had been bad, and then turned good. Within minutes more, he had shot at, perhaps killed, some of the best men there ever were, better men than Delaney had ever known, far better than he had dreamed of being himself. Damrick Fellows. Murk. Stock. Lye Mogene.

He looked around at the tall grasses, and they rustled. He heard low voices, mutterings. How long had this activity been going on? He didn't care. "I never knowed it," he said aloud. "I never knowed what I done, ye cursed Hants!"

The reeds went quiet.

But the sense that he could justify himself on any point evaporated with the echoes of his words. He was a stupid, blundering imbecile, wandering from bad to worse, doing things that had consequences he didn't understand, didn't want to understand, and pretended he could ignore. Not knowing wasn't an excuse. It was just more proof he deserved to be condemned. His stupidity was in his soul, not in his mind.

Delaney sniffed, wiped the corner of his eye. Damrick died right. Avery died right. Just as they should have, somehow, even though it was unjust and they didn't deserve it. And now the image, the memory, rolled back. Not Ham's story, but the actual event. The memory he'd kept at bay, at all costs, never to let back into his mind. The one he knew was always there, always waiting, waiting to condemn him. It looped around his ankle and pulled him down.

And there it was.

"I'm sorry, young fella," Delaney said to Wentworth. As he said it, his mouth went as dry as a hot summer wind. Conch's pistol hung like an anchor at the end of his arm. The sun beat down, but he could feel the humidity of the storm brewing, moving in. A crow squawked, flapped its lazy wings upward. And the sickly man's head came up, slowly, his eyes like lanterns in the dark, searching, searching, finding Delaney. They were not accusing. They were soft and distant and thoughtful. Mournful. Like a man who'd seen too much.

The pistol was a lump of hot iron in his hand. The sweat of his palm made it slippery, too. The thing was far too heavy to hold, much too heavy to raise up. But Delaney did it anyway. "If I don't, ye see, I'll get shot, too," he explained to the quiet man. "And then, well, someone else'll jus' shoot ye anyway."

Wentworth cocked his head just slightly, as though listening to something. Then for no reason Delaney could fathom, he said, "I forgive you."

It was a stab, a sword that flashed straight into Delaney's chest, cutting him deep. It made him want to do anything else in the world but pull that trigger.

"Time's a wastin'," Conch rumbled from behind. The voice cast a shadow of death across Delaney.

Wentworth lowered his head, and he prayed. Delaney couldn't make out the words, but saw the lips move. Delaney heard. He knew this time what it was.

The sweat of his palm, the slipperiness of the pistol butt, the weight of the weapon, the stubbornness of the trigger, the wobble of the barrel as it tried, tried so hard to move away from the matted hair on that dry, dusty scalp…these were things Delaney recalled vividly. He remembered them just that way, right before the flash and the crash and the blood and the thump of the body hitting the earth, emptied of spirit.

Now the drums began. Distant, rhythmic, but with offbeats that countered the main beats, giving them an eerie sound. Delaney listened, and a chill ran through him. They were not up close, where the rustling was. But they made that image, that flash of powder and the body slumping away from him, come to his mind over and over again, like they were calling it up inside him. Over and over. They kept doing it for a while, a long while. And then they stopped.

Delaney sighed. Wentworth had died right. Delaney could have done the same. But he'd killed instead. And now he would die wrong.

Then it hit him. He wasn't going to die wrong, not at all.

The Blaggard's Hole. The *Kwy Dendaroos*. Doorway for the Doomed. The Hants weren't wrong. Belisar the Whale wasn't wrong. This wasn't a penalty that he didn't deserve. This was exactly what he deserved. This ceremonial, ritual torture, this tearing out of his bones, this complete and utter mortal destruction in the most horrifying way imaginable…it wasn't a crying shame, inflicted on a poor soul who hadn't earned such a terrible fate. He wasn't being unfairly punished for doing a good deed for a little girl. No, he was being judged for all the evil he'd ever done and got away with. Or thought he'd got away with. Every secret, every evil thought, every ugly word.

No, this wasn't wrong, it was right. It was just.

He sat up straighter. He raised his chin. He suddenly felt, instead of afraid or angry, almost…what was it? Grateful? No, that wasn't it. But it was something. Somehow, knowing he deserved all this, it made it…easier. No, not easier. Truer! That was it. Sort of.

He looked up at the hole in the canopy. Three bright stars were visible in the deepening blue. And then he knew what this feeling was. He felt worthy. Not worthy of being rescued. No, he felt worthy of damnation. But within that he felt, for the first time in his life, that what he'd done had meant something. It meant something so deep and so profound that God Himself had ordained this end for him. His life had been empty and evil. But it hadn't been meaningless. A man couldn't go around shooting people and stealing and robbing and turning his back on Maybelle Cuddy and the children he was supposed to have, and then just drift away into darkness and nothingness like it hadn't happened. Like it didn't matter. No, there was a God after all. A God who saw. A God who judged. A God who cared. There was a God who would clean up the world.

And that was a God Delaney would be proud to get crushed by.

"Come get me, then!" he announced, not to God, and not to the Hants, but to the mermonkeys. "I'm here! God's will be done, ye pointy-toothed little bone-munchers! Come and get me, I'm yer man!"

He meant it, too.

But they didn't come.

And after a while the drums didn't come back, and then the reeds didn't rustle. And then the feeling faded, and Delaney was left just where he'd been, sitting on his post in his pond, with a crick in his back and a backside that needed a stretch. But he didn't stretch. He left his mind to wander.

And wander it did…back to a tale where Conch Imbry tasted one last, great victory. Just before the wind shifted on him and drove him toward the shoals.

The men in the forecastle were anxious, their patience worn thin by long interludes of dying love when the great and final battle loomed. Delaney remembered that. And then Ham indulged them. He went on and on, describing every detail, shot by shot. He told how the *Shalamon* led a flotilla of ships from Mumtown, a small fleet of Cabeebs and pirates promised gold and shares, out into the rain and wind of Cabeeb Bay. He told how they surrounded those three Ryland ships, how the furnaces on the *Ayes of Destiny*, the *Lion's Pride*, and the *Blue Horizon* glowed red, how cannon boomed and hot shot flew in all directions, tracing and hissing through the rain and the mist. The men saw it all in their minds' eyes, saw the wind kick up, felt the rain come lashing down, heard cannon and thunder, saw the gunpowder smoke plume out, and get kicked by the wind, and then dissolve into nothing in the rain and the storm.

Delaney listened, too, pulled along, engrossed. Who wouldn't be? Conch Imbry proved a brilliant, calculating admiral. He directed the small ships into the fray first, bobbing and crashing on the waves, just so he could watch and learn from their destruction. Then, having unlocked the secret of the Gatemen's success, he trained his long-range guns on the furnaces, only on the furnaces, booming from a distance while the Gatemen wore themselves ragged against a host of quick, light sloops and yachts and catamarans that would not stay still. Whenever an oven was hit square, it roared its flames and coals sky high. Then the fires of hell engulfed their own Gatemen; flying coals and white-hot shrapnel, smoke and brimstone and black grime choking and burning and maiming and killing. And the heat of those coals, now strewn across wooden decks, would hiss and steam but would not be quenched by a little rain.

Seeing the way the Gatemen used their swivel cannon, Conch ordered his powder stores moved from the main hold to the Poker Deck astern. When that was done, he singled out the *Ayes of Destiny*. He brought the *Shalamon* in close. She took a shelling from the Gatemen's four guns, and they did some damage, but not enough; those guns were quickly silenced by the *Shalamon*'s big cannon. And against muskets and pistols, even when the shot was heated, the black ship's rock-hard hull held firm, deflecting glancing musket balls, burning slow even when hit square. And then there was the rain, quenching whatever small flames took root and tried to grow.

The Gatemen fought on, slipping on wet soot and blood, breathing the reek of fumes, taking fire and grapeshot until their *Destiny* was but a hissing, smoking ruin, sinking swiftly into the darkness and the cold at the bottom of the bay.

And Ham told the end of Hale Starpus, a hard man and a harder man to kill. He kept cannons booming and muskets barking until there was hardly a deck left to stand upon. And even when the ship keeled over, gasping and gurgling and creaking into the drink, he swam at his enemies with a knife clutched in his teeth, determined to sever the throat of any pirate unlucky enough to be in the water, fool enough to come within his reach. Thus he fought until a musket ball stopped him, and he slipped under the waves.

Successful at last against the Gatemen, Conch turned the same tactics on the *Lion's Pride*, and she went down as well—a simple freighter after all, her crew mere mortals. After the *Lion's Pride* it was the *Blue Horizon*. With cannon long since silenced, with furnaces in ruins, without hot shot, and with a decimated, bleeding, desperate crew, the Gatemen's ship was boarded. And it was here, when the *Shalamon* slid up from port astern and hull scraped hull, that Delaney made his reputation sure. His feet moved him up and over rails, down decks, up decks. His sword could sing and dance, and it severed many a red-plumed hat from a defeated head. Here, too, Spinner Sleeve and Mutter Cabe made good their pirate vows—Sleeve with a reckless joy that heartened his new captain. And it was on these decks that big Nil Corver, as slow of hand as he was of mind, breathed out his last, a pirate for a day.

In the end, ten ships went down. The Gatemen had sunk eight of Conch's to two of Ryland's. But those two ships took all their cargo, all Ryland's sailors, and all the Gatemen with them. The *Pride* was saved and taken prize, her bounty looted and divided back in port.

Every Gateman died. They were shown no mercy; they expected none. Wives and children, mothers, fathers, sisters, brothers, all would mourn the passing of good men who stood against the evil of their time, and for their trouble left the world too soon. Their memories would live on, hundreds of miles away, burnished in glory. But their remains would sink into the sea in hundreds of feet of cold blue water. They would decompose, be eaten by the sharks, or rise again and wash ashore in the grimmest of reminders for all Cabeebs in Mumtown…here's what happens to a man who crosses Carnsford Bloodstone Imbry.

Spinner Sleeve could not contain his glee. He leapt from his hammock and did a little dance. "Been a long time gettin' to the payoff!" he crowed. "But there's an end of it…them Gatemen finally got what's comin'!" Sailors laughed at him, and then swapped stories of their own. Ham's tale was done for the night. But only for the night.

"The tale of Damrick Fellows has come to an end," he explained the very next evening. "But there is much yet to tell. For Jenta lives on, and so does the secret of Conch's gold."

Eyes popped wide.

"She's goin' after his gold?" one asked.

"A' course she is!" a big voice fairly shouted. This was Blue Garvey, whose comments were few, and generally brutal. "Conch killed her husband. Might as well steal and have a little somethin' to remember him by." He laughed. No one else joined in.

"Conch waited in the port of Mumtown two more weeks," Ham continued, "hoping something familiar might wash ashore." He sucked his pipe, and the crackling filled the forecastle, followed by the smell of sweet tobacco smoke. "But of all the bloated bodies that ever surfaced, not a one could rightly show as either Damrick Fellows or Jenta Stillmithers. So finally he decided they were dead, and if not dead, they were dead enough. He sailed the *Shalamon* out of Mumtown to much cheering from its citizens, almost all of whom were at least somewhat richer for the dark ship's visit."

Conch Imbry was in splendid spirits on the return trip.

"All Hallow's Dance is comin'," Conch said to Mazeley as they stood on the weather deck, soaking in the sunshine. "It may just be my favorite. Costumes, all them ghosts around and all. And me, why I'm expectin' breathless beauties to come 'round to comfort me in my time a' great sadness and loss." He grinned. "See, I'm over her now, Mazeley. I'm a new man."

"Delighted to hear it, sir."

The *Shalamon* took her berth at the docks of Skaelington, and the usual crowd of well-wishers and hangers-on was there to greet them, waving, calling out, soaking up the presence of the city's most famous son. The new pirates aboard watched in fascination. The docks were gray and weathered, nothing to recommend them, but the crowd that gathered seemed quite enthusiastic.

"They think we're famous," Mutter muttered.

"Because we are, ye dolt," Sleeve instructed.

"Not too many women today, for some reason," a veteran of Conch's crew interjected. "Usually more'n half of 'em are females, wantin' the Captain's attention."

"Get a move on!" one of Conch's lieutenants now called out. The men grabbed the nearest mooring line, and though it was overmanned, still they helped play it out.

Within a few minutes Captain Conch and his man Mazeley, as was their wont, strolled down the gangway side by side. Four or five pirates, including Motley, walked with them as bodyguards.

"Ryland's dead. So he's out," Conch was saying thoughtfully. "I'll miss his money. But let's get that fat banker back to the poker table. I enjoyed thinnin' down his accounts, though it don't seem to have had much effect on the rest of 'im."

Mazeley smiled.

"Conch!" one of the few female admirers called out, a bright-eyed young woman who pressed in close, pushing past Motley and the other bodyguards. "Did you catch Damrick Fellows?" she asked, eyes aglow.

The Captain grinned. "We did! We nailed the Gatemen but good!"

A small cheer went up, and others pushed in, all calling Conch's name and asking him questions.

"Okay, back up now…" Conch raised his hands, still smiling as he warded them away. Only Motley pulled his gun. The young woman tried to grab it and he fired. She fell to the ground, holding her chest. Then she lay still.

Conch turned his ire on the goon. "Motley!" He snatched the pistol away from him. "Look what you gone and—"

"Now!" someone shouted, and in an instant five or six in the crowd had Imbry by the arms.

"Treachery!" he shouted, struggling against his attackers until a club came out and struck him from behind, across an ear and a cheek, thudding like it had hit a sodden sandbag. His knees buckled.

"The Conch!" Calls came from above, from aboard ship. But sailors at the rail only watched, dumbfounded, unable to make sense of the scene. The crowd was swarming around their captain. But they were friendly. Right? They were always friendly. They'd disarm anyone fool enough to try to attack Conch Imbry. And if they didn't, his guards would.

And in fact two of Conch's guards did manage to fire their weapons, but they were quickly overcome as well. In the commotion Mazeley somehow wriggled free and slithered through the crowd. He nearly got away, too, until someone recognized him. Then another club went up and came down hard, a direct crack to the skull. Mr. Mazeley crumpled.

It was Sleeve who recognized the danger, and was the first to fire from the deck. His musket shot took down a bystander. But almost immediately, answering gunfire came from the dock. Suddenly the entire crowd was armed, more than thirty pistols came out, aimed, and fired. Pirates fell from the railings, slumped down on the floorboards. Without a command or a commander, the pirates rushed the gangway, intent on going to their leader's rescue. But the citizens rushed up at the same time, jamming their descent.

More gunfire erupted from the deck of the *Shalamon*, as now the sailors aboard began to understand the full extent of the danger, and the damage being done. Conch and Mazeley were gone, hustled from the docks, taken who knew where? But even as the sailors opened fire the dock was swarmed. Hundreds of people came running now, pouring from the streets, from behind buildings, from within shops and taverns. All of them were armed. Most of them began firing on the *Shalamon*. Pirates who jammed the gangway dropped where they stood, and then as the press grew worse from crewmen behind and citizens in front, they stood where they should have dropped, dead men packed and jostled together like a fishmonger's barrel on a market cart. Citizens below now pulled bodies away from the gangway, shooting or stabbing those cutthroats not already shot or stabbed. And then they began to push upward, to board.

The pirate crew took cover. The docks were jammed now, crowded thick with shouting, shooting, saber-waving men and women. Those aboard who dared risk the storm of musket fire to raise up their heads saw leather lashes tied to many arms. Red feathers everywhere. And still more coming. Thousands of them.

"Looks like the city's all turned Gatemen," Sleeve said, aghast.

"More like the whole world," Mutter answered.

And standing on a rooftop, looking down from behind a jutting façade, was Runsford Ryland, assessing his own handiwork. But he took little pleasure in seeing his plan play out. He couldn't help but wish he'd done it while Wentworth yet lived. And after he'd thought about that for a while, then he couldn't help but think about how much harder it would be to maintain his shipping kingdom now, without the chief of pirates on his side.

By the time the initial volley of musket and pistol fire slowed, the pirates understood their peril.

"Shove off!" one shouted.

"Jet the gangway!" another called.

"Cut the lines!" added another.

"Wait! We can't leave the Conch!" Spinner Sleeve shouted, waving his pistol.

"Throw that one overboard, and leave 'im!" The cutthroat who shouted this was pointing his sword at Sleeve.

"We'll come back for him, then!" Sleeve decided quickly.

In the lull, others loaded grapeshot into the muzzles of the cannon, but they quickly drew more fire from the docks. Only three cannon shots were fired before the dark ship *Shalamon* drifted away from her moorings, but each cut a wide swath of destruction. Small arms fire was traded in great waves of smoke and crackling flame. Sailors fell from the rigging as others climbed to take their place, sure that their lives depended on their work. But somehow sails were dropped and the *Shalamon* fled, flying with unusual grace for so big a ship.

The Gatemen on the docks all cheered their newfound victory. They had been prepared to overrun the ship, but they were unprepared to crew another, and pursue.

The forecastle went silent. Sleeve swore once, but made no further comment.

Ham sighed. "Many of you gents remember that day, those of you who sailed with the Conch. But not all know what happened ashore in Skaelington, in those dark days that followed. So I'll tell you now. Conch Imbry was put in prison. And though he swore he'd never see a trial, he did. Sheriffs, judges, jailors, men with big houses that previously had been bought, footing and trim, by bribes paid out by the pirate king suddenly could not be tempted by his gold coins. They say Runsford Ryland grew poor in those few weeks. But his plan held, and so did Conch's chains.

"'I paid ye good wages all my days,' Conch complained to the judge after the verdict was read to him. 'And this is all the loyalty it buys me?' But the justice brought his gavel down. Within a week of his arrest the Conch was marched up a gallows before a cheering throng. The very population, politicians, police, and public alike, who had sung his praises all those years, those who danced whenever he played a tune, and played a tune whenever he danced, now sang songs to his demise.

"Some women wept, but more wept with joy that their children would not grow up in the pirate's thrall. And those children quickly learned new games, replacing Round-the-Monkey with something they called Pirates-and-Gatemen. And in this game, the pirates always lost, dying dramatic deaths, or getting themselves hanged.

"'To blazes wif ye all!'

"Such were Conch Imbry's final words. And then he looked to Mr. Mazeley, standing to his left, a noose around his neck as well. He shrugged, the doors beneath them creaked, and both men fell through the gateway of the doomed, dying together at the end of a hangman's rope."

A long moment of silence filled the close space, the confines of the forecastle, interrupted only by the creak of timbers, and here and there a sniff, or a muffled sob.

"Runsford Ryland was careful to give credit," Ham continued, "if not where it was due, then at least where it would do some good. In speeches and toasts on as many public occasions as he could manage, Runsford Ryland praised the heroism of his son, the first businessman to stand against the corruption and debasement that had been forced on them all by cutthroats like Conch Imbry.

"'Of course,' he would say modestly during a pause in the festivities of the New Moon Ball or standing at the head table of the Great Christmas Banquet, 'when I first told Wentworth of my idea to hire the Gatemen, he balked. He would only agree to go along if he could be the one to carry the banner, and keep his father from the dangers of Conch Imbry's wrath. That was the sort of man he was, and the sort of son.' And the whole room cheered."

The pirates in the forecastle booed. Ham cleared his throat.

"'Wentworth could not be bought,' Ryland would go on. 'But sadly, such was not the case with Damrick Fellows, who started out so well, and should be remembered with generosity for that. I must tell you, it was only by the grace of God that I was able to escape from the good ship *Success*, before he led it and my son's three worthy ships, and all their worthy sailors, to their doom—Gatemen delivered on a platter to Conch Imbry in Cabeeb Bay.'"

The pirates in the forecastle expressed their disgust with varied and colorful enthusiasm.

"'But again,' Runsford would say, 'let us not judge Damrick too harshly. He was, I believe, and as some of you witnessed, deeply in love with that treacherous, unfaithful woman who first caught Wentworth in her snares, then quickly tired of him and ran to the arms, or should I say the pockets, of Conch Imbry. From there she did his bidding, convincing Damrick Fellows to lead the Gatemen to their wretched demise. We must pity Damrick's weakness, for who among us has none? All the while we must thank our Heavenly Father for the good that Damrick did in establishing the Gatemen, the worthy organization it is now my privilege to lead.'"

"Lead? Did you say lead?" a shocked pirate interjected.

"Aye," Ham answered. "For Ryland became the Master of the Gatemen, a title he made up himself."

Pirates growled, and various epithets arose. Even Spinner Sleeve swore at Ryland.

"What do you care, Sleeve? You hate the Gatemen," a pirate challenged.

"True. But worse, I hate fer a snake like Runsford to muddy the name of a great enemy who we beat down in a honest battle. Weren't fer Damrick, why Conch'd sail the seas yet."

"But what about Jenta?" Dallis Trum asked. "What happened to her?"

"Forget the woman," Mutter Cabe intoned. "What happened to the gold?"

Enthusiastic agreement ensued.

"Ah. Well, that's what we're leadin' up to, isn't it?"

And with that, the pirate's mourning ended. After all, Conch was gone. But his gold remained.

"Mayor Runsford Ryland's heroics are well known these days," Ham said. "For sure enough, he was appointed to that role in Skaelington. But there are few alive who know what happened to our Jenta, after *Success* was sunk. As luck would have it, I am one of those. And soon, so shall you be…tomorrow night when we continue. That's all for tonight, lads. More tomorrow if I've a mind and you've the time."

But the next day, Ham didn't have a mind. When Belisar the Whale learned of what Ham Drumbone had promised his listeners, he had Blue Garvey whip the storyteller thirty lashes and throw him in the brig.

Ham recovered and returned, eventually. And he told many tales after that, but not a one about any Gateman, or about Jenta, or about Damrick. And after that no one heard him give the slightest shadow of a hint regarding the whereabouts of Conch Imbry's gold.

Chapter Eighteen

AUTUMN

DELANEY TOOK A deep breath and almost sensed a bit of a coolness in the air. He sniffed around, but couldn't find it again—only the fetid closeness of these dank woods. Probably it was all in his head. The stars were out now. The dusky blue circle of sky above was all but black.

The drums in the distance started back up. They seemed louder, or at least more insistent. Or maybe the evening air carried the sound better. He didn't know. He also didn't much care. In fact, there was very little right now that caught his fancy. His mind had wandered and wondered, flitting along through the tale just as Ham had told it, stopping here and there to ponder things too big for him. And now he was ready for whatever came. The events after Ham had quit the story, they'd kept rolling on, of course, even without a storyteller. They were what had led Delaney here. And now, in the end, he'd got where he was going.

The details were hardly worth thinking on. He would die here, and he knew why. God had no reason to reach down and pluck him up. There would be no idea tomatoes that would grow fat and ripe in his head, showing him how to hop over to dry land. And even if he could, the Hants would just catch him and put him back. Or cut him up like they did to Father Dent. And then to Jenta.

Delaney sighed. He put an elbow on his knee and a palm under his chin. He really hoped that Hant chieftain hadn't sliced Jenta all up, like what happened to the priest. She was a woman after all. But she was good, and so she'd get whammed, and there was nothing to be done about it.

The reeds were moving again. And this time, he saw faces. It was dark, and they were in the shadows, but it was the Hants. Definitely the Hants. Their painted faces like skulls peered out of the long grasses. About a dozen of them, ringing him all round. They looked at him with curiosity and distrust. Then they looked at one another. Then one of them made an odd clucking sound. That was their leader, the only one whose face had been painted up last night. Tattooed, is what Delaney thought. Then another answered with a clucking sound. And pretty soon they were all just clucking away at one another like a bunch of crazy chickens.

"Kinda rude, ain't it?" he asked. "Talkin' in front of a man like that, and me not knowing a lick what yer sayin'?"

They suddenly went quiet, and ducked back into the reeds.

"That's better manners." He was quiet a moment. Then he added, "Though I'd rather ye'd stay and chatted, normal-like."

But he didn't really feel like chatting. He was just making conversation.

He closed his eyes. He pictured Jenta, with her long amber hair and sad eyes. He hoped she was okay. That chat he'd had with her, that wasn't just making conversation. That was a real, honest-to-daylight talk. That was one for a lifetime. He knew her so much better now, so much better than he'd known her back when Ham told his tales. Back then, four years ago it was, or almost that long ago, she'd been just a person in a story. But now that he'd met her, all these years later, and talked to her, she seemed different. Older, maybe. Quieter. Anyway, different than he had imagined.

Of course, she was a mother now. That would likely make a difference.

He had been on watch, him and Lemmer Harps, ordered by Belisar to sit outside the ship's brig where Jenta and her daughter were locked up below decks on the *Shalamon*. He'd approached her first with great wariness, as though she was some magical person, or royalty, someone to whom a small, no-account sailor like Delaney might not even talk. But she was kind, and said hello, and so he said hello back.

"You're staring at me," she said after a few moments.

"I'm guarding you," he answered. He stood a little straighter, to better make his point.

"Ain't suppose to talk to the prisoner," Lemmer Harps reminded him. Lemmer had got there before Delaney, and he had his stool pulled up to the brig, his back against the bars, his big floppy hands resting in his lap. Relaxing. But he knew Lemmer was right. So he looked around and saw the small stool that the guard before him had used on the last shift, and made a show of moving it around to get it just right, so that she'd know he knew his business, and then he sat facing her. He watched her carefully. So that she'd know she was under guard.

For some reason, this seemed to amuse her. "What's your name?" she asked. Her blue eyes were very kind. She was as beautiful as they said, though dressed now in peasant clothes, like a farmer's wife. But she wasn't a farmer's wife, that was plain. And now at last he knew what "hair like fine sherry" looked like. And it was fine, just as Ham described it.

"Ain't supposed to talk," Lemmer reminded her. Then to Delaney, "You talk, I got to report ye," he intoned. "Cap'n's orders."

Delaney shrugged in her direction, to apologize. She winked.

He blushed.

It was about two hours later, when Lemmer started snoring, that they spoke again.

"What's your name?" she asked again, gently this time.

"I still ain't supposed to talk, ye know." He eyed Lemmer, whose head was leaned back against the bars, his mouth open. "Rules don't change just 'cause someone else falls asleep." He said it in a knowing way.

"I don't follow rules very well," she confessed.

"Me neither," he replied quickly, but then wondered why.

"Is that your daughter?" he asked. He pointed to the girl who was sound asleep on the bench, with her head on Jenta's lap. She wore a bright yellow sundress. Delaney knew it was Jenta's daughter. He was just being polite. He figured, now that he'd told her he was one to break the rules he'd better break one, if only to show her he was a man of his word.

"Yes. Where are they taking us?"

"I can't say, ma'am," he said, honestly enough. He didn't know.

"Are they taking us to Conch Imbry?"

He looked at her strangely. "Conch Imbry's been hanged these four years."

She took a deep breath, and let it out. "That's what the last one said. It's just hard to believe it's true."

"Oh, they hanged him, all right. Big to-do there in Skaelington."

She patted her little girl's hair, then stroked it.

Delaney noticed that the daughter had blonde hair. Damrick's was dark, they said, maybe even black. It was Conch that had yellowish hair. Almost that same color. Delaney didn't know how to remark about that, so he didn't.

"So, you're a pirate?" she asked.

"I'm guarding you, ain't I?"

"You don't act like a pirate."

He furrowed his brow. "Now, what's that mean?"

"I don't mean to insult you. It's just, you seem like a dear little man."

"Well, I ain't," he assured her, and crossed his arms. "Ain't never been dear to no one." He paused, then added, "Except maybe my own Poor Ma."

"Your poor ma?"

He brightened. "You know her?"

"I don't think so. What's her name?"

Confused now, he didn't answer. So instead he asked a bold question. "That Damrick's little girl?"

Now she stared hard at him. "Yes," she said. "Did you know my husband?"

"Of him. Never met him myself. I suppose I'd be dead if I ever did. He didn't take much to folks like me."

They were both silent for a while. Then she asked, "What was it like to be a pirate, and to know he was out there?" She seemed to want to know, but only to be talking about him. Like she still missed him.

He scratched at an ear. "Oh, I'd been a pirate less than a day when he died. I was up on the wall of the castle…" he trailed off. "Maybe I shouldn't be talkin' about that."

"You were there? You were in Mumtown that day? You fired on us?"

He sat a moment, then said, "I told you I wasn't a dear man."

But she didn't seem to mind. "You have questions about me," she guessed.

He shrugged. "Belisar will give me the lash, I keep talkin' to ye."

"Not if he doesn't know." Then she said something he couldn't ignore. "You probably want to know about Captain Imbry's gold."

Then he knew for sure that she'd been talking to the last guard about it. How else could she guess that? He looked around at Lemmer, who was still snoring. A fly was walking around his chin. It walked right up to his lip, but didn't go in. Rather, it walked back down his chin again. Delaney looked back at Jenta. "Did you keep that map?"

"Map?"

"Aye," he whispered, leaning in. "The one you stole from Conch's cabin. We heard all about that."

She said nothing, but her look seemed a bit sly to him.

"When you was in the tin box, and got saved from us shooting at ye, and got yer dress ripped, I always wondered, did ye keep the map, or did it rip away?"

She shook her head, but she didn't seem upset at all. "You have quite an imagination. No part of my gown ever ripped away, that I recall. And I do think I would have noticed."

"Oh." He blushed. "That's what I was told." If Ham would lie about that, what else might he have lied about? Now Ham's whole story was in doubt. "Did you say goodbye to Damrick under the boardwalk? The dock, I mean? Where he died?"

She looked down at her little girl, and stroked her golden hair.

Delaney was afraid the question was too harsh, so he rephrased it. "I was just wonderin' if ye really did choke up and all that, with you tellin' him stories and such just afore he cashed in." Still too harsh. "I mean, passed out." But that wasn't right. "I mean passed over." He turned red. "You know, afore he died away."

She said nothing, then after a moment she looked back up. She didn't seem angry or upset or anything. "What's your name?"

It was the third time she'd asked. This time he said, "Smith Delaney, ma'am."

"Some things are private between two people, Smith Delaney."

"I know that, ma'am." Ham did know the truth, then, though he'd added some details of his own. Better to ask simple questions, get her mind off all his fumbling around. "How'd you get out a' Mumtown? How'd you get back to Mann?"

"I saw a boat with a ladder, and it seemed like no one was looking, and so I climbed it. But no sooner was I aboard then a man with a blunderbuss appeared from inside the cabin. He was angry. His wife came up behind, glared at me."

"What'd ye do?"

"I said I needed to get to Nearing Vast. The man and his wife took me. I was very fortunate that they were secretly enemies of Conch Imbry. They hated him, and loved the Gatemen."

"Good luck that."

"Before we left, late that night, we went back under the dock. The three of us. We wrapped Damrick in canvas and took him with us." Her look was far away now. "I haven't spoken of it but once before, to his father."

"Ye took him home to bury him?" Delaney asked.

"No. Far, far out to sea, somewhere between the Warm Climes and the City of Mann, we gave him to the ocean. Buried in salt water and tears."

"Amazin' thing," he said. It actually wasn't much different than he would have guessed, but he liked to hear it from her and wanted her to know he appreciated it. "So what happened back in Nearing Vast?"

"I asked after Didrick Fellows, of course, and was eventually introduced to those who knew him. They took me to my father-in-law, who worked a tiny farm he'd bought with the gold he earned on his one, last voyage as a freighter. He took me in."

"As Damrick knew he would."

She paused, then said, "The next summer I gave birth to Damrick's child, this little girl."

"Ye named her Autumn."

She looked puzzled. "Yes."

"Then Belisar found ye."

"Four years we had." Her face seemed drawn. "But I couldn't hide forever."

"He'd been looking all that time?"

"You tell me, Mr. Delaney. You sail with him. Has he been looking for Conch's gold for four years?"

Delaney knew he had been, though it was the sort of thing that seemed like it should be kept secret. Soon as there was talk of gold, he needed to keep mum. But he remembered well how Belisar had come aboard and taken over the *Shalamon*, and he told her the story.

"I weren't any good at it," he informed the *Chompers*. Not that he could see them now. He couldn't. But he hoped they were still there. "Never should try and tell a story. Should leave it to Ham and others." There were many good storytellers in the world, and he'd heard a few. Ham was the best, of course, but on many ships everyone took turns. Delaney didn't like to, and Jenta found out the reason why. He could never seem to get things to come out straight. He'd be sure he had it right, and then she'd ask the craziest question. And then he'd answer it, and she'd ask something else completely odd. Eventually he figured it was probably him, not her, but it was hard to know, when you were the one telling it.

"We flew all ahead flank out a' Skaelington harbor, we did, for the men agreed on that point. But only for a league or two, and then the agreements come to an end. Some wanted to go back for the Conch, some said go get more help. They started arguin' about whether, and there was shouting, then the boys started working out the answers with their knuckles. And then their knives."

"They fought about the weather?"

"Nah. About going back for the Conch or not. I stayed out of it, 'cause I knowed early on that the answer to that question would be bloody. I was right, too. But only two died, and they didn't want to go to Mumtown. But one who got killed was the first mate, so that's where we went."

"You went to Mumtown?"

"Aye. Like I jus' said. But anyways, ever' bad thing that can happen asea happened on that voyage. We had shootings and whatnot. Regular hands like Gunner Steep and Boom Saller, who'd sailed with the Conch fer years, they were the worst about always saying what Conch would want, and backing it up with fists or daggers if no one agreed. See, there was no captain or first mate or Mazeley left to step in and send that one to the brig or that one to the grate, so it never got set straight and all stayed catawampus. And then it got bad."

"It got worse than that?"

"Ye don't know." He shook his head.

"I guess I don't."

"There was the lookout who called out seeing a Firefish, which jus' got everybody mad and him going crazy, foaming like a rabid hound and pointing and yelling, but no one believed him but he swore it was so, until they dangled him out over the sea like a worm on a hook and proved it."

"They proved there was a Firefish?"

"No! That it wasn't no Firefish, just a man hanging from a rope with no beast to eat him. But they let him hang there a good while, and then they draggled him through the water until eventually they pulled him in dead, and they ate him."

"Who ate him?"

"The sharks, a' course."

"Oh. Thank goodness. I thought you meant the pirates."

"It *was* the pirates."

"The pirates ate him?"

"No! The pirates pulled him in and the sharks ate him."

"You mean they'd already eaten him?"

"Good bits of him. Anyways, we made port in Mumtown. That was where we knew we'd be safe from Gatemen. At least, everyone but knucklebrains here," he glanced at the snoring man. "Lemmer, he got ribbed good for the way he shook and muttered as we sailed in. He was fearing that every last Cabeeb would be wearing one a' them leather armbands like what happened in Skaelington. Had nightmares about it, I believe."

"Poor man."

"But Mumtown was as it ever was. None of the boys knew what to do there, either, no better'n aboard ship. But instead of fightin' on deck, at least they were fightin' in the pubs. So that was a mercy. Though a few of 'em did land in *Horkan* Meeb's prison. But since they was already pirates, they got out after a day or two, and that's when Belisar the Whale comes in and straightens us all out." Delaney grew almost cheerful. "He come in from Skaelington in a stole ship, for he'd lost his own recently, and he climbed right aboard and called for the men to gather. It took a devil of a long time to get everyone back from town or jail, but he finally did get most, and he lined us all up, black eyes and bleedin' lips and all, and he delivered the happy news. I remember jus' what he said:

"'Gentlemen, your Captain is dead. He's hung in Skaelington, along with Mr. Mazeley. I therefore claim this ship as mine, and you as my crew.' That's his words exactly," Delaney confirmed.

"That was happy news?"

"It wasn't to a lot of 'em, who left there on the spot. But it was happy to me. I didn't know Conch well, and I was glad to get shed of him since he's the one made me shoot..." Delaney stopped.

"He made you shoot what?"

"He made me..." Delaney's face went pale—he could feel the blood drain from it, even as his heart seemed to slow to a crawl and pound at the same time. "I can't say, ma'am."

"You don't need to say."

Delaney felt enormous relief. "Thank ye kindly. The Captain, I mean the new captain, Belisar Whatney, he brought a few men with him. Blue Garvey, meanest man I ever knew."

"I've met him. He visited my father-in-law's farm recently."

"Right. He was one of those what went to get you. And a few others. We lost a good bit a' the crew that day, who didn't want to sail for no

Belisar What-not, as they called him. But new crew was easy to pick up in Mumtown. Except for Ham Drumbone. He's the storyteller, came with Belisar. He gathered up your tale from bits and scraps, you and Damrick, and told it all to us from the start."

"That explains why so many people seem to know who I am."

"Yes, ma'am. We all know all about you."

"But you were telling me about Belisar's search for Conch's gold."

"I was?" Delaney couldn't remember. But then, he couldn't remember talking so much before in his entire life. And then to a woman. And then to a woman he wasn't supposed to talk to at all. "I think I said enough." He glanced at Lemmer.

"I understand," she said. "Belisar probably didn't let anyone know that he was in search of the gold all that while."

Delaney said nothing, but thought hard. Then he said, "I remember thinkin' it odd that Belisar wanted to give the *Shalamon* a thorough cleansin', right away." Delaney stroked his chin. "He started that right after he shot Jubal Turley, who was the only man fool enough to speak up when Belisar asked if there were any questions. After he shot Jubal, and there were no more questions, he said he wanted every inch of the ship swabbed out and washed of all its grime. And that's why," Delaney said knowingly. But he stopped there. Belisar had been looking for the map. Belisar didn't care much about keeping a ship up to some naval standard, as he proved in the years since.

"He was searching for the map, no doubt."

"Did ye give it to him? When he found ye on the farm?"

"If I had, I wouldn't be alive."

"Well, I'm glad ye didn't then." Delaney said it with a full heart.

"Thank you, Smith Delaney. But I don't have it. He and his men ran-sacked our house, and tore up all the farm buildings. They shot our dogs and the cow, then burned everything that would burn."

Delaney nodded. It was the way of pirates. Delaney hadn't gone with Belisar on that particular mission; it was just Blue Garvey and Spinner Sleeve and a couple of others. But word was, they'd done all they could to get her to talk about where the map was, or short of that, where the gold was. They would have even shot Didrick Fellows if he'd been home, but he'd gone to Mann to sell some sheep.

"Glad they didn't hurt the two of ye," Delaney said at last.

She seemed to think that was an unusual thing to say. "Thank you, Mr. Delaney. But the only reason they didn't hurt me, or Autumn, was that I told them if they did I'd never say a word and they'd be without their treasure."

"So they took ye with 'em."

"I'm sure your captain has something horrible planned for us."

Delaney couldn't argue with her there. "So there's no map?" Delaney asked.

She looked at him with that sly look again. "I didn't say that, did I?"

"Really? Where is it?" he asked.

She laughed. It wasn't much of a laugh, or a very loud one. But it was enough. Delaney heard with his own ears the reason so many men had been drawn by that sound, even from across a room. "Smith Delaney, I'll tell you what. If you'll help me escape, I will tell you."

This sobered him up. "Ma'am, I can't do that. I'm sworn to the service of Belisar the Whale, and if you tell me where the gold is, I'll just have to tell him."

She shook her head. "A loyal man."

"I am that."

"And honest."

"Honest?"

"Yes. You could have made me promises, heard my story, and then gone to tell Belisar everything. That's what a loyal but dishonest man would do."

"He would?" Delaney didn't say it, but he thought that mostly he didn't do that because he didn't think of it.

Just then the little girl stirred. She raised her head, and sleep was in her eyes. She sat up and rubbed them with chubby, delicate little hands. "Where are we, Mama?"

"On a ship. Still on a ship."

Autumn looked at Delaney. "Are you a bad man?"

Delaney's mouth dropped open. Those little eyes, so sweet and innocent, and trained on him with a question that seemed like bright sunlight shining down a well. "I'm not gonna hurt ye, if that's what yer asking."

"Is he bad, Mama?" Autumn asked, turning to the authoritative source.

"We don't know yet," Jenta said simply.

Autumn looked at Lemmer. "Is he bad?"

"We don't know. He's asleep."

"Should I sing a lullabye?"

"Yes. Yes, I think you should."

The little girl stood up and walked toward Delaney. Putting her little hands on the rusted iron bars, and her face between them, she looked up at Delaney with blue eyes shining, little white speckles in the blue parts, and began to sing the song.

> *A true lang time,*
> *A lang true la*
> *And down the silver path to a rushing sea,*
> *Where moons hang golden under boughs of green,*
> *A lang true la, 'tis true,*
> *And the true heart weeps*
> *As her song she sings,*
> *A true lang time for you…*

He was dumbfounded. It was the voice from his dream. The dream he'd had in Mumtown. He never thought he'd actually hear it, but there it was. And the song…it was the same song. Even more beautiful, more haunting than he'd dreamed it. Had he dreamed it into being? Or had he dreamed of what was to come?

The girl kept singing, verses he hadn't heard before…

> *Oh, carry my burthen, and carry her true,*
> *For she steers for the south and the east*
> *And the few,*
> *A lang true la,*
> *The drum and the yew,*
> *A true lang time, my sweet.*
> *A true lang time and we shall meet*
> *On the silver path to the rushing sea*
> *Where moons hang golden, and boughs are green,*
> *A lang true la, 'tis true.*
> *'Tis true, and lang, and lang true la,*
> *A lang true la, and you.*

The song went on, but Delaney was lost. He was lost in those eyes, in that voice, and in not knowing whether he dreamed or was awake. He was down in that well with the sun shining bright above, and couldn't seem to climb up out of it. There was beauty here he had never known,

Blaggard's Moon

and sadness, and longing, but it felt like perhaps he had known it all once, long ago. It was the beauty of a lullabye, sung from behind the cold iron bars of this world.

Finally the girl finished her song, and looked up at him. "My mama taught it to me. Would you like me teach it to you?"

Delaney had nothing to say. So Autumn turned to her mother and put a hand on a hip. "He's not a bad man, Mama. He's just afraid."

"Come here, Autumn," she said. And the girl ran to her mother, and jumped up on her lap.

"If you change your mind, Mr. Delaney," Jenta told him, "you let me know."

Delaney looked at her and nodded. They said not another word for the rest of the shift. Somewhere in there, though, as his mind clarified itself, he realized that Jenta's last comment was meant to be about setting her free in exchange for the map to Conch's gold, and not about her daughter's offer, which was to teach him that song. He didn't know which offer was more troubling.

Delaney was never so glad to finish a watch as he was on that night. "Don't talk to her," he intoned to the man who relieved him. "She's dangerous."

Their destination became a matter of great speculation and much debate, though this time without the flying fists and the flashing knives. But the farther they traveled south with Jenta and Autumn aboard, the easier it became to guess. Perhaps Belisar had not found Conch's map, but in tearing the ship apart and putting her back together, he had certainly pored through all of Conch Imbry's papers, and read the Captain's log in great detail, and with great interest. There, everyone agreed, he would have learned all about the Hants. He would have learned, there or elsewhere, that Conch had kept his very own Hant, the chieftain he'd installed in that ruined castle outside Skaelington. That was a man who could make any man talk. Or, they surmised, any woman. But as Skaelington was off limits now, a shining example of ruthless liberty from the influence of pirates, there might be another option. And their heading certainly tended to confirm it.

Not many aboard had been to the Forests of Sule. Some had. A very few could tell of the time they'd traveled there to cut the trees and stack the lumber of the night-oak, from which the *Shalamon* would be built. As the sun rose and set, and the ship's course remained true, the speculation gave way to certainty. A certain amount of dread crept into conversations. Belisar would do anything, go anywhere, for a shot at the legendary hoard of coins amassed by Conch Imbry. He'd risk anything, including all their lives.

The drums stopped.

Delaney sat up straight and looked around him. There were no sounds. Even the bullfrogs had quit croaking. He peered down into the black water below him, but could see nothing. He waved his arms around, then stuck out his toes. "Where are you, boys?"

No *Chompers* surfaced.

Swallowing hard, he pulled his feet up under him. His knees creaked and his muscles ached. But nothing else happened. He peered around at the reeds that surrounded the pond, but they were black and still. For an instant, just an instant, it seemed that he'd imagined everything, that none of it was real. That he'd been dreaming the whole thing, all of it: the *Chompers*, the Hants, the drums, everything.

He put a hand, palm down, on top of the post under his buttocks, and flipped himself around again, and shinnied down. The post rocked unsteadily, but his grip was sure. With his toes about two feet from the surface, he leaned out and peered down again. And there they were, his little fishies, roiling the water, their big front teeth agape, little bear traps intent on sailor meat. He sighed, content. "I was worried about ye," he told them affectionately. "But yer all good to go. You jus' hang tight, now, and old Delaney will feed ye soon enough." And he climbed back up the shaft and took his accustomed seat.

It was odd. He felt ready to die. But when it came to it, it turned out he really didn't want to die. It was the pain, he told himself, not so much the actual dying, that caused the fear. Who wanted to go through all that, having bones extracted? Had to be like having a tooth pulled, which he'd had done more than once. Just thinking of it made his jaw ache—the surgeon grabbing on with a pair of pliers, and two or three men holding him down…even being drunk as a skunk, which was the only civilized way to do it, it was like they were ripping out his skull through his jaw. Having all his bones pulled out, all at once, that had to be the same. Probably worse.

He thought of the priest, Carter Dent, and how horribly carved up he'd gotten. That might be even worse, Delaney thought, but he didn't know for sure. That Hant had poisoned him, just for good measure. They said the Hant had given the poison because it made everything hurt worse.

Just the opposite of whiskey or rye or rum. It had made images come into the priest's head, too, scary images, while it made every little touch feel like a red-hot knife blade.

That poor priest.

And poor Jenta. She had not agreed to talk, though Belisar had given her chance after chance. And so he'd taken her to the Hants.

Delaney remembered how the *Shalamon* arrived in port, at Sule City.

"Looks like a bunch a' mud huts on a beach," Delaney noted, peering over the port rail.

"They're havin' fun over there," Mutter noted back, pointing across the deck to the one other ship at anchor here, a small topsail schooner with a Nearing Vast flag. It was named the *Flying Ringby*. Her crew did seem to be enjoying themselves immensely, swimming in the water, swinging wide over it on halyards and then letting loose with a great bellowing, turning somersaults and landing, usually, on their backs or bellies with an enormous splash and a horrendous slap, much to the delight of all onlookers.

"Just stopped to refill some water barrels, I reckon." And Delaney wished that was the only reason the *Shalamon* was here as well.

There was plenty of fresh water, for Sule City sat at the mouth of the River Lambent, which the locals called *Arbetoh*, "The Path." This river was called that, they quickly learned, because it was the only road that led anywhere. No man or group of men could manage to trek through these forests, thick and tangled as they were.

"Get the skiff and the shallop ready!" Belisar ordered. "Mr. Garvey, you'll come along with me. I want Spinner Sleeve, Lemmer Harps, and Smith Delaney as well. Load up ten days' rations."

"What about the prisoners?" Blue asked.

"They're coming with us," Belisar answered. He ignored the slavering grin of his first mate, Blue, wiped beaded sweat from his own forehead with an already wet handkerchief, and then turned his great bulk toward the shore. "I'll need to make a deal with one or two of these natives to guide us. Mr. Sleeve, you come with me for protection."

"Aye, sir!"

Most of the crew were quite content to stay aboard, and so they were extra-eager to help load the two boats for the journey upriver. Belisar returned from shore in less than an hour, reporting success, though he did not bring the guides back with him. After inspecting the boats, he ordered them away.

The shallop was little more than a rowboat, and was lowered with the Captain and the two prisoners in it. Belisar, drenched in sweat, sat with a wineskin on his lap, taking frequent drinks. The skiff was even smaller than the shallop, and though it was winched down from the davit arms, too, when empty it was light enough that two men could lower it with almost any weight of line, hand over hand.

The other men in the party climbed down the mooring lines and into the boats. With the Captain in the stern of the shallop, Delaney sat beside Blue Garvey, and each took an oar. The two prisoners sat in the prow. Lemmer and Sleeve took the skiff.

Their two guides joined them on the water, paddling up in little one-man pods that skimmed around the surface like dragonflies. They used ingenious paddles, a single shaft with a blade at each end. Delaney was amazed at their skill with these boats, but even more amazed that one of them managed this at a very advanced age. Old and withered, he looked like he wouldn't last another day. But he could paddle that little pod like nobody's business, just as well as the other native, who was young and fit.

Even with the lightest boats they had, it was slow going up the river. They made good progress while the river was wide, but before nightfall they had faced a catalog of difficulties: unruly bugs of various unpleasant descriptions, piranha, snakes, rapids, and of course, heat. Once they even had to shoot a big cat out of a tree. The thing roamed back and forth up in the branches overhead, just daring anyone to paddle underneath. Blue took it down with one shot, and then they all watched as the piranha turned it into a boiling feeding frenzy. They'd have stripped it down to bones, too, except that a big croc came along and snapped it up, as though the fish had been just so many gnats.

"I'd like to seen how that cat planned to kill us without gettin' et herself," Delaney said aloud. No one responded; they just kept paddling upstream.

That silent pause was unusual because for most of the trip, little Autumn kept up a steady stream of questions and comments. "That's a really big bird, Mama. What's it called?" "Why is the water so brown?" "Is that the mosquito's nose?" "Why do those men have such little boats?" "Look at that tree, Mama. It's all bent over. Is it an old man tree?" And of course, "Where are we going?" and "How long till we get there?"

Jenta did her best to answer all the questions, and to keep her daughter calm. This wasn't too difficult; it was all an adventure to Autumn. Jenta didn't once seem afraid, and Delaney watched her closely. Now and then her sadness came through, though, in a sigh or a longing look. Then Autumn would ask, "What's the matter, Mama?" And she'd put a little hand on her mother's cheek.

"It's all right, baby," Jenta would say with a smile. "The world is a hard place sometimes."

"Not for me," Autumn would say cheerfully. And then she'd sing. It wasn't always the same song. She had several songs. But all of them were haunting to Delaney. All were young and innocent, and all out of place here, echoing through canyon walls or absorbed into the rain and mist, or just rolling out over the gurgling river.

They slept in the boats, the crewmen taking turns guarding the prisoners and their own lives. The guides didn't seem too worried about anything, stretching out on shore with a rock for a pillow and a long knife by their sides.

On the second night, though, Delaney was on watch when Jenta stirred. He was looking at her face, pale in the starlight and the small sliver of moon overhead. In the rippling shadows she could have been any woman, and he thought of Maybelle Cuddy. Her little boy would be what, ten or eleven by now? He had lost count. Maybe older.

Then Jenta spoke. "Save my girl, Delaney."

Delaney whipped around, looked at Captain Whatney. But the Whale was sound asleep in the stern, sawing away peacefully. He turned back to Jenta. "I wish I could, ma'am."

"Then do."

"I cain't."

"Why not?"

"Well, lots a' reasons. But mostly, I'm a pirate now." He didn't know why he added that final word.

She was silent. "Damrick saved me." She waited a while, then said, "I didn't even want to be saved. I didn't think it was possible. But it was. He loved me when I didn't love him. When I didn't love myself. When I'd given up on everything, that's when he redeemed me."

Delaney was miserable. "Ma'am, why are ye telling me all this?"

"I know you can't save my life, Mr. Delaney. If I die, I will be with Damrick. But she's so young. Save her. Protect her. Please."

Delaney just looked up into the sky. Then he looked back down. "You go back to sleep, ma'am."

"If you can't save her," she said after a pause, "…please be sure she dies quickly, and without pain."

Delaney was sure that a more sorrowful sentence had never been spoken on earth.

After three nights and four days, they arrived. The place where the guides stopped looked no different from any other stretch of the *Arbetoh*, the Path, as far as Delaney could tell. He wondered how on earth these guides could pick it out. But they were utterly confident, and so everyone pulled their boats up onto shore. The younger guide stayed with the boats, while the old man led them through the dense, wet forest.

"If this is a path," Delaney said to Sleeve, "it's doing a good job of disguisin' itself as a forest." They had to hack through vines and thick-stemmed, scaly plants that Delaney was sure were growing fast enough he could see them coming back soon as they were chopped. But after a few hundred yards, they arrived at the camp just as night was falling.

CHAPTER NINETEEN

THE HANTS

"HUMMA COM NOOMDUM," the man who was certainly the leader of the tribe said. He had the painted skull permanently tattooed on his face, though it looked so fresh it almost glistened. And he had so many sticks and briars poking out of his backpack, or what looked like a backpack, he might well have been mistaken for a hedgehog.

"You not welcome here," the old man translated.

"Coulda interpreted that myself," Spinner Sleeve said under his breath.

The visitors, all but Jenta and Autumn, were seated in a rough semi-circle around a fire pit, facing the chieftain. The Hants had taken away all of their weapons before a word had been spoken or a gesture made, except for the shaking of, and prodding by, pointed sticks, rough iron knives, and the large, flat-bladed swords that looked more like paddles or oars. Mother and daughter were placed off to one side, seated on the ground and surrounded by warriors. These spent more time examining the confiscated weapons than they did watching their prisoners.

The Hants wore few clothes, but much paint. Human bones seemed to be the style of the day, as all the men and women had them painted on their skin. But the chieftain was the only one whose face was blackened and then whitened again in the image of a grinning skull.

"Tell him we come in peace, and we bring gifts," the Whale offered in answer.

The old man translated. Then the chief responded with, "Com hoob ano gooblee dom."

The translator shook his head. "He say he not want gifts from strangers of the dark world."

Belisar turned to smirk at his men, slinging sweat as he did. "We're the dark world. That's a good one." Then to the translator, "Tell him, these are gifts for your dead."

When that was translated, the chieftain's interest level noticeably improved. "Oom com say noss rum," he offered quickly.

Belisar looked to the drawn old man.

He shrugged. "He says, let's see what you have."

The Whale then snapped his fingers, and Blue Garvey handed him the squared-off leather pouch he wore on a lash around his neck. It looked like it might have been half of a set of old, weathered saddlebags. Belisar opened the flap and brought out a vial of liquid, a covered jar, and a cylinder wrapped in a soft cloth. He held out the vial first.

"These are the tears of the wronged."

The chieftain clapped his hands even as the words were translated. A young man, a warrior by the look of him, took the vial from Belisar and handed it to his chief. The Hant held it up to the light, and looked at it carefully. He took out the stopper and smelled it. He closed his eyes. He opened them, put the stopper back in. "Kanna com toom."

"What else do you have?" the old man asked.

Belisar held up the jar. "The ashes of the innocent."

"What does that mean, Mama?" Autumn asked. She was paying little attention to anything but her rag doll.

"Hush," Jenta told her. "Hush now."

After another inspection, the chieftain seemed equally accepting of the jar.

Belisar unrolled the cloth, revealing a single bone, broken in two. "The bones of the faithful."

The chieftain examined this one for a long time. Then he looked up. "Goo ha benna deem oh rah. Doo hamma id, com ben day ho."

"The gifts are good," the old man said. "He asks what you seek from the Hants."

"Tell him that the woman hides a secret known but to the dead. I am her chieftain. I want to know that secret."

After the translation, the chieftain nodded. "Hoobatoon," he said.

Delaney didn't know what this meant, but he figured it out soon enough when the warriors behind them produced several long pipes, each about as big around as a man's forearm, and lit them. They gave the first to Belisar, who smoked, and handed it back. Then they passed the others around to the men. The smoke was strong and harsh and tasted of pinecones. Several, including Delaney, coughed at the first puff. Lemmer gagged and clamped his mouth shut, looking like he might vomit.

"Andowinnie," the chieftain said.

"Drink of the marsh yew," the translator said, motioning toward a particularly scraggly bush that grew in the underbrush. It had long needles like a pine tree, but they drooped and swayed like willow leaves. The warriors passed out the smallest cups Delaney had ever seen, not much bigger than the cap of an acorn. Everyone got one of these. They drank it together. It had the same piney taste, and left a flavor of pine tar in his mouth. It also left a sticky residue on his tongue. Lemmer's face turned white, then red, and then he broke out in a sweat. But he kept it down.

That accomplished, the chieftain grew serious. He looked directly at Belisar. "Noo blay honto emssay kwy dendaroos."

The translator spoke. "The doorway to the other world opens tomorrow night. You bring *dendaroos*. The doomed."

Belisar nodded his understanding, and pointed at the woman. The others looked at one another quizzically. All but Jenta, who seemed to understand exactly what was being discussed. She watched in silence as she let Autumn spin around in circles while holding onto her finger, held above Autumn's head.

"You know of this," the chieftain said through the old man. It was not a question.

Belisar acknowledged that he did.

The translator listened, then said, "It is required tomorow night. The Rippers of the Bone must be satisfied."

And then the chieftain began speaking in a low monotone. It seemed to Delaney like he was speaking something he'd memorized, like he was reciting a poem, or something from church. But the translator's words, spoken right on top of the chieftain's words, were unlike anything Delaney had ever heard coming from a priest. He spoke of the mermonkeys. He described in detail their attacks. He described what they looked like. He planted those images—white flesh, sharp teeth, white-hot eyes...

Jenta began singing softly into her daughter's ear, filling her head with music to drive out the dronings and the translated dronings. As she sang, she caught Delaney's eye and he saw her plea once again.

The chieftain paused, and listened. Then he stood. He walked to Jenta and squatted before her, so that he could look at her. He reached out and felt her hair.

"What's he doing, Mama?"

"He wants to know a secret."

"Do you know the secret?"

"Yes."

"Will you tell him?"

A tear welled in her eye. "I don't know, baby."

"Con ben doom."

"It is a fair exchange," the old man translated. "He will find her secrets."

Several of the warriors took Jenta by the arms. She rose with them. "You be strong, Autumn. Go now, stay with Mr. Delaney."

"Is he a good man, Mama?"

"Yes," she answered. Then she looked at the Whale, a plea and a demand at once.

Belisar didn't move from where he sat, didn't change expression. But then suddenly his cheeks rose, and that pleasant, highly unpleasant look came over him. He said, "Delaney, go take care of the girl."

"Go, Autumn," Jenta said.

To Delaney's shock, Autumn left her mother's side and ran to him. She stood looking at him for a moment, and then sat on his lap.

Belisar raised his bulk awkwardly, stumbled once, caught his balance, and then followed the chieftain and Jenta off into the woods. Blue Garvey followed Belisar. Then Lemmer and Sleeve looked at one another. Sleeve stood and followed as well, while Lemmer hung back.

"Where is Mama going?" Autumn asked Delaney.

"I…don't know."

"Don't be afraid, Mr. Delaney."

Delaney looked at her, wide-eyed. "I ain't afraid. I'm jus'…I'm jus'…"

"It's okay to be afraid. Mama says so."

"I suppose she's right about that," Lemmer said. "Sometimes a man jus' cain't help it."

"It doesn't matter if you feel afraid," Autumn told Lemmer, looking into those pinpoint eyes of his, so close to the bridge of his nose, "but what matters is doing brave things. Mama says Daddy was brave."

"Oh, she's right about that," Lemmer offered. "Hardly a man braver."

"He went to heaven," Autumn informed them both. "He left us behind, but he still loves us."

"I'm sure he does," Lemmer said. "Yer Mama ever say you'll go see 'im someday?"

"Yes, that's what Mama says."

Lemmer gave Delaney an ugly grin. "Maybe soon?"

Delaney moved Autumn off of his lap very gently, then stood up beside her. He took her hand. "Come on now," he said gently. "Let's get you safe."

"You'll need a knife or somethin'," Lemmer offered. The grin had not lessened.

"No, I won't," Delaney answered.

Lemmer looked at Delaney as though impressed. "Glad I don't have to do that job."

"Ye want to come with?"

"No!" Lemmer said immediately. "I'm fine right here."

Delaney made for the path back to the boats, but following it turned out to be difficult. He hadn't brought a sword or a knife, and the scaly plants had grown back considerably. He kept wandering into underbrush too dense to pass, and having to double back. "I ain't a woodsman, that's fer blasted sure," he explained to Autumn more than once. But any path through this thick tangle was noticeable, as otherwise it was nothing but thick tangle, and eventually he and Autumn emerged at the riverbank. The young guide was asleep, but he awakened and stood up like a jack-in-the-box as they approached.

"Ye speak any a' the Vast tongue?" Delaney demanded. He'd heard this guide mutter a few phrases, all in his own language, but he'd also seen the man respond to things said in Vast.

The man nodded.

"Good. Take this here little girl back downriver. Ye understand me?"

"Not wait for others?"

"Not wait for others. That's jus' exactly right. Not wait for others. You take her down fast. Ye get 'fast'? Quick-like?"

"Yes," he said, pantomiming paddling his little pod at a high rate of speed. "Fast."

"Put 'er on the *Flying Ringby*. Not the dark ship, the *Shalamon*. Get me? Give the girl to the captain of the *Flying Ringby*. Not the dark ship. The light brown one."

He looked confused. "Not you ship?"

"Not me ship. That's right. And tell the captain to get her out of here. Tell him, get the girl home."

"She go with you?"

"No! She no go with me. She go without me. She go with *Flying Ringby*."

"She go no with you."

"Right. No with me. Now. You go no with me." He gestured as though flicking crumbs away from his place at the table.

The man didn't move.

"Go! You get 'go'?"

"I get pay," he said, and held out his hand, pointing to his palm.

Delaney grimaced and grunted, fished in his pockets, pulled out his coin purse. He opened it. He took out a whole gold coin and gave it to the man.

He looked at it.

"Well, what're ye waiting for now?"

He shrugged. "Maybe I wait for others."

Delaney growled. He pulled out another coin. Then he put it back and grabbed the man's hand, poured all the coins he had, another gold and six silver, into the man's palm. "Good enough?"

"Now I get go!" Then he scooped up the girl and put her in the pod, stepped in behind her so she was in front of him.

"Where is he taking me, Mr. Delaney?" Autumn asked. Her big blue eyes were pleading, an expression just exactly like her mother's had been. Except with the little girl, the clouds within them shone like a sunny sky just before a rain.

Delaney waded into the water to stand next to her, ignoring the possibility of snakes and piranha. He leaned down, put his hands on his knees. "You gotta go back. Ye got to. Yer Mama wants it. She'll come when she can. But you gotta go."

Tears welled in those eyes. The rains came within those clouds.

"Be a brave girl, and all will be fine," he said, as the guide paddled away. Delaney watched, feeling sick to his stomach, wishing what he said was true. The girl was in tears, her little face all bunched up and red. But she waved at him, her little hand coming up. A little blue-eyed girl in a yellow dress, sad and scared and yet trying so hard to be good.

Delaney raised his hand to wave. But he didn't wave. He just held it there, watching the pod skitter away around the bend. Then he looked at his boots. They were filled with water. Then he turned slowly and walked back up the path.

He took his time. He didn't want to know what the Hant chieftain was doing to Jenta Fellows. He didn't want to be a part of this. But he was a part of it. The slower he walked, the angrier he got with Belisar. "What kind a' man does such a low thing?" He meandered. He kicked at tree roots. He yanked on hanging vines, which stung his hand. He broke off sticks, swung them against tree trunks. But eventually, he made it back to camp. By that time, he hated Belisar the Whale. He hated him with a burning passion he didn't quite understand.

"Ye did it?" Lemmer asked, his narrow eyes fixed on Delaney.

"Sure I did. What d'ye think?"

"She's dead, then?"

Delaney shook his head. "Go stuff yerself."

"No need to get all fired up."

There was a crunching sound in the woods, footsteps. Lemmer stood, wiped his pants. They watched as Belisar and Blue Garvey emerged, followed by a couple of Hants and Sleeve. The chieftain wasn't with them. Nor was Jenta.

"What happened?" Delaney asked.

"I got it. She gave up the location of the map." The Whale seemed very pleased with himself.

"Where is she?" he asked.

Belisar laughed. "Where is she...that's a good one. The Hants have her. She should have given it all up back in Mann, saved us a lot of trouble. She'd still be dead, but at least she'd be in one piece!"

Blue and Sleeve laughed.

"Where is it?" Lemmer asked. "The map, I mean."

"Hmm." Belisar was still smiling, but his look grew darker and more distant. "That map is worth about half the gold in the world, I figure. And I've spent four years and many a coin finding its whereabouts. I sailed across the ocean and risked my life to gain that knowledge. And you expect me to tell you, just because you asked?"

Lemmer's look fell. "No," he said conclusively. Then he looked to Delaney, trying to find some help. "It's worth a bunch," he explained to Delaney. "That's why Jenta wouldn't tell no one. She wanted the money for herself."

"No, she didn't," Belisar said.

Lemmer's face went slack. "She din't?"

"She was a good soul," the Whale continued, "for all the good that did her. Her secrecy was meant to protect others. Bad luck for them! She left the map with people who don't even know they have it. They have no idea what wrath is about to descend on them."

Delaney said nothing, but he thought of the couple on the boat, the ones who had saved Jenta and brought her to Nearing Vast.

"Where's the girl?" Belisar asked suddenly.

Delaney straightened, raised his chin. "I took care of her, just like you ordered."

He looked at his sailor with suspicion. "You have an odd demeanor, Mr. Delaney. Is the girl dead, or not?"

Delaney considered lying. But he couldn't stand that smirking countenance, couldn't stand what his captain had just done, and the evident pleasure he took in doing it. "No, she's alive."

"Where is she?" He looked around him.

Delaney crossed his arms. "You told me to take care of her, and I did."

Belisar motioned to Blue Garvey, who walked up to Delaney and looked down at him, much like a bear on its hind legs might look down on a fox. Or a squirrel. "Make him talk to me, Mr. Garvey."

"I'll talk!" Delaney hissed. "I took her to the boats. I paid the guide to take her back downriver."

Belisar blanched. "You did what?"

"You told me to take care of her, and I obeyed."

Belisar turned on Lemmer. "Were you part of this?"

"No, I swear! He told me he killed her."

"I said no such thing. I said I took care of her."

"You're a fool, Delaney," Belisar breathed.

"Did I do something wrong? Sir?"

"Don't think for a second that I am also a fool. I've seen your sad little puppy dog eyes, looking at that harlot and her spawn. Perhaps you've forgotten how many of your mates she and her...husband...killed. Perhaps you haven't noticed the trouble she's caused us, or how many of our kind, your kind, have been dying on the gallows lately, all because of Damrick Fellows and the Gatemen." Then he smiled that cold, reptile-like smile that made the folds of flesh rise up and almost hide his eyes. "Have you forgotten?"

"I ain't forgot."

"You just chose to ignore. To ignore your duty to your captain. But you know, this might work out quite well. There's a little place up here that the Conch discovered some years ago. Perhaps you heard the chieftain mention it. The Hants keep it just for such an occasion as this. I had timed our arrival here, expecting to offer up Mrs. Fellows. But she broke rather easily. Now, I think that the Blaggard's Hole is calling your name, Delaney. Let me have a word with our hosts. Wait here, won't you?"

Blue Garvey grabbed Delaney from behind, a thick, hairy, sweaty arm under his throat.

The drums had begun again. Delaney had been deep in thought again, and had missed when they started up again. But he heard them now, louder than ever, pounding away with their rhythmic beat, their odd offbeats. He looked around him. It was dark. He couldn't see the shore-line. He couldn't see where it met the water. He couldn't see the reeds, nor the faces peering from them, if in fact the Hants were still there. He couldn't see the river, the little creek that flowed from the pond straight in front of him. He couldn't see the trees. He could only see the stars in one small patch of sky above him. The tiny circle of light they illuminated was the only part of the water he could see. He couldn't see the *Chompers*.

Darkness had come.

He sighed. He'd saved the girl. He'd known just what he was doing, though he told the Captain, and himself for a while, that he'd only obeyed orders. He knew better. He'd always known better. He'd just lied to himself. He wondered how often he'd done that and not ever paid attention again. Over his lifetime, he'd probably lied to himself more than he'd lied to anyone else. Maybe more than he'd lied to everyone else combined. It seemed to him now that he'd gotten quite good at it, so good he didn't hardly even notice it anymore.

He'd saved the girl, but he hadn't been able to save Jenta. No, that wasn't right. No more lies. He'd saved Autumn, but he'd let Jenta die. No, that wasn't quite true enough either. He'd killed Jenta. He was a pirate, serving Belisar, and before Belisar, the Conch. Delaney had helped those two captains kill off Damrick, and then Wentworth, and now Jenta. All their most powerful, dangerous challengers.

His heart sank very low. He knew the mermonkey would come soon. He remembered the fear he'd felt earlier when he saw that thing. And then he felt it again, less than an hour ago. And he knew the next time he felt that fear, it would be the end, the real end of everything.

He didn't want to die. He was ready for it, maybe, but he didn't want it. Anything else was a lie.

He was afraid to die.

He was afraid of death.

He thought some more, wondering why. And he had to admit that it was not just fear of the unknown. Or the pain of crossing over. It was hell. He was afraid of hell. He was afraid of a place of eternal torment, the only place he was sure he deserved. *Hell's Gatemen*, Damrick called his men. They called themselves that name to scare pirates, as though that armband and that red feather gave them the right to open the very gates of Hades and usher pirates like Delaney inside. It was a name designed to strike fear into the heart of the lawless. And it did.

It did because it was true. They did send pirates just like him straight to hell. And that's where he was going.

But not straight there. First, he'd have to be eaten by monsters.

Where was that sense of peace, of knowing it was right? Of knowing it was God's judgment and therefore good? It was gone, is where it was. God being just didn't make hell any better.

And then he remembered what Jenta had said. She said that Damrick had loved her even when she didn't love herself. He'd rescued her, even when she didn't know it was possible. When she was sure she hadn't deserved it.

If only he had someone who loved him that much.

If only.

A sudden thud, and the post on which he sat rocked like it had been struck by a...

He gripped the wood tight with his feet. His bowels clenched up within him. His jaw squeezed shut until he heard a tooth crack. His heart clattered in his chest, and he heard the blood pounding through his ears.

He felt claws bite into the wood, deep under the water.

He felt, he heard the scraping as those claws moved upward. He could feel the hands as they clenched again, climbing. He could see the mermonkey in his mind, just as clearly as if it were broad daylight and he was looking at it with his eyes. More clearly, more terribly, because his mind's eye would not close. It stayed open, showing him the horror, the terror, that climbed toward him.

Then he heard the water move. Just a ripple at first, and then a dripping.

Then he heard a hiss, like a cat. It was the scream, the silent scream of the monkey that he'd seen but not heard. Now he heard, but did not see.

But he did see. He saw nothing else—his eyes were blank but his vision was filled with it. The sharp teeth bared, the white flesh pasty like dough.

He felt the vibration as one clawed hand moved, and then heard the clink of the pointed claws, heard them bite the wood above the surface with the merest of squeaks. The post shuddered. It shook, not a little, but like it was whipping back and forth, vibrating like a flag caught in a storm. And he knew that he was shaking it, not the mermonkey. His whole body was shaking.

And then noises came from him, from his chest, his throat. Gurgling at first, as his chest constricted, and he could not breathe in. Then, as he felt the hand of the monster move again and the claws squeak into the wood again, he heard a whine, a high-pitched, ragged sound that he could not control, that came from inside him, that would come out from within him no matter what he wanted, no matter what he tried, as though the noise wasn't just coming *from* him, but it *was* him, his being, leaking out, forced out by the horror below.

His legs were pulled up tight, his heels now digging into his buttocks. Pain raged through his thighs, his calves, as they knotted up like a monkey's fist. And the thing kept moving, claws gripping. And then it hissed again. And the noise in his chest became a wail, then a moan, then a long, low howl. He wanted to cry out for help, to plead to God to save him, but no words came. His howl became his final prayer.

And then he felt its cold hand on his ankle, and his chest seized up, his cry ceased.

It was a gentle touch at first, just a soft, frigid hand sending a shiver of cold fear shooting through him.

Then it grabbed him, the cold, clammy paw wrapping all the way around his ankle and tightening like a vise, until he thought it would squeeze right through to crush his bones.

And then it whipped him off the post, snatched him away and threw him out over the water like he was little more than a rag. And just before he hit the surface, he heard it hiss again.

He managed one breath before he submerged, and then only because he opened his mouth to scream again and his chest cooperated, suddenly sucking in air...and then water. He smacked into the surface of the pond, a painful slap, and was under in an instant, and it was dragging him down.

He coughed once, a single bubble, and then he went limp.

The thing had him. It still had him by the ankle. It hadn't let go. Now it pulled him under, and down. Now it grabbed his wrist, and a hand on his chest pushed him roughly into the muck on the bottom of the pond. He felt the mud, the cold muck on his back. He felt the claws on his chest. He knew now it wasn't one, but two. More.

And he saw them. He opened his eyes, and saw the glow, just a faint glow, like lightning buzzing in the rigging. But in this light it was enough. They were not white, but golden. A faint yellow-gold color. One grabbed his arm above the elbow. He looked at his chest and saw another, with claws on his rib cage. He felt claws on his skull. The hard, pointed nails bit in.

The ripping had begun.

He didn't fight it. He closed his eyes.

He let it happen.

And then he heard the song. It was the girl again. Her song. And he was glad to hear it. It was sorrow and joy and peace. It sounded like prayers, and the answer to prayers. And the fear fled from the song. It fled from him. The song had come for him. It was sent to soothe him, to help him. There was warmth in it. And he was grateful.

The words came with the song, soft and far away, but clear, too, somehow.

> *A true lang time,*
> *A lang true la,*
> *And down the silver path into a rushing sea,*
> *Where moons hang golden under boughs of green,*
> *A lang true la, 'tis true,*
> *The true heart weeps*
> *As her song she sings,*
> *A true lang time for you…*

And he saw twin lights. Small, bright, shimmering above him, like welcoming stars.

And then it was over.

There was no pain. He could feel no claws. He felt nothing but peace. He was rising up, up from the muck and the dark, floating upward.

The stars grew larger, and larger, until they weren't stars at all. They were moons. Golden moons, and he rose toward them. The music was clearer now, and more beautiful. He saw, as he rose, the trees, and was content. The moons hung golden, under boughs of green. He was inside the song. And it was wondrous. The voice…it was no longer the little girl who sang, but a richer voice, richer and warmer and wiser, pure and sorrowful and…he recognized it, somehow.

And then he broke the surface, and he saw her.

It was Jenta.

But it wasn't Jenta. Her skin was marked, and it glowed with light where it was marked, as though someone had carved beautiful lines to emphasize every curve of her cheeks, patterns along her chin, across her jaw, around her forehead, her shoulders, her arms, her hands. She held torches, twin torches, one in each hand. And she looked down at him as she sang. And her eyes were blue, and full of light, a warm flickering of flame.

And then hands reached out to him, blocking his view of her. And they pulled him from the water. They were rough hands, and they hurt him.

And then he knew that he had not died. He knew that he had been rescued. She had, somehow, saved him.

He coughed, and then gagged, and then coughed some more, and murky water flowed out onto the floor of the boat. He had swallowed a great deal of it. He turned over, and lay looking up at her. She was standing, wrapped in light, in a wispy fabric that seemed to flow, and to glow in the firelight. She had dropped her hands, though she still held the torches. Flame fled upward, and he feared it would burn her. But hands took the torches from her now and held them high.

She kept singing, softly now, as though she could barely remember the song, or why she was singing it. Her eyes were far away, not looking at him anymore.

"What happened?" he asked her. Her voice trailed off, and she hummed. But she did not stop singing, and she did not answer him.

He looked away from her. These were Hants in the boat, two warriors, painted like skeletons, and the old chieftain, his face a glowing skull in the dark, his hedgehog bristles sticking out from behind. The two warriors looked at the water, and held the torches over it.

He sat up. The boat wasn't the skiff, and it wasn't the shallop. It was made of dark wood, covered in what looked like leaves. It was the Hants' boat. He looked over the lip, and down into the water. He saw men below, two of them, swimming underwater. They weren't mermonkeys, but men painted like skeletons, and the paint glowed, like the lines in Jenta's skin

Blaggard's Moon

glowed, like her garment glowed, like the mermonkeys had glowed. As he watched, they swam beneath an outcropping of rock, down under the water, and they disappeared.

They swam into a cave.

The Hant chieftain spoke. "Nooloo hah mowbray."

"You go," a voice said. He squinted past Jenta, past the chieftain, and saw the old man, the sickly translator, in the shadows at the back of the boat. "Go to the treasure," he said.

Delaney looked at him curiously. He didn't understood.

"The gold you seek," the old man explained. "It is below."

It took him a moment more to sort it out. Then he understood. Conch's gold, that's what he meant. It was in the cave, in the mermonkey's cave. That's where Conch had put it. He had put it where it could never be found, could never be touched. Belisar wanted the map. He would go to find the map, but the map would only lead him back here.

But where were the mermonkeys? He couldn't see them.

Jenta sang.

> *Oh, carry my burthen, and carry her true,*
> *For she steers for the south and the east*
> *And the few,*
> *A lang true la,*
> *The drum and the yew...*

And then he knew. The song was the map. She had written the map into the song.

He rolled over the edge of the boat and splashed into the pond. He took a deep breath, and then swam down, down, below the lip of the rock, and into the cave. Within ten feet, he could swim up, and he did. He broke the surface. At first he didn't understand what he saw. Everything was golden and glowing. Then he realized it was a lichen, a plant of some sort that glowed. It covered the walls. He saw the two Hants who had swum down before him, now standing above him. They motioned to him. He climbed out of the water and stood beside them. They pointed.

He looked.

What he saw was a nest. A wide nest, twenty feet across, thirty feet wide, five feet deep. It was filled with coins. It glowed. He saw the crates, and splinters of crates, rotting barrels. Conch had carried his gold in here, to be protected by *Onka Din Botlay*. The monsters had made their bed out of Conch's gold. Hundreds of thousands of coins.

"Oh hahn fooh." One of the Hants pointed at him. Then he squatted down, and put his hand into the golden glow. He held it up to Delaney.

Delaney knelt down and did the same, scooping up the gold with both hands.

But it didn't feel like gold. The coins were sticky, and spongy, and melted away where he touched them. And now he smelled it. It was putrid. He tried to drop the golden mess, but much of it clung to his skin. He climbed back down to the water to wash it off. He scrubbed at it, but it stuck to him. He feared it would never come off, but then suddenly it dissolved away, glowing, disappearing into the water. He wiped his hands on his pants, hoping the stuff wouldn't poison him.

And then the two men dove into the water and swam away. Delaney took one last look at Conch's gold, worthless gold, and he followed.

The torches were burning down when he surfaced. Jenta's voice was ragged, as though she was tired, sleepy.

> *A true lang time and we shall meet*
> *On the silver path to the rushing sea…*

The silver path. The river, what the locals called the Path. What the Vast called Lambent, another word for silver. She didn't keep the map because she didn't need it. She had the lullabye.

"Come," the translator said, after the chieftain had whispered something. "Your time is up."

Delaney treaded water near the boat, looking up at Jenta. The lines on her face and hands were fading. He wondered if they were cut deep, deep like the cuts into the priest's face and hands.

Jenta quit singing.

The chieftain looked across the pond. "*Onka Din Botlay*, hoon ah roo."

"They return!" the old man said. And the Hants in the boat reached out for Delaney and snatched him up from the water.

Delaney sat dripping, heard the hiss and turned his head, saw the mermonkeys, three of them, glowing softly golden, glowing with Conch's gold, he now knew, and clinging to the post. His post. They were angry now, or terrified, eyes wide, watching Jenta. Only Jenta.

"The widow's song," the old man said. "They cannot bear it."

"Why don't they go back in the water?" Delaney asked.

"The tears of the wronged are there. The ashes of the innocent. The bones of the faithful."

And now Delaney saw the vial, the jar, and the cloth at the chieftain's feet.

The Hants picked up paddles and propelled the boat to the shoreline, back to the reeds. "They will return soon," the old man said.

When they reached the edge of the water, Jenta stopped singing, and collapsed into the boat, caught gently by the Hants. She lay quiet. And then Delaney heard her sob.

They carried her out of the boat, and through the reeds, through the forest, and back to their camp. They laid her down on a bed of cut reeds. Delaney knelt beside her and took her hand. In the light from their campfires he could see that every inch of her hands and arms was carved, just like her face. The lines, the patterns still glowed golden, though now the glow was fading fast. Her eyes were closed, but tears streamed from them. She was crying.

He lay down beside her, holding her hand, patting it, not knowing what to say or do. The Hants watched, and talked low. He was wary, keeping his eye on their movements. But he had the feeling they were protecting Jenta. And him. After a while, Jenta's breathing became smooth.

Delaney was on dry land. He had been rescued. She had saved him. God had picked him up and put him on dry land. He had saved her, too. Yet he felt nothing but deep, unending sorrow.

Soon he fell into a black, dreamless sleep.

"Come. The chieftain wants you."

Delaney struggled up to the light. His body felt like it was weighed down, like every muscle was made of lead. But he sat up and blinked around him. It was daylight.

Jenta was gone.

He leaped to his feet, suddenly alert and awake. He felt for his sword, or a pistol, or a knife, but he had no weapons. The old man looked up at him calmly, still kneeling.

"Where's Jenta?" Delaney demanded.

"Come. Speak to the chieftain."

The events of the previous night came roaring back to him. "Where's the Captain?"

The old man stood. "Follow me."

Heart racing, cursing himself for falling asleep, Delaney followed. He found the chieftain, still painted, seated in the same spot he had been sitting the day before, where he smoked and spoke and made his devilish deal with Belisar the Whale. He looked up as Delaney approached, and gestured for him to sit.

Delaney stood with hands on hips. "Where's Jenta? What'd ye do with her?"

"Boom."

Delaney felt outrage. "Boom? I'll give ye boom, if ye've harmed that woman again!"

"Boom," the translator said gently, "means 'sit.' He'll tell you all."

"Oh." He sniffed, rubbed his nose, then sat cross-legged facing the elder.

"Your chieftain," the Hant leader said through the translator, "said the woman kept secrets known only to the dead. What the dead tell the living must not be hidden."

Delaney withheld comment.

"The Hants found many secrets inside her."

"Tortured her, ye mean," Delaney said.

"Shall I speak these words to the chieftain?" the translator asked.

"Aye. You can tell 'im I don't appreciate it, what he done to her, and he'll pay if I can get my weapons back."

The old man hesitated, then translated. The chieftain looked at Delaney grimly, and replied.

"Your chieftain, the fat captain, is dishonorable. We gave him one secret, and then he dishonored us."

"How?"

"He gave us gold." The old chieftain shook his head grimly.

Delaney made a knowing face. He wasn't sure where the dishonor was in that, but he didn't want to say it.

But the chieftain explained through the translator. "Hants care for the dead. We learn their secrets, and pass knowledge to them. We do not exchange such for shiny trifles. When your chieftain left, we continued to find her secrets." He paused. "She is a great soul."

He looked into Delaney's eyes for so long, he felt compelled to say, "I ain't arguin' the point."

"We learned much about her. About her husband. About your Captain. About you."

"Me? Uh-oh."

"You saved her daughter."

"She couldn't a' knowed that."

"But we know. For we heard, and we watched. These forests are ours. It is because of this deed that we rescued you from *Onka Din Botlay*."

So he had saved the girl. But it felt like the other way around. "Jenta, is she all right?"

"She is in the healing."

"What's that mean? She goin' to live?"

"She will not die at our hands."

Delaney relaxed. "So what was all that, with her singin' and whatnot, and them critters lettin' me go and climbin' up the pole like that?"

"They are not people, the *Onka Din Botlay*. But they are not animals. They have spirits. Their spirits roam freely among the dead. Twisted, bent, and ancient they are. They flee from light. They flee from heart." He put a fist to his chest. "The song of a woman in mourning…this they cannot bear."

Delaney nodded. He understood that. Who could bear it? "Can I get her? Can we go? Her daughter's way downstream and I know she'd like to catch her up."

"It is done."

"What's done?"

"We have caught up the little girl. She awaits at the mouth of the Silver Path, where it rushes to the sea."

"Well, that's kind of ye. So where's the captain, Belisar, and the rest of the crew?"

"Your chieftain is raised up. The rest have gone."

"Raised up?" No explanation seemed to be forthcoming. "Raised up where?"

"High above, where he belongs."

"What, in heaven?"

"I do not understand heaven."

"Where the good dead go."

"No. He is not where the good dead go. But he is high up."

"I don't take yer meanin'."

And the chieftain pointed upward, behind Delaney.

When he turned and craned his neck, he saw the body of Belisar the Whale, stripped and painted with bones, hanging by his ankles from the treetops.

"Well," Delaney said after a long pause. "That must a' took some doin'."

Then after another pause, he asked, "What happened to the gold? In the cave, I mean?"

"The trifles? Rippers of the Bone protect it, as promised to the great captain of the dark world."

He meant the Conch. "Well, I reckon that works. No one's going to cart it away like that. Can it be changed back?"

"Kanha roo boh," the chieftain said. "Day ho noss."

The translator intoned the answer. "He says, the creatures have the power to turn worthless trinkets into sunlight, and it will shine like this forever more."

Delaney sighed. "I guess that's a good power to have. Though folks out there in the dark world ain't likely to see it quite that way."

EPILOGUE

JENTA'S SCARS FADED. By the time she was reunited with Autumn at the mud huts of Sule City, they were lines barely traceable by the little girl's finger. The healing, whatever that treatment was, had been remarkable.

They found to their relief that the *Shalamon* had sailed. She had pulled anchor not long after Lemmer Harps returned, waving the bare bones at the end of his arm where once a hand had been. With him was Blue Garvey, paddling for all he was worth. Lefty, as he was forever called after, muttered incoherently about ghosts and Hants and Belisar being spirited away before their eyes, raised up into the darkness of the forest above. Blue reported that Sleeve had been caught up too, but in a different way. Late that night the Hants had taken to admiring his boney limbs, and he tried to fight them off. But they carried him away, him cursing and them saying over and over, *Onka Din Botlay*. And in their own tongues, "the Ripper of the Bone must be satisfied." When it became clear to all that Blue was just as spooked as Lemmer, nothing was going to keep that crew from fleeing the Hants and Sule City.

The *Flying Ringby* had long since sailed as well, so Jenta and Autumn and Delaney waited for the next ship, spending their time swimming and fishing and relaxing. Soon enough a ship pulled in. Her captain was known to Delaney, and though he had a cruel reputation, he claimed to have set pirating behind him since his days under Conch Imbry. He was after a greater prize than what could be found in the holds of merchant ships. He needed hands at the moment and after a brief negotiation, he agreed to take Jenta and the girl to the next port, where they could catch a ship out of the Warm Climes, back to Nearing Vast. Delaney signed on, grateful to serve a man who was not a pirate, but who would not hold a man's pirate past against him.

Delaney's new captain was true to his word, and at the next port, Jenta and Autumn were placed in the care of a kindly merchant captain headed north. Before she left him, though, she said her goodbyes to Smith Delaney, on the docks of a port unfamiliar to them both.

"Where will ye go?" Delaney asked, standing at the foot of the gangway. She had been called to board, she and Autumn, but Delaney wasn't quite ready to see her depart, somehow.

"To the farm in Nearing Vast, I suppose," Jenta answered. But her look was distant, as it had been since that night. Her thoughts seemed to be somewhere else—not distracted, precisely, for she was always present, and never missed a turn in a conversation or even a shade of meaning. But more like she was in two places at once, and the other place, wherever it was, was calm and serene and inviting and she wanted to be there fully. "Though I don't know. A cabin up in the woods, perhaps." She looked down at Autumn's sweet face, and placed a hand on her daughter's cheek.

"Well, I guess it's goodbye then," he said slowly. "My ship's sailin', too." He hooked a thumb behind him, toward the great, sleek ship he'd signed on to sail.

"I'm glad you've found your friends," she told him.

"They ain't exactly friends." The crew of the *Shalamon*, captainless again, had fought like badgers during the voyage from Sule City. When they had made port here, half of them had looked for a different ship to sail, figuring the *Shalamon* was cursed. Blue and Mutter and a few others had found the same opportunity Delaney had. They were now aboard the same ship under the same captain, and would be on crew with Delaney once again. "But I thank ye." He put out his hand.

Jenta ignored it, and embraced him. He smelled her hair, his face buried into her shoulder. It was not just honeysuckle, as Ham had described it, but some other sweetness, too. Like mown grass on a summer morning, or the breeze off the ocean right before a rain. He didn't hug her back, but stood straight up, like a board, waiting for it to end. But when it did, he wished it didn't.

"Goodbye, Mr. Delaney," Autumn said, and took her turn hugging him. He picked her up so she could do it more easily, and she planted a kiss on his cheek.

"It's scratchy, Mama," she said, still in his arms, her hand on his cheek.

"Need a shave," he informed Jenta, running his free hand over the stubble of his face. He never did get his knife back, though he would think about it for a long time, wishing he'd been clear enough in his mind to scout along the floor of the pond while he was swimming around down there. But he hadn't been, and nothing could be done about it now. He had to let it go. Sometimes things just had to be let go, he knew, no matter how bad you wanted them to stay. He set the little girl down.

And then he watched as Jenta and Autumn boarded the merchant vessel, bound for Mann. When Jenta turned back and waved, and he saw the sadness in her eyes, Delaney thought about Damrick. He even wished for a moment it was Damrick standing there, and not himself at all. He figured she probably wished the same. But he wasn't Damrick, and that was that. After a while, when Jenta and Autumn were long gone, he turned and walked away.

He had work to do.

Delaney was quickly happy to have signed on, and realized with a great thankfulness just how fortunate he was. He had much to think about, much to ponder. He had gotten down to the bottom of himself and found a darkness deeper than he knew could be. And yet he'd been raised up again—and not like Belisar was, but truly. All of that meant something, and he purposed in his heart to find out what.

But in the meantime his new duties would keep him busy. This ship was a dazzling thing, and he was thankful for that as well. Sleek and long, she looked like she was running at full speed even when standing still. Delaney's heart had pounded from the first moment she cleared the reefs and sandbars of Sule City and he felt her under his feet on the open ocean, running with the wind. He knew he would grow to love her dearly. She was built for a singular purpose, by a singular captain, and seemed destined for greatness.

Her name was *Trophy Chase*, and under Captain Scatter Wilkins she was headed out to the Vast Sea in a favorable wind, leaping like a cat over and through the billows, in headlong pursuit of the legendary Firefish.

The End.

What happens next to Smith Delaney? Find out by reading the...

~ TROPHY CHASE TRILOGY ~
George Bryan Polivka

BOOK ONE: *THE LEGEND OF THE FIREFISH*

Packer Throme longs to bring prosperity back to his fishing village by discovering the trade secrets of Scat Wilkins, a notorious pirate who now seeks to hunt the legendary Firefish and sell its rare meat.

Packer begins his quest by stowing away aboard Scat's ship, the *Trophy Chase,* bound for the open sea.

Will belief and vision be enough for Packer Throme to survive? And will Talon, the Drammune warrior woman who serves as Scat's security officer, be Packer's deliverance...or his death? And what of Panna Seline? In her determination not to lose Packer, she leaves home to follow the man she loves, but soon she is swept up in a perilous adventure of her own.

BOOK TWO: *THE HAND THAT BEARS THE SWORD*

In the midst of their joyous "honey month," newlyweds Packer and Panna Throme are once again thrust unwillingly into high adventure.

Pirate Scat Wilkins, no longer in command of his great ship, has returned with evil intentions for Packer as the *Trophy Chase* sets sail for deep waters once again.

While Packer is away, Panna, his bride, faces danger at the hands of the lecherous Prince Mather.

And a deadly peril has arisen across the sea. A new Hezzan in the Kingdom of Drammun now has diabolical designs on Packer and the Firefish trade, which catapults all of Nearing Vast into the horrors of war.

BOOK THREE: *THE BATTLE FOR VAST DOMINION*

Packer Throme, determined to demonstrate that power comes only from above, leads his people in a war against the dreaded Drammune. The evil Hezzan of Drammun will kill without remorse for the secret of the Firefish...and so will dark forces lurking within Nearing Vast.

As army faces army, and navy faces navy, all are drawn inexorably to the source of the epic struggle...the feeding waters of the Firefish within the Achawuk Territory. One final surprise awaits Packer Throme there in the foreboding place where the struggle for the dominion of the world will be settled at last.

About the Author

George Bryan Polivka was raised in the Chicago area, attended Bible college in Alabama, and ventured on to Europe, where he studied under Francis Schaeffer at L'Abri Fellowship in Switzerland. He then returned to Alabama, where he enrolled at Birmingham-Southern College as an English major.

While still in school, Bryan married Jeri, his only sweetheart since high school and now his wife of more than 25 years. He also was offered a highly coveted internship at a local television station, which led him to his first career—as an award-winning television producer.

In 1986, Bryan won an Emmy for writing his documentary *A Hard Road to Glory*, which detailed the difficult path African-Americans traveled to achieve recognition through athletic success during times of racial prejudice and oppression.

Bryan and his family eventually moved to the Baltimore area, where he worked with Sylvan Learning Systems (now Laureate Education). In 2001 he was honored by the U.S. Distance Learning Association for the most significant achievement by an individual in corporate e-learning. He is currently responsible for developing and delivering new programs for Laureate's online higher education division.

Bryan and Jeri live near Baltimore with their two children, Jake and Aime, where Bryan continues to work and write.

Be sure to visit his website at www.nearingvast.com.

To learn more about books by George Bryan Polivka
or to read sample chapters, log on to our website:

www.harvesthousepublishers.com

HARVEST HOUSE PUBLISHERS
EUGENE, OREGON